JERRY

Jerry -

JERRY

By
Arthur Stanwood Pier

*With Illustrations
by Christine Tucke Curtiss*

Boston and New York
Houghton Mifflin Company
The Riverside Press Cambridge
1917

CONTENTS

[v]

CONTENTS

CONTENTS

CONTENTS

ILLUSTRATIONS

❧ JERRY ❧

THE HERO PAYS FOR HIS BEER: AND SHAKES HANDS WITH A CANDIDATE FOR CONGRESS

THERE was the usual Saturday six o'clock crowd in Grady's saloon. But instead of being ranged in a thirsty double row along the bar, they were grouped at the farther end round a man whose hat, tilted on the back of his head, exposed the edge of his thick, smoothly brushed black hair. He was not, like the others, a workingman; he carried no dinner pail; if you entered late, like young Jerry Donohue, and stood, like him, on the edge of the crowd, you could just get a glimpse of this gentleman's striped blue-and-red waistcoat. When Jerry came in the door, he was flourishing above his head a fair white hand on which gleamed a large seal ring.

But Jerry arrived too late to get any idea of what the speech was all about. He heard only a sentence, meaningless without the context — with it very funny, for the crowd exploded in laughter — exploded literally, shooting its units out along the bar.

"A round of drinks on me, Mr. Grady," called the gentleman of the waistcoat.

Jerry stepped forward, not to avail himself of this opportunity, but to ask Dave Scanlan who the gentleman was.

JERRY

"John Maxwell, running for Congress," said Dave. "Don't you know him by his pictures?"

Now that his attention was called to it, Jerry recognized the resemblance. The mill town was placarded with bills bearing Mr. Maxwell's picture. There was a bill on nearly every telegraph pole; often there were clusters of bills. Jerry had been absorbed in the waistcoat; he studied now the face of the gentleman leaning so nonchalantly against the bar. Jerry was quite thrilled with admiration for Maxwell's youth; it was much greater than seemed to him compatible with Congressional dignity. Thirty, perhaps, were the gentleman's years; his eyes, small, dark, and sharp, glittered in a pale face; he laughed much and genially, showing very good teeth.

Jerry himself had just come of age and in another month would cast his first vote. He drew nearer.

"That smells like a good pipe tobacco." Maxwell addressed a workingman at the bar. "Let's have a pull, will you?"

Reaching out, he abstracted the man's clay pipe from his mouth and inserted it between his own lips. The man grinned rather foolishly; Maxwell pulled on the pipe. "Fine," he said, "fine! I'd like to get some of that." He returned the pipe to the owner. "What's the name of it, please?"

"Red Boy."

"I'll just put that down, so I won't forget. Thanks ever so much." He scribbled in a notebook.

When he glanced up, his eyes fell on Jerry; and Jerry, suddenly embarrassed because he had been staring so

hard at the gentleman, turned away and stepped up to
the bar.

"A beer, please," he said, and tendered a coin in payment.

Grady waved it back.

"It's on Mr. Maxwell," said the barkeeper.

"I'll pay for mine," said Jerry.

Grady shrugged his shoulders and took the money.
While Jerry drank his beer, Grady, lolling across the
bar, conversed with the candidate.

"Smart-looking fellow, ain't he?" said Dave Scanlan
to Jerry.

"You bet. Did you speak to him, Dave?"

"Yes — shook hands. Say, do you want to meet
him?"

Jerry was shy. "Oh, I guess not; what's the good?"

"Well, you can say you done it, you know. That's
something to be able to say — 'specially if he gets to be
President some time."

"I guess I won't bother him," said Jerry.

He drew away from the bar, and with Dave Scanlan
and two or three others cast admiring glances at Mr.
Maxwell. Then Jerry's open, boyish face flushed pink
up to the roots of his blond hair, he twisted his big
hands together behind him like an awkward child, and
dropped his eyes. For Grady was pointing at him in-
delicately, and Mr. Maxwell's eyes were scanning him
with apparent interest.

In another moment the candidate had approached.

"Grady tells me you would n't come in on my invitation."

"I did n't see why you should pay for my beer." Jerry was more red with embarrassment than ever.

Maxwell laughed. "Shake hands," he said. "Can I have a few words with you somewhere?"

"In Grady's back room —"

"Pretty much at home here, eh?"

"I know my way round."

Grady's back room was unoccupied; nevertheless, Maxwell talked in a confidential undertone.

"One thing first," he said. "Are you with me or against me?"

"With you."

"That's good. It saves me time. I'd have had to get you in the long run. Now I tell you. I want to meet some of the young men of your neighborhood. I want to meet them through somebody that stands well — somebody they respect. You're the man. That crowd in there" — he jerked his thumb towards the door — "they're most of them not your kind. I did n't need Grady's hint to see that. And you're the man I'm looking for."

"To do what?" Jerry asked. He was much flattered.

"I want to hold some parlor rallies. That is, get some of the young fellows together in the house of one of their number and talk with them, get to know them, have a nice social evening. Touch on the issues and make it a kind of informal and instructive occasion. And I want to have one of these parlor rallies in this neighborhood and especially for young voters. I was wondering if you'd be willing to lend your house and get the crowd together."

"Why, yes, I guess so," said Jerry dubiously. "It's for mother to say; I don't believe she'd mind."

"You see, there won't be a particle of expense to you," explained Maxwell. "I'll set up the cigars for the crowd."

"Could mother be on hand? She'd like to meet you, I know. Would that be all right?"

"Why" — Maxwell hesitated, — "some time I hope to meet your mother, — but I don't really believe it would be very pleasant for her that evening — house filled with a lot of men smoking — kind of rough for her, don't you think? I guess she'd better be out visiting that evening. But I'll drop round some other day and meet her."

"That'd tickle her to death. What night do you want to have the party?"

"This is Thursday. How about next Tuesday? Could you get a crowd together for that evening?"

"Easy enough."

"Then we'll call it a date — and if your mother objects you'll notify me at once, won't you? That's my address. And what's yours?"

"Eighteen O'Gorman Street. I guess mother won't kick. And you'll come and see her some time, sure — I can tell her so?"

"Sure." Maxwell gave Jerry a friendly pat; and with his hand on the doorknob, remarked: "I'm mighty glad you'll do this for me. I wanted to have this rally in a house where I'd be sure things were sort of nice."

"Our house ain't very fancy," Jerry warned him.

"I'm not worrying. And if you'll round up as many

fellows as you can, I'll be ever so much obliged. Awfully good of you anyhow to do this for me, old man."
He opened the door and shook Jerry's hand warmly in full view of the staring workingmen, who seemed to ruminate upon the incident over their pipes.

When he had departed in his automobile, the crowd slowly converged upon Jerry.

"What'd he want? What'd he tell you?" clamored Dave Scanlan.

"Ah, go on." Jerry pushed his way through to the door. "He just ast me to be his secret'y in Washington — and I turned him down."

Jerry entered his house whistling; from the kitchen his mother's voice greeted him.

"Ah, such a good supper as I have for you to-night, Jerry, and getting cold this fifteen minutes. What makes you so late, child?"

"Stopped in at Grady's for a drink," said Jerry; he strode across the room, seized the small woman, and kissed her.

She did not respond to his kiss; the eyes that had welcomed him, bright with vivacity, lost their blue sparkle, the lips that had been laughing drooped; she sat down at the table humbly, silently, a dumpy, dejected little person.

"Ah, tut," said Jerry. "Don't be vexing yourself about me, mother. I'm all right. Try a bite of the steak. It's good — even if you did cook it."

"I wish you would n't go to Grady's, Jerry."

"Not for a glass of beer after the day's work at the mill?"

"You might have it here at home."

"Oh, you don't begrudge me the bit of a social time with the boys. 'T was grand luck I dropped into Grady's. Mr. Maxwell was there — you've seen his pictures all over the place; him that's running for Congress. He's a fine man; I talked with him. He asked me could he hold a parlor rally here next Tuesday night."

"A parlor rally! What's that?"

"Oh, just getting together a lot of the fellows. Giving them a chance to meet him and hear him talk. Say, mother, it's great, ain't it? He'll be elected to Congress, sure. And getting close to him this way now — it's a fine start for me; I'll be doing something in politics myself some time."

"Well, now, think of that!" exclaimed Mrs. Donohue. Her face shone again, eager and youthful, as Jerry's own; her dread of the saloon was forgotten. "Isn't it the fine chance for you, Jerry! A Congressman! I wonder can I get the curtains all washed and the carpets beat and a tidy crocheted to hide the grease spot your head makes on the red plush chair. And my best black skirt needs turning."

"What would you bother with a lot of things like that for? This is just to be a rough men's party, mother; and you'll spend the evening with Mrs. Driscoll or Mrs. O'Toole — and some time later he'll come out and make you a social visit; he declared he would, nothing could stop him from it, upon his soul, he thought that well of your boy."

"Then I won't get to see him next Tuesday at all, at all!" cried Mrs. Donohue.

"Ah, well, you might hang about the house till he comes and then dodge out the back door — if you're that set on it."

Jerry had a desire to talk over the exciting prospect with some one else besides his mother; he had a desire to talk it over with the most exciting person he knew, and that was Dave Scanlan's sister Nora. He could n't help feeling that in Nora's eyes he might derive a little more importance from the fact that he was about to entertain so distinguished a guest. And when he mentioned to his mother that he thought he would slip down and see how the Scanlans were bearing the news, she was possibly not deceived.

"It's the jealous pair that Michael and Delia Scanlan will be, no doubt," she commented. "'T would be the grand thing for them if they could get Mr. Maxwell into their parlor. But don't you be making Nora feel too bad over it, Jerry."

Somewhat self-consciously Jerry grinned and took his departure.

Calling on Nora was not an unmixed pleasure; for it always meant calling on the Scanlan family. Now Michael Scanlan glowered at Jerry over his newspaper and muttered a greeting so faint that it perished in the thicket of his black whiskers; and Mrs. Scanlan, gaunt and shrewish, opened at once with a note of envy and derision in her voice.

"Well, I hear you're in luck, Jerry, what with a politician taking a shine to you, and little enough you deserve it, for spending your hours in a bar-room. It's a good punishment to Dave that it was n't him that was picked on. Though why it should have been you and not him is more than I can see."

"It was just a chance shot, I guess," said Jerry.

"I've no reason to suppose it could have been anything else," replied Mrs. Scanlan; her indignation was causing her to rock vigorously.

"How silly you are, both of you!" Nora looked from one to the other with mischievous eyes. "He liked Jerry's looks the best, and that was all there was to it. Going to invite me to the party, Jerry?"

"I'll invite you to come and peek in through the window. That's what mother is going to do. I'll watch a chance to slip you some ice cream."

"That's a nice kind of an invitation."

"I'll invite you to come now and have a soda with me."

That invitation she was willing to accept. It was only by the employment of such artifices that Jerry was ever able to enjoy her society alone. This evening he felt he was especially fortunate; so often of late, when he had stopped in at the Scanlans', had he found Charley Corcoran, of Corcoran's Drug Store, seated there.

So they walked down the street together, he a stalwart six-foot figure of a young man, honest-eyed, clean-lipped, straight and strong; she a slim, young girl, with dark eyes that shot merry glances and a voice that made every syllable she uttered music in Jerry's ears.

Jerry escorted her to Bundy's Drug Store, not Corcoran's.

II

ON Friday and Saturday Mrs. Donohue energetically
conducted a house-cleaning; she took up the parlor and
dining-room carpets, draped them on a clothes-line in
the front yard, and with her head swathed in a blue
polka-dot handkerchief, beat them with a rattan stick.

"If he's good enough to go to Congress, he's good
enough to have this house fixed up for him a bit," she
would say. She could not help exhibiting her pride over
the distinction that had been conferred on Jerry. "And
it the first chance he's ever had to vote in all his life!"
she would conclude. "And a Congressman making up
to him right off! Ain't he the lucky boy!"

By Saturday night she had put down the carpets and
washed the parlor and dining-room curtains; these on
Monday had to be darned, for they were old and did
not well endure her vigorous cleansing. On Monday,
too, she washed the windows and dusted the furniture,
the pictures, the chandeliers — singing all the while.
She finished crocheting the tidy and hung it over the
stain on the red plush chair. The paper roses on the parlor mantel had become soiled after six months of decorative service; unwilling to throw them away as having
outlived their beauty, she went over them, petal by
petal, with a bit of damp cloth. No gardener ever tended
living roses with more care than that which she had

bestowed in trying to preserve the fresh appearance of these flowers. Likewise, though an object of even greater solicitude, had the white memorial dove been grimed and flecked. Against a sheaf of rushes and enclosed in a frame lined with white satin, it hung head down, wings outstretched, transfixed by an arrow which was issuing at its back. Beneath it, worked in red worsteds, was inscribed, "At Rest."

"I declare, Jerry," said Mrs. Donohue, surrendering to despondency on Monday evening, "if there's been one thing that I've tried to keep free from spot and stain since your father's death, it's that dove. But what with the soft-coal smoke, the soot, the dust a-flying in from the street, that dove is no longer the pure white bird it ought to be. I hope Mr. Maxwell won't notice the specks on it, and think we've failed in our duty towards the dead."

"You have n't!" Jerry cried, folding her in his arms.

"I've tried not, Jerry." She got a hand free from his embrace and wiped her eyes. "It ain't a room that's been used much, certainly. And when I have come in here, I've always had a thought of him. I've always tried not to have thoughts or say words in here such as — as he would n't like if he knew. And I've felt you've always tried to do the same, Jerry."

The young man nodded; he was old enough to vote, but there were even yet times when he could not be sure of his voice.

"Now stop your worrying," he said at last soothingly. "You're just played out. You've made the house look fine — but you need n't to have."

[11]

"I wanted it as your father would have liked it if ever a Congressman had come to sit with him. But I *am* tuckered, and there's things to do to-morrow — so I guess I'll go to bed. Good-night, child."

Jerry stroked her cheek.

"You ought n't to work like this for me or anybody else — not even for dad," he said gently. "Good-night."

Tuesday evening, when Jerry came home from the mill, he found his mother in a state of triumphant exhaustion.

"I did think at one time I never would get through," she said. "I hope I've froze up enough ice cream and fried enough doughnuts. How many do you think will come, Jerry?"

"You mean to say you've been freezing ice cream and frying doughnuts! Well, if you ain't a wonder! Mr. Maxwell did n't mean we should do that kind of thing."

"I don't know as that's Mr. Maxwell's affair," replied Mrs. Donohue with dignity. "If you're going to have folks, be hospitable. I borrowed the Driscolls' freezer, and that along with our own makes four gallons. So it ain't as if you'd been inviting your friends to an empty house. I'll spend the evening at the Driscolls' — and say, Jerry, Mrs. Driscoll asked if we might n't slip over some time during the party, her and me, and peek through the window — she'd so like to see the Congressman. I told her we could."

"Sure," said Jerry. "And if you'll make some kind of signal, I'll sneak you out some ice cream."

In his black suit and stiff collar, with a salmon pink necktie which flared violently against the deeper pink of his neck and face, Jerry descended the stairs. His mother had just finished putting the dishes away in the kitchen.

"My, but you do look nice!" she assured him. "Now I'm going up to change my dress, so I'll be ready to run over to Mrs. Driscoll's the moment he comes. Don't stir round and get yourself all mussed up and excited, child; just sit still and be calm."

Obediently, but with an uncomfortable consciousness of his collar, Jerry sat in the parlor and endeavored to give his mind to "Ben Hur." The doorbell jangling violently summoned him.

A brewery wagon was waiting at the curb; the teamster was waiting at the door.

"Two kegs for J. Donohue," said the teamster. "This the place?"

"Yes, but I did n't order any —"

"Sent by John Maxwell."

The teamster strode down to his wagon and lifted a keg out in his arms. Jerry held the door open for him dumbly.

"In there." Jerry pointed to the dining-room.

"Jer-ry!" The call came from upstairs just as the teamster had departed for the second keg. "Did you go to the door?"

"Yes, mother."

"Who was it?"

"Oh, just a — just a mistake."

The brewery wagon was turning away when another

wagon drew up at the curb. At the door Jerry waited apprehensively. The driver lugged a bushel basket filled with tumblers up the steps.

"In there," Jerry murmured, pointing to the dining-room.

On a second trip the man brought in four quarts of whiskey and two boxes of cigars.

Jerry closed the dining-room door upon these contributions; then, as if at a loss, he inserted his forefinger down the front of his collar and gave his chin three or four meditative hoists. He returned gravely to the parlor and resumed his reading of "Ben Hur."

His mother descended the stairs. "What in the world have you been tramping about so for, when I told you to sit still and be calm?" she demanded. "I thought the house was coming down."

"Oh, I wanted to make sure everything was all right," he answered. "And it is. Now I'll read you a chapter out of this book."

And thus placidly were they engaged when the jangling bell proclaimed the first arrival.

"I guess I won't wait to see Mr. Maxwell after all," said Mrs. Donohue nervously, "unless this is him."

From up the stairs, whither she retreated, she saw Jerry open the door and admit Dave Scanlan and four or five other friends. Then she took her departure undetected by the guests.

Until the arrival of the candidate, there was an atmosphere of dismal decorum. The young men, assembling at last to the number of twenty-five, conversed in funereally low voices.

JERRY

At last an automobile puffed up the street and stopped before the house. Instantly the two front windows were blocked with heads; the front door was flung open.

"It's him!" Jerry announced with excitement.

Mr. Maxwell was a believer in dash, in "snap." He ran up the plank walk and divested himself of his fur overcoat as he ran.

"Hello! hello! hello!" he cried; he grasped Jerry's welcoming hand and tossed his overcoat into a corner by the door. "Say, old man, I'm sorry to be late. I've brought with me these friends of mine — Mr. Donohue, this is Mr. Tracy, Mr. Jenks, Mr. Tiffin. Darned good fellows, the whole bunch. And, say" — he caught Jerry's arm and dropped his voice to a whisper — "there are half a dozen more coming up the hill now — saw my machine, gave me a cheer, and invited themselves. One of them's Jimmy Burns, running for the Legislature. You won't mind letting 'em in? I guess there's stuff enough for all."

"Oh, sure," said Jerry. "The more the merrier."

He was quite exhilarated; the candidate's bounding manner reassured him after the gloomy tension of the last half-hour.

"Now introduce me all round," said Mr. Maxwell. "And then," he added in Jerry's ear, "open up the stuff."

It was wonderful how Mr. Maxwell's entrance invigorated the assembly. "Well, boys, here we are again," was his happy, general greeting. To individuals he was more than kind; he held hands affectionately while he endeavored to recall the Christian name. To his host he vouchsafed an ecstatic moment, calling him "Jerry." "And I remember you too," he said to Dave Scanlan. "You were with Jerry the other day at Grady's — and you're — Scanlan. Yes, to be sure, Scanlan. I tell you, I don't often forget a face — though sometimes I go a little shy on names."

Jerry flung open the door into the dining-room.

"Fellows," he announced, "Mr. Maxwell has kindly provided some liquid refreshments and cigars for this evening; if you will kindly step this way."

"A-ay!" cheered the crowd, surging forward.

"And," shouted Jerry, "there's ice cream and dough-nuts on the house."

Mr. Maxwell got inside the dining-room door. He worked his way into the corner where Jerry was ladling ice cream out of a freezer.

"Jerry," he said, "I'll bet this was your mother's doing."

"It was that."

"Well, I want some of that ice cream in a moment."

He turned; some one passed him a glass of beer.

"Gentlemen! Friends!" Mr. Maxwell raised his glass above his head, and they all listened. "I want every one here to fill his glass and then join me in a toast that I will propose."

The activity in the neighborhood of the kegs was resumed. But at last every one was supplied.

"All ready, Congressman," shouted Dave Scanlan.

Mr. Maxwell mounted a chair. "Gentlemen, I want you all to know that Mrs. Donohue with her own hands froze this ice cream and fried these doughnuts for you boys to-night. She wanted you and me, coming here to-night to welcome each other, to enjoy ourselves; and so she did all this for us. Now I say that when the women come into the campaign and give us their support in this way we're bound to win. And I want to propose the health of Mrs. Donohue — God bless her!"

There was great cheering; they all drank with avidity. Jerry in his gay excitement accidentally slapped a chunk of ice cream on the floor. He gathered it up with his hands and chucked it into the freezer upon the salted ice, complimenting himself meanwhile on his discretion in withholding from his mother knowledge of the beer. Now knowledge could come to her unaccompanied by any sting of disappointment or disillusion.

Jerry was at last free to go into the parlor. Mr. Maxwell hailed his entrance — waved him forward and put his hand on Jerry's shoulder. "Fellows," he said, "I want you all to join with me in singing the praises of our host, Mr. Jerry Donohue." He seated himself promptly at the piano and, playing the accompaniment, began, "For he's a jolly good fellow"; soon all except the blushing Jerry were hilariously challenging a denial. At the end, when Mr. Maxwell was about to leave the instrument, the man whom he had introduced to Jerry as Mr. Tracy spoke up.

"Gentlemen," said Mr. Tracy, "I move that Mr. Maxwell continue playing this piece and that we continue singing the same words with reference to him."

"Second the motion!" shouted Jerry enthusiastically.

So Mr. Maxwell amiably yielded to the demand.

JERRY

In the midst of the uproar there entered the delegation that the pianist had warned Jerry to expect. They were six or eight in number, rough young men who had not, like the other guests, arrayed themselves with scrupulous care, and who had been drinking — were, in fact, slightly inebriated. They bunched themselves in the doorway and shouted rapidly in unison: "Rah, rah, rah, Maxwell!"

"Jimmy Burns!" cried Maxwell, joyously springing from the piano stool and going forward with outstretched hand. He led the dissipated-looking, unwashed leader of the gang up to Jerry and introduced him as the next member of the Legislature from the district. Jerry hospitably showed the newcomers into the dining-room; the whiskey bottles engaged their interest. Jerry returned to the intellectual center.

"Mr. Maxwell," he ventured to speak up boldly in a lull; "I'm sure we'd all like to hear you talk on the tariff and the other issues."

Maxwell assumed a conventional posture, resting his arm negligently on the mantelpiece.

"Friends," he said, "I don't want to talk to you to-night about the tariff; I'd rather take that and similar matters up later in the campaign, on the stump. In this Congressional election I don't look on the tariff as much of an issue. The important issue for the voters in this Congressional district is the character of the man that's to represent them in Congress. The all-important thing for this district is to send a man to Congress who stands close to the heart of the people — a man who mixes with you, who sympathizes with your life, who

does not hold himself aloof from you and your joys
and your sorrows. The man who takes a human interest
in his constituents, my friends, is the man who will best
serve them. No matter whether he belongs to the Republican Party or to the Democratic Party, the effi-
cient representative must be a democratic man. Now,
my friends, in all modesty I wish to contrast myself
with my opponent. You know what sort of a man he is
— or if you don't know I can tell you. Rich, prosperous,
arrogant — one of the aristocracy. He lives in a big
house, he has his automobile and his horses, he wears a
fur overcoat. Well — some of the rest of us may have all
those advantages. But that does n't make us hold ourselves aloof. We mix in with the people just the same.
But my opponent — he's one of these silk-stocking poli-
ticians. He's not what we call a 'mixer.' You'd never
see him coming down here to talk to you fellows this
way and having a nice social time with you all. Now,
how does it work out — that type of man and my type
of man, when we get to legislating? A comparison of .
our records, made when we served together last year
in the State Senate, will enlighten you. During that
time I was always accessible to my constituents, always
glad to see them and help them, no matter how unimportant or how destitute of influence they might happen
to be. During that time I was in a position to grant no
less than two hundred and forty-seven favors — and
I granted them, every one. I'm only sorry that this
district here was n't included in my Senatorial district,
because then some of you boys might have got some of
these plums."

There was hearty laughter at this.

"Or maybe you would n't have, because I guess most of you were n't voters then."

This sly sally was also much appreciated.

"And now, what was my opponent doing in the same time for his constituents? He had as many opportunities as I to grant favors. Did he grant a single one? No. Did he get a single job for the needy? No. Did he take the slightest interest in his constituents or seek to do them the slightest human service? No. They bored him. He denied himself to them if they came to see him. He had no time for the man in trouble. He associated only with the men of his own set. He neglected his constituents; and as he neglected them then, he'll neglect them if they send him to Washington; and as I served mine then, I'll serve them if they send me to Washington. As Congressman I'll be able to do more favors to my friends than I could as State Senator; don't you forget it. Now, my friends, when I'm on the stump, I'll talk tariff and other national issues; but I want to impress it upon you, and I want you to impress it on your friends, that the important issue in this Congressional campaign is the personality of the two men who come before you asking for your votes."

"And you'll get 'em!" cried from the dining-room doorway Jimmy Burns.

"A-ay!" shouted the crowd, and they clapped and whistled.

Jerry did not at first make any demonstration; then, with a dull idea that his position as host imposed the duty, he feebly clapped his hands.

"Don't you think it was a corking little speech?"
said Dave Scanlan in his ear.

"No," said Jerry, "I don't."

Dave looked at him in amazement; he had great respect for Jerry's opinion.

"Why not?"

"Oh, I'll tell you some other time."

He turned away from Dave; he was really quite miserable. His sensitiveness had rebelled against the unworthy, cheap appeal; his intelligence had detected the fraud; his pride was hurt. It galled him to be told in such plain and insolent terms that Maxwell in coming to his house had performed an act of condescension; it angered Jerry to feel that he alone appreciated the impudence.

At another time he would have been amused by the diversion in which the lanky, crafty-eyed Jimmy Burns and the chunky, red-faced follower known as "Bill" became engaged. They had temporarily given their attention to doughnuts rather than to whiskey, and were endeavoring now to utilize one of the stout circular confections in a game of ring-toss; they stood several feet apart, and each took turns in trying to circumvent with the missile the other's gravely upraised forefinger.

"Bill, you wiggled it," complained Burns after a failure.

"I did not; you can't pitch because you can't stand," retorted Bill.

"Can't stand! I'm standing for the Legislature, my son, and you don't want to forget it."

"You for the Legislature! Go on! If you get more than one vote, it'll be because you're a repeater."

"Ah, you're sore because they handed you the lemon. You thought you was going to run yourself."

"Ah, crawl under the sink along with the other pipes."

"Say, does anybody smell gas?" said Burns.

"You first, with your nose above the leak," replied Bill.

"Your valve's flappin'; it needs a new washer. Try this."

Burns slammed the doughnut into his friend's face.

Bill sprang forward and seizing his assailant by the shoulders propelled him violently backward through the parlor. Too late Jerry perceived the disaster that impended and sprang to avert it. The two went crashing into the corner where hung the memorial dove. Jerry flung them apart and exposed the ruin. The satin-sheathed frame was crumpled and broken; the bird lay crushed upon the floor. Jerry said nothing; he stooped and picked it up and carried it from the room. As he bore it up the stairs he caressed it with his hand as if it had been a living, wounded thing. He laid it on his bed and looked at it for a little while; he lifted the torn wing and turned over the crushed body; it seemed to him past mending. Then he went down again to his guests.

Apparently the mishap had quieted them; when Jerry entered, they were gathered about Maxwell listening. Jerry had no longer the eager desire to crowd into the front rank of the speaker's audience; he stood a little apart, leaning by an open window.

Then, as he caught the drift of Maxwell's story, his cheeks reddened, his lips set angrily. The young men crowded closer round the narrator, chuckling at intervals, more and more intent. And by the window Jerry's face darkened and grew stern.

The climax of the tale delighted the gathering. While laughter filled the room, Jerry turned his back and looked out of the open window. Then with a start he leaned out. Two women were hastening away from the house across the grass; and though their backs were turned he recognized them — Nora and his mother.

Jerry faced about and walked up to Maxwell, thrusting his guests unceremoniously aside. He overtopped Maxwell by three inches, and he looked down into the man's pale face with blazing eyes. Even before he began to speak a hush had fallen upon the company.

"Mr. Maxwell" — Jerry's voice was harsh and rasping — "my mother washed these curtains, beat this carpet, cleaned and swept this room so that it should be fit and decent for you to come into. And you come here and talk smut — here in my mother's room. Now get out."

Maxwell drew back a step. "Oh, look here," he said appeasingly, and he tried to laugh, "don't take it so hard. Why, if I'd known —"

"I don't want to hear one word out of you," said Jerry inexorably. He addressed the others in a quieter voice. "My mother and a friend — a friend of hers wanted to have a look at this great man that's been favoring us. They got a look at him — through that window just now while he was telling his story. The man that shames my mother does n't stay under this roof."

Maxwell, very pale, shrugged his shoulders and achieved a smile.

"Come along, boys," he said. "I had no idea this was a Sunday-school class — and I don't know that I've ever before been insulted by my host."

No other voice was raised; there was a forbidding look on Jerry's face. Less than half the company followed Maxwell from the house; the others lingered.

There was an awkward silence.

"Well, I guess I'll be going," said Dave Scanlan. "Say — I guess you're all right, Jerry. I'm with you."

"So'm I," muttered sheepishly some of the others. "Good-night, Jerry."

"Good-night."

When Jerry called at the Driscolls' for his mother, she looked as if she had been crying. She looked at him with mingled appeal and reproach. He merely said, "They've gone, mother."

But out of doors he asked abruptly, —

"What did you think of him? I saw you and Nora leaving the window."

"Oh, Jerry!" She dabbed her handkerchief to her eyes.

"I kicked him out of the house," said Jerry, "when I heard that. I'm sorry, mother."

Then in her joy and contrition that she should ever have doubted her son, she stopped, flung her arms about Jerry, and wept on his breast. A few moments later, ascending the steps of the house she said, —

"And now, Jerry, child, you're done with politics, I hope?"

"Oh, no," he answered. "To-night I've just begun with politics."

She paused on the threshold to look at him. There was a new confidence and knowledge in his eyes, in his smile. Then with poignant sorrow and exultant pride she understood; this night she was present at the passing of the boy, the awakening of the man.

III

Two nights after the parlor rally, Jerry, according to his
custom, was assisting his mother in the drying of the
supper dishes. When he had wiped the last saucer, he
remarked with an impromptu air, —

"I guess I'll be going up the road a piece. I told
Dave Scanlan I'd see him."

"It's a wonder it's Dave and not some other in the
family you'd be seeing," replied Mrs. Donohue. "Working with Dave day in, day out, as you are. It's for him
you put on your new tie and your best coat, I suppose."

"What'd be the use of teasing me?" said Jerry with
a grin. "You don't think Nora would look at me —
after her spying upon me with you the other night and
seeing the kind of company I keep."

"I'm thinking Dave has set her straight upon that.
If he has n't I will."

"You're a good creature, but you must not always
be so possessed to be helping your son along. Hold up
your cheek now, till I give it a smack." He held it up
himself in his two hands and smacked his loudest kiss
in the middle of it.

"Go along then with you, and don't be plaguing the
heart out of me," cried his mother.

Then, when he had gone, she sat down in the parlor in her rocking-chair and rocked and lamented to herself aloud. Grown up he was, indeed, when he was for leaving his mother in the evenings to be going to see the girls. Better that, to be sure, than to be hanging about the saloons. And yet if he could but be contented at home after supper always, forever and ever. She looked at the square clean spot on the wall where the memorial dove, now in the taxidermist's hands, had hung, and her eyes filled. If only her man Jim had lived.

Meanwhile, Jerry walked briskly up the foggy street. The electric light ahead, caught in a spider-web of mist, glowed like a great moist topaz. The windows in the little wooden houses shone in the wetness and the dankness, all hospitable and pleasant; each one that he passed had an encouraging message for the young man. From the mills at the foot of the town came the heavy, slogging vibration and clang, vibration and clang, that continued without intermission, day and night. Just now it seemed to Jerry a rather cheerful sound; he fancifully translated the beat of it into the adjuration, "Steady that does it. Steady that does it."

A still more cheerful sound reached him presently and thrilled his heart, for it proceeded from the house towards which his steps were directed, a house planted on a knoll above its neighbors and accessible by means of a zigzag flight of steps. To the accompaniment of a piano a girl's voice was singing, "Kathleen Mavourneen"; at the foot of the steps Jerry stopped and listened. Never, he was sure, had he heard, never would he hear, any one sing more appealingly. His young heart thrilled to the melody, to the vivid picture of the singer with which his imagination presented him — the rich, red cheeks and dark, curling hair and lovely, fluctuant, trilling throat.

He mounted the steps and knocked on the door. It was opened by Nora herself — Nora, with her quick, startled smile. The prettiest girl that Jerry knew, she was also always the best dressed; she wore this evening a white muslin gown with short frilled sleeves, and her hair was banded with a black velvet ribbon. The hand that she gave Jerry was white and soft, the voice with which she greeted him was clear, uncorrupted by the harsh and shrill intonations of the neighborhood. Slender and delicate, she had a round little chin, a sensitive little mouth, a fastidious little nose — all uniting with the flash of her smile and the color in her cheeks to endear her to the young man.

"I heard you from the street, Nora," he said, "and of course I had to come in."

"Oh, that was it, was it? I had hopes you'd strolled up to see me on purpose."

"So I had. Nora, you've a great way of guessing what I'd be at."

"It must be because I give it so little thought. I'd be guessing now you'd be at speaking with father and mother; it was just them I was amusing."

"Keep on with it, keep on with it," said Jerry. "I shan't mind."

He followed Nora into the sitting-room, in the middle of which Michael Scanlan and his wife were occupying an S-shaped "conversation chair." Michael, facing the door, nodded to Jerry in silence; Mrs. Scanlan glanced over her shoulder and remarked, "Oh, it's you, Jerry," in a manner that was distinctly more fretful than welcoming.

But Jerry was not easily dismayed.

"Sure it might be any other creature that was happening to pass along the road. It would be a fine struggle a man would have with himself, not to get drawn in by the sound of Nora's voice. Now has she sung you 'The Widow O'Toole,' Mrs. Scanlan?"

"I don't care for Nora to be singing them vulgar songs," replied Mrs. Scanlan, over her shoulder.

"Oh, now, would you be calling it vulgar!" Jerry exclaimed. "Just a bit of cheerfulness, to my way of thinking. Will you let me see what songs are there, Nora?"

While he stood beside her at the piano, he was aware that her parents watched him with lazy hostility. They were North of Ireland people and Protestants, and the Donohues had come from Cork. But Jerry did not feel very much depressed by the parental antipathy. Nora had a mind of her own, and he ventured to think it was favorably disposed toward him. So he continued to chatter in his lively manner: "There's 'Father O'Flynn'; the sight of it makes me almost feel I can sing myself. And 'Mulligan's Musketeers' — that's another I can hear inside my head, but I've got it safe shut up there; don't be scared. — You know, Nora, you look fit to sing in grand opera to-night — is n't it a fact, Mrs. Scanlan?"

"She may be doing that yet," responded Mrs. Scanlan severely. "We expect great things of her."

[29]

"We do," agreed Mr. Scanlan, with equal severity.

"Sure," said Jerry. "And don't you be disappointing us, Nora."

"I think there's no great danger," observed Mrs. Scanlan with a malicious pungency that Jerry affected not to notice.

"Well," Jerry said, "let it be anything you please Nora. Just sing."

"I'll have time for only about one song. Maybe not for that. I told Charley I'd be ready at eight and it's that now."

"Where is it you're going?"

"To a dance at McCabe's Hall."

"Who with?"

"Charley Corcoran."

"Oh!" said Jerry. "Well, you're dressed more fit for grand opera than for McCabe's Hall."

"I always like to dress up when I go to a dance."

"I always want Nora to look like a lady wherever she goes," interjected her mother.

"Them that are of a low class will be less likely to get familiar with her," added Mr. Scanlan.

"She won't find many of a high grade at McCabe's Hall," replied Jerry.

"As good maybe as what some young fellows have in their mothers' parlors," said Mrs. Scanlan.

Jerry reached hastily for a sheet of music. "Come on, Nora," he said. "'Kathleen Mavourneen.'"

She had sung only one stanza when her mother interrupted.

"Nora, there's some one at the door."

JERRY

It proved to be Charley Corcoran. Jerry had always felt antipathy if not animosity towards the light-haired, scorbutic young man who was frequently standing in the doorway of Corcoran's Drug Store. It was more than the mild, generic antagonism that the man in workman's clothes extends towards each member of the class that habitually wears white collars and tries to keep its trousers creased. That stronger feeling, innate and indefinable, was intensified in Jerry while he watched Corcoran's debonair entrance and observed his mannered greetings of Nora and her family. "Dude!" Jerry thought, and in his mind the word was charged with the energy of rancor and contempt. "Dude!" He wanted to cry it aloud when Corcoran addressed him with patronizing suavity: "I hear you had quite a political meeting at your house, Donohue."

"The less it's talked about the better," Jerry replied ungraciously.

"You may well say that," observed Mrs. Scanlan.

"Well, you know, Mrs. Scanlan," said Corcoran confidentially, "when you mix into politics you've got to put up with all sorts. Finding that out, eh, Donohue? Your man Maxwell is all right, though; he can have my vote."

"I thought likely." In his extreme aversion Jerry could not permit himself words enough even to make sarcasm effective.

"Oh, sure, he's the fellow. — Well, Nora, all ready to come and trip the light fantastic with me?"

Jerry wondered how Nora could endure a man who talked to her in that fashion. It seemed to him a hack-

neyed and objectionable form of smartness. And yet
Nora seemed smiling and eager; she would be ready in
a moment; she had only to get her wrap; she had n't
been to a dance in weeks and she was awfully excited.

While she was out of the room Corcoran addressed
himself to her father. What did Mr. Scanlan think of
the rumor that the Works were to be sold? Mr. Scanlan grunted his contempt for the rumor. The Purroy
Steel Works were a family affair; they would never be
sold.

"I'm sure I hope not," said Corcoran. "For of course
if they were to be sold, there's no telling what might
happen to all the men there. They might be laid off,
they might be turned out of their jobs. A man is lucky
in these days if he has a good business of his own, that
can't be sold over his head."

"You don't need to do any worryin' on my account,"
Mr. Scanlan replied testily.

"Oh, certainly not; oh, I don't suppose there's any
real danger," Corcoran made haste to say. "Only, as
I look round and see the other young fellows, like
Donohue here, I can't help feeling I'm pretty lucky, to
be fixed as I am."

"Them that are satisfied with what they've got have
a right to feel lucky," retorted the formidable Mr.
Scanlan. "Them are the ones generally that have got
more than they deserve."

Corcoran threw up one arm and pretended to dodge.
"Never touched me. You and Mrs. Scanlan know I
must have more than I've got if I'm to be satisfied. I
hope you folks wish I may get it."

The severe and tight-lipped silence on the part of both Mr. Scanlan and his wife intimated no enthusiastic assurance that they would forward their visitor's desires. Corcoran was so little abashed, however, that he laughed indulgently and remarked, "I believe Donohue has got you all hypnotized."

Incensed beyond endurance by this charge, Mr. Scanlan brought his fist down on the arm of the conversation chair and vociferated, "No man can do that to me. No, sir. No man."

And Mrs. Scanlan looking malevolently over her shoulder admonished him, "It seems to me you'd better think what you're saying, Mr. Corcoran."

In Jerry, who was silent, disdain triumphed over anger. He walked to the table at one side of the room and, picking up the copy of "Ben Hur," bound in alligator skin, began to turn the pages.

Mrs. Scanlan, impartial in her favors, at once admonished him: "I always tell Dave to be careful how he handles that book."

Jerry put down "Ben Hur" and turned to the music rack. And then Nora entered, radiant and eager, with a gray cloak over her shoulders, new white gloves on her hands, and a scarf encircling her face.

"We're off," said Corcoran, stepping forward to meet her. "By-by, people."

He took Nora's arm and steered her by the elbow in a manner that enraged Jerry. Nora, however, did not resent it; the sound of her gay laughter seemed to linger in the room even after she had gone.

Jerry felt obliged to linger also for what should be

a decent interval. Mr. Scanlan, however, commanded him to sit down, so he took a chair in front of Mrs. Scanlan's section of the conversation chair, unwilling to receive any more of her Parthian glances. Mr. Scanlan, short-necked and stiff, screwed himself round to address the young man.

"I will have it understood," he said, "that Nora is not for no drug clerk."

Though encouraged by the statement, Jerry felt it unwise to offer any comment. After a brief pause Mr. Scanlan continued, —

"She is not for no mill-hand, either. She is not for the likes of any one around here. That is not what we have been raising her for."

"No," asserted Mrs. Scanlan with dyspeptic vigor, "it is not. Would I have raised her like a little lady just for that? Twenty she was last month, and her two hands still that white and soft that she might have been raised in a big house with a large lawn around it and an automobile to take her riding whenever she wished. Never a thing about the house have I let her do with them hands, neither cooking nor scrubbing nor washing nor ironing; 't is my own I have worked all these years, and without complaining. No fit wife would she be for a poor man, Jerry; mind that."

"I guess if she fell in love with a poor man she'd be a good wife to him," Jerry ventured to say.

"She understands she is not to fall in love with a poor man," replied Mrs. Scanlan.

"How is she by way of meeting the rich?"

"By means of her talent. If she does n't be singing

before long in grand opera, she will be singing anyway in grand houses. I said to her only this very night, 'Nora,' I said, 'you'll be a millionaire's wife before you die.'"

"Well," said Jerry, "you need n't try to discourage me by telling me that, Mrs. Scanlan. Maybe one of these days I'll be that millionaire."

He rose, and Mr. Scanlan rose also.

"Jerry," he said, laying his hand on the young man's shoulder and speaking not unkindly, "you'd better be putting the notion clean out of your head. I'm wishing you well, but my girl is not for you, and that's the fact. Instead of laying up money for my old age I've spent it giving her the best I could — she's had her piano and her clothes and her lessons in music and singing, and I've been glad to give them to her, for I want her to better herself in the world. Now you understand how we feel."

"Yes, but of course it can't alter my feelings, Mr. Scanlan. And if I found that Nora cared for me, you could n't expect me to hold off, just for the sake of obliging you and Mrs. Scanlan."

"I'd like to know where you get your impudence," Mrs. Scanlan exclaimed. "Not from your ma; she never would talk back like that. And your pa, he was a mild, quiet kind of man."

"Of course I don't mean to be impudent, Mrs. Scanlan." Jerry's voice was as placating as he could make it. "If ever I can get Nora to consent, I hope I can get you and Mr. Scanlan to do the same. I should feel badly if I could n't."

"Well, you can't," snapped Mrs. Scanlan. "And anyway Nora has too much sense to listen to you."

Jerry flushed. "I'll say good-night," he remarked, and he left the room.

Mr. Scanlan followed him apologetically, hospitably, into the hall and opened the door for him.

"We can't back you up on this, Jerry," he said, "but you're a good boy, you are, and if I had another daughter you could have her and welcome. But not Nora — no, not Nora."

Out in the dampness of the night Jerry felt disconsolate. He wished that Mr. and Mrs. Scanlan had n't forced from him a declaration of his intentions with regard to Nora. He wished that they had never suspected his intentions, that they had limited their opposition to Charley Corcoran, that they would n't try to influence Nora in any way. It seemed to him that, considering the foolish standards they were always holding before Nora, she was quite wonderful to remain her lovely, sweet, unspoiled self. He wanted her to go singing through life, of course; but he felt that she herself wanted to do more than that, and that she would be happier if given work as well as play over which to sing.

If she married him, she would have work enough; Jerry admitted that somewhat ruefully. Of course his mother, who would live with them, was a great housekeeper and would no doubt insist on doing more than her share. Still, a husband earning four dollars and a half a day could n't provide his wife with servants and an automobile and the other luxuries that Mr. and Mrs. Scanlan seemed to regard as essential to Nora's happiness

in the married estate. And yet four dollars and a half a
day was a good wage, and Jerry thought that in the
course of another six months, when old John Flannery
retired on a pension, he was pretty sure to get Flannery's
job, and that meant seven dollars a day. And he didn't
see why, on such an income, he couldn't make Nora
happy.

After all it was silly to put such aggrieved questions
to one's self, especially as it was not Mr. and Mrs. Scanlan so much as Charley Corcoran that was dangerous.
Corcoran's jaunty manner, his air of knowing the world,
his hands, so different from those of a workingman, his
subtle assumptions all excited Jerry's fears and hostility; all seemed to him quite likely to have a potent influence upon Nora. He walked on slowly, more and
more dejected; it occurred to him that, although Nora
might hold him blameless for the scene on which she
had looked two nights before, she must regard his part
as having been one of boyish incompetence — and by
contrast she probably felt that Charley Corcoran was
a person of wisdom, experience, and balance.

And perhaps he was; and perhaps he was right in
giving credence to the rumor that had in the last week
been circulating through the mills and exciting uneasiness and apprehension. A year before, when old David
Purroy had died, there had been, besides mourning,
uneasiness and apprehension. But as time had passed
and the son James Purroy, who had inherited the Works,
gave no sign of making a change in his father's policy,
the sense of security returned to the mill-workers and
their families. David Purroy alone among the mill-

owners of his generation had established the practice
of employing three shifts of men instead of two; he had
paid the highest scale of wages and had surrounded himself with the pick of the iron and steel workers. They
were Scotch and Irish mostly; in the other mills, where
men worked twelve hours a day, were to be found
Poles and Lithuanians and Hungarians.

Now, with the rumor that had within the last few
days mysteriously made its appearance, a chill of anxiety
had passed from house to house. Every one recognized
the probability that if the mills changed ownership,
the liberal and yet none the less successful policy of the
Purroys would be discontinued.

Upon Jerry, walking slowly in his mood of dejection,
these considerations pressed now with special force;
from the confident contemplation of Flannery's job
at seven dollars a day he turned to the dismayed
imagining of himself with no job at all. So precariously
placed, how could he hope for success in any rivalry
with one so independent, so well aware of the advantages of his position, as Charley Corcoran?

His musings brought him to the crest of the hill,
whence he looked down into the pit of strange, irradi-
ated fog that concealed the sprawling steel works and
the sluggish river. Now and then with a grim detona-
tion a burst of flame would lick through the haze and
vanish, leaving the vapors to seethe and simmer up-
wards towards the dim aura that overspread the heav-
ens. Jerry plunged on down the slope, more absorbed
in fighting the vapors within him than in contemplating
those without. He strode briskly on to the mill gates,

swung off for half a mile through the lower part of the town, ascended the hill until he reached the main street, and then struck off along it towards home. But as he passed McCabe's, the sound of dance music from the upper windows came to him; after he had gone by a few steps he stopped, turned back, and mounted the stairs. He paid twenty-five cents for a ticket and entered the hall.

It was crowded with dancers, bumping one another, shrilly exclaiming, shrilly laughing, above the sound of the tinny piano and the two raucous violins. Naked gas-jets flared from brackets high along the walls; those more distant were encircled by a dim effulgence, owing to the dust that swam thick above the dancers' heads. The more rowdy of the young men of the town, the more brazen of the young women, were conspicuously present, pushing, shoving, dancing boisterously, wooing and responding to advances with flagrant publicity. Jerry stood watching for Nora to make her appearance, fair as a lily among the blowzy, loud, robust young women; he saw her presently, her slim, white figure and sweet, flushed face emerged for one shining instant, and then the profaning mob shut her again from view. From time to time he had glimpses of her, twice she passed near him but without seeing him; Corcoran, holding her close, was laughing, and talking in her ear with an effect that was to Jerry of odious intimacy. And she seemed to be enjoying it, to be responsive; Jerry saw her swing her head round and look into her partner's face and laugh gayly.

The music ceased, the dancers swarmed in search of

seats, Jerry held his tenaciously. The length of the room away Nora and Corcoran established themselves; Jerry kept his eyes upon them until the music began again and they again were lost in the throng. They reappeared, they came circling down the room, they passed within a few feet of Jerry; three times he watched them pass him thus and did not move. But when they made their fourth approach, he sprang up, shouldered his way among the other dancers, and confronted Nora. "My turn," he said; and Nora, with a little cry of surprise and pleasure, slipped from Corcoran's arms into his. "Look here!" cried Corcoran, stupefied; but Jerry whirled her away and laughed exultingly.

"He kissed me," she suddenly murmured in his ear. "I did n't like it, Jerry."

"I 'll pound his face." Jerry stopped dancing, to sweep the room with angry eyes.

"No; it was n't bad enough for that." She tugged gently at his arm. "Dance with me a moment and then take me home, Jerry."

He held her more closely, more firmly, in the proud consciousness that she was seeking his protection. And soon Corcoran appeared in their path, with the smile of one who has been good-naturedly tolerant. He spread out his arms and shouted, "That's right, Donohue, bring that ship into port."

Jerry was for sweeping by him and giving him a good bump as they passed, but Nora stopped.

"I feel you 've had me on your hands enough this evening, Charley," she said. "Jerry's promised to see me home."

"I thought I asked you to this dance."

"Yes, and it was nice of you. But Jerry's asked to take me home, and I was sure you would n't mind."

"Oh, sure; I don't mind who takes you home."

Corcoran turned his back and walked away. The next moment he was dancing with a young woman conspicuous for her unnaturally yellow hair, vermilion cheeks, and generally meretricious effect.

"I did n't want him to get mad," Nora confided plaintively to Jerry. "I don't see why he had to go and get mad."

"I don't see why you care if he did."

"Oh, I don't care very much. For, after all, he'll soon be all right again."

Jerry thought it curious and trying that she should derive satisfaction from that prospect. He suggested that if she was ready to go home, he was.

"Well, I suppose so." She seemed now more than half reluctant.

"It's not a very good crowd for you to be mixed up in," Jerry said apologetically. "That was why I was thinking —"

"Oh, all right, let's go."

If she had been for a moment a little reluctant, the first breath of cool fresh air outdoors seemed to dissipate all regret. She slipped her hand into Jerry's arm, drew close to him confidingly, and said: —

"Oh, Jerry, I'm glad you're taking me home."

The little speech, the slender, gentle, clinging creature made Jerry's heart thump excitedly. "I'm glad too," he said, and stopped there, throbbing, inarticulate.

"I did n't like it in there. I did n't like Charley Corcoran as well in there."

"How about me?"

"Oh, you, I liked you just as well. Better." She glanced at him and seemed to cling a little closer. "Yes. It was so good to see you."

He turned with her from the main street into one that was more quiet, less brightly lighted.

"Why, Jerry, where are you going? This is n't the way home."

"Don't you want to walk for a little while? I'll take you home after I've talked with you."

She did not reply, and he knew then that she was ready for what he had to say. It made the saying of it easier.

"Nora, I love you. I want to marry you, Nora. I'll work for you and love you as long as I live."

The words flowed from him in a tremulous undertone, the more appealing, the more convincing, perhaps, for their quivering, breathless eagerness. She did not withdraw her hand from his arm; she murmured, "Oh, Jerry!"

"Oh, Nora, don't you love me?"

She was not disposed to answer that question. Still she did not withdraw her hand; intent upon exacting all the perquisites of a young woman in her situation, she said: —

"Why do you love me, Jerry?"

Why should n't he? When she was the prettiest, the smartest, the best? Did n't the sound of her voice hang in his ears and make its own soft music there all day long while the hammers were pounding and the blasts were being blown off? Was n't she just a darling through and through? Was n't she, though? — and suddenly aware that the street was as deserted as it was dark, and that she had not withdrawn her hand, Jerry seized her in his arms with a wild and joyous courage, and kissed her, kissed her, kissed her. She stopped him at last with a gentle reproof: —

"Why, Jerry, I did n't say you could do that."

"Yes, but you did n't mind it, really? You — you liked it a little?"

"Why, I don't know. It was such a strange thing for you to do, Jerry."

"Yes, but you liked it?"

"Well," — she hesitated, — "I suppose I sort of liked it — a little."

And now that need for courage was all past, it was with a wild and joyous confidence that Jerry seized her in his arms.

They walked on through the more dimly lighted and less frequented streets of the town, Jerry pouring himself out earnestly, Nora reticent, receptive, yet persuaded to unfold herself by shy degrees. No, she had n't thought he cared for her so much — well, perhaps sometimes she had suspected it — no, she could n't say just when she had begun to care for him; in fact, she did n't know that she really did care for him; well, yes, — in answer to Jerry's grieved upbraiding, — she supposed she did. And she guessed that the first she knew of it was that very night; yes, when he had come into McCabe's Hall and she had seen him, she had wanted to run right up to him.

"I almost feel sorry for Corcoran," Jerry cried triumphantly. "And how I hated him a few moments ago!"

"I wonder if I'm being mean to him."

Jerry, in some alarm, assured her that she was not.

"I think maybe I am. It was just because he liked me so that he kissed me. The same reason that you did."

"Yes, but you did n't like it from him and you did from me," said Jerry jealously. "So don't be thinking of him any more, Nora darling."

"I won't be thinking of him the way I do of you, Jerry."

That qualification pleased him better even than an obedient promise of full renunciation could have done; his soaring spirits had to find expression in another rapturous hug and kiss.

"Oh, Nora! I did n't dare hope — I was afraid you with your talent and all —"

"I have n't any talent — that's all dad's and mother's foolishness."

"They think you have — and anyway they count on your marrying something more than a mill-hand. This will be an awful blow to them — but you don't care — not too much, do you, Nora?"

"I could never have married some swell, the kind they wanted me to." The calm crudity of the statement grated a little on Jerry, even in the extremity of his adoration. "How was I to get the chance? It was n't as if I could ever be a great artist and have society men always at my feet."

"But even if you could, you would n't want to — not now, would you, Nora?"

She laughed and pushed him away. "You must n't be expecting me to be too crazy about you all at once."

"Yes, but I do. I want you to marry me all at once."

"Oh, my goodness, no. Such a time as I'd have with the family! I don't dare."

"Waiting won't make it any easier."

"Maybe it will. When they see that nothing else is likely to happen. Besides, I could n't tell them now, Jerry. Dad's paid for a full term for me at the Conservatory, and I've got to go ahead just as if I meant it. I would n't dare not to."

"Anyway we can give them fair warning what to expect."

"Indeed we'll not, Jerry dear. It's me that has to live in that house, not you. We'll give them no warning at all, not until the time comes."

"When will the time come, Nora?"

"Ah, now, Jerry, how can I settle a thing like that at the moment? It's got to be thought over."

"All right, let's begin to think about it. Here it is, the end of October; what do you say to next spring? Your music term will be over, and maybe I'll have a raise by then, and — anyway I can't wait any longer, Nora darling."

"Well, maybe by the time it gets to be June."

"It's a month in midsummer. Spring, I said."

"I'll see how I'm feeling, perhaps, when it gets along towards April."

That answer pleased him better, the more because he had slipped his arm round her waist and she let him walk with her so. She was his, she was his, she was his!

That was what the night sang to him, that was what the deep voices of the mills were crooning, that was what the train pulling out of the station was panting. What joyous thrills and memories would these common sounds forever have power to stir! Fog and dampness, slimy pavements and blurry lights, what immortality of romance was henceforth theirs! How everything in life was suddenly enriched for him — all by the trustful surrender of this little creature to his encircling arm!

So they walked and talked in whispers, all up and down the quiet streets, and up and down again. He could n't take her home, for there they could n't talk; and she would n't consent to come with him to his house and confide to his mother the happy news. No, she was quite firm on that point; no one should even suspect it until she announced it to her own family. For you could n't trust anybody with a secret like that; if you did, it would be sure to get round. And though it disappointed him that his mother was not to be enlightened and share in his happiness, he was still too happy to argue about that; he was still happy enough just to walk and talk in whispers, and over and over again, when no one could see, to kiss her and feel her sweet, warm kisses on his lips.

And she must have liked it too; that was the exhilarating and exciting thought that he finally bore home with him; for it was late, quite late, when she bade him good-night at her door.

IV

JERRY felt that it was very hard to be as happy as he
was and not let people know about it. There was no
satisfaction in having people see you were happy unless
you told them why. And when you had such a magnificent, such a stupendous reason for your happiness, to
have to keep silent about it was irksome and unnatural,
and made you forget sometimes how happy you really
were.

Besides, the world began to go wrong in various ways.
In the first place, Maxwell was elected to Congress; even
in his radiant condition Jerry took this incident deeply
to heart. To him a Congressman had seemed of necessity a man who towered above other men in character
and intellect and virtue; he had believed that the men
who sat in Congress were all patriotic, earnest students
of public questions, high-minded and sincere. That his
district should choose as its representative a shallow
charlatan chagrined him, made him feel humiliated; the
district was guilty of profaning and polluting the Capitol.
It was no mere personal resentment in Jerry that cried
out at the news of the honor conferred on Maxwell; it
was the inborn sense of respect for law and lawmakers,
and of reverence for the institutions of liberty.

Then there was the renewal of relations between Nora

and Charley Corcoran — a renewal indicating to any casual observer that Corcoran was again a suitor, and that Nora was again willing to be wooed. Of course, as she explained to Jerry, she was n't, and it was n't serious, and there was no need for him to get jealous; she just had to keep her family from suspecting that she was engaged, and she could n't do it unless she saw something of other men.

As for Corcoran, he had become persistent, even insistent in his attentions; Jerry encountered him frequently at the Scanlans' house and sometimes had the satisfaction of withdrawing Nora from him for a walk round the block or for a visit to one of the phonograph galleries where penny-in-the-slot machines retailed through rubber tubes the voices of the world's greatest singers; sometimes, however, he endured the miserable pain of seeing Corcoran's escort preferred and of remaining behind to receive the sardonic hints of Mr. Scanlan and the toplofty blather of his wife. Yet it was n't these informal dallyings with Corcoran that caused Jerry the greatest uneasiness; it was her quite regular weekly engagement with him. Every Wednesday night while Jerry was drilling in the Y.M.C.A. Hall, she and Corcoran went into the city to some play or other. Jerry remonstrated with her, told her it was unfair to Corcoran and very disturbing to himself; but she only laughed and said that he need n't have Corcoran on his mind. She was going to have what fun she could while she was still unmarried, and as for Charley Corcoran, he was perfectly well able to take care of himself.

To Jerry all this was perplexing — the more so when,

in a further endeavor to elucidate and justify her behavior, Nora explained to him that they were n't really
engaged yet, were just expecting to be. Such a distinction was too fine for him to grasp, especially as he was
permitted the endearments that he had always supposed existed legitimately only between those whose
intentions were quite definite. He concluded that girls
had different ideas from men about things, that was
all; and so, when he caught himself, as he sometimes
did, questioning or criticizing in his own mind Nora's
course, he hastily erected over her that large, vague,
sheltering excuse.

Yet even so, all through this winter there rested a
blight upon his Wednesday evenings, those evenings
which in the autumn had been the most pleasant. In the
evolutions of the drill he would be wondering about
Nora and Corcoran — where they were, whether Nora
was having a better time with Corcoran than she usually
had with himself, whether she was sparing him a single
thought; he would go through the manual of arms quite
mechanically with his mind thus distracted. There was
one thought more recurrent and more repugnant than
any other; Corcoran had kissed her once, and undoubtedly Corcoran would kiss her again. And Jerry was
afraid that the next time she would not tell him about it.

She was in the habit of telling him how much she had
enjoyed the play to which Corcoran had taken her, what
good seats they had secured, how late it was when they
got home; it appeared that in Corcoran's company she
never saw a dull play, sat in a poor seat, or arrived at
home at a seasonable hour.

JERRY

"If he'd just do something so that I could smash him!" Jerry often thought while he marched and countermarched with his company in the Y.M.C.A. Hall; and the desire made him shout out his orders with an extraordinary ferocity. Roger Trask, the drillmaster, colonel of the third militia regiment, watched him and thought, "There's a fellow that would make a good soldier — a good officer."

Trask had a special interest in Jerry, a special feeling for him. It had been Jerry who had induced Trask to undertake the training of this company; one evening in the preceding September, at the invitation of the superintendent of the local branch of the Y.M.C.A., the officer had given a talk on the discipline and service of the militia. He often recalled his satisfaction when after the talk a stalwart, eager-faced, blue-eyed young man came up to him and said, "That's fine, what you've been telling us. And it would be the making of a lot of us if you'd only come out now and then and give us some real lessons about drilling and soldiering." The company which at first had numbered only about thirty men had doubled in size. It was still a varied assortment of old firearms that the privates bore; Trask had wanted them to dispense with weapons, but Jerry had pleaded so hard for them that he had conceded the point.

Jerry's feeling for Trask was nothing less than hero-worship, qualified only by the secret sense of kinship that humble appreciation claims. Trask was exactly the kind of man that Jerry aspired to be — straight, vigorous, commanding, yet genial, too, with a geniality that never compromised his dignity; contemplating him, Jerry felt in himself all sorts of similar potentialities, and at the same time more than ever despaired of outgrowing his coltishness.

A circumstance chronicled on the first page of the *Daily Press*, the favorite newspaper of the workingman, confirmed and emphasized Jerry's secret sense of kinship with the drillmaster. The engagement of Colonel Roger Trask and Miss Claire Desmond was announced in an article richly biographical and illustrated by photographs of the pair. Miss Desmond was not only very beautiful, as appeared from her picture; she was the daughter of Benjamin Desmond; and locally that name was as significant as that of Vanderbilt or Astor. When, on the Wednesday night following, Trask entered the Y.M.C.A. Hall, there was a spontaneous outburst of applause, at which he laughed and turned red; and that encouraged every one to come forward and shake his hand. Jerry, performing this ceremony, could hardly keep back the words, "I know exactly how you feel." Yet afterwards he reflected that he did n't know exactly how Trask felt at all, and permitted the thought to depress him for a moment; how inconceivably delightful it must be to free one's joy and happiness and love to all the world!

It was not long after this episode that the figure of Benjamin Desmond began to loom portentously alive to persons for whom his existence had hitherto been as mythical as that of Crœsus. For the rumor that had been disturbing the community there proved to have been a solid foundation; one morning early in Janu-

ary the announcement was made that the banking house
of Desmond and Company had purchased the Purroy
Steel Works. The price, though not made public, was
stated in the newspapers to be in excess of twenty mil-
lion dollars. It was also stated that Desmond and
Company now controlled all the important rod and rail
mills in the vicinity and were organizing a corporation
to be known as the American Foundries Company to
take over the ownership and management of these
properties. In effect, the employees of the Purroy
Works found that they had changed masters over-
night.

Grim speculation at the Works, foreboding and panic
in the homes of the workmen, followed promptly upon
this disclosure. That evening, on going home, Jerry
found his mother in a completely pessimistic yet de-
spairingly resourceful frame of mind. She was waiting
for him in the hall; she clung round him and he felt
the trembling of her arms, the nervous clutch of her
fingers.

"Now don't you feel blue and cast down in your
mind, Jerry," she entreated him. "It's just when you
least expect it of them that things have a way of coming out all right in the end. I've been thinking what
a blessing it is that I have my health and strength. If
things come to the worst, we can maybe sell or rent the
house, and we've still got your father's life insurance
money. Then in the city I can find washing to do, and
that will keep us till you get a new job. Of course if we
can't sell or rent the house and there's the mortgage
to pay and you don't get something to do right off —

His Mother.

well, then I suppose we'll lose pretty much everything we own. At least we can keep body and soul together through my washing; it's a mercy I learned to wash well when I was young, and that I've kept my health and strength."

"It's a mercy to you to let you run on until you run down," said Jerry. "A fine sight you'd be, taking in washing and the like of that, and a fine sight me for letting you. Sit you down, you excited old body, and get possession of your five senses. And now mind what I'm telling you. Divil a doubt but I could get a better job any day that I chose to quit the Steel Works and go into the city. Divil a doubt now, I'm telling you."

"Oh, Jerry, is that the truth? Indeed, if it is, you're taking a great load off my shoulders."

"Of course it's the truth. A great strong lad like myself! In half an hour I could land any job that I wanted. Divil a doubt now."

"It does me good to hear you say it. But I wish you would n't say that word 'divil,' Jerry dear. Your father never used it."

"All right, mother. I'll do my best. And now don't be pulling that long face any more; it don't look right on you. Your face ought to be broad and good-natured like a Dutchman's."

She smiled doubtfully. "Have you honest the heart to be joking with me, Jerry?"

"Yes, and the heart to be eating a fine supper, if there's such a thing to be had in this house —"

"Well, there is then." And she bustled away, and

presently Jerry from his room upstairs heard her singing to herself while she put the dishes on the table.

But her cheerfulness was short-lived; even in the midst of supper forebodings settled again upon her, she was sure that Jerry had just been trying to comfort her, some big and ominous change affecting all the employees of the Works was impending. It did no good for Jerry to deny, to ridicule, to cajole, to declare; she had sunk into one of the blue moods that came upon her seldom, but that always filled Jerry with fear and distress. No, Jerry would lose his job and they would lose their house; they were to be cast out, wanderers on the face of the earth; for her, an old woman, it did n't matter so much, but it was hard, cruel hard, that she should n't be allowed to die in the room where her husband had died. So she continued to talk, more and more gloomy, more and more depressing, while Jerry with wrinkled brow and entreating eyes ate his supper and kept jumping up from it to put his arm round her and say, "Oh, now, mother, don't you now, don't you; no, it's not so, indeed it is not." "Ah, well you may say that, but I've lived longer in the world than you, Jerry, and it's been but to see things go from bad to worse; that it has. But never did I think to see the day when we should be driven from door to door, begging our bread —" "Mother, mother!" Jerry cried imploringly; it frightened him to hear her, so unheeding, so unreasoning. She had been subject to fits of depression ever since he could remember; she plunged into them without warning from the crest of her usual happy exuberance, and they seemed to come now with increasing frequency.

She left her supper almost untasted, and Jerry ate
without satisfaction or enjoyment. Afterwards while
he helped her with the dishes, he tried to turn her
thoughts into more pleasant channels, but she would
not be diverted; she was for the most part glumly
silent and spoke only to lament or to reiterate dismal
predictions. Jerry's heart sank lower and lower; he fore-
saw that what he must soon say would provoke her to
despair in a new quarter. His instincts in dealing with
his mother were fatally accurate. Yet there was no way
of avoiding this disaster.

"Now, mother," he said when the last dish had been
put away, "you content yourself for a minute in the
parlor, in the big chair; do. I've got to run down to the
Scanlans' on an errand, but it won't take me the short
part of a minute to get it done; you'd not know I had
left the house before seeing me again."

It was of no avail; he knew that when she fixed him
with her solemn eyes.

"What errand have you at the Scanlans', Jerry?"

"Oh, just to say that I'm not going to a lecture."

"What lecture is it, and who were you going with?"

"It's just an illustrated lecture on Africa, and I told
Nora I'd take her, maybe. But I'd rather stay at home
with you and —"

"Oh, no, you would not, Jerry. It would be a mercy
to you if I was dead this minute —"

"Oh, mother, mother!"

"Oh, yes, I'm nothing but a drag on you, just in
your way. You have to think of what you ought to be
doing for me when all you want to think of is Nora

Scanlan. But I'll not have it, Jerry; I'll not be blocking your happiness. God knows what you'll live on when you marry her, and she's not one that can do with little. But I'll not be here to trouble you; have no fear of that."

Jerry stepped forward and took possession of her. He did not speak; he clasped her in his arms, drew her head against his shoulder, and then with one hand caressed her hair and her cheek. He held her so in silence, and at last she began to sob. He knew now that he had conquered the unhappy spirit; he cast an anxious glance at the black marble clock on the mantelpiece. It pointed to half-past seven, and that was the hour at which he had engaged to call for Nora. His mother seemed to divine his perplexity; she said, —

"Now, Jerry dear, I'm all right, and you must hurry along to take Nora to the lecture."

"I'll hurry along to tell her I can't —"

"Now, why would you be letting my foolishness spoil your pleasure? Go along with her, do."

"Talk, then, till you're blue in the face, but I know it's an evening when the old woman needs me."

He slipped out of the house; she heard him go whistling up the street. But though he made such cheerful and confident haste, he was by no means easy in mind as to the outcome of his mission. There were times when he felt rather afraid of Nora, and this was one of them.

Dressed for the street, expectant, mildly welcoming, she greeted him at the door, if greeting it could be termed which began with a reproach.

"Well, I thought you were never coming. Are we going to be late? I always hate to be late and miss the beginning of a thing."

"I'm awfully sorry, Nora, that I can't go with you after all," Jerry answered. "Mother's all upset to-night, and I've got to run right back to her. Here are the tickets; I hope you can get Dave or some one to take you."

"Oh, Jerry, what's the matter? Is she sick?"

"Not sick exactly, but she's in a state over the news about the Works."

"My goodness, is that all! As if my folks were n't all stirred up too! I don't see as that's any excuse."

"You would if you knew how much it's affected her. I can't leave her alone this evening, Nora."

"If she's not sick, I don't see why you should n't. She can't be any more worked up than dad and mother, and I don't mind leaving them alone — goodness, I want to get away from them! Such talk! It drove Dave out — and he'd been bad enough himself."

"I'm sorry to disappoint you; I'm disappointed too."

Nora was frowning, not listening. "I don't know who I can get — at such short notice — it's so late now. Oh, dear, I do think you might have let me know earlier, Jerry."

"I could n't; I did n't realize till just a little while ago how this thing had taken hold of mother."

"Well, I don't see what good you can do. Most likely she'd be better off if you were n't there to stir her up to talk about it."

"No, honestly, Nora dear, I would n't feel right to

be leaving her alone this evening. And if you don't want to use the tickets and would come and sit with mother and me —"

"There would n't be much fun in that. Oh, I suppose I can use the tickets; I suppose I can get Charley Corcoran anyway to go with me."

"Or maybe your father or mother."

"Thanks for the idea. But I don't know as it would be safe for the other one to be left alone."

"Ah, Nora," Jerry pleaded, "don't be sore on me."

"Oh, I'm not sore on you. But it's time you were getting back to your mother, and time I was walking down to Corcoran's store. Charley and I will be late enough as it is."

"Good-night, then," said Jerry stiffly, and he withdrew, thinking that the women a man most cares for make the world a hard enough place at times.

But his mother was grateful to him for his return, glad to sit by him on the sofa while he read to her from "The Old Curiosity Shop," which he had taken the day before from the town library; and when finally she kissed him good-night she said, "I'm sorry I was such a silly old woman, Jerry."

"You've a good right to be sorry," he answered jocularly.

"What was there for me to be going off my head about?" she asked. "Just because the Works have been sold, why has an old body got to be lepping at once to conclusions? No doubt they'll go on just as they've always done."

"Not a doubt in the world. And just you be doing

the same, mother, and I'll thumb my nose at the devil himself."

"Ah, Jerry darling, don't use that word. And don't be thumbing your nose either; it don't look nice."

"All right, mother. I keep forgetting."

He kissed her; she liked, without really understanding, the twinkle in his eyes.

V

It was a sunny morning in early March; the wind blew
softly from the south, and people opened doors and
windows to welcome Spring. Jerry Donohue, starting
to his work four minutes ahead of his schedule, strolled
and swung his dinner pail blithely. It was just a morning to assure one that all one's doubts and apprehensions
had been vaporings as tenuous as the smoke that
floated and drifted and broke to let the sun shine
through. So long a time had passed since the absorption
of the Purroy Works by the American Foundries Company, with no foreshadowing of any change in policy,
that anxiety was giving place to confidence throughout
the town. And Jerry's sanguine temper was invigorated
by more than the fresh sweet air of the morning. The
night before he had found Nora in her most responsive,
confiding, affectionate mood. Never had she been so
completely, so assuredly the girl that he loved — with
her hand pressing his arm, her slender self drawing close
to him, her eyes upturned to his, her laugh trilling a
pleased response to the speech of admiration, to the
sudden, impulsive caress. He was as puzzled by this
new hospitality of manner as he was elated.

Indeed, had he but known it, the influences that he
counted most hostile had advanced his cause; the bitter
reproaches which she had that evening undergone at

the supper table from her parents, who were exasperated
by the failure of the musical education they were be-
stowing upon her to produce the expected results, had
increased her conviction that life at home could not be
much longer endurable; and the boldness of Charley
Corcoran's behavior that afternoon had somehow revealed to her more glaringly his scorbutic unattractive-
ness. Jerry's kind and humorous eyes, honest face, and
big, stalwart frame had seemed more than usually
welcome and likable — and Nora, while she vaguely,
emotionally responded to the admiration in his eyes,
had more distinctly and concretely felt that, quite
apart from any emotional considerations, she could not
do better than marry Jerry Donohue. More than any
one else that she could think of, he seemed to her to
have a man's full strength, a man's full power to confer
security.

Jerry, thrilled by her unaccustomed readiness to let
the conversation take a practical turn, had spoken
with vigor and decision. He had been patient, he had
waited, but it was time now for a definite understanding.
Very well — and the promptness and explicitness of her
answer had left nothing to be desired; the term at the
Conservatory ended on April 9; on the next day she
would announce her intentions to her family, and within
a month thereafter she would marry him.

Jerry, transported with joy, had been by turns bois-
terous, exalted, demonstratively affectionate, jovially
serene; his ancient foes had sallied forth to play cards
with some neighbors, and Dave was presumably en-
livening a billiard hall with his presence. So there was

none but Nora herself to impose a curb on the swain's high spirits. And this she did not seek to do; the higher they mounted the better she liked it, the more readily and gladly did she yield to the charm and domination of her lover, brighter grew her eyes, gayer and freer her laugh; it came upon her suddenly, with a sense of surprise and delight, that she no less than he would look forward to the wedding day. And only a few minutes before she had named the date with resignation rather than enthusiasm, just as one might do who had finally been cornered after a long and wearisome flight.

So it was in a blithe spirit that Jerry Donohue set forth the next morning to his work. Indeed, his head was so shrouded in the clouds, his nose was so cast upward, happily sniffing the balmy air, that he had got some distance down the slope leading to the Works before he perceived the unusual proceedings at the entrance. Groups of men stood on either side of the mill gates examining large printed notices that were affixed to the fence; those who had finished reading passed inside, walking slowly; as he drew near, Jerry became definitely aware from the behavior of the men that the printed notices were of grave import. Standing on the edge of the crowd, he read the following: —

IMPORTANT

On and after April 1 work in the Purroy Mills will be in two turns of twelve hours each instead of in three of eight hours each. Under this new arrangement the number of employees will of necessity be reduced. Those who are not to be retained will be given one week's notice.

J. F. Drayton, *Superintendent.*

JERRY

Like most of the other men, Jerry turned away in silence. But it was not the silence of stolidity or of apathetic despair; anger was burning hot within him, the anger of the oppressed. The Purroy Works had always made money for their owners; the avarice that prompted a scaling down of the working force and an increase of the working hours was inhuman. That was the crude generalization that presented itself after the first moment in more concrete form — in a fanciful contrast of Benjamin Desmond, a beneficiary, no doubt, of the new scheme, and of himself, a sufferer from it. There would be Desmond, deriving from the increased toil of Jerry's hands the price of a case of champagne or of a gratefully received and publicly acknowledged subscription to a charity, or a month's rent of a pew in his aristocratic church; and there would be Jerry Donohue, deprived of all his youthful pleasures, of the freedom to enjoy life that he had thought he would share with his bride, of the cheerful leisure that had always marked the latter and best portion of each day — nothing left him but to drudge, to eat, to sleep. Oh, that would be permitted him; he would not be one of those to be dropped; that would be the fate of the old, half-broken men.

He came up abreast of one of these who was plodding with slow steps, head sunk on his breast. It was Jim Dobbins, a friend of his father's, and at the sight of his haggard face Jerry's wrath was submerged in pity. For more than a year Dobbins had been in failing health; his flushed skin, drawn tight over his cheekbones, was that of the consumptive; his wife was wasting away with the same disease. He had three children, the eldest a girl of fifteen.

"They've watered the stock, and we've got to pay six per cent on it," said Dobbins. "It's for you young fellows, Jerry, to decide whether you'll fight or submit. We old ones are about done anyway. We're all in the hands of bloodsuckers."

He turned aside into the open-hearth mill where he worked.

In the rod mill, Tim Brophy of the night shift, whom Jerry relieved, had just heard the news. He was a few years older than Jerry and had a wife and two babies. His usually welcoming face was now scowling and sullen; he hardly looked at Jerry, but put on his coat, picked up his dinner pail, and walked off silently.

All the morning Jerry plied his tongs, caught and drew the hissing, white-hot, writhing serpents of metal out across the rolls. More mechanically than usual he was performing his task; his mind was preoccupied with his problems. What should he do? Implanted in him by his father was the sturdy principle that a man ought to stick to his job — that to seek to better one's self by change was to gamble recklessly. And it wasn't as if a choice were open to him; the twelve-hour day ruled in all the other iron mills, and iron working was the only thing he knew. He could learn something else, but to do that would take time and would mean a great reduction of income; it would mean the indefinite postponement of marriage, and the surrender of the house that had so long been his mother's home. He thought of all these things, and he thought, too, of the effect that the news would be likely to have on his mother and on Nora, and unaccustomed lines of worry and care furrowed his young brow.

In the noon intermission, while he was eating his luncheon, Dave Scanlan came in from open-hearth mill number two. "Going to have a mass meeting in Y.M.C.A. Hall to-night," he said. "Be on hand, Jerry; tell every one to come."

Dave bustled off, a brisk, important emissary; his manner and his message were encouraging. To Jerry and, no doubt, to many other young men cheerfulness returned; the sound of a mass meeting was hopeful; at least it promised excitement. So Jerry deferred consideration of his problems; his chief concern during the afternoon was the condition in which he should find his mother. He hastened home at five o'clock, apprehensive lest she had collapsed utterly, yet not unprepared to discover that she had already dismantled the house and was awaiting him in a tearful triumph of resignation.

To his great relief she had committed neither of these excesses; in fact, she was sewing in her rocking-chair and greeted him calmly. She had heard all the news; she had gone about the neighborhood, visiting distracted women, and distracted women had visited her; the sight of them, she explained to Jerry, had made her resolve not to go "lepping" into the air like she was a wild creature. Now that she knew what the worst was to be, she was n't afraid of it; of course, twelve hours a day in an iron mill was too much for flesh and blood to stand for a whole lifetime, but for a short while now, till he did be getting hold of a better job, it might be borne; and if not, there was always the washing to fall back on. And as for their home, well, it was themselves that made it, themselves and a few things they prized — not the four walls of the house; if they had to move away, they could take the spirit of their home with them. It was n't as if they would be worse off, more unlucky, than anybody else; trouble would n't seem nearly so bad when all their friends and acquaintances had to share it. She reinforced this cheerful philosophy with an unusually good supper: "We may be economizing soon on our victuals, Jerry, but not tonight."

So it was a hearty, well-fed, optimistic young man that sallied forth to the mass meeting. That proved less exciting than he had anticipated; there was no dissent from Dobbins's proposal that a committee be appointed to confer with the management and plead for a revocation of the new order. The committee was instructed to contrast the efficiency of the employees of the Purroy Works with that shown in any other mills in the country; to point out that this efficiency was due to the homogeneous character of the working force, composed as it was of men of straight English or Irish descent, and not of Croats, Lithuanians, and "Polacks"; to declare that the imposition of greater burdens upon a reduced force must decrease the efficiency of labor, and that the overworking of employees meant economic waste; and finally to convey the warning that if the order was not withdrawn a general strike of all employees would be called. Dobbins was appointed chairman of the committee that was to present these considerations to the management.

Then began the series of conferences that were prolonged for ten days unavailingly. The management disputed the claims of the employees, yet professed reluctance to adopt so severe a policy of retrenchment; that, however, had been dictated by the directors. Dobbins and his committee sought an interview with Benjamin Desmond, who was recognized as the controlling force in the Purroy Company's affairs. Desmond referred them back to the management. The management deprecated the idea of a strike; all parties would be sorry, very sorry, if any such development took place. Not because of the threat, but because the management was sincerely desirous of holding the good-will of its employees it would endeavor to reopen the question with the board of directors.

Meanwhile, Roger Trask, without the knowledge of the workmen, had been pleading their cause. At the weekly drill he had heard from Jerry and from Dave Scanlan and others vigorous statements of their grievance — made, he well knew, with an understanding of his relations with the man whom they held accountable for their plight. Trask did not intimate to them that his sympathies were enlisted with their cause, but the next day he called upon Desmond at his office and relieved himself of all the arguments that he had heard and that had appeared to him sound. Desmond, a dark, wiry little man with a sharp nose and an aggressive under jaw, shook his head decisively at intervals during Trask's protest.

"You're dealing with intelligent English-speaking workingmen," urged Trask. "That means, your mills have an advantage over those that employ largely foreign-born, ignorant, half-skilled men —"

"Americans don't work in the mills nowadays; it's only the foreign-born who think of doing that," said Desmond. "Americans prefer to be plumbers, gasfitters, carpenters, electricians, clerks, and labor agitators. If Americans want to work in the mills, they must accept the conditions that the foreign-born impose."

"I think that these Americans will not accept such conditions."

"In that event I have no doubt that their places will soon be filled."

"To me it seems a short-sighted policy — to refuse to American workmen fair wages and reasonable hours and fill their places with miserable aliens who have never known either fair wages or reasonable hours. It's a horrible economic blunder. You can't think that men are mere subsidiaries of machinery. You must believe that machinery should be an auxiliary to men."

"If a mill were an institution like a hospital or an art museum, supported partly by private contributions, there might be something in what you say. I'd a good deal rather myself see the men accept the conditions that are enforced on us and make the best of them. But so far as they themselves are concerned — well, I don't know that it would n't be better for them to clear out — seek other occupations. Improved machinery in these mills has rendered a man's work less arduous and wearing than it used to be — also less interesting. Men can work longer hours — and it is n't now work for Americans. For doing a dull, stupid, monotonous job day in and day out, I don't want an American; I want a Slav or a Hungarian."

He was scarcely less frank in expressing his views when the committee of workingmen waited upon him for the second time. Their persistency and their intimation that punitive measures must follow if the management adhered to its published intention annoyed him; he remarked sarcastically, "You men at the Purroy Works seem to feel that you are the aristocracy of labor."

From that interview the committee returned discouraged and indignant. At the mass meeting called to hear their report Dobbins mounted the platform. He narrated the efforts that had ended in the failure of all negotiations; his recital of Desmond's cynical speech provoked a wrathful, inarticulate roar. Dobbins, haggard, tired, feverish-eyed, made an impatient gesture imploring quiet.

"Your committee feel," he continued, "that the only course left to us is to strike. We recommend, therefore, that a vote be taken to call a general strike throughout the works at midnight on March 31st. You must remember that if you vote to strike, you must all stand together. You must fight your own battle. You can look to no organization for help or support. Because we've had higher pay and worked shorter hours than union labor, we shan't now get any assistance from union labor. In order to win this fight, we've got to be willing, not only to suffer ourselves, but to see our wives and children suffer. We've got to be willing to help every one his neighbor, even when we're at the last gasp ourselves. Your committee want you to look the facts in the face before you take action."

In the back of the hall Jerry Donohue had sat and listened with grave intentness. The hopefulness that he had nursed that somehow things would come out right had received its death-blow. In its place arose a desire to take his part in the struggle; he did not think of Nora, he did not think of his mother; he was animated only by eagerness to give his service to the common cause. He tried impatiently to get the chairman's eye, but others were recognized and made halting or fiery speeches, all in favor of resistance to the oppressive order; at last he was given the floor.

"We can't just loaf round here idle," he said. "I say we keep on in our three shifts just as we've been doing — only, instead of working in the mills, let's patrol the mills. There's a company of us that's been drilling here once a week. Let's have each shift organized to do regular patrol duty — have them drill regularly every day. It will keep us out of mischief — and it will help to keep other fellows out of the mills."

The proposal was greeted with applause. Dobbins rose and said, —

"It's a good idea, that of Jerry Donohue's. But I would advise that the patrolling be done without weapons of any kind. I understand that when the boys have been drilling here, they've had firearms. Let's have it agreed that they are to be left at home."

The unanimous sentiment of the meeting was crystallized in formal votes, providing that a general strike should begin at midnight on March 31st, and that thenceforward the approaches to the mills should be patrolled, night and day, by unarmed squads. The chairman named an executive committee of five; Jerry Donohue was the youngest member. Then, before the meeting adjourned, Dobbins made one more proposal.

"To get this strike started right, I say that on the morning of April 1st we march in a quiet and orderly parade through the streets of this town carrying the American flag."

That proposal was executed. At nine o'clock on the raw April morning, when the accustomed clangor of the mills was stilled and the accustomed smoke no longer ascended from their chimneys, the parade of the workers was organized. Dave Scanlan headed it importantly as flag-bearer. Jerry assisted Dobbins to form the men in line. Volunteer musicians arrived with fifes and drums, and to an inspiriting march that already proclaimed victory the procession started. Up and down the muddy, hilly streets it marched, while wives and children and well-disposed shopkeepers stood upon the sidewalks, and waved and cheered. Jerry marched at one side, casting a keen eye on the ranks, calling out orders, receiving good-natured chaff — "Right you are, General" — "Keep step with the Colonel." He saw his mother on her doorstep, a sturdy, sober-faced little figure; she did not smile as he passed, but only looked more sad. He saw Nora Scanlan, black-haired, dark-eyed, slender, fluttering a handkerchief to him from her front porch, and for one wild, ecstatic moment while he marched by, he felt that he was a soldier going to the front, saluting for the last time the girl that he loved. Then he glanced at the shambling, rough battalion and down at himself, and all the romance shriveled.

VI

In the neighboring city public opinion did not exert itself very heartily on behalf of the strikers. Most of the newspapers were owned by capitalists averse to approving the course of workingmen who disputed the decrees of their employers. In defending the action of the men Trask made little impression. Railroad officials, bankers, manufacturers were unsympathetic with his arguments. "This is America," they reminded him. "We're all workers here. This is n't a place for a man who is n't willing to work his hardest." Instances were given of various rich men, railroad officials, bankers, manufacturers, who had died young in consequence of their magnificent industry. "Twelve hours a day; I work twelve hours a day myself," declared the editor of a newspaper. "Why should those fellows expect easier terms than are made in any other mills?"

Meanwhile, the management refrained from taking any aggressive measures. Times were dull; the company seemed content to have the mills shut down indefinitely.

In a situation so unsettled, so unpromising, Nora Scanlan told Jerry that they must abandon their plans. "We can't get married while you're not earning anything," she said. "That would be foolish. Besides, I've got to do something to help my family pretty soon.

After the term at the Conservatory closes I must try to find work. So we'll just have to postpone things, Jerry."

"Yes," he assented. "I suppose we must."

His disappointment was somewhat colored over by loving admiration for her spirit. She was no mere frivolous, decorative little girl; witness her talk of going to work in order to support the family. That was like his mother; she was a girl with character as well as charm. He tried to let her see that his admiration was greater than his disappointment, that she shone more brightly than ever his heroine. His attitude pleased her; she said, "Oh, you don't think I'm as splendid as that, Jerry!" And when he assured her that he did, she sighed contentedly, "Well, we must make what sacrifices we can." To begin with, they would have to sacrifice the pleasure of declaring their engagement. The news of it would, in all the circumstances, afflict her parents bitterly; she felt that she mustn't add to their troubles — and she didn't want them to add to hers. Jerry acquiesced — with less enthusiasm. He could not declare himself in sympathy with the sensitiveness of her parents, and he would have liked the stimulus and support to be derived from public recognition of his success in winning Nora's heart. "Oh, you don't think there's any glory to you in it!" laughed Nora, when he explained what he would be sacrificing; and she gave him a kiss because he asserted emphatically that he did think just that.

The days of idleness grew into weeks, and meanwhile the discipline maintained by the strikers discouraged the occasional strangers who came to the Purroy Mills seeking work. Always there was a patrol in front of the gates; the advice to strangers that they should not try to enter was usually heeded. Sometimes one more temerarious than the rest would walk up to the line and attempt to push through; he would be hustled roughly out into the street. "No violence," which had been the first watchword of the strikers, was changed after a month of privation to "No unnecessary violence." The six policemen of the town were not disposed to interfere with the operations of the patrol.

For a time the workingmen held together, firm in their purpose. Many of them owned or partly owned their houses; to these the winning of their fight was a vital matter. Others persisted from a sense of loyalty or from inertia; to start out and seek work will always be for some men less easy than to sit and wait for it.

But as time drifted by and reserve funds diminished, the number of the men who stayed to fight dwindled. Their faces were sharpened and anxious. They had begun to feel the pressure of hunger and of hopelessness.

James Dobbins's wife collapsed under privation and died. Her three children lay awake sobbing throughout most of the night after her death, but James Dobbins, sitting by her side, shed scarcely a tear. In the morning when Jerry Donohue and his mother came to offer their help, Dobbins paid no heed to their words. The skin was drawn tight over the sharp bones of his face and looked dry and livid. In his feverish eyes there was an insane malignity. He spoke in a husky monotone.

"It's the women that suffer. They go to heaven. Most men go to hell. It's men that kill women. She'd have lived longer than me — much longer — but they've killed her; I helped them. She's got three children; only one is a boy. There will be two for her in heaven."

Jerry stood scared and silent, but his mother placed her hands on the man's shoulders and said: —

"Jim, do you mind how you tried to comfort me when my man died? You must let me do the same by you now, my poor boy. Come into the next room, where there's a bed for you to lay yourself, and I'll sit by you. Come, Jim."

He submitted and let her lead him out through the door. Jerry went downstairs and found the three children in the kitchen. He drew the younger little girl and the boy to him, one under each arm, and began to talk. They were all coming over to his house for dinner; they were going to make him and his mother a visit. Their father was coming, too, and his mother had made doughnuts — the kind they always liked; lots of them.

Kate, the oldest girl, stood at the window unheeding. She was a brown-haired, slim little creature, with cheeks ivory pale and features sensitive and clear. With the two other children looking up at him quietly expectant, Jerry stood in perplexity. Then Mrs. Donohue came down the stairs, went over to Kate, and kissed her.

"Your father's sound asleep," she said. "Poor lamb, you're all tired out. And the little ones too. Aren't you, dearie? — Yes, there, there!"

Kate had suddenly flung herself into Mrs. Donohue's arms and safe in their embrace had burst into passionate weeping. That started the two other children crying; Jerry, distressed and sympathetic, vainly strove to comfort them. It was Kate who, still sobbing, brought about a slackening of the wails, for upon hearing the lamentations of the younger she resolutely detached herself from Mrs. Dononue's clasp and coming over with a little moist ball of a handkerchief wiped her brother's and then her sister's eyes. "Don't cry, Peter; don't cry, Betty," she besought them; and then with a certain dignity she turned to Mrs. Donohue and said, "They're awfully tired, and maybe if you'd help me to put them to bed, they'd get some sleep."

"Indeed, I'm going to put every last one of you to bed," said Mrs. Donohue. "And when you wake up, there will be something good for you all to eat; mind now, that there will."

So the children obediently accompanied their friends to the house next door and climbed the stairs. "Kate, you and Betty can lie on the big bed, and Peter, he can have the little bed," said Mrs. Donohue. "Just take off your little shoes now, and stretch out. Look at these two beautiful patchwork quilts to cover you with. Ain't they handsome? And they feel as nice as they look. Now just snuggle down and close your eyes."

Soon she reported to Jerry, who had waited below, that they had dropped off to sleep. "We've got to take care of them from now on, Jerry," she said. "We must watch Jim; he's not himself."

Jerry nodded cheerfully, but when his mother turned away, his brow wrinkled. Already they were almost at the end of his savings; to be sure, there was still to his mother's credit the thousand dollars from his father's life insurance, but he did not like to think they must draw on that. He stood looking out of the window; presently he saw Nora Scanlan approaching and went out to meet her. They walked on together for a little way, talking in subdued voices.

"That means we'll never be married," she said listlessly, when he told her of the responsibility that he and his mother had undertaken.

"Oh, yes, we will," he declared. "Why, Nora, you won't get tired waiting, will you?"

"I don't know. Maybe I'm tired now."

"Oh, Nora, don't say that."

"I guess it's true. You can't go on caring very much for a person when you're always worried and anxious and unhappy."

Jerry's head drooped. More than ever he felt his impotence. Then he straightened up hopefully.

"If only we can win this fight. Or even if we don't and I get another job. You won't always be worried and anxious, Nora; I know I can keep you from being so — some day."

"Oh, yes, if you can get a job, Jerry. I know I can't get one myself. I've tried and tried, but there seems to be nothing I can do. And we're all so miserable and worried at home — so unhappy."

"Oh, but things will be more cheerful some day. And you mustn't be drawing your pretty face all up into wrinkles."

"Why don't you all give in and take the hard life that's offered you?" Nora asked listlessly. "Or else go away and start in fresh somewhere altogether? What's to be gained by carrying on this siege?"

"It's justice we're fighting for, Nora. A man hates to quit, even for his own good, when he's fighting for justice."

"There's no use in being obstinate. Dave and father are just as obstinate as you."

"You'll be glad we were when it's all over. I don't believe you'd want to marry me if I quit, Nora."

" I don't believe I want to anyway. We might as well stop talking about that. We both of us have too much else on our minds."

"Nora dear, you're not right about it at all. The mere sight of your face puts all those gloomy things clean out of my mind, and starts me to singing in my heart."

"It is not the same that the sight of you does for me. Nothing starts any singing in me any more. And I don't in you, Jerry, — no, no, it's no use trying to pretend."

"Oh, Nora, if you'll just keep your courage up and be cheerful!"

"I'm not the person that can, Jerry. And it's well for you to be finding it out now — instead of after we'd made such a blunder as to get married."

"Nora, you'll not be feeling like this for long."

"Why should I not? It's the way I'm always feeling. And you're no good to me in these days, Jerry — not the least bit in the world. So I know there's no use in our planning to get married — when you can't help me now. No use — not the least bit in the world."

Jerry was silent. He felt disheartened and crushed. If Nora wasn't willing to give him in the struggle such support as his mother gave him, she was no doubt right in breaking the engagement. Yet after a while he resumed desperately the effort to convince her that she was wrong.

"Oh, Jerry," she answered, "don't try to throw dust in my eyes — and your own. There's dust enough flying to-day without that. I should like to get away from this town."

She set her lips and narrowed her eyes against the puff of wind that caught up the dirt of the roadway and sent it swirling upon her. "Such a filthy, shabby, nasty little place!" she said. "Don't you hate it, Jerry?"

"I never have," he answered moodily. "I don't know but what I may."

"I'm tired of walking," she declared after a few moments of silence. "I'm going home now. And if you knew how I hate my home!"

"If you knew how I want to take you from it — make a home for you!"

"But you can't, can you, Jerry?"

"No. Not now. But if you will only wait, Nora."

"I don't know, Jerry. All I know now is that I don't care much about you. I feel too sorry for myself. By the time things are better — if they ever are — you very likely won't care anything about me. Anyway it's better that we should stop thinking about each other."

"I suppose you're right — and I'll do my best to control my thoughts."

"I don't know that I want you to, Jerry."

"Then you mean —"

"I don't mean anything except that I'm a pig. I'm

not going to think any more about you, but I don't care how much you may continue to think about me."

"Then I'll come for you some time, Nora."

"You may not find me."

At the steps of her house she bade him good-bye. "Don't come to see me any more, Jerry. For the present at least."

"I've never liked anything the way I've liked loving you, Nora. I can't stop it off short, you know."

"I wouldn't have you do that, Jerry. Perhaps it will be some help to me to feel that for a while anyway you'll still go on caring for me — all to yourself."

She shook hands with him and turned away. It was a long time before he spoke with her again.

VII

A MOTTO IN WHICH THERE IS A DISTINCTION WITHOUT
A DIFFERENCE: AND A VICTORY WHICH MAY TURN OUT
TO BE NO VICTORY AT ALL

In the last week of July a notice was posted at the entrance to the Purroy Steel Works announcing that the mills would resume operations on the first Monday in August, and that the places of those employees who had not by that day signed the new wage scale would be filled. Dobbins called a meeting of the men; they voted, with no dissenting voice, to remain firm. Most of them held the opinion that the threat on the part of the management to introduce new workmen would not be executed; nevertheless, there was earnest discussion of the tactics to be employed for the frustration of such a measure. Dobbins made a bitter speech. "You'll not let any outsiders get a foothold in the Works!" he cried. "You'll keep them out — by force, but not by violence!"

The distinction appealed to the audience. They went home, chuckling sardonically, ejaculating, some of them, with pleasurable anticipation, "Force, but no violence!" That there was now a day to which they might definitely look forward, a day containing possibilities of climax and excitement, was an inspiriting thought. The routine of picketing which had been maintained with failing zest called out fresh alertness. Off duty the younger men discussed eagerly the action that they might properly take to prevent invasion. As the day approached, their talk grew more reckless. "Anybody that comes looking for trouble will find it," was a frequent assertion.

At seven o'clock on the morning designated fifty men hired by the Purroy management arrived by train. They were of various nationalities and various ages — haggard, anxious, elderly men and aggressive-looking youths, all poorly dressed, armed only with dinner pails. Drayton, the superintendent of the mills, led them from the station to the Purroy Works. The news of their arrival had preceded them; at the mill gates the full force of the strikers was assembled and barred the entrance. Drayton addressed the hostile gathering persuasively.

"For every one of you men, if you'll come in now, there's the old job — nobody blacklisted — wages as good as are paid in any other mills in this section. There's a living for you here. It may not be as good a living as you think you're entitled to, but it's the best that the company offers or is likely to offer. I honestly think — and I've tried hard to be a friend to you all — that most of you will make a mistake if you don't accept what's offered. Now I'm going to ask you to make a passageway so that I can enter with these men."

He paused and looked expectantly at the sullen throng. The answer to his speech was an inarticulate murmur of defiance. He scanned the faces in silence; there was not one that was not forbidding.

"Step aside, fellows, — fall back now." He advanced, motioning to those in the front rank to clear a path.

JERRY

One young man quailed under his eye and stepped aside, only to be flung back into place by his neighbors. The treatment stiffened his courage, and he resisted when Drayton pressed against him.

"Come on, you men!" Drayton shouted. "Break a way through."

The example that he set, burrowing with his own broad shoulders into the mass, thrusting with his powerful arms, inspired his hitherto hesitant followers; in a moment there was a lively scrimmage, which soon deteriorated into a number of separate fights. Jerry, back in the middle of the throng, did not see clearly what was happening, but with an ardor equal to that which filled him when he took part in football games he heaved and pushed and struggled, and presently to his astonishment found himself with three or four others free of the throng and rushing Drayton across the street. They all desisted with a somewhat chastened sense of triumph, but when Drayton again strove to advance they blocked him off stoutly. There was a lull in the fighting; the strikers obviously held the upper hand.

"I warn you men," said Drayton, breathing hard, "you'd better open up a passageway."

"We'll let you go through any time you want, Mr. Drayton," said Dobbins. "But we won't let you take that gang of Huns with you."

Resenting the epithet, one of the invaders stooped and hurled a brick. Outraged Anglo-Saxon nature rose to that brick. Fists only — no brickbats; those were the weapons of Huns. In the course of the disorder the town police dutifully made their appearance and after an unimpressive effort to assert their authority were deprived of their clubs and good-naturedly told to go about their business; they remained, interested and not unsympathetic spectators of the final triumph of the defenders.

It was soon achieved. The Huns were unorganized and offered a spiritless resistance; their leader, isolated against a house wall and firmly held there by four sturdy young men, of whom Jerry was one, vainly shouted adjurations and imprecations. In a few moments the invading force was retreating down the road, pursued merely with threats of dire punishment in the event of another attack. Jerry and his comrades released the superintendent.

"We're sorry to have to hold you up this way, Mr. Drayton," Jerry said.

The superintendent looked him sternly in the eye.

"You will learn, young man, that lawlessness never wins."

"Not even when practiced by corporations?" Jerry asked, still respectful.

Drayton kept his eyes on him. "I'm not likely to forget you. And you'll have reason to remember me." He stepped forward and again addressed the mob, which out of interest in what he might have to say, ceased for a few moments its uproar of jubilation.

"You men have done a very foolish thing. You may realize it by to-morrow, and if in that case you disperse quietly and make no further trouble, I shall be willing to let the matter drop. But one fact you have got to recognize: you can't bully the company."

"No, and the company can't bully us," cried a voice.

"It has no desire to; it offers you terms that are recognized everywhere as fair. If you choose to go on fighting us, it will be a fight to the finish; I warn you."

The newspapers of the neighboring city that night and the next morning magnified the riot; not only had the strikers beaten men who were peaceably endeavoring to assert the right to work, but they had cruelly assaulted the superintendent of the mills and attacked and driven away the police. Public sentiment was aroused against the strikers; the sheriff of the county was called upon to act and restore order, so that those who wished to work should not be intimidated and prevented by violence.

Under this censure the temper of the men at once became more ugly. Some of them appeared for guard duty carrying shotguns and protested against the order to go home and disarm. But on this point Dobbins was firm: "Force, yes, but no bloodshed. Put away your guns, boys; they might tempt you to murder. Hold them off, fight them off — but with your own strength and hands."

To Dobbins, emaciated, weak, his cheeks burning and his eyes bright with fever, there belonged a spiritual vitality that, stronger by contrast with his physical feebleness, dominated and stirred his followers. They were ready to obey him and to vindicate him; he personified visibly for them the consequences of oppression, and he made them feel that he counseled them as one who no longer had any selfish ends to serve.

The next morning Drayton and another trainload of

workingmen arrived and marched up to the Purroy
Mills, under the escort of the sheriff and his deputies.
At the gates an even stronger guard was assembled to
oppose them. The sheriff read a proclamation calling on
the mob to disperse under penalty of fine and imprisonment. The mob remained stubborn and sullen; the
sheriff called on his deputies and the strike-breakers
to follow him; the clash of the preceding day was re-
enacted. But the resistance of the strikers was of a
rougher character; instead of hustling and shoving, they
battered freely with fists; clubs made their appearance
in the hands of the attacking party. A deputy, feeling
that his weapon was being wrested from him by one
ruffian while another seemed bent on throttling him,
dropped the club and drew a revolver. Suddenly, then,
in the midst of the throng there was an explosion; a
striker dropped with a bullet in his thigh; the deputy
who had fired the shot was hurled to the ground, kicked
and beaten; his comrades, drawing revolvers, closed
round him and by threatening his assailants secured his
release; meanwhile, several of the strikers who had
hurried to their houses near by had returned with guns.
Their example inspired others; in a few minutes it was
a formidable armed mob that confronted the officers of
the law.

"We were n't the first to shoot, and we won't be the
second," said Dobbins. "But we'll shoot if we have to."

Jerry Donohue, in the front rank of the strikers, tingled with excitement and suspense. Such a stillness had
fallen that he heard the breathing of the man next to
him. Fascinated he kept his eyes fixed on the sheriff, a

bulky, red-faced man who had lost his hat in the scrimmage and whose bald head glistened in the hot August
sun. The officer was panting from his exertions; sweat
was streaming down his face; but with the revolver in
his hand he was not quite an object for derision. Jerry
watched him with the absorption of a mere spectator,
one not himself involved in the drama, and wondered
what he would do.

The sheriff looked about him; his forces were over-
matched. Reluctantly he returned his revolver to his
pocket.

"I don't propose to engage in a pitched battle with
you men," he said. "You defy the civil authorities; very
well. In a day or two you are likely to find yourselves
under martial law."

Thus with dignity he admitted defeat; again the
superintendent had to lead his discouraged host from
the scene of action. The victors, still fearful of surprise
and trickery, strengthened their patrol about the
Works; notwithstanding the precaution, they were
nearly all exultant over their triumph. Jerry was one
of the few who were silent and thoughtful. Doubt had
sprung into his mind for the first time when the sheriff,
an unheroic, rather absurd figure, had pocketed the revolver and unexpectedly achieved dignity. That little
speech of his had communicated to Jerry something like
a shiver of consternation. He had never really contemplated coming into violent collision with the higher
forces of the law. To resist the officials of the Purroy
Works, to disregard the perfunctorily issued commands
of the local constabulary, was not to invite the disap-

proval of his conscience; now, however, he began to wonder to what extreme resistance might rightly be carried. This question involved others that had not arisen in his mind before; most unsettling of all, a doubt concerning the inherent justice of the cause. If the men the company were seeking to employ were professional strike-breakers, thugs, members of the strong-arm fraternity, there would be little reason for compunction; but the appearance and behavior of most of them permitted no such classification. With an uncomfortable stirring of sympathy, Jerry confessed a recognition of them as men earnestly seeking work, desperately needing it. The enthusiasm with which he had thrown himself into the sacrifice for the common lot withered away.

But once you had cast your fortunes in with hundreds of others, of what use were belated subtle perceptions, glimmerings of light, yearnings to undo?

VIII

THE group on duty before the gates knew that the end
was near. The whole town was aware of it — had been
since the night before, when the governor's decision
to call out the National Guard had been published.
Immediately upon the receipt of that news many of the
strikers had slipped away. They realized that further
resistance was hopeless and they dreaded punishment for
past resistance if they remained. But most of the men,
though admitting the futility of prolonging the fight,
were animated by a resolve to make no premature surrender. Even though they all knew that their rebellion
had been already overcome, they chose to compel the
effective demonstration of the fact.

It was not a stimulating prospect, however, and the
drizzling rain that dripped from their hat-brims and
trickled down inside upturned coat-collars made it difficult for them to maintain the desirable spirited appearance. They stood about discussing the course that
after the capitulation it might be best for each one to
follow. Most of them were disposed to seek again their
old positions in the mills.

"Not for me," said Jerry in response to a question.
"Drayton has a black mark down opposite my name.
I'm going to get a job in the city, and then I'm going

to night school; if you don't have an education you're bound to be somebody's man all your life."

"An education's no guarantee either," replied one of the group. "A job that you can save money in — that's all that counts."

"Where will you find one of those?" asked another. "Unless you've got a rich friend to help you to it."

"Sure, that's the thing," declared a third derisively. "A rich friend! And where would we be getting a rich friend!"

Smoke ascended from meditative pipes and was dissipated in the moist air in hopeless inquiry.

Jerry shrugged his coat more closely round him, settled his chin in his collar more doggedly. Nothing to do now but wait it out. His thoughts at the moment turned, not to his own and his mother's uncertain outlook, but to the difficulties of the Scanlan family. He had not seen Dave or his father for two days; when he had last seen them, they were both unsteady from drink, unfit for picket duty, and had been led away to sober off. There was talk among the men that the Scanlans were especially hard-pressed — without funds and unable to get credit any longer at the local stores. To Jerry, remembering the extravagant aims and expenditures of the family, the gossip seemed only too likely to be well grounded. He thought of Nora in the unfamiliar atmosphere of squalor that must now surround her, with a drunken father and brother sprawling before her eyes and a bitter, shrewish, and discouraged mother berating them and her alike, and a hot desire to be her rescuer, to bear her away to peace and comfort and happiness, burned in him, only to leave him, with the quenching of it by common sense, more miserable than ever. He could n't serve her, he could n't marry her, even if she were willing; he had nothing to offer. He was himself a dependent now on his mother's little hoard — a dependent as much as the three motherless children that she had taken into the house — motherless and, as Jerry thought, soon to be fatherless; Dobbins was now but a tottering shadow of a man.

Yet the thought of Nora in misery, the misery of actual want, drove him apart from his fellows; he paced up and down bending his brows upon the problem, striving to originate some method by which he might come to her aid. A full-grown man, a man of his exceptional vigor and strength — surely it was preposterous that he should be as incapable as any child of giving support to one in need — to the one he loved. It could not long be so; youth, enthusiasm, strength, they must find a good market. He chafed even now at the delay in running to seek it that loyalty to his fellows imposed upon him; he longed for the hour of deliverance.

He raised his eyes and, looking down the road, knew that it was at hand.

There through the rain the troops came marching, a dull brown line.

Jerry rejoined his comrades; silently they formed in front of the mill gates, true to their standard of military discipline. Thus in dignity they waited; then the advance of the troops was halted and the officer in command came forward alone.

When he drew near, there was an exclamation of recognition, then a stirring of excitement and uncertainty in the ranks of the men. For he proved to be that officer who had been their friend, who had inspired in them their zeal for military discipline and instructed them in the manual of arms.

Roger Trask came on briskly and seemed to search the throng with eager eyes. He was not checked by the stiff alignment, but saying, "Hello, boys, I want to have a talk with you," he came up close and then greeted three or four by name. "Hello, Jerry; how are you, Donaldson; come on; don't hold off; gather round and let me talk to you — and then you talk to me, just as straight as you like." His manner was magnetic, there was sincerity in his voice and eyes, they all of them knew that he had been their friend. Neither Jerry nor Donaldson offered resistance when he took their arms and turned them so that standing on either side of him they faced the others; neither of them sought to escape from a position of such doubtful honor. And as he spoke, the others gradually closed about him and listened in silence.

"I'm sorry I've been chosen for this duty. My sympathies have been with you in your fight. But we're sent here to prevent disorders such as may arise from violence or intimidation —"

"You mean," said Jerry, "you're sent here to hold us away from the gates while outsiders walk in and take our places."

"We must see that the law is enforced and that there is no interference with personal liberty. Yes, Jerry, you've stated what our function must be. These gatherings at the gates must be discontinued; and I would a great deal rather have you decide to disperse quietly now at my request than be compelled to order up the troops and clear the street by superior force."

"You're here just as the agent of the mill-owners."

"It's an unfortunate fact that the preservation of order is likely to benefit them rather than you. But it's only the preservation of order that we concern ourselves with."

"Have they got another gang of strike-breakers that they're going to run right in under your protection?"

"I don't know anything about their plans, Jerry. I sympathize with you people. But it's my duty to see that you disperse."

"What if we don't?"

"Then we shall have to march up with bayonets. You'll find it better in the end that you should be on good terms with us. Now I don't want to have to make it a military command; I ask you, as a friend, to break up this gathering."

"Well," said Jerry, "there's no use trying to stand out against bayonets. I'm done."

He detached himself from Trask's grasp and walked away. Donaldson followed; the movement became general. When a few moments later Trask brought up his men, the space in front of the gates was clear; only on the neighboring street corners groups loitered and watched with unfriendly eyes. Trask stationed a guard and led the rest of his men to the vacant land on the hilltop where they were to pitch their tents.

That afternoon the importation of foreign labor was

resumed. Trask stood at the gates and watched the procession pass. Among the faces he recognized a few; some of the young men that he had drilled had fallen into line and were seeking reinstatement in their old jobs. He looked in vain for Jerry Donohue. He noticed one man, elderly, haggard, emaciated, who walked with feeble steps and coughed feebly.

The next afternoon when the guard was being changed, Trask was again at the gates. A man came running out, crying that there had been an accident. Not waiting to learn the cause and thinking that a riot might be in progress, Trask took two of the guardsmen and hastened through the mill-yards. He came to a group gathered behind one of the great corrugated iron sheds. Lying dead on the slag was the man who had drawn a pitying glance from Trask when he stood in line for work the day before.

"He was consumptive," said one of the men in reply to Trask's question. "Toppled over at his furnace. Poor old Jim."

IX

ORDER was restored, the mills were running full time,
Millvale was prosperous again. The regiment which had
accomplished so much for the place was breaking camp
— and on the same day a number of families were moving away from their homes.

Walking through the town for a last survey, Roger
Trask paused in front of a house that was being dismantled. Chairs and bedding stood on the sidewalk; at
the curb, attached to an open wagon, a gaunt horse
eyed the furniture dejectedly; a small boy stood at the
horse's head. The thing that had caught Trask's attention was a white dove, a triumph of the taxidermist's skill, with an arrow thrust through its breast; it
reposed against a background of rushes and was encom-
passed by a gilt frame. Underneath the bird in illu-
minated characters were the words, "At Rest." This
memorial emblem had been placed for the moment on
a table.

"Where are you going, son?" Trask asked the boy.

"Into the city."

"What will your father do there?"

"My father's dead."

The gulp that followed the words told Trask that

the bereavement was of recent occurrence; he touched the boy's shoulder and said sympathetically: —

"Oh, I'm sorry. Have you any sisters?"

"Two."

"And a mother?"

"Mother's dead too."

"Who looks after you all?"

"Old Mis' Donohue."

"Well, will you give this to Mrs. Donohue and tell her it's for you and your sisters?" He slipped a five-dollar bill into the boy's hand.

The boy looked at him, then at the money, and said gravely, "Thank you."

Just as Trask was starting on his way, Jerry Donohue, carrying a rocking-chair piled high with pillows and blankets, came out of the house.

"It's you, Jerry. What are your plans?"

Jerry set the rocking-chair down and drew his sleeve across his moist forehead.

"I think some of getting a job in a blacksmith shop. I guess an ironworker might get a chance in such a place. If I don't, I'll find something. We've rented our house here to a woman that's going to take in boarders. I tell you, that's a load off our minds. Now that we've got to move, mother's quite keen for going into the city. She has a good spirit. Oh, I'll find something to do. Got to. I've got quite a family to bring up and educate — two girls and this boy."

"Relatives of yours?"

"Well, no," Jerry admitted. "But they've got nobody else. — Hello, what you got there, Peter?"

"He gave it to me," said Peter, showing the bill.

"Very kind of you," said Jerry. "What are we going to buy with that, Peter?"

Fingering the fortune, Peter confessed himself at a loss.

"Shoes, maybe," suggested Jerry. "And a hat for Kate and a dress for Betty? Lots and lots of things maybe that we'll buy. Only don't be losing it; you'd be the wise fellow if you took it in to my mother now."

The boy seemed willing to earn a reputation for wisdom; at any rate, he went indoors obediently, walking with solemn steps, not running like a boy at all.

"You're a well-set-up fellow, Jerry," observed Trask. "Why don't you try for a place on the police force?"

Jerry rested his hand against the horse's flank and meditated a moment.

"I would kind of like to be a cop," he said at last. "How would I go about it, Mr. Trask?"

"You'd have to pass a civil service examination — physical and mental. I haven't any doubt that you could — with a little training and study. The Police Commissioner calls on the Civil Service Board for men as he needs them, and chooses from the list of those who have passed."

"It might be worth trying," Jerry admitted. "Studying for it needn't interfere with my working at some other job?"

"Not in the least. When you get settled in your new quarters, come and see me. I know the Police Commissioner, and I'll get you all the information you need."

"Well, I'll do that, Mr. Trask. And I thank you very kindly."

They shook hands; turning the corner a few steps away, Trask looked back and saw Jerry carefully packing the memorial dove between two pillows. If a little later he could have peered into the dismantled house and heard what passed, Trask might have been both amused and touched, might have felt, too, the compunction of the careless benefactor who finds his services overvalued. Mrs. Donohue, after working briskly all the morning, had suddenly collapsed with grief. In the stripped upper room that had held her most sacred possessions she rocked and lamented, while the three children stood about her, interested and overawed.

"It's taking the heart out of my body to be taking me out of this room," Jerry heard her cry as he climbed the stairs. "'T was in this room my man died, with his head by yonder window, where he could be looking to the sun in the west; and so it was I have been thinking to die all these years myself, with my fingers plucking at the same quilt that his hands went straying and wandering about on, and the same bit of sky sending the last light to my eyes as to his. When you're old, you want no change whatever to come to you, and when you're poor, it's only a change for the worse that does come to you."

"Well, there you're wrong now," Jerry broke in cheerfully. "Do you know what kind of a change is coming to me? Wait till I tell you. I've just found it out this minute, from the colonel of the regiment, him that handed Peter the five-dollar bill that you cling to so

miserly. I'm to have the look-in at the job of a cop.
It's wearing a blue coat and brass buttons and a helmet
that I'll be, with a small club hanging at my side in
great dignity. And from being a cop I'll be made a lieutenant, and then I'll be a captain, and after that, no
doubt, a general or an admiral or something of that nature, with gold lace as well as brass buttons on my blue
coat. And you'll be a very important and respected
family, so there's no use whatever to sit here lamenting
for the good old days. Get up now, and we'll go out
and meet the grand good new ones."

"What kind of a rigmarole is this that I'm hearing?"
said Mrs. Donohue with asperity. "From a cop to an
admiral! If our ill-fortune has gone to your head, it's
no more than I've a right to expect."

"It's the sober truth I'm telling you; it's the look-in
at the job of a cop that's promised me. And he's one
of the most influential men in the city, so they say. Now
won't you be the proud woman when first you see me
in uniform?"

"When that time comes!" Yet in spite of her accent
of skepticism Mrs. Donohue's face had brightened; and
she rose quite cheerfully when Jerry said, "Now I must
be stealing the chair out from under you, for we've got
to be on our way; it's a job maybe that won't wait for a
lazy man."

"I don't believe you're going to be a cop," said Peter.

"Why not?"

"I guess you're only fooling."

"I believe you, Jerry," said Peter's older sister, Kate.
"I know you're going to be a cop."

"And what makes you know that?" Jerry asked curiously, pausing with the chair hung on one arm.

"I know that you'll always be what you say you'll be." The trustfulness in Kate's gray eyes was as calm as in her voice.

Jerry felt absurdly embarrassed by the admiration of the little girl. "Much obliged, Kate; you're my friend," he said. "Come on now, everybody, and set sail for the Cape of Good Hope."

That amused Peter, who had recently rounded the Cape in geography, and confirmed him in his belief that Jerry was a great joker. And at the same time it made Kate even more sure that Jerry always meant exactly what he said.

X

At the corner half a block away Jerry saw his family
take the trolley car for the city, where they were to
enjoy the hospitality of his aunt, Mrs. Murphy, until
he should arrive with the furniture and distribute it
among the four rooms of the apartment that they had
hired. "I do not wish to be beholden to Bridget Murphy
for one minute longer than is necessary, Jerry," had
been his mother's parting words. "Though your father's
own sister she is, she has never been sisterly with me;
never have I liked her since the day when she as good
as told me that if her brother had married another kind
of woman he and his would not have been mill-hands.
Mill-hands, that was the word that Bridget Murphy
used, and your father an expert puddler and earning
twice what Dan Murphy ever earned at his genteel job
of copying in the City Hall. And now that young
Maggie is a stenographer in a business office — a pert
one if ever I knew pertness — and you're out of a job
entirely, the less I see of Bridget Murphy, the better.
She is like to be choked by her pride, and her sympathy
will be of a triumphing kind and that plentiful it would
turn an angel in heaven against her. So make what
haste you can with the load, Jerry, without, of course,
endangering it with reckless and headlong driving."

Jerry, glancing back at the gaunt and drooping horse,

assured his mother that he would be prudent and bade her not to fret herself if he seemed long upon the road. The mention of this possibility started her upon another voluble statement about the limits to her endurance, which was cut short by the arrival of the trolley car and the necessity of getting aboard.

It had been Jerry's pious intention to respect his mother's wishes and not dally by the roadside with his freight. But as he drove past the Scanlans' house, he felt that he must run in for just a moment and find out what Nora had in mind to do and bid her good-bye; he wanted to let her know that suddenly he had some prospects and that he would be working and waiting for her. So he stopped his wagon and ran up the steps, and presently Mrs. Scanlan opened the door to him. There was even less cordiality in her visage than usual, and very much less charm; she looked cross and tired, and her slatternly dress and disheveled hair betokened a dejected spirit.

"You see we're moving," said Jerry. "I thought I'd stop in and say good-bye."

"It's soon said," replied Mrs. Scanlan. She held the door and gave him no opportunity to enter.

"You're going to stay on here?"

"I don't know."

"Has Dave found a job yet?"

"He has not."

"I have n't either." Jerry tried hard to conciliate her. "But I guess we'll both land something pretty soon. Is Dave at home now, Mrs. Scanlan?"

"He is. But he's not to be seen by any one — neither

him nor his father. I suppose, though," — there was a
gleam of sly malice in the woman's eyes, — "it's really
Nora that you're wanting to see?"

"Yes, of course I hoped to see Nora," Jerry said
eagerly.

"I've got to disappoint you. Nora's gone off this
morning with her husband. They're buying furniture
for their new house."

"Nora's not married!" Jerry's eyes no less than his
voice expressed incredulity.

"Married she is, as the Reverend Fitch, who performed the ceremony in this house last night, will be
telling you."

"Who?" asked Jerry with an effort; his voice sounded
strange in his own ears. "Who was it?"

"Her husband you mean? Oh, 't will be no surprise
to you at all. It's Charley Corcoran."

Jerry gazed at her in silence, striving to detect in that
taunting face the evidence of untruth. She recognized
the doubt in his eyes.

"It's nothing to me whether you believe it or not,"
she said. "But if you want to make sure I'm no liar
you 'can stop in at the Reverend Fitch's house, or at
Corcoran's Drug Store."

"It's hard to believe," Jerry said slowly, "but I can't
be doubting your word, Mrs. Scanlan, about your own
daughter. Yet I never thought to hear she was Corcoran's wife."

"Of course I hoped she'd do better than that,"
said Mrs. Scanlan. "But I was afraid she was going to
do worse. So I don't know as I can complain."

Jerry made no reply. He turned and descended the steps, and Mrs. Scanlan closed the door with a triumphant slam.

After climbing to his seat in the cart Jerry sat listless and held the reins in a listless hand. That promising future of which he had been so cheerfully prattling was extinguished; the city that he had thought of as glowing with opportunity lay now before him dark and hostile, and he felt robbed of the courage to attack. How could Nora have done it? he asked, and his imagination supplied the answer. She had done it in order to escape poverty and want. Well, perhaps she would be happy.

Behind the old horse, while it passed at leisure through the town, Jerry brooded in wretchedness. Suddenly the blood rushed to his face and his heart quickened its beat. Nora and her husband were gazing at some placarded oak chairs exhibited in the window of R. & H. Black's Furniture Emporium; a moment more and he would be passing them. He choked down the unsteadying lump in his throat and looked hard ahead, yet watched them from the corner of his eye; he was unutterably relieved when without noticing him they passed inside the store. Nora was wearing her blue suit and the little hat with the garland of pink rosebuds that she wore only on festive occasions; Jerry could not see her face.

It was late in the afternoon when, having unloaded his cart and put up his horse, he arrived at his Aunt Bridget's; he knew from the first glance at his mother and his aunt that there had been a passage at arms. Mrs. Donohue had gathered the two little girls into one arm and Peter into the other; the children were tearful, her eyes were snapping, and Mrs. Murphy wore the satisfied and martyred expression of one who has performed without flinching an unpleasant duty. She was severely gracious in bidding farewell to her guests; a spirit of foreboding seemed to accompany her wishes for their welfare. Mrs. Donohue's expression of appreciation for the hospitality enjoyed was not effusive.

She and Jerry walked to their new lodgings, the three children following behind. "She upbraided me with my folly in taking them to live with us," she said to Jerry in an indignant undertone. "And them right there to hear it. I'll never go near the woman again. Why were you so long upon the road, Jerry? I thought you'd never come."

"Was I long?" said Jerry.

"So long I was sure something had happened to you. Did anything get broke?"

"Nothing of value. Only my heart." Jerry looked at his mother with a humorous grin.

"Now what's your nonsense?"

"Yes, that was it. My heart got broke soon after I started, and I had to drive slow to keep the pieces together. That's why I was late."

"Jerry, what are you talking about?"

"Well, I stopped at the Scanlans' to say good-bye to Nora. But she was out with her husband — Charley Corcoran. They were married last night. So I just sort of jogged into town after that."

"Oh, Jerry!" His mother looked up at him with love and sympathy, and he knew that she wanted to press his hand. "She was n't worthy of you, Jerry; I — I hate her."

"Don't do that, mother." He turned and said briskly to the children following behind, "You're going to like living in here. School's just round the corner, and you'll make a lot of friends, and sometimes in our building you can go up and play on the roof."

Kate smiled gratefully. "Peter will like that, won't you, Peter?"

Peter agreed that he would like it, and little Betty declared that she would like it too.

"And it's the snug little place that you'll have to live in," said Jerry. "Kind of like a doll-house, it's so snug."

They were obviously pleased at hearing that. And soon they all ascended the two flights of stairs in the narrow brick building and entered their domain. It consisted of three little rooms, a bathroom, and a kitchen; and although the belongings of the family were not numerous, they left, as Mrs. Donohue observed, little space to stir about in. Jerry had done his best, but his mother pronounced some rearrangement necessary, and by the time they sat down to their cold supper the children and Mrs. Donohue were tired. So very soon after supper they all went to bed, the two girls in one room, Jerry and Peter in another, and Mrs. Donohue in the third and best room, which was to be parlor and sitting-room by day. Peter was soon asleep, but Jerry, lying close to the thin partition, heard the sound of a girl's sobbing; it was subdued, but it continued for a long time. He wondered what caused it — whether it was that Kate found herself afresh missing her father and her mother, or that the new quarters were strange and unhomelike to her, or that the unkind words of his Aunt Bridget were rankling in the little girl's mind. He lay there wishing he might comfort her and wondering how he might; he supposed it would only frighten her and be interpreted as a reproof if he rapped on the partition, though ever so gently.

But by and by the sobs ceased, and he heard nothing but Peter's even breathing from the little bed beside him, and he wished that he could go to sleep too.

XI ·

JERRY did not allow many days to go by without seeking an interview with his friend Roger Trask. He found
that Trask had been mindful of his promises and had
obtained all the information that a candidate for the
police force might need in order to prepare himself.
Trask in fact accompanied him to the offices of the
Civil Service Commission and saw him enrolled as an
applicant.

"And now," Trask said, "all you can do is to wait
your turn and meanwhile make yourself fit."

"I've got to do more than that," said Jerry. "I've
got to find a job. You don't know of one, do you, Mr.
Trask?"

No, Trask could not help him there. He tried to help
him; he made inquiries among his friends who were
employers of labor, but met with no encouragement.
Business was in a depressed condition, the number of the
unemployed was increasing, no one seemed to have need
of a skilled ironworker. Jerry, making the rounds of
blacksmith shops, machine shops, iron foundries, grew
more and more disheartened. He became more sensitive about going home at night with no success to report;
he thought his mother must soon begin to lose confidence in him, and he wondered if with all his health and
strength there was no work that he might be permitted

to do. He wondered how men got jobs; he was willing to serve an apprenticeship at anything, but wherever he applied he was told that there was nothing then, but that he might inquire again in a month or two. Never before in his life had Jerry known what it was to envy a fellow man — and now there was scarcely a man that he passed on the street without envy — without the thought, "I suppose you have a job." There was Armstrong, who with his wife and two children occupied the first-floor suite of the apartment house and who, as Jerry soon discovered, came home tipsy every Saturday night — a mean-looking, ferret-eyed creature, yet he earned good wages in a plumbing shop; Jerry ventured to ask him one day if he would be willing to use his influence with his employer to get him received as an apprentice — a request that drew the coolly insolent rejoinder, "Nothing doing." Jerry flushed to the eyes with mortification, choked down his wrath in silence, and thereafter when he met Armstrong passed him without a glance of recognition. Indeed, he had further reason to regret having approached his ungracious neighbor, for as it happened on that same day, when he had returned discouraged from the search for work and was sitting weary and with vacant mind in his mother's room, he heard the trampling of children outside on the stairway and then the shrill voice of the older Armstrong girl.

"Paddies! Paddies! Irish Paddies!"

"We're not Paddies!" Jerry heard Peter cry; and then the voice of Kate, more loyal, rang out: "Well, what if we are Paddies?"

"My mother won't let me go with Paddies," declared the shrill voice triumphantly. "My mother says it's a shame Catholic Paddies should live in this house."

"We're not Catholic Paddies."

"Your folks are."

"Well, I'd rather be a Paddy then than what you are."

"My mother says they're all liars and they'll burn in hell fire."

"Don't you dare say such things!"

"Who'll stop me?"

It was Peter that replied: "Jerry's going to be a policeman and he'll arrest you."

An uncontrollable cackle of laughter attested the amusement of the Armstrong progeny. "Policeman nothing. He's just a loafer, my mother says."

"He is not — and when he's a policeman he'll arrest you," Peter screamed; and little Betty began to cry.

"Come, Peter, don't speak to them any more," said Kate.

"Paddies! Paddies! Irish Paddies!" rose the taunting chorus, and it was still sounding when Kate, flushed and with eyes blazing, pushed her brother and sister into the room. She did not see Jerry, seated near the window.

"You just wait there," she said, "till I finish off those two limbs —"

"Oh, Kate," said Jerry, and she turned startled and stood motionless. "I wouldn't pay any attention to them; just let them alone — that's best."

"But you did n't hear what they said, Jerry."

"Yes, I did. The best way to treat people like that is to have nothing to do with them."

Kate was reluctant to abandon her design of revenge. "I'd have slapped them, I'd have pulled their hair, if Betty had n't got frightened and started to cry."

Jerry delivered a wise lecture on the advantage of bearing one's self with dignity. "I've got to practice it against the time when I get to be a cop," he said. "And a cop's family has to be just as dignified as he is. You just remember that when kids give you their sass; just walk away with your nose in the air."

"I hope, anyway, when you're a cop those Armstrongs will do something so you can arrest them," exclaimed Kate; her eyes were still snapping and her bosom heaving with indignation. "Oh, Jerry, do please be a cop soon, just to show them."

"Just as soon as I can, Kate; but I tell you, a cop's family has got to learn to be patient as well as dignified."

"Well," said Kate, "I suppose that's so. But I'd like to claw those Armstrongs — yes, I would — claw them."

Even Jerry found it hard to endure with patience and dignity the annoyances that his impish neighbors were constantly devising for him. He would find the door of the apartment placarded with the sign, "Cheese It The Cop"; above the stairway would be posted the announcement, "Irish Paddies up one flight," and drawings of an insulting character would frequently decorate the walls. It was evident that an older hand had helped to frame some of these posters; Jerry wondered at the idle malice that inspired the Armstrong family. It was some time before he realized that it was all a part of a campaign to force him and his mother out of the house; he had never before encountered sectarian and race hatred in a virulent form.

Irritations such as these, and the great and increasing anxiety as the days went by and the little hoard diminished and still no work was to be had, left Jerry small opportunity for the more luxurious unhappiness to be experienced through dwelling on the sorrow and disappointment of a blighted romance. There were times, of course, when he thought of Nora and gave himself the painful pleasure of visualizing her as she had appeared to his eyes in his happiest moments; but that life now seemed so remote as to be almost unreal, to have belonged, indeed, to another person; he accepted with resignation the fact that a penniless man out of a job has no right to think of marriage — has hardly the right to love. And it was better that he should not think of Nora's marriage, a marriage where there had been nothing but lust on one side and nothing but a desire to be supported on the other.

In the evenings Jerry became a frequenter of the Y.M.C.A. Building; there he prepared himself for the civil service examination by exercising in the gymnasium and by joining the class of candidates that received instruction twice a week from various lecturers. He learned to know the difference between a mittimus and a subpœna; he became able to tell what a felony is and why it is worse than a misdemeanor; he learned that a simple assault is not assault and battery, and that perjury is not subornation of perjury. He learned when a patrolman may arrest and when he may not, when he needs a warrant and when he does n't — and after he had learned these and many other puzzling, necessary facts, he found that there were still many more that he must be prepared to know. The more nearly he became qualified for membership in the police force, the higher rose his respect for those who already wore the uniform; he had never before realized what a fund of knowledge it was necessary for the ordinary patrolman to acquire. "I'm almost a lawyer already," he said to his mother after about a month of such study. "Sure, to be a cop is to belong to one of the learned professions."

In the gymnasium there was no other candidate whose rivalry he feared. Jerry had both strength and quickness; in chinning himself on the bar, or handling the seventy-five-pound dumb-bell, or doing the high jump he was excelled by none of those who practiced these exercises with him. Yet as time passed the knowledge of this fact gave him little satisfaction. "I get stronger and stronger," he muttered to himself, "and what's the good of my strength?"

It finally proved of use, for one day when he was strolling along the river wharves a foreman to whom he had often applied in vain beckoned to him. There was a cargo of molasses and cotton to be unloaded; Jerry went to work cheerfully at twenty cents an hour. From that day he was sure of at least intermittent employment upon the wharves, so long as navigation continued; but winter was approaching, and with the closing of the rivers this resource must fail him. And even in such humble employment he was not free from molestation; one day when he was bending under a heavy grain sack and passing the grating at the end of the wharf, he saw two young, obnoxious faces grinning through the bars and heard the snickering comment of the elder Armstrong, "Ain't he the dandy cop!" Thereafter hardly a day passed on which these two amiable young persons did not repair to the wharves and gaze at him through the grating, convulsed with merriment over his performance of his tasks. It was an indignity with which it seemed impossible to deal; he could have borne it with equanimity had it not soon come to his knowledge that the Armstrong girls were using their discovery to plague Kate and Peter at school.

Kate drew him out into the hall one evening to whisper, "Jerry, can't I lick those two Armstrongs to make them shut up? They're always teasing Peter because you're working down at the river instead of being a cop, and they've set a lot of others on to tease Peter about it too. I don't care what they say to me — I'm older — but it is n't right they should pick on Peter so. It's making him hate school."

"I'll have a little talk with Peter," said Jerry. "But you would n't mend matters by fighting with them, Kate. Just try to hold your temper and keep your dignity; some time things will come our way. It's a pity, of course, that I ever made that remark about what I was going to be —"

"No, it is n't, and you *are* going to be a cop!" the girl cried; and as she clung with both hands to his arms he felt her wiry little frame quivering as with passionate conviction.

"If I ever am, I could n't do better than have your spirit, Kate." And Jerry laughed and stroked her shimmering brown hair affectionately. She did n't understand quite what he meant, but she looked at him with pleased and grateful eyes.

Jerry had the talk with Peter that he had promised, and showed him that no matter what the provocation might be, a boy could never have a row with a girl — that however insulting she might be a man could n't lay his hand on a woman. "But cops sometimes arrest ladies," Peter reminded him. Yes, that was true, but it was never by way of gratifying any personal resentment, but simply because, for the safety of the world at large, the ladies had to be put under restraint.

"And if you've ever noticed a cop arresting a lady, Peter, you've noticed that the lady does all the talking. The cop never bothers to answer back. Now you want to get in training to be a cop some day, so just bear this in mind when the girls taunt you. Just say to yourself, 'I can't arrest them yet because I'm not a cop, but I can do one thing a cop would do, and that is keep my mouth shut.' Just remember always to say that to yourself, Peter."

The little boy's face cleared with satisfaction; he felt that his course would now be much easier.

XII

GLIMPSE OF A BENEVOLENT PERSONAGE: WHOSE SECOND
APPEARANCE BODES NO GOOD TO A CANDIDATE

NOT all the neighbors were as unpleasant as the Armstrongs. On the floor above Jerry and his mother lived a young compositor and his wife, Bennett by name; and from the first they had shown a friendly disposition. Mrs. Bennett had confided to Mrs. Donohue her expectations — a hardly necessary formality — and had pleased her by saying it was a comfort to have her on the next floor; she and Mrs. Armstrong had never "got on," and in case of trouble it was always so unsatisfactory to have to call in a person that you did n't get on with. Now she would n't have that to worry about any longer, thank goodness — and Mrs. Donohue would be willing to help her, would n't she?

Of course, Mrs. Donohue's heart at once went out to the girl, who was a delicate, pale, blue-eyed creature, with a pretty, wistful mouth, and she was lavish of promises and comforting assurances and speech that imported competence and knowledge; for though she had never been lucky enough to have more than one herself, there were many and many that she had assisted, and if she said it who should n't, 't was hardly likely that any hospital trained nurse could be of more use in such a matter. The two women passed much time in each other's company, and it was no doubt partly to show some recognition of Mrs. Donohue's kindness that

JERRY

Bennett invited Jerry one day to go to a ball game. Jerry hung back at first, unwilling to accept favors that he could not return, but Bennett, understanding, laughed and said, "It's a cheap treat all right. The sporting editor's a friend of mine, and he gave me the tickets." So Jerry's scruples vanished, and sitting high up in the stands he and his new friend smoked their pipes, followed the game with enthusiasm, and arrived at a greater liking for each other.

"I tell you, it's a fine thing to have a job on a morning newspaper," observed Bennett. "Lots of ball games I get to see in the summer, and matinées in the winter. Night work's not so bad when it begins at six and ends at three. And the *Standard's* a fine newspaper to work for. — Say, see that fellow in the gray felt hat down on the aisle? Take a good look at him. That's Patrick Maguire. You've heard of him, I guess?"

"Oh, sure," said Jerry, to whom the name and fame of the local political boss had been well known for years.

"You'd ought to have gone and settled in his ward," said Bennett. "Then you'd be sure to be in line for a job. Patrick certainly does look after all the residents of the Fourteenth. If a man will live there for three months, he'll find work for him — and if he likes his looks he won't make him wait as long as that. He's kind of good-hearted to all the folks in need outside of his ward, but to them that's in it — well, they think he's next door to an angel."

Jerry studied the back of Maguire's head with interest and in a moment was rewarded with a profile view of his face. It was a good-humored, alert face, and it seemed just then to be eyeing its companion quizzically. Jerry's attention was directed to this person, whom he recognized as John Maxwell, the Congressman. He imparted the information to Bennett.

"I'm not surprised," was Bennett's comment. "He picked Maxwell to run for Congress. Nobody does anything or gets anywhere without his sanction. The *Standard's* the only paper in town that dares to oppose him. And you know, from all they tell me, he's not such a bad lot. He lives as strict as a preacher — does n't drink, does n't smoke; and for all he's supposed to have made a fortune out of politics, you'd never know it except by what he does for the poor. He gives 'em picnics and buys milk for their babies and sends sick people to hospitals at his expense; and he lives in the same little house he's always lived in down on Moran Street. Regular old bachelor, and looks after his sister and her kid; you'll see him running them round in his automobile. Don't you suppose you know anybody that could introduce you to him?"

Jerry shook his head. "I'm afraid not. I once met the Congressman down there, but he would n't remember me — and he would n't help me if he did."

"Well, now, I tell you" — Bennett spoke earnestly — "you go and call on Maguire some day anyway. Tell him your name's Donohue and let him look at you. I'll bet he'd do something for you. He stands by the Irish and he's a good judge of men."

Jerry thanked his friend for the suggestion, but had no idea of acting on it. He was n't going to put himself under obligations to the boss and feel for the rest of his days that Maguire had a right to count on his support. From what he had read in the newspapers he had conceived a prejudice against Maguire, and it was not diminished now that he had learned that Maxwell was one of his creatures. "I will ask favors of no man that I don't respect," he said to himself, and as he glanced down the aisle at Maguire and Maxwell his jaw became unconsciously more set. Then a two-base hit by a member of the home team brought the joy of life back into his face.

It was nearly two months later that the postman one morning left in the Donohues' letter-box a card from the Civil Service Commission. Peter brought it up to Jerry, and Jerry when he had glanced at it cried, "It's waiting that does it! Look at that now, mother, and give your fine boy a smack on his two cheeks." He held before her a notice to the effect that candidates for the police force would be examined on the following Tuesday at the headquarters of the Commission.

It was with high confidence that he presented himself for the test; even the sight of the fifteen or twenty other candidates assembled did not reduce his hopefulness. Some of them were taller and heavier than he, most of them looked "tougher"; but Jerry, studying them one after another, told himself that he would be willing to wrestle or box with any of them. They were called out of the waiting-room one by one; at last his turn came, and he entered the dressing-room, stripped off his clothes, and put on his gymnasium suit. In a few moments he was summoned to appear before the judges; and no school or college youth ever entered the field for any athletic contest with more eager excitement than he felt as he passed into the next room. Then he instantly became aware of an ominous fact; in the group of judges and spectators who gazed at him with curiosity he saw in his first glance Maxwell and Maguire.

"Your name is Gerald Donohue?" said one who appeared to be in charge of the examination.

"Yes," Jerry answered.

He saw Maxwell look at him with sudden intentness, and at once knew that the Congressman had recognized him. No doubt it had been foolish to entertain the momentary hope that he would fail to do so; such political success as Maxwell had achieved had been owing to a rather unusual talent for remembering both names and faces.

Keeping his sharp eyes fixed on him, Maxwell whispered to Maguire. Jerry felt that evil influences were leaguing themselves against him, and the angry suspicion tautened his muscles. "Chin yourself, dropping each time to the full reach of your arms," said the examiner.

Jerry sprang up, grasped the horizontal bar, and set to work. He was accustomed to do fifteen or sixteen "chins" in practice; now he did not drop to the floor until the nineteenth had been tremulously, painfully achieved. He was allowed to stand quivering for a few moments.

"Take the parallel bars," said the examiner.

On these also Jerry excelled his best record, for he "dipped" twenty-three times as against a former high mark of twenty-one.

In the lifting tests he was unable to measure his performance; he heaved and pulled at a cross-bar that seemed fastened to something immovably embedded in the floor. "That will do," said the examiner, who had been bending over the registering disk. "I'd like to have another crack at it," said Jerry, for he felt that he had not got his full leverage into the effort and that the faint smile upon Maxwell's face was invigorating. "One chance is all we allow," replied the examiner, and handed him the grip machine, on which Jerry clenched his fist and tried to crush it. He had to give up without accomplishing his desire. "Try the left hand," suggested the examiner. The machine remained unbroken.

Next Jerry was asked to show what he could do with a seventy-five-pound dumb-bell. That was a thing that he had practiced with, and he put it up with either hand quite easily. Also he lay upon his back and rose to a sitting posture, carrying a fifty-pound dumb-bell behind his neck. After he had engaged in some weight-pulling to show the strength of his pectoral muscles, the examiner said, "That will do," and turned to the chart on which he had been figuring.

"That's all, Donohue," he said brusquely. "Yours is the best record yet."

He said it so that every one in the room might hear, and Jerry passed out of the door thrilled with delight, feeling as fresh and eager as if he had taken no exercise at all, and thinking to himself, "You can't get back of that, Mr. Maxwell, nor you either, Mr. Maguire." He put on his street clothes and was then directed down a corridor to the oral examination room, where three grave and rather severe gentlemen questioned him upon a variety of subjects. He stood up to them pretty well, and under his blithe and engaging confidence their manner towards him thawed somewhat. And when they had finished with him, one who seemed to be the chairman said kindly, "I hope that you did well in your physical examination, Mr. Donohue. In other respects you seem to me just the type of man that we want on our police force."

Was it any wonder that Jerry Donohue hastened home that afternoon, weaving in and out among the crowds on the sidewalk, and where they were too thick, skipping down from the curb and striding along past them in the street? Was it any wonder that he went bounding up the stairs of the apartment house, and to his expectant and assembled family cried, "Well, I don't want to be raising any hopes, but I guess I landed it."

"I'm not going to get my hopes up yet," said his mother conservatively.

But Kate paid no heed to pessimism.

"When are you going to get your uniform, Jerry?" she asked.

"Oh, it is n't settled; we must n't do any more talking about it until it's a certainty," Jerry explained.

"Yes, I know. But I'm just living to have those Armstrongs see you in uniform."

"Never mind about that. You go on standing at the head of your class, Kate; that's the kind of thing that counts."

She looked up at him in a pleased silence of gratitude, her face flushed at his praise, and then she bent, as if in sudden embarrassment, to kiss and cuddle Betty.

XIII

EVENTUALLY Jerry received a letter from the Civil Service Commission notifying him that he had passed the tests for patrolman and that his name had been sent to the Police Commissioner, to be acted upon at that official's discretion. And then the days and weeks went by just as they had done before.

At last Jerry visited the Police Commissioner's office and asked the clerk when he might expect appointment. The clerk gave him an unsatisfactory, vague answer. Jerry derived the impression that the recommendation of the Civil Service Commission by no means insured appointment to the police force. Disquieted in mind, he went to the headquarters of the Civil Service Commission and asked for an interview with the chairman. That kindly gentleman remembered him, looked up his record, and told him that his name had stood at the head of the list submitted to the Police Commissioner.

"Since that date," said the chairman, "I find that there have been four new patrolmen appointed. We sent on the names of seven candidates. Your turn ought to come soon."

"If I stood at the head of the list, why should n't I have been appointed first?" asked Jerry.

"You will have to put that question to the Police Commissioner."

[124]

"His clerk would n't let me see him, and made me feel that my chances of ever being appointed were pretty doubtful."

"Well," said the chairman regretfully, "it's quite true that it is n't mandatory on the Police Commissioner to give an appointment to every one passed by our Board. He can't appoint any one whom we don't recommend; our control stops there."

"I understand," said Jerry. "I should like to ask one other question. Why are Patrick Maguire and Congressman Maxwell allowed to be present at the physical examination of candidates?"

"The idea has always been that there should be a few outsiders invited to attend the examinations — as a guarantee that they are conducted in good faith. Patrick Maguire" — the chairman hesitated and smiled a trifle ironically — "perhaps I violate no confidence if I say that Mr. Maguire was invited by a member of our Board who values highly his services to the city. I may add that two of the other guests at your examination were gentlemen who are not in sympathy with Mr. Maguire."

"Well, now, I'm thinking it would n't be strange at all if Mr. Maguire and Congressman Maxwell between them had the ear of the Police Commissioner?"

"As to that, Mr. Donohue, I can only say that I'm so busy trying to keep politics from creeping into our department that I don't know what influences may be at work in other quarters."

"You've been very kind to me, sir," said Jerry, "and I thank you."

"Not at all," replied the chairman. "And I hope that you get your appointment."

"Plain as the nose on your face," muttered Jerry to himself when he was outside the door; and he turned his steps at once to Roger Trask's office.

Trask gave him a friendly welcome. "I was thinking of looking you up — so long since I've heard anything about you. I've been away for a couple of months — my wedding trip, you know — just got back last week. — Now tell me — have you landed that job on the police force yet?"

Jerry stated his case and his suspicions. Trask's cheerful face grew troubled.

"Of course Bridges is a strong party man," he admitted. "I've never believed that he stood in quite so closely with Maguire as his political opponents have charged him with doing, but I suppose their relations are more or less friendly. Maguire, you feel sure, would use his influence against you simply to gratify Maxwell's personal spite — he'd have no other reason?"

"None that I can imagine."

"I don't know as much as I should like to about city politics, but I do know that all kinds of trades are going on," said Trask. "Bridges is a friend of mine; maybe he'll listen to me rather than to Maguire. — Have you found anything else to do all this time?"

"Nothing steady."

"Business is better than when you were in before. We ought to find work for you now." Trask took up his telephone and in a moment was talking with some one. "This you, Jim? Yes, Trask. Got a job in your shipping-room or anywhere else for a friend of mine? Yes. All right, I'll send him down."

He turned to Jerry. "James Murray and Company, down on Front Street — wholesale grocers. See Murray himself — give him this card; he spoke as if he might do something. And if you're up against it in any way, drop in and see me; drop in and see me occasionally anyway."

It was for Jerry a quite rejuvenating interview. And an hour later he was going home with the blithe news for his mother that he had at last secured a regular job.

"It just shows what a man with influence can do," Jerry observed. "I might have gone on trudging the streets for months while you were all starving to death. And here it's a mere word over the telephone and another on a visiting card, and I'm signed on at once at fifteen dollars a week. And I should n't be at all surprised if to-morrow or the next day the postman would be bringing me a letter from the Police Commissioner asking me would I be so kind as to become his private secretary."

"Indeed, he'd be doing that and more too if he knew all that I know about you," declared his mother. She was in a state of high elation. She felt that now all the worries were at an end.

Kate and Peter, returning from school, rejoiced also in the news.

"And you'll be working indoors, where those Armstrongs can't see you and holler at you, won't you?" said Kate.

JERRY

So Jerry settled down to the work of packer in the shipping-room of James Murray and Company. Eager to learn and quick, he soon overcame his first awkwardness, and after a week was performing his tasks as rapidly and competently as any other man in the room. Now that he was again earning money he decided that he could afford to take the law course in the night school. The law interested him; perhaps some time he could become a lawyer. If he could n't do that and yet became a policeman, his studies would be useful; a policeman could n't know too much law.

So in these days Jerry led a busy and happy life. Yet with all his occupations he found time to be curious and eager about the result of the interview between Trask and the Police Commissioner; and one day during his lunch hour he made another call at Trask's office.

"Yes, I've talked with Bridges, and it's about as I supposed." Trask leaned back in his chair and clasped his hands behind his head. "I don't want you to have any wrong impression about Bridges, Donohue. He's absolutely straight; I've known him for years. When I put your grievance before him, he admitted frankly that both Maxwell and Maguire had stated their preferences to him about appointments, and he had deferred to them. He said there were a good many reasons why he thought it wise in the administration of the department to consult Maguire's wishes when he could; they may or may not be good reasons, but I'm sure they're honest. I told Bridges that from my own personal knowledge I was certain you would make a fine policeman and that for this once I wished he would do me a favor even if it meant displeasing Maguire; I intimated to him what was back of Maguire's hostility. He promised me then that as soon as a vacancy occurred he would see what he could do. I'll keep after him to see that he does n't forget."

"You're certainly a good friend to me, Mr. Trask," said Jerry. "And I must be the tiresome kind of a plague to you."

When Jerry got home that evening he reported the conversation to his mother and added, "So it does look more and more as if I'd be a cop some day. But it might be to the credit and the peace of mind of both of us if we were to cease talking of it from now on."

"I would n't be finding it hard to hold my tongue on the matter," said Mrs. Donohue. "But it's different with a child that has once been filled up with hope. Kate and Peter — their minds fair run upon the notion of seeing you in a cop's uniform, and thinking what those young ones on the floor below will say then."

"It's a great pity I ever put the notion into their heads, though it was with the idea of giving them something grand and cheerful to think about. Let's not be stirring them up again. They'll be as well pleased, if not better, if I was suddenly to appear before them in a cop's uniform after they had in a manner given up all hope of it."

"You're quite right about that," said Mrs. Donohue.

That same evening Jerry returning late from his studies at the night school heard the Bennetts' door open as he ascended the stairs. In the dim light that reached out into the hallway he saw a face peering over the banisters.

"Is that you, Mr. Donohue?" It was young Mrs. Bennett who called down to him; and when he answered she said, "I suppose your mother's asleep, and I hate to ask you to wake her, but oh, I do wish she'd come up and sit with me. And then would you please go for the doctor? It's Dr. Ray, 25 Dillon Street. And if you'd fetch Jim home to me too."

"I will. And my mother will be with you in a moment," said Jerry.

He had only to whisper in his mother's ear, and instantly she was awake and alert. Then he went springing down the stairs and racing through the quiet streets. From the shadow of a building a policeman stepped out, checked him, and putting his hand on his shoulder peered suspiciously into his face. He was a grim-featured man of middle age with a brown mustache; he held Jerry and while he looked at him in silence he slipped a hand down over his pockets.

"I'm running for a doctor," Jerry gasped. "Woman in our house having a baby —"

"Go along," said the grim policeman, and Jerry renewed his breakneck pace.

He turned into Dillon Street and had to strike a match in front of three different houses before he was able to identify number 25. Then he pulled the bell vigorously; he heard it jangling for a while, and then he pulled it again.

A man poked his head out of a third story window.

"Dr. Ray?" asked Jerry.

"Yes."

"Mrs. Bennett, 34 White Street, needs you right away."

"She does n't need me as quick as you think," replied the doctor grumpily. "Husbands are always in a rush. All right, go back and tell her I'm coming."

Jerry did not think it worth while to enlighten him as to his error, but hastened on to the office of the *Standard*. By the time he reached it he was pretty well winded, in spite of his gymnasium training. Bennett, on hearing the news, demonstrated the truth of Dr. Ray's assertion about husbands; after a few moments Jerry fell behind. "Don't wait for me," he called; and Bennett, who had no intention of waiting, quickly disappeared.

It was a fine winter night, still and clear, with the stars shining in the cleft of sky above the narrow street and the moonlight washing the house fronts on one side and flowing down over the roofs on the other. The peaceful stillness and the nature of the errand that he had just performed united to induce in Jerry, as he recovered his breath, a meditative mood. How splendid to be Bennett, racing home to welcome the arrival of a child! How important to be a father! How unimportant not to be one! Jerry recalled the sense of vicarious significance with which he had stood on Dr. Ray's doorstep and heard the physician make his slurring comment on husbands; in that moment Jerry had enjoyed being disparaged as a husband.

A figure appeared out of the shadow on the opposite sidewalk and crossed over towards him. It proved to be the policeman who had examined him a few minutes before.

"Your friend's going home as fast as you went after him," said the policeman. "I had to stop him like I did you. Fellows running through the streets at night as fast as you two — kind of a suspicious circumstance."

"I suppose so," Jerry answered. "But you see how it was."

"I know; got three of my own. All came in the middle of the night too. Well, I guess my delaying you and your friend won't make any difference. Good-night."

"Good-night," said Jerry, and walking on he resumed his meditations.

When he got home, he found that his mother had not returned. He went to bed, but lay awake thinking of the extraordinary and enviable thing that was happening to Bennett just overhead. The episode of childbirth had never before been brought so closely to his attention, and it was masculine inexperience that caused him to center his thoughts upon Bennett instead of on Mrs. Bennett. What an exciting time it must be!

He heard footsteps ascending the stairs and knew from the leisurely sound of them that they must be Dr. Ray's.

Then after a while, just as he was falling asleep, he was aroused by a commotion and trampling overhead. It lasted for some minutes, and then suddenly and quite distinctly he heard a shrill crying.

"Gosh!" he said. "Bennett's got a real live baby."

Then he went to sleep, and the next morning his mother told him Mrs. Bennett had an eight-pound boy.

XIV

MRS. ARMSTRONG'S DAY ON THE ROOF: THE KNOCK
ON MRS. ARMSTRONG'S DOOR

IT was three weeks later that the notification came from the Police Commissioner. Mrs. Donohue handed it to Jerry one evening when he returned from his work, and watched his face eagerly while he read it.

"What does he say? You're the provoking fellow — you've not got the expression of a fish," she clamored after a moment. "Have you got it or have n't you?"

"The expression of a fish? Sure I have."

"Oh, don't be teasing me. Have you got the place? Let me see that letter."

"I have," said Jerry. "So quit up now on your impatience. There, read it."

"Impatience, when it's but a decent bit of interest I'm showing! — 'Gives me pleasure to announce —' I will say for him he has a polite way of doing things. 'Report for duty on the 21st.' That's a week from to-day, Jerry."

"Yes, it begins to look like the real thing now," Jerry answered. "But let's not say a word to Kate and Peter, mother. Just leave me to walk in on them some day in my cop's uniform — that will tickle them more than hearing all about it in advance."

"You're right it will — and, indeed, I'm wishing I had learned it the same way myself."

"Now listen to that! And you at me to tell you about

it before I had fair read the words myself! You're a contrary kind of a woman."

"I'm as I was made. Your father used to say I was terribly curious about the concerns of all them I was fond of, but a wonderful hand at minding my own business in all other respects."

"He knew you like a book, did n't he, mother?"

"He was a smart, clever man. And there's no getting away from it, Jerry; you might be glad to have me different, but I'm as I was made."

"Well, we've all got to pretend to be satisfied as far as possible with our relatives and our surroundings," said Jerry.

"Ah, don't talk to me in that cold-blooded kind of way, Jerry."

"Don't you ever know when I'm joking!" Jerry drew her to him and caressed her. "Sometimes I think you've got an idea of a joke, and sometimes you have n't. You're a contrary kind of a woman."

"I'm as I was made," Mrs. Donohue repeated with comfortable resignation. And then she added in a tone of deeper feeling, "Ah, Jerry, would n't your father have been proud of you this day!"

He must n't smile at her any longer; he held her face up between his hands and kissed it — kissed the tears from her eyes. When he released her, she turned and pointed to the memorial dove.

"To this day, Jerry, as often as I look at that bird, I feel the arrow's really in my heart."

"I know, mother. Often and often I feel it too."

They heard footsteps approaching from the kitchen.

"Mind, don't say a word!" Jerry whispered, and Mrs. Donohue nodded understandingly.

Kate summoned them to supper. "Oh, I hope you'll like it, Jerry. It's the first time your mother's let me do it all myself. Peter and Betty set the table. I hope things will be good."

He caught her eyes watching him anxiously, eagerly, at frequent intervals through the meal; and when he praised the coffee and asked for more of the beans and commented favorably on the fried potatoes, the little girl seemed to glow with pleasure. Afterwards she washed the dishes and Peter and Jerry raced to see who could dry the most; Kate had to take a towel and go over a good many of those that Peter dried. Then she helped Betty to undress and get to bed; she came out into the sitting-room to study her lessons with Peter just as Jerry was about to leave for the night school.

"Good-night, Kate; good-night, Peter."

"Good-night, Jerry."

"'Night, Jerry."

"Be sure you're both in bed and asleep before I get back."

That was the formula on which they parted every evening; then Jerry swung away with a mind striving to recall what had been said in the last lecture about real property, and Kate sat dreaming over her grammar of what little girls of fifteen who have their eyes on their books are very apt to dream of. But Kate was a sensible girl and never dreamed very long; and she was a shy girl and was quite sure that nobody and certainly not Mrs. Donohue, who was usually dozing in a chair or else was upstairs visiting with the young convalescent mother, ever guessed of what she dreamed.

At the warehouse the next morning Jerry had unexpectedly to deal with what he recognized as a crisis in his life. Mr. Murray sent for him, and after speaking in complimentary words of the manner in which he was doing his work said that one of the shipping-clerks was leaving and he might have the place. It would mean a little more pay, and he would be in line for further promotion.

Jerry thought rapidly and declined the offer. "In fact, I was coming in to tell you, Mr. Murray, that I'll be leaving myself; I've got a place promised me on the police force, and it's that I've had an ambition for this long while."

"Are you sure you're not making a mistake? Do you think it's wise to sacrifice what may be a good opening in business and take a job as patrolman?"

"I have a feeling," said Jerry, "that it's always wise for a man to do what he most hankers after."

"If he feels that the work and the remuneration for it are such as will always satisfy him."

"A patrolman has a chance to be some day more than a patrolman."

"That's true. And yet I'd advise you to think twice before choosing the police as a career."

"Well," Jerry said firmly, "maybe from the worldly point of view I'm foolish. But from my own I'm not. If I did n't take the job of cop when I had a chance I'd be disappointing some folks that I don't want to disappoint. And what's more, I'd be disappointing myself.

I'd never be happy, figuring costs and keeping books and doing office routine. I want to be in something more active, with adventure in it and a chance to use my muscles. And then"—a certain shyness crept in to Jerry's voice—"it would be kind of a satisfaction to feel you were doing what you could to—to protect the public."

"I won't make any further attempt to persuade you. A man who talks like that is able to determine such a question without help from outside. You look as if you had plenty of muscle, and what's more you look as if you had plenty of backbone—and that's where most of the policemen in this town need stiffening. I hope you won't have all the bloom rubbed off your ideals."

"If it's rubbed off in one place it soon grows in another with me," said Jerry cheerfully. And he and Mr. Murray parted with a sense of considerable respect on each side.

Every day Jerry expected his mother to confess that she had been unable to contain the great secret; each evening when he came home he would say to her, "I guess now that your tongue has at last got the best of you and you've been blabbing to Kate," and Mrs. Donohue would reply spiritedly, "Indeed, now I have not." But one evening upon his arrival he found her with such a cloud of wrath darkening her brow that he forbore to make the customary accusation and asked instead, "What on earth has happened to give you that look?"

"It's that Armstrong woman," replied Mrs. Donohue

and rocked rapidly in her chair. "You know, it was her day on the roof."

"Her day on the roof? What would she be doing, spending a day on the roof?"

"Use your mind, Jerry. Is n't it Monday that Mrs. Bennett hangs out the wash on the roof? Is n't it Tuesday that we do? Is n't it Wednesday that the Armstrong woman hangs out the wash? Well, then!" Mrs. Donohue rocked more fiercely. "It was nothing that any woman would n't have done — nothing that any decent, friendly kind of a body would have minded. With a lot of little baby things to be washed every day — and her not strong yet either! I would n't have believed it of a soul."

"I don't yet get at the straight of it," remarked Jerry.

"Why, as I said, with a lot of little baby things to wash, Mrs. Bennett thought no harm, even though it was the Armstrong woman's day, to slip up on the roof and hang them out. So up she climbed, and it so happened the Armstrong woman was n't there, but there was a long length of clothes-line with nothing flying from it at all, and in the space of a minute Mrs. Bennett had pinned up all her little things and come down again to her rooms as innocent as a lamb. A couple of hours later when she went up after her wash, there were all the little things pitched in a heap on the dirty gravel roof, all smooched and grimed; and that Armstrong woman had just moved and spaced her things wider apart so they'd take up the whole length of the line. A nice kind of a neighbor! I happened to go upstairs to see the baby, and there was Mrs. Bennett in tears, with the heap of smooched little duds on the floor beside her. She's not strong yet, poor thing."

"I hope she told the Armstrong woman what she thought of her," said Jerry.

"No, she did not. She was afraid to make a scene over it, for fear she'd get upset and it would be bad for the baby. Her husband was out at the time and won't be back till late to-night, so he knows nothing of it. I've just been aching to put my oar in, but I felt it was fair he should have first chance. What a woman!"

"A grand outfit, the whole family. But now don't you be getting into a row with them. There's no use of it at all."

"I'm not saying what I may be doing," said his mother darkly.

"It's Bennett's row, not yours; mind that. He might n't be thanking you for your help. And now to turn your mind to another subject — I'll be getting my uniform to-morrow; I'm to be sworn in at noon, and after that I'll be a member of the force. So you need to keep a firm grip on yourself for only one more day."

"It's no such hardship for me. But it will be the great sight to see you in a cop's suit at last — and to see the eyes of all the children at beholding it."

"To say nothing of your own, opening out like saucers. — I'll bet now you took those soiled baby things of Mrs. Bennett's and washed them again yourself and dried them in your own kitchen."

"Well, what if I did? It was n't as if I was that driven

with work I had no time to be doing a friend a small favor."

"I was n't criticizing you, you quick-tempered body. I was just by way of proving to you that I know you like a book."

"Oh, indeed, you 're a very smart fellow, that I 'll own." She continued her emphatic rocking, but a smile flickered about her lips.

The next morning after breakfast Jerry slipped upstairs and held a brief interview with Mrs. Bennett. And that afternoon, having been enrolled at Police Headquarters as a patrolman, he bore home a box containing his uniform. Kate and Peter had arrived from school, and Peter made inquiry as to what was in the box and how he happened to be home so early, to which Jerry responded, "Ask me no questions and I 'll tell you no lies," and proceeded to lock himself in his room. Peter, after some further expression of his curiosity, was for going to the park to see if there might be skating on the pond, but Mrs. Donohue told him to wait a few minutes till Jerry came out; perhaps Jerry would go with him.

It was, indeed, a wonderful, resplendent, and grinning Jerry that emerged. Kate shrieked and Peter shouted, and then both children danced round him, and Mrs. Donohue, beaming and happy, walked round him too and exclaimed, "Well, it certainly does become you, Jerry; it certainly does become you."

"You really are a cop, Jerry?" Peter asked in a moment of fearful skepticism. "It is n't just a fake?"

"No, I really am a cop," said Jerry. "Here, look at

my shield." And he exhibited the insignia that bore the number 71.

Peter examined the helmet, which he tried on, and the club, which he flourished. Meanwhile, Kate, who had been silent and enraptured, found her tongue and began to ask Jerry how he had achieved his appointment.

"Oh, I'm crazy to have the Armstrongs see you!" she cried.

"They soon will. Are the Armstrong kids at home now?"

"Yes, I think so. They were just behind me coming from school, and as we came up the stairs they called after us, 'Good-bye, Irish Paddies.'"

"Well," said Jerry, "I'm going to bring Mrs. Bennett down here, and then maybe you'll see me make an arrest."

"Jerry!" cried his mother in mingled consternation and delight, but he stepped out of the room without explaining himself.

Presently he reappeared, accompanied by Mrs. Bennett, who was giggling with excitement.

"Does n't he look grand!" said Mrs. Bennett. "And oh, my goodness, what is it he's going to do?"

"I'm going to exercise my authority," said Jerry. "Step out into the hall now, all of you, and hang over the banisters and you'll hear. Only be quiet, and don't be laughing and chattering."

So very quietly they went out and hung over the banisters in the manner prescribed, and he descended the stairs. They heard him give a tremendous knock on the Armstrongs' door; Kate emitted a convulsive, joyous laugh. "S-sh!" said Mrs. Donohue, who was trembling with eagerness.

They heard the door open; there was a moment of silence, and then Jerry's voice, stern and ominous, ascended to them.

"Is your mother in?"

Subdued came the answer, "Yes, sir."

"Tell her to come here."

Peter's mouth was open in breathless ecstasy; Kate wanted to jump up and down and clap her hands. Oh, if they could only see as well as hear! What bliss! Now, listen!

"Mrs. Armstrong, I've called to warn you against any further malicious interference with Mrs. Bennett's washing. I have told Mrs. Bennett that for a second offense of such a nature you can be brought before a magistrate. Malicious mischief is punishable by fine or imprisonment. I want to give you this warning so that you won't make trouble for yourself."

"Say, look here, is this a joke?" The question rose in uncertain but sufficiently angry tones.

"No, it is not a joke. Look at this badge. And remember after this that you've got no exclusive right to the roof, Wednesday or any other day."

Abruptly Jerry turned and ascended the stairs. For the next few minutes his descriptive powers were taxed to the utmost. Which Armstrong girl was it that had opened the door? And how did she look when she saw him? Was she all goggle-eyed? And Mrs. Armstrong; I bet she was scared; I bet you could see her tremble.

Anyway the warning proved effective; Jerry and his

family received no further annoyance from the Armstrongs. And Mrs. Bennett was sufficiently human to find always upon Mrs. Armstrong's day on the roof a number of little baby things that needed to be hung out to dry.

XV

DURING the first month of his service Jerry was placed
under the tutelage of various veteran policemen. He
accompanied them on their patrols in different parts
of the city and became familiar with their routine duties. They displayed towards him varying degrees of
kindness, indifference, and churlishness. Only one
seemed to have a real interest in teaching him; that
was Sheehan, the officer who had stopped him on the
night when he was running to summon the doctor.
Sheehan remembered him, and the first time that they
started out together said immediately: —

"Was it a boy?"

"Yes," Jerry answered. "But it was n't mine, you
know."

"I remember; too bad. You 'll make a better policeman when you have one of your own. You 're fast on
your feet anyway. Some of the men on the force
could n't run thirty yards — unless there was a keg of
beer at the end of it. How much do you know about
this city?"

Jerry answered modestly that he still felt pretty ignorant.

"I don't doubt you 've got all the nice, clean, respectable knowledge," said Sheehan. "You could direct
a woman to Bell's store, and you could tell a stranger

how to go to the Union Station, and what cars run to Oakmont, and what corner Norris's candy shop is on. But could you find your way about the red-light district?"

Jerry felt very young and innocent as he replied, "No."

"And could you take me to any one of the swell gambling-houses? Do you know where Tim Coogan's bar-room is — and if you do, do you know it's the headquarters for a gang of North End crooks? Do you know Jake Rubinski's pawnshop — the biggest fence for stolen goods in the city? Or Tony Lapatka's place on Condon Street?"

In reply to each of these questions Jerry had to shake his head.

"Well," said Sheehan ominously, "when you've learned all about those places and the gangs that infest them, you have n't even begun to learn what's rotten in this city."

"What is?" asked Jerry.

Sheehan looked at him and then smiled, Jerry's eyes were so ingenuous and so trusting.

"We'll come to that by degrees," he said. "Now we'll stop in at Tony Lapatka's joint for a minute. You want to fix in your mind every face that you see there, for it will be that of a crook or a suspect."

Condon Street lay back a block from the river front and was lined with bar-rooms, cheap restaurants, pawnshops, and men's outfitting shops. At eight o'clock in the evening, the hour when Jerry and Sheehan walked along it, the street presented an aspect of liveliness and gayety; men and women thronged the entrances of the moving-picture places or strolled arm in arm; their faces were usually expressive of a stolid sensuality; the uncurtained windows of the saloons revealed lines of men standing at the bars; over the window displays of clothing stores and pawnshops the electric lights cast a glamour that did not exist by day; the drug stores with their brilliant liquids and warm enticing odors seemed at night to take on a new allurement.

Tony Lapatka's "place" was a combination restaurant and bar-room. At the entrance of the two policemen talk and laughter ceased, and silent, watchful tension prevailed. Jerry was uncomfortably aware that he was an object of sullen hostility.

"It's all right, boys; we have n't come for any of you to-night," said Sheehan, and the reassuring words brought a cold smile to some of the faces. There began then a whispering conversation at the tables, but all the eyes remained hard and watchful. Sheehan in a low tone sketched the different characters: — "That fellow with the fat face and the hair slicked back is Heinie Schwartzfelder, known as 'Heinie the Dip' — just out of prison where he's done a five-year term for robbery. Next to him the big-nosed, lop-eared guy is Owney Burke; he's done time for burglary, but got pardoned out. There's a couple of gangsters over in that corner, Marty the Nib and German Otto —"

But at this moment Jerry's eyes fell upon Dave Scanlan, who was sitting at a distant table; and without waiting to hear more of Marty the Nib and German Otto he made his way eagerly to his old friend's side, unmindful of the scowling glances that were shot at him by those he passed, and of Dave's sullen, unwelcoming face. His hearty greeting overbore Dave's reluctance; "Come and tell me all about the family, Dave; I have n't seen any of you for nearly a year "; thus he drew him away from his two unsavory companions and led him to a corner of the room.

"Is it going to queer you with your friends to be seen with a cop, Dave?"

"No." But Dave was red and ill at ease. "I did n't know you'd got this job."

"I've just got it. How are things going with you?"

"Lost my job a month ago for drinking. Been on the bum ever since."

"What's happened to the family?"

"Dad works when he's not too boozy."

Dave's voice was defiant; his eyes, now that he raised them to Jerry's, were hard and cynical.

"How's your mother, Dave? How's Nora?"

"Mother's about as you might expect. I don't deny it's hard on her; still, a place where all you get is a tongue-lashing ain't much of a home. Nora's living out at Millvale — going to have a baby next month. I don't know as she's any too happy."

"I hope she will be. Look here, Dave; I think maybe I can help you to get a job. I was working for Murray, the wholesale grocer; you come round to my flat, 34 White Street, to-morrow morning before nine, and I'll give you a letter to him; — no, I'll go with you and see him. He's a fine man, and there's plenty of good chances in his business. — Now I've got to be moving

[147]

on; Sheehan's waiting for me. Don't forget, Dave; 34 White Street, and come before nine."

"He'll want to see my references; when I say, 'Fired for drinking —'"

"Maybe he'll take me for a reference. Try him anyway."

"Oh, I'd just as soon try it. All right, Jerry, much obliged."

They parted; and Dave had to rehabilitate himself in the esteem of the two companions who during this interview had been eyeing him with distrust and contempt. There was only one means at his disposal; in a short time all three were gloriously drunk. Later in the evening he separated from his two friends and after wandering uncertainly through the streets chose to pick a quarrel with a man whose stare he regarded as insolent. The man knocked him down, and Dave found the recumbent position so comfortable that he chose not to get up. He remonstrated with two policemen who finally bundled him into the patrol wagon.

In the morning, under an assumed name, he pleaded guilty to the charge, "Drunk and disorderly," and was sentenced to the reformatory for thirty days.

So Jerry looked in vain for him, blamed himself for having failed to get his address, searched for it in the city directory without success, and ended three days later by writing to Nora at Millvale and asking for it. Then a week passed before Nora answered the letter; Jerry's daily expectancy and daily disappointment when the postman made his rounds were surely not owing to his interest in Dave. He confessed to himself that a

token from Nora's hand would still have magic for
him; he wanted a letter from her for its own sake, more
than for Dave's. When it came, it was a brief, even a
formal little note, that betrayed nothing about herself
beyond the fact that she had been unwell and so had
neglected to answer his question promptly. She gave
him the information that he asked for and added, rather
sadly he thought, that she had n't seen any of her family for a month, but supposed that if they had moved
she would have heard of it.

Jerry felt that she would not have written so imper-
sonal a note if she had been happy.

He read it a second time, wistfully lingering over the
delicate strokes and graceful curves of Nora's writing;
they were characteristic of her, so pretty, fragile, sensitive; he was unaware that across the room Kate was
watching him. He looked up startled when Kate said: —

"Some one been making you feel badly, Jerry."

"Yes," he admitted. "An old friend of mine seems
unhappy, and there's nothing I can do to help."

"I guess if you just went and showed him you felt
badly because he did it would help."

"Sometimes we can't do that; sometimes that might
do more harm than good."

Kate looked puzzled. "I know if I was ever unhappy
and you showed me you felt badly about it, I would feel
better."

"That's because you're such a nice little girl, Kate."
He walked over to her and stood for a moment caressing
her cheek with his hand. And suddenly she seized the
hand and pressed it hard to her warm lips, then let it

go. He laughed. "You're a funny little girl, Kate —
just as funny as you are nice."

But he really was embarrassed by her sudden unac-
countable demonstration and by the affectionate look
in her eyes as she turned her flushed face up to him.
After all, Kate was growing into quite a big girl, and it
was time to stop treating her like a little one. She had
always been a sensible young creature; he hoped she
was n't now about to go through a phase of romantic
nonsense. The thought made him draw away; and
thenceforth there was less warmth and playfulness in
his manner towards her. And from her there were no
more alarming outbreaks of affection; she kept herself
always so busy when he was near that he could not but
realize the groundlessness of his apprehensions. At the
same time he was conscious of a vague disappointment,
not remote from pique. He had been so in the habit of
having her look up to him that the more level gaze of
her eyes seemed almost to imply disparagement.

Jerry found Mrs. Scanlan at the address that Nora
had given. His appearance in uniform impressed her and
seemed to cow her, at least for a time. Instead of inter-
viewing him in the doorway, she let him enter and even
pushed forward a chair for him. Discouragement had
aged her and had reduced her defiant manner; Jerry
could not help feeling sorry at the evidence of a broken
spirit, and at the pathos of her surroundings. She was
living with only a few remnants from her ambitious
past; gone were the lambrequins and the tidies, the
vases and figurines and Rogers groups, the piano and
the superfluity of furniture that had given the parlor

of her former home its air of opulence. The S-shaped conversation chair in which Jerry and Nora had often sat she still retained, and the large easel with its crayon portrait of herself, the ormolu and onyx clock, and the squat-bellied lamp with the large globular glass shade; but everything else was by comparison mean and battered and poor. The sight of the conversation chair touched a sentimental chord in Jerry's memory. He remembered just how Nora used to sit in it, with her arm along the back and her head propped on her hand while she listened gravely to his eager vows.

Mrs. Scanlan did not know where Dave was. He had written a letter to her saying that he was all right, but that he might not be home for some weeks; he was n't coming home till he was earning money again.

Jerry was puzzled. "If you see him, Mrs. Scanlan, send him to me; I may be able to find a place for him."

The intimation of possible power to help galled her.

"And what right have you to be getting up in the world?" she asked bitterly. "I mind it was you was one of the trouble-makers in the mill. I mind it was you that was all for rioting and using guns and beating up the police and them that came in your way. If you and the likes of you had never been born, Michael Scanlan and his son would be working in the Purroy Works today. I hope you're pleased to see what you and the likes of you have brought us to."

Jerry made no answer; his silence seemed to aggravate her bitterness.

"A fine person for a policeman, you that was rioting

and beating up the police! Oh, it's them that are double-faced that get ahead in this world."

Jerry took out a pencil and wrote his name and address on a card. Then he rose and laid the card on a table under Mrs. Scanlan's eye.

"If Dave should ever be wanting a job I might help him to find one," he repeated. He walked to the door, and then turned abruptly and came back. "I tell you, Mrs. Scanlan, I want to be your friend." He held his hand out to her; and then after a moment her face softened, her lips quivered, and she broke into tears.

"Oh, I don't like anybody, I hate everybody," she sobbed. "Everything's gone wrong with me. I don't care any more what happens. I wish I was dead."

And in another moment she was sobbing on Jerry's shoulder.

XVI

JERRY IS ASSURED UPON GOOD AUTHORITY THAT HE IS
ALL RIGHT: AND WONDERS IF PATRICK MAGUIRE MAY
NOT BE THE SAME

It was not Sheehan but another of Jerry's tutors, a
good-natured Irishman named Rafferty, who pointed
out one day Patrick Maguire's abode. He did it reverently. "The biggest-hearted man in the city," Rafferty affirmed. "Rich, too, and look at the quiet little
house that he lives in. Not off among the swells, but
down here in the old Fourteenth Ward, right where
he's always lived. What that man has done for the
folks of the ward won't ever be known. No, sir. Nor the
half of it."

Pressed for information as to a few, at least, of
Maguire's benevolences, Rafferty specified the annual
picnic for residents of the ward, — on which he assured
Jerry the outlay was "tremenjous"; the personal interest that Maguire took in the welfare of his neighbors;
the way in which he kept feeble and superannuated men
on the city's pay-roll; the influence that he was always
willing to exert in order to get jobs for those who needed
them — never asking in return for so much as their
thanks; the needy women and children that he was forever befriending and looking after; the funerals that he
paid for and the wedding presents that he made; it was
a recital of virtues, rather vague in spots, but enthusiastic and credulous.

JERRY

"And a special warm place he has in his heart for the men on the force," continued Rafferty. "He knows us all by name, and he takes an interest in a fellow too. Why, once last winter I met him on my beat, and he turned and walked a couple of blocks with me, drawing me out, kind of. Whenever I see him now he asks after the missus and the kids. The last time he put his hand in his pocket and gave me a jumping-jack to take home to the baby. I suppose he carries things around like that all the time, just to give away."

"Sounds like a mighty nice kind of fellow," Jerry observed artlessly.

"Oh, he's fine — a man to tie to," caroled Rafferty. "Well, now, you take the Chief of Police, Chief Dolan. He and Maguire are great cronies. And they say that Maguire's made him a wealthy man. Done the same, too, by some of the lieutenants that have the inside track with him."

"How?"

"Oh, Maguire's that wise about city real estate that he can tip off his friends to many a good thing. So they say. He's never done it for me. But maybe he will one of these days. If he gives me a jumping-jack for the baby, why should n't he give me a tip on real estate?"

"And loan you the money to win with. Sure. Why not?"

Rafferty laughed genially, as if he recognized the improbability of such good fortune, yet enjoyed contemplating the fantastic hope.

"What made Maguire a wealthy man?"

"City contracting. Paving, sewers, all that kind of

thing. You see, he's always on the inside. He knows
how to get the jobs."

Jerry chose not to debate the merits of a success thus
achieved with one who was so obviously an admirer of
Maguire. He expressed the hope that Rafferty might
some day receive the magic tip, and regretted the fact
that nothing of such a nature was likely to be extended
in his direction.

"Oh, Maguire may take a shine to you too," said
Rafferty generously. "You never can tell."

A week later Jerry was assigned to a patrol which led
him past Maguire's house. That was the quiet end of the
patrol; most of it lay through the saloon-infested streets
of the river front. It was always with a sense of relief
that Jerry turned for the few moments each morning
and afternoon into the pleasant street of small houses in
which Maguire lived. There were ailanthus trees shad-
ing the sidewalks, and the neighborhood was one that
more than any other through which Jerry passed expressed a sense of normal family life. In the morning the
women were busy sweeping the sidewalks or polishing
the doorknobs or carrying on cheerful activities within
doors; in the afternoon they played on the doorsteps
with their babies or sat by the windows reading or sewing. The brick houses, with their green shutters, were
uniform in type, and the uniformity imposed upon the
occupants a rivalry in neatness. A clean, tidy, self-
respecting little neighborhood it was, yet hardly one
in which a commanding figure was to be looked for.
Maguire's domicile was as neat and clean and unpre-
tentious as any other; a green parrot in its cage in a

window was the distinguishing feature. Jerry had a weakness for pets; he was disposed to a less rigorous judgment on Maguire after seeing that parrot.

And he needed to call up all his old predispositions and prejudices in order to be properly stiff in his first encounter with the man himself. Maguire came out of his house one day just as Jerry was passing.

"'Morning, officer," called Maguire. "Just a minute; I'm going your way." And he came bustling up and fell into step with Jerry. "My name's Maguire; I take quite an interest in the force. In fact, I think I know every man on it. Perhaps you'll be surprised, Mr. Donohue, at finding that I know your name."

"Not in the least," said Jerry. "I suppose when you try to block a man's appointment you know him by sight."

"Say, I like a man that's frank." Maguire laid a friendly hand on Jerry's arm and halted him while he delivered his explanation. "I'll be equally frank with you. It's perfectly true that I did oppose you, Donohue. There was another fellow that I had in mind; he hadn't passed as well as you had done, but still he was pretty good and he was one of my friends. But you got influence to working in your behalf, and that was too strong for me. I had nothing against you, you understand."

"I don't see how you could have," Jerry replied.

"Well, then," said Maguire, dropping his hand and resuming his brisk gait, "there's no occasion for hard feeling. I had to work for my friend, but you had influence that was too much for me."

"That remark is almost too much for me," said Jerry with a grin. And Maguire went into a convulsion of almost noiseless laughter.

He laid his friendly hand again on Jerry's arm.

"Donohue," he said, "you're all right."

He walked on then at his brisk gait, taking nearly two steps to Jerry's one, and talking at an equally lively pace. He questioned Jerry about his history, asked him whether he was married or single, where he lived, how he happened to think of becoming a policeman — and made Jerry's curt replies seem ungracious by contrast with his own freely volunteered information about himself.

"I've been so busy with one thing or another all my life I've never had the time to get married," he stated. "It doesn't make much difference so long as a man has some good women folks of his own to take care of, like you and me. I've got a widowed sister that I live with — her and her little girl. — You live alone with your mother, do you — no small kids around the house?"

Jerry explained that he and his mother had a kind of an adopted family.

"That's a mighty good thing to do," said Maguire. "I tell you, it's only nice people that adopt kids. You're all right, Donohue."

Jerry was strongly disposed to feel that Maguire must be fundamentally all right too. The rotund figure supported by the brisk little legs induced a kindly regard — pleaded for it even, exhibiting as it were an innocent comicality. In the large head, behind the bland, large face, may have been the wisdom of the ser-

pent, but to Jerry it seemed merely a humorous shrewdness that looked out of the small bright eyes, and a
kindly, sensible judgment that balanced itself on the
firm, smooth-shaven lips. The short, stubby nose was
indicative both of good-nature and pugnacity; and the
little man's way of cocking his head while he talked or
listened might be bird-like and alert or exasperating
and impudent. His clothes advertised both his oddity
and his vanity — a soft green hat worn at an angle, a
greenish suit, and a yellow-green necktie — each shade
of green clashing with the next and producing an effect
of a strange rarity and queerness. And to a man so
genial and confidential no friendly-hearted Irish youth
could long be antagonistic.

"My little girl is just getting over a sickness," said
Maguire. "She's only six years old. Her father died
two years ago, and when she took sick her mother —
my sister, you know — was like to go crazy. I tell you,
the last couple of weeks I've not had those two out of
my head a minute. But yesterday the turn came, and
this morning the little girl is doing fine. I tell you, it
makes me feel like going out and doing good to all the
world."

"I'll bet it does," said Jerry.

"There's no question about it, I like the kiddies,"
observed Maguire, in the tone of one confessing to a
weakness. "And a little sick kid — especially one that
I'm fond of — it breaks me all up. Seeing our baby's
playthings lying round just the way she left them —
I did n't want to have 'em touched or put away; I felt
somehow if anything happened to her I would n't want

to have 'em moved, ever. But she's all right now, and I tell you the world seems a different place."

Walking along the street, Maguire greeted nearly every one that he met. Jerry could not but be impressed by the pleased expression on the faces of those whom he thus recognized or by the democratic salutations of many obviously unimportant men and women, — "Hello, Pat." There must be something genuine and meritorious about such a man.

The next time that Jerry accompanied Sheehan he was taken to see some of the homes of protected vice. Gambling-houses and brothels flourished behind as fair a front as that of any respectable dwelling.

"Take note of 'em; write down the numbers in your little book," said Sheehan. "It's a wise thing to know all the joints, even though you're not given the power to go in and smash 'em."

"Why are n't we?"

"I guess it's because it's profitable to some of our bosses to have 'em do business."

"Are n't they ever raided?"

"Oh, once in so often there's a raid, after every one in the district has been tipped off."

"What's the reason? Who is it that's crooked?"

"I've only got my suspicions."

Jerry did not press for information, and after a moment Sheehan continued: "I know I can trust you not to repeat what you're told. I've been a patrolman for ten years. There's nothing against my record, and there have been occasions when I've come in for a word of praise. But promotion — not for me. In my early days on the force I was too zealous; that was my trouble. I was all for closing up the illegal joints. I went to my lieutenant about it, and he turned to the sergeant and said, 'Sergeant, here's a man that thinks there are gambling-hells and dives right here in this town. Now what do you think of that?' And the sergeant grinned and said, 'Can it be possible?' 'Well, Sergeant,' said the lieutenant, 'I'll detail you and a squad to go to-morrow night with this active young scout to these places that he's been observing. Let no guilty man nor woman escape, Sergeant. Horrible, to have such goings-on in our town.' Well, what might you expect after that? The next night I took the squad round to the different places, and everything was as quiet and decent as a church. No gambling, no rum, no vice. When we got back to headquarters the lieutenant gave me a tongue-lashing. Told me I was a disgrace to the force, a false alarm, no better than an amateur reformer, a hot-air artist, a pipe-dream fakir — oh, he laid it on. That lieutenant is Chief of Police to-day."

"Is there graft all through the department?"

"I don't know. Maybe I'm soured, but I can't help suspecting every man that gets ahead. Of course the chief has to divide up. Maguire gets a rake-off; I'm sure of that. All the grafters pay tribute to Maguire."

"How about the Police Commissioner? If things are so bad, why does n't he do something? He seems honest."

"He's honest, but he's in politics and he wants Maguire's friendship. He would n't graft himself, but he sees no more than he wants to see."

"I met Maguire the other day. He does n't seem like a crook."

"No, he 's too smart to seem like what he is. You 'd better look out for him. He 's probably going after you to make you one of his gang."

Jerry felt a strong impulse to defend Maguire. But he only said: —

"What is there against him anyway?"

"Everything — from the way he got his start to the way he keeps on going. Ten years ago, before the subways were built, Maguire was bossing a gang of Dago laborers for a firm of contractors. When the subways were planned, he came forward and offered to hire all the diggers that would be needed, and the street-railway company accepted his offer. He got more than six hundred men to working on that subway — all foreigners that knew mighty little English; and the company kept him on as foreman to boss the Dagoes. He held the job for a year, and then he was fired. But by that time he was a rich man. He had levied tribute on every one of those Dagoes that he had working under him. He had made each of them pay him two dollars to get the job, and then he made each of them pay him a dollar every week to hold the job. And it was n't till he got grasping and began to demand two dollars a week from them that some of them complained to the management and Maguire was given the sack. Then he organized the Ward Fourteen Maguire Club, and he 's got richer and more powerful, and now the management of the street railway that fired him ten years ago do business with him whenever they want to get any measures through the city government. That's part of Maguire's record. I guess that Chief Dolan could tell you a lot more of his record if he wished."

"He did n't seem like such a bad sort of a fellow," said Jerry. "Why, he talked to me about his sister's little kid, and honest, he almost had tears in his eyes."

"You're young at this job yet," replied Sheehan. "You'll be surprised to find how many crooks and criminals are good to their folks."

Jerry wondered if Sheehan could be right about Maguire. He could not bear to think of that agreeable little man as a crook or a criminal. The designation seemed especially preposterous one day when Jerry saw him driving a touring-car in which a young woman and a little girl were seated. Maguire recognized Jerry and waved to him genially.

Jerry was assigned to duty on the Front Street wharf the morning that Maguire gave his picnic for the children of the Fourteenth Ward. The big side-wheeler *Susan Myer* was alive with clamorous youngsters; they crowded to the rail and waved and screamed to friends or relatives on the wharf below. Maguire was bustling about, now on the boat, now on the wharf, giving a jolly word here to a child and there to a mother, burdening himself with lunch-baskets and rushing up the gangway to deposit them and return for more, mopping his face frequently with the handkerchief that hung like a bib from his collar, reassuring parents as to the care that would be bestowed upon their children and exciting the expectancy of the children by pointing out the great freezers of ice cream that were being carried on board, leading the band while it played "Dixie," and afterwards waving his hat in acknowledgment of the applause; — Jerry wondered if he would maintain such continuous activity throughout the day. "Now don't you worry about your child," Jerry heard him say to a woman who clung apprehensively to her little girl. "There's two trained nurses aboard and half a dozen other women, and we'll all look after her. This is a holiday for the mothers as well as for the youngsters; if we took the mothers along they wouldn't have any fun. I'm giving a picnic for the grown-ups two weeks from to-day; then you'll have your turn. Come along, kidlet." The mother, reassured, smiled and surrendered her daughter, who clasped Maguire's hand and trudged away with him willingly.

When he had stationed her on the deck where she could wave to her mother, he returned to the wharf and passed back and forth through the crowd, shouting, "Last call for the picnic! All aboard that are going aboard! Don't let any kids be left behind. Last call for the picnic!"

There were no belated youngsters in sight. So the philanthropist returned on board the steamboat, the whistle blew, the gangway was hauled in, the moorings were cast off, and then, while the band played and the children screeched and fluttered their handkerchiefs, and Maguire waved his hat with one hand and used his bib with the other, the pleasure craft moved slowly out into the stream.

The woman in front of Jerry sighed and said to her neighbor: —

"I hope I done right to let Sadie go. But I'll be that anxious till I see her safe home again."

"You need n't to be," responded her friend confidently. "She could n't be in better hands. Why, Pat Maguire, he'll be like a father and mother both to all them young ones."

Jerry remained, watchful and meditative, until the wharf was cleared. Then he went upon the tour of his duty; and while he walked he wondered what kind of a man Pat Maguire really was.

XVII

ONCE or twice a week Jerry made it a practice to look
in upon Mrs. Scanlan and ask if she had news of Dave.
After a time he stopped asking if she had news, and
instead sat and talked with her and told her all the
cheerful anecdotes he could think of. She made him see
very soon that she was grateful for these visits, and she
usually tried when he was with her to affect a responsive cheerfulness. But always before he left her she
would say, "You don't think anything has happened
to Dave, do you, Jerry?"

Occasionally on these visits Jerry saw Michael Scanlan. It was never an agreeable experience to find Scanlan at home. He sat in surly silence, sometimes listening with apparent contempt to the talk of the others,
more often oblivious of it. Jerry never saw him when
he did not diffuse the stale odor of liquor, and yet Jerry
could never have said that he had seen Michael Scanlan
drunk. There was a look in Scanlan's face that Jerry
did not like. It was particularly noticeable when the
man's glance was turned on his wife. Then the scornful
sneer of his lips and the hard malice in his eyes were
virulent. But never once did Jerry hear him speak.

Mrs. Scanlan talked to Jerry of her husband when he
was not present. "I get scared of Michael, he's that
changed," she said. "He was never much for talking,

[165]

but he used to talk pleasant to me once in a while. Now he never does. He barks at me, you might say, like a dog."

"He means nothing by that," Jerry assured her. "I suppose he comes home tired and discouraged. He has n't anything very pleasant nowadays to talk about, and you know when things go wrong the best-tempered people will be grumpy with them that they're used to. I'm that way myself at home very often; I've no doubt my mother would tell you so if you asked her."

"I did think that when Nora's baby came he'd take an interest," said Mrs. Scanlan. "But no; from the way he acts, much as ever he cares whether the child lives or dies."

"Has Nora a baby?" cried Jerry.

"Yes, did n't you know? I thought I told you when you were here last. But I guess it did n't come till that night. I remember now; it was just after you'd gone that I got word to hurry out to Millvale. It's a boy, but not a strong baby. Nora's worried sick over it — and that husband of hers — well, he cares no more than mine."

"I guess they both really care," said Jerry. "And don't you worry, Mrs. Scanlan; Nora's baby will be all right."

"And Dave — I don't understand Dave," continued Mrs. Scanlan. "He knew his sister was soon going to have a baby; you'd think — it's not like him; I feel sure something's happened to him; — and Nora, she's begun to worry about Dave; she says she knows Dave would take some interest in her and her baby, and she cries and cries, thinking first of one and then the other.

And that man of hers — he scolds and curses her just like she was crying only to annoy him."

Jerry gritted his teeth.

"He's a devil, that's what he is," said Mrs. Scanlan. "He's abused her and beat her; he's beat her even when she was more than six months along. No wonder it's a poor sickly little thing. More wonder she and it did n't both die. She did n't let me know the way he was treating her — not until within the last month. But she would n't leave him; she kept saying that after the baby came he might be different. I said to her, I says, 'Babies in the house only make that kind of a man worse,' but she would n't hear to it. Now she knows."

"I'd give a month's pay to be by the next time he starts to beat her," said Jerry. "It's a crime for her to go on living with the brute, Mrs. Scanlan."

"She did n't want to leave him, she was sure he'd be different when she had the baby. And I had n't the heart to urge her, for what could I do for her? Like as not, if I brought her here, her father might pick on her like Corcoran does."

"She can't go on caring for a man that beats her; she's got to leave him."

"She can't be planning about anything now, Jerry; she's that weak and that anxious. And I can't be planning for her neither; things have got clean beyond my power to straighten them. It seems sometimes as if a family that had been going along comfortable enough breaks all of a sudden to pieces. That's what has happened to us."

"Don't you be losing your courage," Jerry adjured

her. "Things run one way for a while, and then they turn round and run the other way. When Dave comes home, he'll be a big help. And I have a feeling he'll come home soon."

Three days later when Jerry next saw Mrs. Scanlan, she told him that Nora's baby had died.

"And her not able to go with it to the grave." Jerry had never before seen Mrs. Scanlan display so much emotion; as for himself, his eyes were filled with tears.

He tried to compose a letter to Nora that afternoon, but after several efforts he decided it was better to say too little than too much. So he wrote on a card, "With the sympathy of your old friend Jerry Donohue," and sent the message with a dozen white roses to the little house in Millvale. And while he paced slowly on his beat that evening, his thoughts were with Nora and her heartrending grief.

They were interrupted with startling suddenness. He had just turned into a street of small shops when he heard some distance away a terrified cry for help followed by a shot. As he ran in the direction of the sounds, he saw two men emerge from a lighted doorway half a block ahead, dash across the street, and dart round a corner. Jerry gave chase; passing on the full run the lighted doorway from which the fugitives had come, he glanced inside, but saw nothing except an apparently empty grocer's shop. He turned the corner and was exultant at finding his men again in sight. This was to be the first important, the first exciting arrest that he had made since joining the force. He felt exhilarated and confident. He was fast on his feet, as Sheehan had said, and he did not doubt his ability to run the criminals down.

Before gaining the next cross-street one of them was lagging. The other turned the corner; Jerry rapidly overhauled the second of the fugitives, who ran more and more weakly. And at last Jerry's hand fell heavily upon him.

"I did n't do the shooting, honest to God I did n't do the shooting!" The man gasped the words, almost in collapse.

Jerry swung him round and looked with dismay into his face.

"Dave!"

For an instant he held him; then he gave him a shove and ran round the corner in pursuit of the other fugitive. But the man had disappeared; Jerry raced for two blocks, looked down cross-streets, and searched alleyways, to no purpose. He hastened back to the store that had been the scene of the crime. In the doorway stood three women, frightened, awe-struck, afraid to enter. From within came the sound of weeping; Jerry went in and saw a white-haired, kindly-looking man behind the counter bending over some one invisible, some one who was sobbing in the low, monotonous key of utter grief. Drawing a little nearer, Jerry saw the woman; she wore a dressing-gown; her hair was unbound; she knelt beside the body of a man who had been shot through the head. The woman looked up, and at sight of Jerry she got to her feet. She was a comely woman of middle age; the tears rained down her cheeks; she cried to him imploringly, "My husband had n't an enemy in the world!

Who could have done it!" And then she cast herself down again beside the body and gave way to a fresh burst of sobs.

On being released by Jerry, Dave had again started to run; he had taken the first turn that he came to and had run promptly into the arms of a policeman. The policeman was Sheehan; he looked Dave over deliberately.

"I've seen you before," he said. "Why are you running through the streets at such a clip?"

"I was in a hurry to get home," Dave answered.

"What have you been doing?"

"Just out seeing some friends."

"Where do you live?"

"On Burke Street."

"If you're in a hurry to get home, why were you running away from Burke Street?"

"Away from it?"

"Yes. It's back in that direction."

"I guess I must have got turned round somehow."

"What's happened to excite you so? Why should you be in such a hurry to get home that you run until you're near ready to drop?"

"Well, I — I run a good deal for the exercise."

Sheehan took a grip of Dave's left arm and passed a hand over him, searching for a weapon.

"I've seen you at Tony Lapatka's place more than once," he remarked. "Your conduct is suspicious. I'll take you along to the station house and give you a chance to tell a straighter story there than what you've been giving me."

XVIII

OVERWHELMED in spirit, Jerry left the store soon after midnight. The widow had been led upstairs to her apartment over the shop; two detectives had made a careful study of the premises, the medical examiner had come and gone, and finally the body had been borne away. Jerry, who had been standing guard all the while, was free to resume his interrupted task.

The sight of the unoffending slain and of the grief-stricken wife caused him to lament bitterly his failure to capture the murderer. That Dave was the guilty man was to Jerry absolutely unthinkable, but that Dave had been a witness and in some degree a partner to the crime there was little room to doubt. And Jerry, as he walked and pondered, was perplexed as to what he ought to do. He did not in the least regret having let Dave go; it was the other fellow, the really guilty one, that it had been his business to catch. And anyway he could n't, he simply could n't have arrested Dave — his oldest and best friend. That is what he repeated to himself, yet his conscience was not easy. He knew that he had now done what he had hoped and believed he never should do — violated the oath that he had taken when he was sworn into the service. He said to himself

[171]

defiantly that it was the only decent thing to have done.
Yet because he had done the only decent thing he
questioned if he was, after all, the right kind of man
for the police force. The right kind of policeman would
have arrested Dave, even if he had been his brother.

Now Jerry recognized the complications resulting
from his act. If the real criminal was to be run down,
it could in all likelihood be done only through information furnished by Dave. And nothing could be more
improbable than that Dave should elect to remain in
the neighborhood, however certain of Jerry's loyalty.
Jerry resolved that the moment he was off duty that
night he would hasten to the Scanlans' rooms and if, as
he hoped, he should find Dave there, he would compel
him to tell the full story of the crime.

At three o'clock his tour of duty ended; and he reported at the station house. The sergeant at the desk
greeted him with interest.

"Do you know a fellow named Scanlan — David
Scanlan?" the sergeant asked.

"Yes," Jerry answered with a sinking of the heart.
"Why?"

"Sheehan brought him in a few minutes after the
murder to-night. Found him running just three blocks
away from Walsh's store, all out of breath and not able
to account for himself. He said he knew you and you'd
vouch for him. Just the same, they're still at it, giving
him the third degree."

"I've known Scanlan for years; I was brought up
with him; we worked together in the Purroy Mills.
He's been down on his luck for the last year — but the

idea of his murdering any one — it's absurd. What do they think they've got against him anyway?"

"Sheehan says he's been traveling with a bad gang, and his behavior was mighty suspicious. And being in the neighborhood of the murder at just that moment — running away from it — they seem to think he knows something."

"I guess I'll go up and have a look at him," said Jerry; and slowly he ascended the stairs to the top floor of the building. His thought was that he might perhaps be allowed to take over the questioning of Dave, and then, if left to deal with him alone, might draw from him all the facts which the merciless persistence of Sheehan and the lieutenant would probably wrest from him otherwise. And Jerry had some idea that if Dave confessed to him he would be able to help him.

As he drew near the top of the stairs, he heard Dave's voice raised in desperation: "Can't you go away and let me sleep? I've told you all I've got to tell, and I'm played out; for God's sake, let me sleep."

"I wouldn't mind a bed myself," said Sheehan. "But we're not going to let up on you till you've made a clean breast of it."

"Not till you've told us all you know about how that man Walsh was killed," affirmed the lieutenant.

"I've told you I don't know a thing about it," cried Dave.

By that time Jerry had reached the top of the stairs; the voices had come to him through an open transom. He stepped to the door and knocked upon it; the lieutenant opened it, and Dave and Jerry faced each other.

There was a moment of silence during which Jerry looked steadily into Dave's eyes and Dave stood haggard and motionless.

"Lieutenant," Jerry said, "I'd like to have a word with you about this man."

The lieutenant came out into the hall and closed the door behind him. He and Jerry talked in low tones.

"I know Scanlan," Jerry said. "He's an old friend of mine. He might tell me things he wouldn't tell any one else. What would you say to my questioning him?"

"You can come in with us and ask him any questions you like," said the lieutenant.

"I think I'd get more out of him if he and I were alone."

The lieutenant considered a moment.

"You wait here; I'll see how he meets the idea," he said; and he returned into the room.

Then Jerry heard him say: —

"Officer Donohue tells me he knows you from the ground up, and says if he is allowed to question you he's sure you'll make a clean breast of it. Shall we have him come in?"

Jerry listened eagerly for the answer. When it came, it startled him.

"Oh, I might as well tell you the truth. I was with the fellow that did the shooting. But I didn't know he was going to do it, I didn't dream of it — and that's God's truth, every word."

The lieutenant opened the door triumphantly. "Come on in, Donohue," he said. And then as Jerry entered, he turned to Dave and spoke persuasively. "Now just get it off your chest. What's the whole story?"

"I had nothing to do with the shooting — nothing at all." Dave, while he talked, paced nervously back and forth across the room. "The fellow that did it — I didn't know him very well. We were both of us down and out; he told me it would be a cinch for us two, working together, to clean up some money. He said if we picked small stores in quiet neighborhoods and went in late at night when the owner was closing up, we'd be safe enough and maybe make some good hauls. He was to cover the fellow with a revolver and keep him scared while I went through the money-drawer; and if there was a safe we'd make the fellow open it. We thought we could pull off several such jobs before this town got too hot for us; and then we could beat it to another place and work the same game there, and so on; and at last we'd have quite a pile; that was the way we figured it. Of course we supposed a fellow would always throw up his hands with a gun pointed at his head. But this fellow — he was the first we tried it on — he was reaching up to one of his shelves and had his back to us when we walked in; my partner had him covered before he turned round, and when he did, he looked right into the muzzle. And right off he let out a yell and ducked behind the counter, and then there was a bang and we ran; that's the whole story as true as I'm standing here."

"It's not the whole story," said the lieutenant. "You've not told us who your partner was."

"I can't do that."

"Do you think you're under any obligation to protect a murderer?"

"I don't believe he really meant to kill him. I think he was just so startled when the fellow let out that yell and ducked, instead of throwing up his hands like we both expected, that he got rattled and the gun went off kind of without his meaning it."

The lieutenant sneered at the defense. "Anyway it's not your business to decide whether he meant to kill or not. What we want of you is his name."

"Well, I'm not going to give it." Dave's mouth grew sullen. "You've got all out of me now that you'll get — and it's enough too."

Jerry spoke up. "Lieutenant, why don't you leave me alone with him for a while? I think maybe I can make him see things differently."

"All right; do what you can with him, and don't let up on him till you have the information."

The lieutenant and Sheehan withdrew. Jerry stood with his back against the door and waited in silence until the sound of their footsteps on the stairs had ceased. Then he approached Dave, who had sunk upon a chair; he pulled a chair up beside him and seated himself.

"How did you happen to get caught, Dave?"

"Just after you saw me I beat it round the corner into Ninth Street and ran right into the cop that was here a moment ago. He got me all confused when I tried to tell him where I was going, and when he got me here they guessed right off I'd had something to do with the shooting. When they told me you'd come to get me to confess I knew the jig was up. Somehow I had n't thought you would turn against me."

"The chances are that as long as they'd caught you and suspected you and you were guilty, they'd have succeeded finally in bringing the charge home to you. And the fellow that confesses is always treated more leniently than the fellow that's convicted. That's why I wanted to talk to you; that's why I want you now to tell all you know. You did n't kill the man; I feel sure you could n't have done that. But the people who don't know you won't feel sure. You're not justified in shielding a murderer — and, moreover, you'll suffer for it if you do."

"But I can't split on him, Jerry."

"Why not? You've said you never would have gone into this thing if you'd had any idea he might shoot. He was willing enough to put you in a hole — and it was a cold-blooded murder; you need n't try to excuse it. You have no right to shield the fellow; and besides, you'll be a fool if you do it, for it's bound to be at your own expense."

"I would n't want to feel that maybe I'd brought him to the chair."

"Suppose he shoots some one else. He probably will if he's left at liberty. How will you feel then? It will be your fault, you know."

"Just the same, you would n't split on him if you were in my place, Jerry."

"I certainly would. I'd come to my senses mighty quick."

"Would n't you always despise a fellow that split on another?"

"Not in a case like this."

"You'd really tell if you were in my position?"

"I would."

Dave hesitated. "Well," he said at last, "it was Red Schlupfe."

"Was he one of the fellows that you were with the night I saw you at Tony Lapatka's place?"

"Yes."

"Why did n't you look me up the next day? You promised to, and I might have got you a job. Then this would never have happened."

"I got full that night and they pulled me in. They sent me up for thirty days. I gave an *alias* so the folks would n't know. When I got out, I struck Schlupfe right off, and I looked at things kind of different from the way I did before they put me in jail. The way Red pictured it, I thought it would be some exciting, wandering round with a gun and scaring the life out of a fellow now and then. I never had the least thought it might mean murder."

"Well," said Jerry, "it ought n't to go so hard with you, now that you've confessed everything; the jury will see you're innocent of the killing. The chief thing is to get a good lawyer. I'll see Mr. Trask. Of course, you'll have to make up your mind to take some punishment."

"Oh, yes, I realize that. I wish I could get it without having mother and Nora punished too."

"It will be a hard blow to them — especially Nora, coming on top of what she's just been through."

"What's that, Jerry?"

"Her baby's just died. It lived only a couple of days."

"That's tough, is n't it! Poor Nora! She's drawn the short end of the stick all right."

Then after a pause Dave asked: "Do you know anything about the man that was killed?"

"He left a wife and four children."

"Is n't it terrible! Is n't it awful! Somehow I can't believe I'm mixed up in anything like that."

Dave's head drooped and Jerry's heart went out to him more than ever. "I'll try to get to your mother first thing in the morning — before ever she reads about it in the newspaper," he said. "And now, Dave, what you want is sleep, and I guess you'd better have it right off. Come along, old fellow."

So Jerry conducted his friend to the cell, in which he saw him locked for the night, and then delivered to the lieutenant the information that he had obtained.

XIX

WHEN Jerry took his way to the lodging-house where
the Scanlans were domiciled, the laboringmen had not
yet started for their morning's work; only the milk carts
were abroad. Ascending the dark stairway of the tene-
ment, he heard the voices of those he sought raised in
anger; Michael Scanlan was demanding money and his
wife was refusing to give it. "Not one cent," Jerry heard
her say; and then again in a taunting drawl that seemed
to add emphasis to the refusal, "Not — one — cent."

Jerry knocked on the door, and after an interval
Mrs. Scanlan opened it. She wore a soiled pink wrapper
of canton flannel, her hair hung untidily about her
shoulders, her face was flushed and wrathful from the
controversy in which she had been engaged. Michael
Scanlan in undershirt and trousers sat at the scantily
provided breakfast table, and on seeing who the visitor
was concentrated his gaze on the chunk of sausage before
him.

Anxiety had sprung instantly into Mrs. Scanlan's eyes.
"Jerry," she said, "have you got news of Dave?"

"I have," Jerry answered. "Not very good news, and
yet when you hear the whole story you'll have reason
to feel glad it's no worse."

For the first time since Jerry had been coming to the
house Michael Scanlan took notice of him. Scanlan

[180]

rose and said in his old, masterful way, pointing to the conversation chair, "Sit there and tell us what you know."

"Dave is in trouble," said Jerry. "He got mixed up in an attempt to rob a store last night; the storekeeper was killed; Dave was arrested."

"There must be some mistake!" cried Mrs. Scanlan. "You know, Jerry, no matter what bad habits Dave's got into lately, he would n't steal."

"I'm sorry to say there's no question about it. He was caught as he was running away. He's made a full confession. He and a man named Schlupfe went in to rob a store; Schlupfe held the storekeeper up with a revolver and when the man called for help shot him. Dave had nothing to do with the shooting. But they've caught him and they have n't caught Schlupfe yet."

"You say he's confessed all this?" Scanlan looked at Jerry unbelievingly.

"Yes. I was in the room when he told the whole story."

"You were one of those that dragged it out of him?"

"No. I did n't do that. But soon after I came he made up his mind to confess."

"And you think he's guilty, do you?"

"Not of the murder; he had nothing to do with that. And that's why I said it's not so bad as it might be. If we can get the murderer, as we soon will, Dave ought to be let off with a light sentence."

Mrs. Scanlan, who had listened hitherto as if stupefied, broke into a wail. "Oh, my God, what's to become of us, what's to become of us!" She rocked from side to side in her chair, clinging to the seat with both hands, careless of the tears that began to stream down her face. Her bosom heaved with her sobs and lamentations.

Michael Scanlan sat indifferent to the outbursts; he lighted his pipe and smoked stolidly. Jerry endeavored to comfort the woman; he told her that he had in mind a good lawyer who would look after Dave's interests and that he would consult with him that day; he urged her to go to the police station and have a talk with Dave. Gradually he prevailed on her, so that at last, though still weeping, she stood up. "Yes, I'll go to him, I'll go to my boy," she said through her sobs.

"I will not go to him," said Michael Scanlan. "He's no longer son of mine. He's a crook."

In the painful scene that ensued between husband and wife Jerry felt that his presence was neither valuable nor desired; when he left the room Michael Scanlan was still seated in the conversation chair, sullen, malevolent, smoking his pipe, and his wife was lying face down across the bed, crying out amidst moans and sobs that she hated him and wished he were in jail instead of their son.

XX

THREE days after the murder Schlupfe was arrested in a town fifty miles away. He stoutly declared his innocence and clamored for an opportunity to confront his accuser.

Within two weeks both he and Dave Scanlan were indicted for murder.

Trask, who had readily consented to serve as counsel for Dave, was chagrined by the action of the grand jury. He remembered Dave as a member of the company that he had drilled; he had liked him, and he believed his story now, just as Jerry believed it. He had thought that Mulkern, the District Attorney, would not, in Dave's case, press for an indictment on the charge of murder, and he was both disappointed and disturbed by the grand jury's finding. It was apparent that the prosecuting official was determined to get a conviction, if possible. In the interviews that Trask held with him, he was unable to convince him of the entire credibility of Dave's story.

That Trask really felt apprehensive as to the outcome Jerry first learned only a few days before the trial. He asked Jerry if he had come upon any clues to connect Schlupfe with the crime and corroborate Dave's story. Jerry said he had not.

"My belief is," said Trask, "that the District Attorney's office will not exert itself to make out a case against Schlupfe. If any evidence against him that seems to you important comes into your hands, I wish you would communicate it to me as well as to Mulkern; otherwise it may not be brought out at all."

"How is that?" Jerry asked.

"I only have suspicions. There seem to be various ramifications to the case. Schlupfe, it appears, is the nephew of a contractor in Ward Fourteen, who is one of Maguire's lieutenants. The contractor has money and influence, and he's using them in behalf of his nephew. He and Maguire have got Congressman Maxwell to defend Schlupfe. And I have n't much confidence that the district attorney's office will make a back-breaking effort to convict any one that has the support of Maxwell and Maguire."

"But surely the prosecution would n't try to discredit Scanlan's confession."

"Not actively, perhaps, but they might allow the defense to build up an alibi for Schlupfe and not attempt to demolish it by cross-examination. I don't say that this will happen; only I don't like the look of things."

Events accurately fulfilled Trask's prediction. The selection of a jury occupied the greater part of two days. Dave followed all the proceedings with an intense, nervous interest; Schlupfe seemed stolid and unconcerned. The two prisoners sat so far apart that direct communication between them was impossible, and from the first they took little notice of each other. Dave, leaning on the table in front of him, concentrated his

attention on the juror who was being examined; Schlupfe
lolled comfortably in his seat as one who had nothing to
fear. Behind Dave sat his mother; at frequent intervals
she would reach forward and touch or press his arm,
striving to communicate her love and faith.

Once the jury was chosen, the trial moved rapidly.
Mulkern, the District Attorney, made a brief opening
address. He was a sallow, sharp-featured man, thin and
tall, and he gave the impression of being both just and
merciless. He outlined the case for the prosecution,
commented on the peculiarly brutal nature of the crime,
and closed by saying that he believed the evidence to be
presented would warrant the finding of a verdict of murder in the first degree against each of the defendants.

He called Henry Morrison as the first witness. Morrison testified that he lived in the house adjoining
Walsh's store, that on the night of September 15, at
about eleven o'clock, he was in bed reading when he
heard a shot and almost immediately, on the sidewalk
under his open window, the footsteps of a man running.
He had wondered about it for a moment before getting
up to investigate; when he reached the window and
looked out he saw a policeman pursuing a man who was
then far up the street. He had not waited to see the outcome of the chase, but had hurriedly dressed and gone
out of his house and into the store. At first he saw no
one; then he looked behind the counter and found
Walsh lying unconscious, with blood flowing from a
wound in the neck. With a handkerchief he had tried to
stanch the flow, and then had telephoned to Dr. Curran
and to police headquarters. And then he had run upstairs

JERRY

and roused Mrs. Walsh, who was asleep in the apartment over the store.

Trask cross-examined Morrison and asked him if he had not seen two men fleeing. Morrison said that he had seen only one; that the policeman was almost under his window when he looked and that he had taken just a glance up the street which had shown him the fugitive, perhaps a hundred yards away, that he had then drawn in his head and got ready hastily to find out what had happened.

"You would n't swear that there were n't two men running away?"

"No, but I saw only one, and my impression is that there was only one."

"You were, of course, very much excited, and did n't observe as carefully as you might have done — you were in a hurry to get away and see what had taken place?"

"That might be," admitted the witness.

Dr. Curran described the wound and explained that it was necessarily fatal. The man was in fact moribund when he arrived, which was within five minutes of receiving the telephone message. The skin round the wound was blackened and burned; the weapon had evidently been discharged with the muzzle almost touching the victim.

Dr. Kelly, the medical examiner, corroborated Dr. Curran and exhibited the 38-caliber revolver bullet that had been recovered in the autopsy.

Mrs. Walsh took the stand. She was a comely, middle-aged woman of character and self-control; she answered the questions quietly, and though her lips

trembled and she sometimes seemed on the verge of
tears, she did not break down. She looked frequently at
the prisoners, from one to the other, with an expression
of sorrowful wonder rather than of vengefulness. Dave
could not meet her eyes, but Schlupfe gazed back at her
hardily. Her testimony was of no real importance; she
said that she had been in the store talking with her husband at a quarter past ten on the night of the murder,
and that a few minutes after eleven she had been roused
from sleep and had come downstairs to find him dying.

Next Sheehan was called and testified to the circumstances under which he had made the arrest and to the
difficulty which he and the lieutenant had experienced
in trying to draw a confession from the prisoner. Court
was adjourned for the day with the lieutenant about to
testify to the details of the confession.

Jerry, who had been in the room for part of the afternoon, walked home with his mind disturbed about many
things. Schlupfe's attitude of indifference and confidence was disquieting. It made Jerry wonder if Schlupfe
knew things that Dave had n't told, and would be able
to prove facts to Dave's disadvantage. Moreover, Jerry
looked forward to his own appearance on the witness
stand the next day with uneasiness. In the two months
that had elapsed since the night of the murder his dereliction from duty in letting Dave escape had troubled
him but little. Now, however, it was giving him concern.
Should he be obliged on the witness stand to narrate
that episode? Would there be any way of evading it? He
had not confided it to Trask; he could n't quite bring
himself to the point of going to a lawyer and asking ad-

vice about suppressing or evading the truth. Yet if the truth came out, it might not only affect most seriously his own future, but it might also be prejudicial to Dave. Not of an introspective habit, and disposed to look on the bright side of things, Jerry made up his mind after some pondering that he could tell a sufficiently truthful story without incriminating himself or doing an injury to Dave's case.

The next morning the lieutenant corroborated Sheehan's story of the confession, and, as Sheehan had done, told how obstinately Dave had resisted the effort to make him disclose his confederate's identity.

"So up to the time when you left Scanlan on that night he had not mentioned Schlupfe's name?" asked Maxwell in cross-examination.

"No, sir."

"When did you first learn that he had implicated Schlupfe?"

"About half an hour later, when Officer Donohue came to the desk and told me."

Officer Donohue was called. Mulkern, the District Attorney, asked him if his patrol on the night of the murder took him into the neighborhood of the crime.

"Yes, sir," Jerry answered. "I had just turned the corner from Ransom Street into Eighth when the thing happened."

"Tell what you saw."

"I heard a shot, and two men rushed out of a house some distance along the block and ran up Eighth towards Weaver Street. I chased them, but they got round the corner of Weaver Street, going south. I was n't very

far behind, and when I turned into Weaver Street they
were both in sight. Where Seventh crosses Weaver, one
of them took the turn to the left, and I went after him.
But he had disappeared; I thought he'd gone into the
alley between Seventh and Eighth, but I could n't find
him. The other fellow had gone up Seventh in the opposite direction; when I came out after searching for the
first man, he was n't to be seen. So I went back to find
out what had happened. There were three women in the
entrance to Walsh's store, kind of afraid to go in;
Walsh was lying on the floor behind the counter, dead;
Mrs. Walsh and Mr. Morrison were both there. I
stayed until Officers Pinkham and Thomas came, and
then I told them what I've told just now."

"What did you do then?"

"I finished my patrol and at two o'clock went to
Station 9 to report. Then I learned that Scanlan had
been arrested and that Officer Sheehan and Lieutenant
Murphy were still questioning him. I thought maybe
Scanlan might talk to me, for I had known him well for
years, so I went up to the room. I waited outside and
heard him tell the story that Officer Sheehan and Lieutenant Murphy have told. Then I went in and asked
Lieutenant Murphy to leave me alone with him a while.
I talked with Scanlan and told him I thought he was
making a mistake to feel that he was under an obligation
not to give the name of the man that had fired the shot.
He was very loath to do it, but after a lot of arguing I
persuaded him. He told me the man was Schlupfe. He
told me that he had just got done serving a month's time
in the reformatory for drunk and disorderly, and he ran

into Schlupfe when he was feeling down and out, and Schlupfe proposed the thing — all just as the other witnesses have described."

The District Attorney had no further questions to ask the witness; Trask rose to examine Jerry.

"You say, Officer Donohue, that you used to know the defendant Scanlan; how well did you know him?"

"About as well as if he was my brother. We were together out at Millvale as boys, and we worked together in the Purroy Mills until they changed hands; Scanlan was about my best friend."

"He bore a good reputation among his fellow workmen?"

"Yes, sir."

"This sentence that he has just served — drunk and disorderly — do you know anything about that?"

"I saw him early in the evening that it happened — his getting drunk. He was in Lapatka's place, sitting at a table with this fellow Schlupfe. He told me that he was out of a job, and I said if he would come to me the next morning I thought maybe I knew where there was one that he might get. Well, he did n't come, and when I tried to get track of him a few days later he'd disappeared. I never learned until the night of his confession what had happened to him — and then I did n't learn much. He only remembered he had been in Lapatka's place with Schlupfe; when he came to the next day he was under arrest, for the first time in his life."

Trask turned the witness over to Maxwell for cross-examination.

Jerry knew, the moment he looked into the Congress-

man's black eyes, that Maxwell had neither forgotten
nor forgiven him. There was a sparkle of malice in them
that was disturbing. Maxwell began suavely enough.

"Now, Officer, you say that Scanlan was reluctant to
make any confession implicating any one?"

"Yes, very reluctant."

"And you were able to overcome his scruples by persuasion — there was no coercion in your methods?"

"None at all."

"You were quite unusually patient with him?"

"I don't know about quite unusually. It's the first
case of the kind I ever handled."

"You're rather a new man on the police force?"

"Yes."

"Just how intimate was your friendship— how well
had you known Scanlan?"

"We used to work together. We lived near each other
and saw a lot of each other."

"Were you and he involved together in some riots
that took place at the Purroy Works?"

"I would n't call them riots."

"The newspapers called them riots, did n't they?"

"Some newspapers."

"And they were bad enough so that the militia had to
be ordered out?"

"The militia were ordered out."

"Do you recollect who was in command of the militia
on that occasion?"

"Colonel Trask."

"This gentleman that you see here as counsel for the
defendant Scanlan?"

"Yes."

"Did he find it necessary to disperse a riotous assemblage in which you and Scanlan were taking part?"

"There was just a group of us in front of the mill gates —"

"Never mind that. Mr. Trask, as an officer of the militia, found it necessary to order you to disperse, did n't he?"

"Yes."

"And he let you know there must be no more such gatherings?"

"Yes."

"Prior to the arrival of the militia there had been violence and threats of violence, had there not?"

"Very little violence."

"Sufficient so that the sheriff was unable to deal with the situation?"

"He did n't deal with it."

"Did you and Scanlan and others arm yourselves and make it your business to keep applicants for work away by force?"

"Yes, we did that."

"And sometimes you found it necessary to beat and maltreat men who were too persistent in seeking work?"

"There was very little beating that I know of. I suppose we handled the fellows a bit rough sometimes."

"Your methods were effective until the militia put a stop to them?"

"Yes."

"Now this intimacy of yours with Scanlan — you were an old friend, not only of his, but also of his family? You knew them all well — had known them for years?"

"Yes, I've known them pretty well for quite a while."

"If it were possible for you in any way to assist Scanlan out of a scrape, you would try to do it?"

"I'd try to do that for any one."

"Still, perhaps you'd make a little special effort for one who was an old friend?"

"It would be only natural."

"Now, just what were the arguments by which you prevailed over Scanlan's reluctance to incriminate any one else?"

"I told him that as he'd been let in for this thing with no idea of murder developing from it, he was under no obligation to shield the man who had committed the murder. I told him that his own chances would be much better if he kept nothing back. Finally he came to see that, and then he made a clean breast of it."

"You did n't prompt him at all — make any suggestions?"

"No."

"Prior to finding Scanlan under arrest in the police station, what was the last occasion when you had any talk with him?"

Jerry looked at Maxwell steadily and repeated in a steady voice, "The last occasion?"

But for all his steadiness of aspect he was clearly, to the keen eyes of the hostile examiner, seeking to temporize. Maxwell, who had asked the question with the design of drawing Jerry back to the meeting with Scanlan and Schlupfe in Lapatka's saloon, seized upon the indication of weakness.

"Yes, the last occasion. When was it? Where was it?"

Jerry hesitated and reddened to the eyes. The disclosure was not to be evaded; and in that moment of delay he saw that it would ruin his career.

"When was that last occasion?" Maxwell's voice was aggressive and threatening; something, he could not guess what, that was to be disadvantageous to the witness and helpful to his client's case, was providentially about to emerge.

"It was a few hours earlier, that same night," Jerry answered.

"What were the circumstances of that meeting?"

"I had overhauled him and grabbed him as he was running away. It was at the corner of Weaver and Eighth. He was one of the two men I chased after the shot was fired. When I caught him and saw who he was, I just gave him a shove and ran after the other fellow."

"You deliberately let him escape, although you had reason to believe he had committed a crime?"

"I knew that if a crime had been committed it was the other fellow that was the really guilty one, and the one I'd better get."

"Did you realize that in letting Scanlan go you were violating your oath as an officer of the law?"

"Yes, but I wanted to get the other man."

"You knew that for such neglect of duty charges could be preferred against you and you could be dropped from the force?"

"I was n't thinking about that. Scanlan was my

friend, and I felt sure he could n't have done anything
very bad. So I went after the other man."

"The testimony you gave a few minutes ago — before
this was dragged out of you — did n't indicate that
you had arrested this man and then let him escape,
did it?"

"No. I just said that one of the men turned north on
Weaver Street. That's the way Scanlan went after I let
him go. I said the other man turned south on Weaver
Street and I followed him. That was true."

"Nevertheless, you deliberately gave your testimony
in such a way as to mislead the jury, did n't you?"

"I don't think I misled them on any vital point."

"You were perfectly willing to let Scanlan escape,
even though it might turn out that he had committed a
murder?"

"On the spur of the moment, without knowing just
what had happened, I let him escape."

"And you're still pretty anxious that he should escape, are n't you?"

"I'm anxious he should n't be found guilty of something he did n't do."

"You're sure you saw two men, of whom Scanlan was
one, running away?"

"Positive."

"You're quite sure this second man was n't an in-
vention of your own — an afterthought?"

"Absolutely."

"You saw him turn south on Weaver Street?"

"Yes."

"And after only a moment's delay with Scanlan you

ran after him and he had disappeared, just as if he had never been?"

"Yes."

"That was a great surprise and disappointment to you?"

"Yes."

"But you did n't immediately take measures to find Scanlan and get information from him that would enable you to arrest the guilty man?"

"I meant to do exactly that as soon as I was off duty. And that's just what I succeeded in doing when I talked with Scanlan later at the police station."

"Now, look here!" Maxwell advanced close to Jerry and shook his finger in his face. "Was n't your conversation with Scanlan in substance about like this: 'Of course you and I both know there was nobody else, but if we're to get you off we've got to hang this thing on some definite person'?"

"Nothing of the sort," declared Jerry with heat.

"Did n't you recall having seen Scanlan with Schlupfe in Lapatka's place one night, and did n't that give you the idea of suggesting Schlupfe's name to Scanlan?"

"No. Certainly not. Scanlan volunteered it of his own free will."

"After you'd talked with him for some time?"

"Yes."

"That will do for you," said Maxwell with a sneer. And Jerry, feeling impotent and humiliated, left the stand.

Immediately afterwards court was adjourned for the day. Jerry, as he took his departure from the building, felt that every one looked at him either pityingly or with suspicion and contempt. He could not bring himself to tell his mother that evening of his dereliction from duty and its probable consequences. She was deeply concerned, as it was, over the account that he gave her of the progress of the trial. When he went to the police station later in the evening the lieutenant greeted him coldly, and the other men had little to say to him. Sheehan alone showed some sympathy, but even he was not consoling. "It was a kind of a human mistake to make," said Sheehan, "but it's the kind you can't afford to get caught at. It's tough luck, mighty tough luck, that's what it is."

Jerry got the newspaper the next morning before anyone else in the family had seen it. Officer Donohue's testimony was "featured" in the account of the trial. At the end of the article it was stated that the Chief of Police had declared his intention of preferring charges against Officer Donohue.

Jerry looked over the newspaper at his mother, who sat on the opposite side of the breakfast table. Kate and the two children were in the hall getting ready to go to school.

"It seems as if I was always having to break bad news to people's mothers," said Jerry.

"Good gracious, who is it now that you must be doing that to?" asked Mrs. Donohue.

"It's the case of a fellow on the force, that was found being too easy and considerate with a friend that it was his duty to arrest. He let him off instead of taking him along to the station house. And now he's likely to lose his job on account of it, and I've got to tell his mother about it all."

Something in his manner and his expression made Mrs. Donohue guess his meaning. "It's me you're to break the bad news to, Jerry," she said quietly; and he answered as quietly, "Yes."

He showed her the passage in the newspaper and explained all the circumstances. Kate came into the room and listened in silence. Peter and Betty called to her, and she told them to run along — that she would overtake them. Jerry was unaware of her consternation until he turned and saw the look on her face.

"Jerry, they can't make you stop being a policeman for that, can they?" she asked.

"I don't know; I'm afraid they can," he answered.

"And if they do, it's a shame to them and not to you," exclaimed his mother; her eyes flashed and she clung to his arm with pride. "You'd have been no son of your father if you'd not tried to help an old friend. And anybody in his senses would know it was not Dave Scanlan that was up to committing a murder. You did just right, Jerry, you did just right, and it would be a queer kind of a man that did n't see it. I'm not afraid that they'll punish you."

"It's more than likely that they will. Of course, deliberately letting a prisoner escape — it's a pretty serious offense; I can see that."

"I can't — so long as it was Dave."

Jerry laughed, and Kate said: —

"I shan't be able to do any studying to-day; oh, I can't bear it if you have to stop being a policeman."

"Why?"

"Because somehow you're just right in that uniform, and you're big and strong and just what a policeman ought to be. It would n't be fair to make you give it up. And besides, just think of those Armstrongs!"

"Well," Jerry said, "there are some things too awful to think of. We'll just hope for the best."

When Jerry talked like that, it was impossible not to feel reassured. Kate hurried away to join her brother and sister. A few minutes after she had gone the postman put into Jerry's hand a letter from the Chief of Police. It notified him that he was suspended from the force, that his suspension was to go into effect immediately, and that he would have to answer on the 10th of the next month to charges to be preferred before the Police Commissioner.

Jerry took off his uniform and put on his old suit; his mother wept.

"It's just laid away for the time being, I guess," he said to her. "I'll talk myself back into it on the 10th of next month, as large as life and twice as handsome. Now I must be off to the courtroom; have a look, will you, my good woman, and see that the coast is clear and no Armstrongs at all roosting on the stairs."

XXI

WHEN the District Attorney called the name of Martin Kemperton, Dave Scanlan looked round with unconcealed alarm. Jerry at least caught the expression on his face and hoped that none of the jurors had noticed it.

A respectably dressed, comfortably stout man of middle age took the witness stand and stated that he was a dealer in small arms and that he was always careful to observe persons to whom he sold revolvers.

"Do you recognize either of the defendants as a person to whom you sold a revolver?" asked the District Attorney.

"Yes. The defendant Scanlan."

"Do you recall any of the circumstances?"

"It was the day before the murder occurred. He came into my store in the afternoon and said he wanted a revolver. I asked him no questions, but he told me he was a night watchman and his employer wanted him to carry a gun. He bought a 38-caliber revolver and a dozen shells."

"You are positive this is the man?"

"Yes. As soon as I saw the picture of him in the paper the day after the murder I recognized him."

Dave was talking in eager whispers with his lawyer, whose face was grave and attentive. The jurors watched them while the witness returned to his seat in the back of the room.

Jerry had listened to Kemperton's testimony with amazement. The man seemed to be telling the truth. Yet Dave, in spite of his declarations that he had made a clean breast of everything, had never mentioned this transaction. Jerry was not reassured by his excited whisperings and the lawyer's grave face; Mrs. Scanlan, pale, nervous, yet bent on comforting her boy, leaned forward in her chair and pressed and patted his arm all unheeded.

The District Attorney had no more witnesses. Maxwell called Hans Bergmann to the stand. A broad-shouldered, thick-chested man of about thirty, with a heavy, Teutonic face, stiff, light hair erect upon his head, skin pale and blotchy, eyes small and shifty, testified that on the night of the murder Schlupfe, whom he knew well, had been in his pool-room until it closed at midnight. Asked how he could be sure it was the night of the murder, he replied that Otto Wangenheim came in at about half past eleven and said that there had been a shooting over on Eighth Street, less than a quarter of a mile away. Schlupfe, who was standing by at the time, had remarked that a fellow was a fool as well as a crook to go into the hold-up business on Eighth Street.

"He said that if he was going out with a gun to rob somebody he'd pick on somebody worth while," testified Bergmann.

Cross-examination by Trask failed to confuse or shake the witness. He declared stolidly that he could not be mistaken, that he knew Schlupfe well, that Schlupfe spent many an evening in his pool-room.

Otto Wangenheim testified that he was a barber and that on his way home from his shop at a few minutes past eleven on the night of the murder he saw a crowd gathered in the doorway of Walsh's store. On joining it he learned that a man had been shot and killed less than a quarter of an hour before. He had tried to see the body, but two policemen were guarding the door and he was unsuccessful. He had gone at once to Bergmann's pool-room and had been the first there to announce the news. He remembered that the men who gathered round him were Bergmann, Schlupfe, Goldstein, and Kupelmayer.

Both Goldstein and Kupelmayer corroborated Wangenheim. Moreover, they testified that they had been playing pool with Schlupfe for at least two hours before Wangenheim came in with the news of the murder. They were unsavory-looking young men; and Wangenheim, with his lopsided head and thick, weak lips, was not a prepossessing person. But they all told their stories with apparent frankness.

Other witnesses were produced to testify to Schlupfe's good character — the liveryman in whose stable he had once worked, the alderman from his district, the butcher who had employed him as errand boy eight years before, the keeper of the bar-room that he was accustomed to frequent and that never saw him drunk or disorderly, and finally his uncle, who had a teaming business and had sent Schlupfe to buy some horses in the town where he had been arrested. The horse dealer appeared and corroborated this testimony.

The prosecuting attorney cross-examined none of these witnesses. Trask's efforts to trip them up or to discredit them resulted in failure.

Maxwell recalled Jerry for cross-examination, and asked him if Scanlan in his confession had admitted the purchase of the revolver as described by Kemperton. Jerry was obliged to say he had not.

"How do you happen to be appearing to-day without your uniform?"

"I object!" shouted Trask.

"If Your Honor please," said Maxwell, "I believe it is competent to bring out any facts that may tend to impeach the veracity of a witness."

The judge allowed the question, and Jerry answered:

"I'm not wearing the uniform because I've been suspended from the force."

"That will do, Mr. Donohue."

Maxwell glanced with a triumphant smile at the jury. He chose not to put his client on the stand. Dave Scanlan took the chair.

Confused, hesitating, making statements and then changing or retracting them, Dave caused Jerry's heart to sink. In regard to the revolver he said that Schlupfe had told him the one who was to use the weapon had better not be the one to buy it. Schlupfe had given him the purchase money and had waited in the neighborhood of the store until he emerged. He never would have bought the revolver if he had believed that Schlupfe meant to do more than intimidate people with it. He had n't included the story of the revolver in his confession to Officer Donohue because he did n't want to make himself appear worse than he was — and in view of what had happened the purchase of the revolver would have seemed a suspicious circumstance, and he had n't felt it necessary to mention it.

Making these explanations, Dave apparently felt that he did not carry conviction; he wavered and stopped upon an uncompleted, halting sentence.

Trask guided him through the story of the crime. He had met Schlupfe by appointment at the corner of Fifth and Tanner Streets at eleven o'clock; they had gone along Tanner Street and then up Burchard Avenue, and then down Eighth Street looking for places where it might seem safe to attempt a hold-up, and finally they had passed Walsh's store, and then, attracted by the deserted aspect of it, had turned back and entered. When he described the shooting, Jerry squirmed and gripped the edge of his chair in painful apprehension; he believed Dave, but he knew that Dave was not making others believe him. The stillness of the courtroom grew more and more ominous, as Dave gropingly, diffidently delivered his narrative. The jurors and the judge were watching him with unconcealed doubt and suspicion; Mrs. Scanlan sat pulling a handkerchief through first one hand and then the other, while she gazed at Dave with an imploring fixity and earnestness; Schlupfe and Maxwell leaned back in their chairs comfortably and smiled in open scorn; Trask stood close to his witness and strove, by question and suggestion and an appearance of calmness and confidence, to steady him.

"Now," said Trask, when Dave had at last finished

his story, "just what were the circumstances under which you met Schlupfe and arranged with him to embark on a series of robberies?"

"I'd just come out of the reformatory where I'd been for a month."

"Why had you been in the reformatory?"

"Drunk and disorderly."

"Was it your first offense?"

"Yes, sir."

"Never been arrested before?"

"No, sir."

"What day was it that you were released from the reformatory?"

"Wednesday, the 20th."

"The day the killing took place?"

"Yes, sir. I got out of the reformatory that morning and came down to the city. I wanted to find a job before I went home and saw my mother; she did n't know where I'd been. But I met Schlupfe and he took me into Pomeroy's saloon and gave me a drink, and then we got to talking together, and he told me his scheme."

"So he persuaded you then to join in it?"

"Yes, after about half an hour's talk."

"This was in Pomeroy's saloon?"

"No; we just had a drink in there, and then we went and sat on a bench in the park in front of City Hall."

"And after that you agreed to buy the revolver for Schlupfe?"

"Yes. He said that if he was willing to make the play with it, I ought to be willing to take his money and buy it."

"After you bought the revolver what did you do with it?"

"I gave it to Schlupfe."

"Did you ever handle it again?"

"No, sir."

Trask had no more questions; Maxwell rose to cross-examine.

"You say that Schlupfe persuaded you to buy the revolver, and that, as you supposed it was to be used to intimidate only and not to kill, you consented to do it?"

"Yes, sir."

"Then why did you buy loaded shells for the revolver?"

"Well, he asked me to and gave me the money."

"And yet you say you never supposed that revolver was to be used except to intimidate?"

"He told me he would n't use it."

Maxwell had no further questions to ask.

Trask was able to introduce evidence discreditable enough to Schlupfe. He showed that Schlupfe had been convicted of theft and had served a sentence of eighteen months; also that he had once been found guilty of assault and battery, and had served for that offense a term of six months. He asked for an adjournment until the next morning in order that he might look up the records of the witnesses who had been interested in trying to establish an alibi for Schlupfe. Over Maxwell's protests the court granted the request and gave Trask until the following morning.

The most industrious efforts during that interval

were unavailing. Schlupfe's witnesses were all of shady
reputation — so much it was easy to establish; but they
none of them had a criminal record. So far as tracing
their movements on the night of the murder was concerned, Trask found it in the few hours at his disposal
quite impossible. He was able the next morning by skillful cross-examination to anger them and set them in a
bad light, but that was all.

With the evidence all in, the District Attorney rose
and addressed the jury. He was aware, he said, of the
solemn responsibility imposed upon him; if in a professional eagerness to gain a verdict he endeavored to per-
vert or misinterpret the evidence that had been given
in this case, he would be unworthy of the office that he
held. He conceived it to be the duty of the attorney for
the State not primarily to seek a conviction, but to establish the truth; and he trusted that so long as he remained
district attorney he would be fair-minded enough, when
the evidence disclosed at the trial proved not to support an indictment, to admit that he had been in error
and to atone as best he could for excess of zeal. In this
case the matter as regarded one of the defendants was
simple. Scanlan had acknowledged a certain measure of
guilt; the only question was whether he had acknowledged the full measure that belonged to him. He had
purchased the revolver, he had purchased the shells with
which the killing had been done, he had been forced
reluctantly to admit these facts; his story implicating
Schlupfe as more guilty than himself might be true.
Only, if it were true, a number of men had lied, had
perjured themselves, had been bought — there could

be no other word for it — to save the neck of a cold-blooded murderer. He could not feel sure enough that this was the case to press for the conviction of the defendant Schlupfe. If the jury felt that the testimony of all those who had appeared in behalf of Schlupfe should be discredited and that he was guilty of the crime in the manner described by Scanlan, it was their privilege and their duty to report him guilty; but he himself could not in justice to his own conscience urge the jury to bring in such a verdict. As to the defendant Scanlan, he would have to press for a first-degree verdict. His confession had been only partial; whether he or some confederate had actually fired the shot could not affect the measure of his guilt. That was complete, and was established by his reluctant admission of the purchase of the revolver and the shells. The murder was cold-blooded, premeditated, and without any extenuating circumstance. A verdict in the first degree against the defendant Scanlan was not merely warranted, but was demanded by the evidence — which the District Attorney then proceeded to analyze.

Maxwell followed the District Attorney. He assured the jury that he would take but little of their time; indeed, considering the argument which they had just heard, he felt it hardly necessary that he should speak at all. He wished, however, to present to them some additional reasons why they should not permit themselves to be greatly influenced by Scanlan's partial confession and the testimony of the suspended policeman Donohue. One hesitated to believe that there was anything in this case partaking of the nature of a frame-up;

but it was nevertheless to be remembered that Scanlan and the suspended policeman Donohue were close
friends of long standing, that they had taken part in
the riots at the Purroy Works, — riots that had been
suppressed only by the calling out of the state troops,
— and that the two men had become intimate, as joint
law-breakers always do. It was not inconceivable that
the suspended policeman Donohue had effected a com-
promise between his easy conscience and the impulses
of friendship and had suggested to Scanlan a means of
evading the extreme penalty for his crime. The testimony fixing an alibi for Schlupfe at the time of the
murder was too varied and complete to be disregarded
or disbelieved; the question why Scanlan should have
tried to incriminate an innocent man and this particular innocent man might never be solved. One could
but offer a hypothetical explanation. The suspended
policeman Donohue had once seen Scanlan and Schlupfe
together; when he found his friend Scanlan involved in
the difficulties created by an untruthful confession, he
had, with the same desire to be helpful which had
prompted him to release the fleeing Scanlan, suggested
that Schlupfe might be the confederate in the crime;
and Scanlan in his cowardly desperation had grasped at
the suggestion. Schlupfe's arrest and indictment had followed. The suspended policeman Donohue had already
been sufficiently discredited by events. Scanlan's confusion on the witness stand, his obviously trumped-up
story about the revolver, were sufficient evidence of the
fact that he had been lying. Maxwell closed by declaring
that he had no other duty or desire than to secure jus-

tice for his client, and that in attacking Scanlan's confession and the suspended policeman Donohue's testimony he was animated by no spirit of vindictiveness.

Jerry sat and listened, wave after wave of impotent indignation coursing through him, his face crimson, his hands clenched. He wished the blood would not rush into his cheeks at the titter which followed each reference to the suspended policeman Donohue. Quite apart from the attack upon himself, the argument disturbed and dismayed him. For the first time he began to fear that the jury might actually find Dave guilty of murder in the first degree. It had seemed too incredible, too monstrous, yet now that dread grew and grew in his heart. That it was in Mrs. Scanlan's heart also Jerry knew, for her face was more rigid and colorless and her eyes more terrified. She sat leaning forward, clinging to Dave's arm through most of Maxwell's argument.

Trask appealed to the jury to believe Dave's confession. His plea was earnest; he was not asking them to bring in a verdict which would enable the defendant to escape the proper penalty for his offense. He took sharp issue with Maxwell over Patrolman Donohue's testimony, which he declared to be that of a transparently truthful man. Would any but a truthful man have narrated facts damaging to himself as Donohue had done — facts which, if he had kept silent about them, could never have been made known? Was it not the story of one duly and deeply impressed with the significance of the oath that he had taken when he went upon the witness stand? There was no justification for the effort of counsel for Schlupfe to besmirch Donohue's

character, and suggest that he had connived at a
"plant"; it was an infamous insinuation. Far more
worthy of belief were Donohue and Scanlan than the
witnesses who had undertaken to prove an alibi for
Schlupfe. One, a dog-fancier of ill repute; another, unable to define his business; a third, a fellow who had lost
four jobs within a year because of drunkenness — all
loafers; were the jury ready to accept the statements of
these men? It was preposterous to think that Scanlan
was maliciously trying to incriminate an innocent man.
The evidence of Schlupfe's innocence was suspiciously
complex and complete; it had been too elaborately put
together; it suggested very careful coöperation on the
part of certain witnesses. That Scanlan had intended to
rob the store he admitted, and for that he deserved
punishment. But it had never been in his mind to kill
the storekeeper, and the hand that had pressed the
trigger and sent the bullet on its fatal mission was not
his.

The judge's charge was favorable neither to Scanlan
nor to Schlupfe. As to Schlupfe, he instructed the jury
that their verdict must be either "Guilty of murder in
the first degree" or "Not guilty." There seemed no evidence which would justify them in convicting Schlupfe
of murder in a less degree. As to Scanlan, his confessed
complicity in the robbery which had resulted in Walsh's
death required the jury to find some verdict against him.
If the story told by Scanlan was wholly true and he had
no intention or knowledge of any intention on the part
of Schlupfe or any one concerned with him in the robbery to use the revolver in any event, then the jury

might find him guilty of murder in the second degree or of manslaughter. If they found that Scanlan had himself fired the shot or that Scanlan had plotted with a confederate and had understood clearly what use in certain contingencies was to be made of the revolver, the jury should then bring in a verdict against Scanlan of murder in the first degree. It was a plain issue of veracity between Scanlan on the one hand and the witnesses who had appeared to establish an alibi for Schlupfe on the other. Whether Scanlan had deliberately endeavored to fasten the crime on an innocent man, or whether Schlupfe's friends had perjured themselves in order to procure his acquittal was for the jury to determine.

The jury were out for seven hours. They found Schlupfe not guilty, and Scanlan guilty of murder in the second degree.

XXII

MICHAEL SCANLAN HAS AN UNUSUAL AMOUNT OF SORROW
TO DROWN: AND NORA RECALLS THE BEST MORNING
OF HER LIFE

DURING his suspension from the force Jerry decided that the best use he could make of his time until the Police Commissioner finally disposed of his case would be in prosecuting his law studies. So he appeared every morning at the law library as soon as it was opened and stayed there with hardly an intermission until it was closed. The librarian, who had hitherto taken a friendly interest in the stalwart, ingenuous-looking young policeman, and had helped him to map out a course of reading, now turned cool towards him. But Jerry, though sensitive enough to every such intimation of distrust, chose to seem thick-skinned, sought the librarian's help when he needed it, never appeared to be aware of the curtness with which it was rendered, and always cheerfully expressed his appreciation.

He was not in the courtroom on the gray December morning when sentence was pronounced upon Dave Scanlan. Jerry read in the evening newspaper that Dave had been sentenced to twenty years imprisonment.

In view of the verdict Jerry had not expected a lighter sentence. Yet to weigh the meaning of it, now that it had been pronounced, appalled him. Twenty years! Almost as long a time as he had already lived in the world!

JERRY

Jerry passed the street in which the Scanlans lived, hesitated, and retraced his steps.

There was a light in the third-floor windows of the shabby lodging-house; Jerry felt his way slowly up the dark stairs. At first there was no response to his knock; but when he repeated it, Mrs. Scanlan opened the door a few inches and stood in the opening as if to guard the premises from invasion.

"It's Jerry," she said, turning and speaking to some one in the room. "I guess he can come in. Yes, come in, Jerry."

She opened the door wide, and then he saw Nora. She sat huddled forward on a low chair, a gray shawl thrown over her shoulders, her elbows resting on her knees. She looked frail and thin and piteous; more piteous than anything else, Jerry thought, was her effort to greet him with a smile. It vanished as he took her hand; tears rolled down from her eyes.

"It's tough, Nora, it's awfully tough," he said, and he found no other words to communicate his sympathy; he tried to comfort her by patting her shoulders. "Mrs. Scanlan, you were a wonder; the way you kept up your nerve in the courtroom; it was fine. And now the case is n't finished yet; Mr. Trask, I know, has hopes that a new trial will be granted, and maybe we can get something on some of those witnesses — if only we can do that, we'll have a new trial sure. Dave was absolutely innocent of the murder, Nora. And I don't believe an innocent man is going to suffer for a crime like that."

He stopped, and felt as he looked at the women's faces

[214]

that it had been the merest babble that he had been uttering.

"Oh, if we had money, maybe we could get him off," sighed Mrs. Scanlan. "But you can't do anything in law without money."

Jerry could not dispute that.

"Can I be of any use to you?" he asked. "Any little thing that you and Nora might like to have fetched in to you?"

"Nothing, unless it's Michael Scanlan you could get hold of."

"Have you any idea where I might find him?"

"Sometimes it's Murphy's saloon on Ninth Street, and sometimes it's Galvin's on Eighth. And sometimes it's somewhere else. He's got an unusual lot of sorrow to drown to-night; so no doubt he'll be worse than usual."

"I'll go out and see if I can't round him up."

"He'll be ugly if he thinks you've come after him."

"If I find him, I'll not bother him too much; I'll just try to coax him along home. Isn't it a pity that he wasn't in when you came, Nora? Then he'd have stayed, most like."

"He was here when Nora came." Mrs. Scanlan looked at her daughter and continued, "It was her coming that made it sure he would go out and drown his sorrows. When he'd listened to what she had to say, he rose up and went out without a word. Not a word to his own daughter, that had been abused by her husband and driven from house and home and —"

Nora put a restraining hand on her mother. Mrs.

Scanlan, who had begun to tremble and to raise her voice became silent.

"I could n't stay with him any longer," Nora said. "He was forever sneering to me about Dave. 'Your brother the murderer' — that's how he always spoke of him — and he managed to speak of him about fifty times a day. This morning he said to me, as if it was something to be happy about, 'So this is the day your brother the murderer gets what's coming to him.' I did n't answer; I packed a few things in a bag and left the house. I'll never go back to him, never."

"And her father had not one word to say, not one word!" repeated Mrs. Scanlan bitterly. "Just got up and went out — to forget it all in drink. He's been earning next to nothing these days. Nora and I have both got to find work of some kind. I suppose Nora's husband could be made to give her money, could n't he? I want her to ask Mr. Trask about that."

"Yes, mother, yes, but please don't talk about it —"

"There's no reason why Jerry should n't know just what trouble we're in."

Jerry flushed at his inability to make an immediate practical response to this veiled appeal.

"I wish I could help, Mrs. Scanlan. I'll go anyway and see if I can't get track of Mr. Scanlan and bring him home to you."

"Most likely you can't. And if you find him and he's far gone, I'd as soon he'd stay away. He has nothing on him that anybody might steal."

Nora followed Jerry to the door; she passed with him out into the dark hallway and closed the door and held

it with her hand, so that she might speak to him and
not be overheard by her mother.

"You don't feel hardly towards me, Jerry?"

"Of course not. How could I, Nora?"

"You have reason enough. I have no right to complain of all that's gone wrong in my life; I brought it
on myself. But when I think of Dave. — Do you remember, Jerry, when he had pneumonia and I nursed
him?"

"Yes. You could n't have been more than fifteen
then."

"I thought if he died I could n't live. I nursed him all
one night when mother and father were both so worn
out they had to sleep. It was the worst night of all.
When the doctor came in the morning, he told me I'd
saved Dave's life. I was so proud and happy. It was
the happiest morning of my life. I remember going out
to breathe the air; the sun was shining and our poor
little house looked finer to me than a palace — and
then you came along —"

"I remember. You ran up and told me that Dave
would get well. I remember just how you looked that
morning, Nora."

"The best morning of my life. And how much better
it would have been if Dave had died that night! And if
I could have died too!"

"Now, Nora!" Jerry seized her hands. "You must n't
give up hope. He surely won't have to serve the full
term. And once he's out, we'll look after him, we'll
see that he has a new start; he'll make something of
himself yet."

"Perhaps. Who will make anything of me!"

"You will; you will yourself, Nora. I'm glad you've left that man. You'll do something now with your music."

She shook her head; he descended the stairs heavy-hearted.

His search for Scanlan was vain. Not at Murphy's, not at Galvin's, not at any other place that presented itself to Jerry's imagination as a likely resort for one with sorrows to drown did he find the errant Michael. His search was so conscientious that it was long after the supper hour when he got home.

XXIII

WHEN Jerry opened the door of the apartment, he was
at once made aware that the domestic conditions were
abnormal. His mother's room, which was also the sitting-
room, was dark, but by the light from the hallway he
could see that a small person had been put to bed there
on the sofa. And immediately the small person sang out
in a voice that he recognized as Betty's, "Look where
I've gone to bed, Jerry. Peter's sick." The tone intimated a pleasurable excitement over the situation.

Kate came out into the hall; she looked troubled and
anxious.

"I'm afraid your supper's cold, Jerry," she began.
"I tried to keep it warm, but —"

"Never mind about the supper; what's the matter
with Peter?"

"He was taken sick in school this afternoon; I brought
him home. He could hardly walk the last block, and it
was all I could do to get him up the stairs. He has a
high fever; the doctor came and said it might be pneumonia. You know he's had a cough the last few days."

"Poor little kid! Can I see him?"

"I'm hoping he'll drop off to sleep. But you might
look in on him."

The little boy's flushed face and heavy eyes that
opened with no sign of recognition alarmed Jerry. He

withdrew and talked again with Kate in whispers. Yes, the doctor had told her just what to do; she had been giving the medicine regularly. If he fell asleep, he was n't to be roused for any medicine.

"Where's mother?" Jerry asked.

"Mr. Bennett came and asked if she would n't sit upstairs with Mrs. Bennett. Their baby is sick and Mrs. Bennett's worrying about it, and Mr. Bennett could n't stay home from his work. You'd better go in and eat your supper, Jerry; I'm afraid it will be stone cold."

Jerry ate his supper, as he was told to do, but he did not really know whether it was cold or hot. He was beset with anxieties; Peter's sudden illness alarmed him. Peter had become to him like his own little brother. He spared a thought for the Bennetts; poor people, if anything should happen to their baby! He had never seen anybody so thoroughly engrossed as Mrs. Bennett in one tiny human being, so enraptured by it and brimming over with happiness on account of it. Peter must surely be all right. If anything should happen to Peter — Jerry's imagination flew instantly to Kate and shrank back appalled.

After supper he went upstairs to make inquiries about the Bennetts' baby. He found that it was better, early in the afternoon it had been seized with convulsions, and Mrs. Bennett in a paroxysm of terror had carried it down to Mrs. Donohue, who had plunged it into a hot bath and then summoned the doctor. Now it was asleep and seemed quite normal, but Mrs. Bennett was so unnerved that she still needed the support of Mrs. Donohue s presence. "If it should have another attack and you were n't here, I don't know what I should do," Mrs. Bennett had said, and the appeal had been irresistible.

This information Jerry's mother conveyed to him in whispers through the half-opened door of the Bennett apartment; and then she asked anxiously about Peter. "Goodness knows I don't know where I ought to be," she said. "But if Kate needs me, you come for me, and I'll manage to get to her somehow. Goodness knows it never rains but it pours. Things always happen in a bunch, or else they don't happen at all. It's always been so, it always will be so, in anything where I'm concerned."

Jerry went back to his own rooms and persuaded Kate to let him watch for a while. The lamp was shaded so that it did not throw its light directly on Peter's face, but Jerry could see that his eyes remained half open and that from time to time his lips were mumbling inaudibly. And as the clock on the mantelpiece ticked on and on, and there was no change, Jerry watched with deepening anxiety. Presently came a strangling cough, forerunner of a paroxysm; Jerry raised the boy's head and shoulders and held him while the terrifying spasm lasted. To feel the little frame so racked and shaken sent a pang of tenderness to Jerry's heart, and when it was all over, before laying the boy's head on the pillow, he kissed the inviting little hollow in the back of the soft white neck.

He put the boy down gently; in a few moments, to Jerry's immense relief, Peter fell asleep.

The watcher's thoughts, at first intent on the patient,

strayed gradually as the boy's breathing continued to be regular and reassuring. They went back to Nora; they returned to that morning, now so many years ago, which she had recalled to his mind and which in the light of this immediate experience took on a fresh vividness. Nora had then been hardly older than Kate was now. To recapture in imagination the Nora of that day, the Jerry of that day, was too poignant an effort. Kate and Peter anyway should be shielded from such misery and shame as had befallen Nora and Dave. But if they were to be shielded, how he must work!

Stimulated by the reflection, he began to review in his mind the law of real property. In this troublesome occupation he was engaged when Kate entered and attempted to resume her place.

He told her firmly that she was to go to bed and not disturb him or Peter again that night. She was going to have nursing enough to do, and she must not use up all her strength at the outset.

When she was convinced that he meant what he said, she showed him the medicine that Peter was to have if he awoke, made him promise to call her if he became alarmed about anything, set the room quickly and quietly to rights, and as quickly and quietly smoothed out Peter's bed without moving him. Jerry watched her with admiration for her noiseless efficiency.

"You're a great little nurse, Kate. I should almost like to be sick so that you could look after me."

Her sober face showed a momentary gleam of pleasure.

"I should like it if you were n't very sick. — I shall love it when Peter is only a little sick."

"That will be soon, I'm sure. Good-night, Kate, and don't lie awake worrying."

He returned to the subject of real property, but after a time found it hard to concentrate his thoughts. Peter was restless and now and then spoke incoherently in delirium. Of what value would a knowledge of real property be if anything happened to Peter? Then, when Peter quieted down again and Jerry's anxiety about him was temporarily relieved, Dave's plight and Nora's plight took possession of his thoughts. He drifted into a sentimental contemplation of the old days when he had been a romantic dreamer and when romance had crowned with its glamour and mystery poor Nora's head. He exercised his will power and set his mind firmly upon the subject of real property again.

His mother came in at midnight and spoke to him in the hall.

"How is Peter, Jerry?"

"Sleeping. Can you go to bed now?"

"Yes. The baby seems all right, and Mr. Bennett has got back, so Mrs. Bennett feels easier. Mr. Bennett is waiting outside; he wants to speak to you a moment. I'll stay with Peter till you come. Is Kate asleep?"

"I hope so. I told her I'd watch to-night."

Jerry stepped into the dimly lighted hall; Bennett came close to him.

"First of all, Donohue, I want to tell you how grateful we are to your mother; I don't know what might have happened to the kid if it had n't been for her. She's a good neighbor all right. — I'm sorry to hear about the boy."

"Yes, but I hope he'll be better in the morning."

"Sure he will. — There's a thing I learned this evening, Donohue — story came into the office just before I left; I set it up. Scanlan's father — you know, the fellow that's just been convicted — his father shot and killed his son-in-law, a fellow named Corcoran, this evening, and then killed himself. Walked into Corcoran's store, went right up to him, pulled a revolver, and put a bullet through his head. Then turned the gun on himself. They say Corcoran and his wife had quarreled, and she'd gone home to her folks — probably excited her father against him."

Jerry listened speechless. "Does she know yet?" he finally asked.

"I suppose they've sent some one to tell her. But that wasn't in the story."

Bennett went up the stairs, and Jerry returned to watch by Peter's bed. Jerry thought no more about the law of real property that night.

XXIV

FOR a week Kate and Jerry and Mrs. Donohue alter-
nated their anxious watch by Peter's bedside. Then
came the day when the fever subsided as suddenly as it
had arisen, and the boy who had so long been either de-
lirious or comatose looked up at the watchers with un-
clouded eyes and a wan smile. "I guess I won't be able
to go to school to-day," he said; and he did not at all
understand the emotion in Kate's voice when she answered, "No, Peter, not to-day, but some day, thank
God." "To-morrow, I guess," said Peter hopefully.

He asked Jerry why he was n't in uniform and seemed
interested in the explanation that when a policeman let
a prisoner escape in order to catch another man it was
a technical breach of duty, and the policeman went
without his uniform for a while by way of atonement.

With the elasticity of childhood Peter rapidly recovered his normal health; indeed, he was again going
to school before the question whether Jerry should ever
again be permitted to wear the uniform had been decided.

With the lifting of the big anxiety about Peter, the
petty anxieties pressed relentlessly upon Jerry's mind.
Once more had set in the drain upon his mother's little
hoard; once more he was eating the bread of idleness and
feeling guilty because he had such an appetite. There

was no work of the most temporary sort to be had at the wharves; the river was frozen over and all navigation was suspended. It took courage to go to Mr. Murray and explain why he should again be seeking a job; but he did it. Murray gave him a not particularly cordial reception and regretted that he could not help him. Jerry came from the interview with flaming cheeks. He kept away from Trask, thinking that he, too, had probably lost faith in him. He called on the superintendent of the street railway, and the superintendent seemed pleased with his appearance and evidently thought of giving him a place as a conductor; but when he asked what Jerry's references were and so learned who he was, his manner too underwent a change and he declared frostily that there was nothing he could offer him. Finally Jerry got work as a porter in a hotel. During the two weeks that he was on duty there he never pocketed a tip without a feeling of deep humiliation.

Life in those days seemed to be a series of minor slights and indignities. The Armstrongs, who had not been in ignorance of his disgrace, exhibited their heartfelt satisfaction. Again the two Armstrong girls hung about the doorway watching for him; and when he appeared they were all giggles and derisive snickers. Armstrong told him that he looked more natural in his old duds, — had never looked as if he was made to wear a uniform, — and as he would probably never wear one again it was just as well. Mrs. Armstrong came out on the stairs one day to greet him and asked him if he expected to find much difficulty in disposing of his uniform at a good price. She also had to laugh — so she informed him — whenever she thought how he had threatened to arrest her for hanging her clothes on the roof. That was too funny. She guessed the next policeman that filled the place that he left vacant would be less concerned about bothering a neighbor and more about getting criminals to jail instead of letting them go.

These evil auguries for his future did not disturb Jerry more than his own apprehensions disturbed him. He realized fully that being laid off from the force might prove merely the preliminary to dismissal. In that case he would have to continue at the uninspiring task that furnished a makeshift for the time being. But he would n't always continue at it; eventually he was going to be admitted to the bar. There would be always a few hours a day that would be his own and that he would n't need for sleep. He was employing those hours now religiously at the law library.

The day after Michael Scanlan had killed Corcoran and himself, Jerry had gone to see Nora and her mother. Groups of boys and girls were idling in front of the house and on the pavement opposite, hoping to get a glimpse of the afflicted family. Three young men followed Jerry to the doorstep and would have entered had he not helped the landlady's daughter, who admitted him, to frustrate their designs. She closed the door in their faces and he held it against them until she could turn the key.

"Tell Mrs. Scanlan who you are when you knock," she said. "Otherwise, you 'll never get in."

Both Nora and her mother seemed crushed by the tragedy. It was as if they had exhausted their capacity for emotion.

"I can't hardly believe it," Mrs. Scanlan kept repeating in a monotonous voice. "I could n't hardly believe it about Dave, and I can't hardly believe it about Michael."

| "If only I had n't said to father what I did yesterday!" lamented Nora. "I shall always feel I drove him to it."

"I don't know but what it would have been better if he'd taken us with him," said her mother. "There's nothing in the world left for us now."

There were things that Jerry could do for them. Because of these things and the obligations they entailed, he was the more willing in the days that followed to accept the gratuities against which his pride rebelled.

As it turned out, Nora was not left so badly off by her husband's death. After the payment of all debts she would have an income of about a thousand dollars a year. The condition of her finances no longer caused Jerry anxiety; it was sounder and more assured than that of his own.

When Jerry appeared for the hearing before the Police Commissioner, he was surprised and pleased to see Trask sitting at the back of the room. The Chief of Police presented the charges in person; he read in a monotonous voice from a typewritten document the stenographic notes of Jerry's testimony at the trial and expressed the belief of the Department that, "the facts being as stated, it was desirable that Officer Donohue be dismissed from the force, for the good of the service."

The Police Commissioner, a spare, severe-looking man,

smooth-shaven, with silver-gray hair neatly smoothed down on either side of the straight line bisecting it, asked Jerry if he cared to make a statement. Jerry replied that he could not conceive of being exposed a second time to such temptation; he was bound to say that he could not feel very penitent for what he had done, and yet that he thought in all ordinary circumstances and emergencies he could be trusted to recognize and perform his duty as well as the next man; he hoped anyway that he might be given a chance to prove that this was so.

It was not much of an appeal to the emotions. When he had finished, Trask stood up and asked if he might say a few words. He explained that he had come to the hearing without any urging from Officer Donohue —who had, in fact, held no communication with him since the trial. It seemed to him that Officer Donohue deserved another chance, especially as he had owned his fault in a manly fashion instead of lying as he might easily and safely have done. So far from being untrustworthy, he had shown a keen regard for the truth. Such a man should not be branded as morally unfit.

Jerry felt embarrassed and unspeakably grateful. He wished he were such a paragon as Mr. Trask pictured him to be. As for paragons, where was one to be found the equal to Mr. Trask! He felt it must be wonderful to be so fixed that you could give such help and encouragement to a fellow who needed it. How he would like to be some day in a position where he could do a thing of that kind!

Almost immediately these pleasant juices of emotion were transformed to gall. The Chief in a bullying tone

objected to having an inefficient, untrustworthy patrolman — yes, untrustworthy, that's what he was —
made a regular hero. In behalf of the efficiency of the
force — of which he conceived himself to be a better
judge than the gentleman who had just spoken — he demanded the dismissal of Donohue.

The Commissioner was evidently impressed by the
reasonableness of Jerry's defense and announced that he
did not feel it necessary to remove him for the good of the
service. He did, however, agree with the Chief that
Officer Donohue ought by no means to be regarded as
a "regular hero," and he felt that some punishment, in
addition to what he had already undergone, would not
be amiss. He restored Jerry to his place on the force, but
sentenced him to serve for one month without pay.

Great was the rejoicing in the Donohue flat that evening when Jerry showed himself once more in uniform.

It came near being his last appearance. Some time
after midnight, when he was passing along a back street,
he saw the flicker of flames through a stable window.
He ran to the nearest fire-alarm box, which was a block
away on another street, and he had just sent in the alarm
and turned back when Sheehan, coming up behind,
called to him.

"Fire on Deane Street," shouted Jerry in reply.
"Stay by the box and direct the engines."

But Sheehan chose instead to follow. He arrived at
the stable as Jerry, working with his night-stick, loosened
the staple of the main door. In a moment they got it
open; there was instantly a burst of flame and smoke;
within, walls and carriages were ablaze. The rear of the

stable was partitioned off from the carriage room, and behind the partition sounded the whinnying and trampling of frightened horses. Jerry and Sheehan sprang through the smoke to the inner door and found it locked as the outer had been. Again Jerry used his night-stick with success; the flames were scorching his back when he got the door open. He and Sheehan entered, and flinging their overcoats over the heads of two of the three horses, led them out of their stalls and through the smoke to the street. The whistle of the fire engines, the gong of the hook-and-ladder wagon sounded in the distance.

"Hold this horse," said Jerry, and he passed the halter to Sheehan and took his overcoat from the horse's head.

"Don't try it, old man," Sheehan advised.

But the horse in the stable neighed piteously.

Although the partition wall was now a mass of flames, Jerry, holding his overcoat up before his face, rushed again into the room of the horse stalls. He muffled the horse's head and got him out of the stall and facing the doorway, but then the terrified animal would not move. The flames were darting across the opening, growing thicker every moment. Snatching up a bundle of hay, Jerry lighted it and touched it to the horse's rump. The animal leaped forward in frenzy; Jerry, holding his hands before his face, plunged after it. He reached the street, with his uniform ablaze, and his arms and neck and hands feeling as if they were being devoured by fire. Sheehan smothered the flames and wrapped his own overcoat round him; then the firemen arrived and took charge of the fire. Jerry walked to the police station and reported and had his burns dressed. The next day he went on duty swathed in bandages. The owner of the three horses that he and Sheehan had saved called at the station house and left a five-dollar bill for him.

XXV

A PLACE TO WHICH IT IS HARD TO COME: AND ONE
THAT IT IS EVEN HARDER TO LEAVE

THE court refused Dave a new trial; probably, as Trask
said to Jerry, it would have done so anyway, but after
Michael Scanlan's violent act the refusal was a foregone
conclusion.

"Just from the point of view of his son's interest, it
was the worst thing he could possibly have done," Trask
observed regretfully. "The chances of ever getting a
pardon have shrunk a hundred per cent. In the mind of
any governor the father's act will create a presumption
against the son, and will confirm the idea that he's a
dangerous man. Scanlan is the victim of a most unfortunate chain of events."

"Yes," Jerry admitted. "I don't see that there's
any use in trying to do more for him now."

"It would only prejudice his chances later. All you
can do for him is to go and see him once in a while, and
keep him cheered up."

It was not easy to keep Dave cheered up. Jerry paid
the monthly visits that were permitted and sat with
Dave in the guard-room for the allotted hour. Each
visit renewed and strengthened his liking for his old
friend, his belief in him, and his sorrow for him.

Dave's grief over his father's end seemed quite to have
supplanted pity for himself, and to have increased the
weight of his remorse. There were tears in his eyes

[233]

when he talked about his father to Jerry. "He was a good dad once — he always would have been if things had gone right and he had n't taken to the bottle. And what he did at the end he never would have done but for me. He was plumb crazed, Jerry; I drove him to it."

"I don't think you need to feel that," Jerry answered. "Set your face to the future, Dave; you'll be coming out some time, you know; and do what you can while you're here so that it won't all be time wasted."

"I know; that's what I've said to myself. But honestly I don't believe I've got the stuff in me. If it was only a year or two years, or even three, I might stick it out and amount to something at the end; but twenty—"

"It's pretty stiff, but you'll see it through. Just keep saying to yourself, 'Some day I'll be coming out, and I've got to be ready,' and don't think how long a time it may be. — It's easy to talk, Dave. I'd help you any other way if I could."

"I know you would, Jerry. Your talk does help."

Jerry looked at the others seated in the semicircle before the officer's table. It was like a schoolroom, with the pupils all culprits and the teacher one whose aim was not to teach but simply to intimidate and control. The convicts, in their gray homespun uniform, were of all types, from the hulking and brutish to the delicate and even aristocratic; their visitors ranged from the dirty Jew of the Ghetto to the woman in furs whose limousine was perhaps waiting at the gate; and Jerry reflected that each one of these friends or relatives was there trying to fulfill the same purpose — trying in some way to help through talk. And in the light of that thought how tragical the silences, and the obvious inexpressiveness of their speech! Into one hour each month they must pack all the comfort and hope and sympathy that they could give — and how little of these could they convey!

The turnkey, whose eye had been on the clock, came up and handed Dave the yellow slip, signifying that he must return to his cell.

Jerry stood for a few moments waiting for the outer door to be opened. With him waited two women, whose visits with their husbands had been terminated at the same time. They were women of respectable appearance, and they looked at each other commiseratingly.

"It's a hard place to come to," said one.

"It's hard to come, and harder still to go," said the other.

Jerry felt that the remark must epitomize the emotions of a convict's mother or wife.

On a subsequent visit he was glad to find Dave in a more cheerful mood — owing to the fact that he had been admitted to membership in the prison brass band. Dave beat the drum with proficiency, and his ability was promptly recognized. The band rehearsed three times a week and gave concerts on the various holidays that, as it seemed to Jerry, formed one of the mockeries of prison life. Anyway Dave was almost exuberant in telling Jerry of his achievement.

"And there are some mighty good fellows in the band," he assured Jerry. "Some crack musicians too. I feel having this just as a recreation is going to help me a lot; it's made the work in the shoe-shop go better. And I get plenty of time to read. I'm to have lessons on the cornet; the fellow that plays that is in here for eight years. I told Nora about it when she came to see me, but she did n't seem much interested. I guess the drum and the cornet are n't high-toned enough to appeal to her."

He spoke with just a trace of bitterness; it suggested that Nora had been less appreciative of the solace of his recreation hour than he had thought she should be.

It made Jerry uncomfortable to have Nora criticized even by implication. He wanted to defend her, and without knowing against just what she was to be defended.

XXVI

OCCASIONS FOR MARVELING NEVER CEASE: ADVANTAGES OF BEING AN OUTSIDER

It seemed to Jerry that he was forever and vainly trying to make good the financial loss that he, or, more accurately, his mother, had sustained through his two months' suspension from the police force. During that period it had been necessary for Mrs. Donohue to dip again into her savings; Jerry's ambition was not only to meet all the expenses of the household, but also to restore the sum that she had withdrawn. Time and again he seemed on the point of making a contribution to this worthy filial purpose only to find his little accumulation engulfed by some unexpected and imperative need. It might be a suit for Peter, or a hat and coat for Kate, or stockings and shoes for Betty; there was seldom any information forthcoming from any of these persons as to their needs or desires, but Mrs. Donohue was not above practicing espionage and was liberal in conjecture. Jerry could not say no to her generous suggestions. Some of them it was possible to execute without confiding in the beneficiaries; in regard to others Kate had to be consulted, and then, unless the necessity was too glaring to be disputed, the good intentions were usually put to rout. For Kate was very stiff in her self-denial; if she could get along without a thing, she did so, even though both Jerry and his mother were for pressing it upon her. They never knew all that her stubbornness in this matter cost her; at school, her hats, dresses, and shoes excited the derision of the modish Armstrong sisters, and their public ridicule of her wounded her as no one looking at her proudly held head and impassive face could have guessed.

And meanwhile Jerry continued to marvel and worry over the amount of money it cost to maintain a not very large and most economical family. The months went by, and it was always a neck-and-neck race between income and expenses — now one nosing ahead and now the other; and so far as Jerry could see, it was always going to be so. He could expect no increase of salary for two years anyway, and there was no certainty of its being granted then; and even if it were, he had to look forward to an increase in expenses; it was to be expected that Peter's and Betty's needs would be a little greater each year. And then Kate — she stood at the head of her class in the high school; she ought to go to college, if in any way it could be managed. A girl as bright as she was could become a secretary or a teacher, she might under favoring circumstances disclose talents or capabilities that would assure her independence and happiness. She ought to have every chance. And Jerry wondered desperately how he was going to give her any chance at all.

These anxious thoughts and even more anxious and pressing calculations were Jerry's most constant companions on his otherwise lonely night patrol; often they intruded themselves between him and the page when he sat reading in the law library. He wished sometimes that he had never abandoned the promising place that

he had won at Murray's. It seemed, as he looked back
on it, one of those errors of immaturity that it was hard
to understand. But he did not dwell unduly on his mis-
takes; he was of too cheerful and hopeful a spirit for that,
and he would comfort himself with the reflection that
for the practice of the law a term of service on the police
force was a better preparation than any position, however lucrative, in a mercantile establishment. The an-
noying thing was that he seemed to have less leisure for
study than before; his assignments were more arduous
and exacting, and when he was off duty he was often so
tired and sleepy that study was impossible. So his progress was discouragingly slow.

One day he confided his intention to Sheehan.

"There's where you show your brains," said Sheehan.
"I never had the ambition or the intellect — wish I had.
There's nothing in this business for an honest man.
There's plenty in it for one that's crooked. You and I
are distrusted because we're straight. The Chief has
surrounded himself with a gang after his own heart and
they want under them only men they can corrupt.
Blackmail, blackmail, nothing but blackmail — that's
what our superiors are after all the time."

"If you've got evidence of this, you ought to lay it
before the Police Commissioner or the District Attorney."

"I haven't got the evidence, but a man can't be a
member of the force for ten years without knowing
what's in the air. And if I had the evidence, I wouldn't
dare to use it. Why, they'd manage to run the steam-
roller right over me. I'm not so young or so independ-

ent that it means nothing to me to lose my job. With four kiddies to feed and clothe a man can't afford to start out on the crusading act."

"No," admitted Jerry. "That's true."

"I've been on the force ten years," repeated Sheehan. "And I'm practically an outsider to-day. As long as *you're* on it *you'll* be an outsider. That's why I say you're doing well now to prepare yourself for something else."

"Why don't you do the same?"

"It's too late. I'll be forty next month. All I can do is sit tight and hope for a pension some day if I'm lucky."

Jerry learned that Sheehan had spoken truly when he said that they were both outsiders. The other officers with whom he was thrown slighted him or showed their aversion. He had violated the oath of office, and he had been exposed; that was damaging enough. He had been reinstated through the intercession of a rich, reforming busybody; that was worse.

When it appeared that sentiment had definitely turned against him, Jerry made no effort to propitiate it. He felt less sensitive than he might have done had any of his colleagues manifested traits that he regarded as likable. He was as little drawn to them, however, as they to him; at times the antipathy was crystallized into sharp antagonism. The spectacle of a bully in uniform kicking and battering a "drunk" who was feebly resisting efforts to drag him to a cell led to an exchange of words that meant lasting enmity. At the police station scenes of brutality were not uncommon, and frequently Jerry's indignation got the better of his discretion. His unpopularity became more than local; the men at other posts heard about him and disliked him without even having the misfortune of his acquaintance. When the captain of Station 9 succeeded in getting rid of him, the men of Station 16, to which he was transferred, showed that they felt they had a grievance. Even Rafferty of Station 14, whom he occasionally encountered, and who in the beginning had displayed a spirit of friendliness, seemed now extremely undesirous to be seen in his company.

For one in Jerry's position such unpopularity had certain advantages. He was not tempted to take part in the diversions of his fellow policemen; he was able with the greater single-mindedness to devote his leisure time to study; and the stimulus to surmount the obstacles to a legal education was stronger than it might otherwise have been. The thought of remaining permanently a member of the police force as it was constituted became intolerable.

Of course Jerry was always facing in his own mind one important question. "After I'm admitted to the bar, how am I to make a living?" He hoped that time and chance would lead him to the answer.

XXVII

NORA PRACTICES MENTAL SUGGESTION: AND PATRICK
MAGUIRE PROVES AN IMPRESSIONABLE SUBJECT

AFTER Michael Scanlan's death, Nora and her mother
did not long retain the rooms in which they had been
living. Nora's inheritance made it possible for them to
seek a more agreeable neighborhood, and in a quiet and
respectable street of small brick houses they found a
haven such as they desired. It was one flight up and
extended all the way through from the sitting-room with
a bay window and rubber plant to a bedroom that looked
out upon an ailanthus tree and a clothes-line. The landlady furnished meals in the front room on the first floor,
where a canary swung and sang in its cage. There were
no other boarders; the landlady — from whom, of course,
their history could not be concealed — proved to be
sympathetic rather than censorious; and she was so
considerate as not to advertise the identity of her
lodgers — except to a few intimate friends, who hovered
about for sidelong glances at them and spread throughout the neighborhood the news of the interesting arrivals
at 21 Gurney Street.

Jerry came occasionally to see them. Mrs. Scanlan
was very much broken by her sorrows and had failed in
health as well as in spirit. The personality that had once
been so dominating had become almost negligible. She
seemed always to be sitting idly, submissively, in the

bay window beside the rubber plant, and looking down the street with apathetic eyes.

Nora had not yet decided what she should do. Of course, there was now no urgent need for her to do anything, but she felt, so she said to Jerry, that she would be happier if she had an occupation. She might try to get some music pupils, though she doubted if she had the patience that a teacher ought to possess. Sometimes she thought it might be interesting to learn stenography; if it did n't take so long she thought she would do it. She confessed that as yet she had n't plucked up heart to seek work of any kind; it seemed to take a long time to get back a normal feeling about things. It did n't seem as if she could ever sufficiently free her mind of the awful experiences she had lived through in the last six months so that it would be fit for work or study — and as for play! She smiled at Jerry pathetically.

He spoke of Dave to her and of his brave spirit, but he felt, even before she replied, that the topic was distasteful; there was a contraction of her pretty dark brows, a thinning of her gentle lips.

"I've been to see him twice, but I don't know that I can go again — not often anyway," she confessed. "It has the most dreadful effect on me — worse even the second time than the first. To see him in those clothes — with all those vile creatures — and those jailers watching us — and the place smells so nasty and looks so hopeless. I could n't even pretend to be cheerful; and when he told me about his playing the drum and having lessons on the cornet and seemed to expect that I would feel that was something to be happy about — I could n't; that's all. To see Dave trying to draw comfort out of such a thing — it was too pitiful."

"Even so — of course your visit did him good."

"I don't believe it did. I think it probably depressed him; I think he was probably unhappier after it than before. If I could have assumed something I did n't feel while I was with him — but I could n't. Sitting in that place I felt as if I was polluted. I don't do Dave any good by going to see him, and I do myself harm."

Jerry questioned that assertion, but she insisted that it was true. Of course, she explained, she did not mean that she would entirely give up going to see Dave. And perhaps in time she might get used to the surroundings and not mind them so much.

Again Jerry had a vague desire such as he had felt when Dave had intimated disappointment over Nora's attitude — a desire to defend and protect her — this time against herself. He knew that she did not do herself justice when she talked in such a strain. He withheld, however, that peculiarly irritating comment, and contented himself with feeling sorrier for her than before. Poor little soul, with her sensitiveness and her softness, it was not to be wondered at that she rebelled so bitterly against this last, this uttermost sordid and squalid experience.

He did not go to see her very often. As he said to himself quite truly, he had no time for calling on people. But his real reason for staying away as he did was that he did not want to expose his affections again to capture, and he feared her power, even involuntarily, to annex them. It would be most unsettling if he again found

Nora-

himself thinking of her and looking at her with desire in his heart, and this was too critical a period in his life to justify his running the risk of such unsettlement. Even as it was, he had her for a while too much on his mind. Her failure to find work to do, her lack of occupation, troubled him. After much apparant wavering, she had decided that she did n't want to teach music or study stenography; perhaps she might trim hats. That was a thing that she thought she could do better than most people who tried to do it. It would be a bright and cheerful occupation, too, — getting hats ready for the spring season; she would enjoy working with colors. But she was easily discouraged, and because the first milliner's shop at which she volunteered her services was unable to make use of them, she promptly abandoned the idea of hat-trimming as an occupation. Besides, as she explained to Jerry, it was n't right for her to leave her mother alone too much; her mother was growing more and more feeble and needed her.

Not until the next autumn did Nora finally secure employment, and then it was desultory and not very remunerative. Twice a week she served as pianist for a children's dancing-class. Among the pupils was Patrick Maguire's little niece Laura O'Brien. Maguire came occasionally with his sister to look on, and was introduced to the dancing-teacher and to Nora, who was ignorant of what a privilege had been hers until afterwards, when the dancing-teacher enlightened her. Nora at once grasped an idea. Patrick Maguire was a power, a political power. Everybody knew that in some mysterious way he had but to command and his bidding was done. He could get Dave pardoned if he chose to. She must improve her acquaintance with Patrick Maguire; she must win his friendship and sympathy and prevail on him to use his influence in Dave's behalf.

She did not think it worth while to confide this brilliant inspiration to Jerry. Fortune favored her intentions; one day when she was the first to arrive at the hall, Patrick Maguire came without his sister, leading his niece by the hand. Mrs. O'Brien, it appeared, was not well; — no, nothing serious, thank you, just a bad cold; and as Laura had wanted to come, he had volunteered to bring her. Nora agreed that it would have been the greatest pity if the little girl had stayed away — she was such a good little dancer — one of those that Nora liked especially to watch. It was quite unusual for a child so young to show such a sense of time; she must be very musical. Mr. Maguire thought likely; she had never taken any lessons. Nora suggested that she sit down at the piano and try a little fingering; the young lady, in an amiable frame of mind after so much flattering, was nothing loath, and almost immediately won surprised, enthusiastic admiration for her natural talent, her manner of touching the keys, the tone that she produced — it was almost as if she had an instinct for the instrument. What a satisfaction to be such a child's music teacher! Patrick Maguire beamed and nodded his approval of such appreciation.

"You really think she's something remarkable?" he asked.

"Think!" exclaimed Nora. "All I can say is, I'd rather teach that child than any ten ordinary children.

I know what I'm talking about," she added. "I've studied both piano and voice at the Conservatory for four years. I always thought that if I could find just the right kind of beginner I'd love to teach."

Mr. Maguire made no response to that, and Nora had a fear that her remark had lacked subtlety. But at the next meeting of the dancing-class he approached her with the proposal that she had longed yet hardly dared to hear.

"I've talked things over with my sister," he said. "She wants to know if you'd be willing to come to the house a couple of times a week and give our little girl lessons on the piano."

"Why, Mr. Maguire!" exclaimed Nora. "How did you ever think of such a thing! Of course I'd love to do it! Why, I never had the least idea of being asked. I know I shall be so proud of my little pupil some day — shan't I, Laura dear?"

She caressed the child affectionately, and the child looked up at her with a serene, self-confident smile.

In her heart Nora felt a little ashamed of her subterfuge. But, as she said to herself, who would n't be just as disingenuous, scheming, and tricky as necessary to get a brother out of prison — a brother unjustly sentenced for twenty years?

How she was going to accomplish her purpose she did n't yet know; but already she felt certain that Patrick Maguire would be her tool.

XXVIII

JUST what burden Nora had taken upon herself in engaging to give music lessons to Laura O'Brien she very
soon learned. The child, so far from proving a prodigy
of promise, revealed a singular inaptitude and a disposition, after the first novelty of interest wore off, frequently sullen and at best indifferent. To teach a stupid
pupil is a supportable trial, one of the commonest, endured creditably by quite unheroic persons; but to maintain the pretense, against all the evidence of one's senses
and the conviction of one's spirit, that the dullest of
scholars is brilliantly endowed and is making extraordinary progress — that was the task that Nora had
recklessly assumed and that grew daily more oppressive. Either Mrs. O'Brien or Patrick Maguire — and
sometimes both of them — sat within hearing of the
lesson; and Nora soon wondered at the blindness to
obvious facts that maternal and avuncular affection
could engender — wondered at it, was irritated by it, and
grateful for it. Without its assistance she could never
have carried through her part; it seemed almost right
to trade upon such serene, complacent ignorance; the
only thing that was really wrong was having to submit
to such a strain upon the temper. Always to be pleasant,
encouraging, and flattering, even when she wanted to
scold and slap, was humiliating to her spirit and de-

tracted from her sense of personal dignity. But she kept
her great aim always before her, and knew that to accomplish it she must win the liking of Patrick Maguire.
And to do that she must always be nice to the little
girl, even in the child's most detestable moments, and
she must never tell the truth about her.

Finding the man so gullible caused her both to like
him and to be contemptuous of him. He was both a
nicer and a stupider person than she had supposed one
of such political power could possibly be. Men were
queer creatures to let themselves be bossed by that
kind of a person. Boss — yes, that was the word usually
applied to Patrick Maguire. She knew he deserved the
name, because he sat at home and had men come to see
him — policemen, tough-looking, roughly dressed men,
and sometimes well-dressed men too — she saw them
all when they passed the open door of the parlor where
she sat giving the lesson. Then the door of Patrick
Maguire's little room at the end of the hall, where he
was an unseen auditor, would be closed, and — if Mrs.
O'Brien was not somewhere about the house listening
— Nora's manner could relax. She was careful, though,
never to let it collapse; Laura, even though feeling
resentful at times of the inexplicable alteration in treatment, never had any grievance to treasure up and make
a ground of complaint.

When Nora knew that Maguire was at home and
unoccupied with callers, she would finish the instruction
period with a singing lesson — which always meant that
by way of illustration she would sing a song to her
pupil. She did not confine herself to songs of a nursery

or juvenile character; they were such songs as "Father O'Flynn," "Kathleen Mavourneen," and "The Wearing of the Green." They would draw Maguire from his retreat as a hurdy-gurdy draws a child; he would come in and seat himself to listen, and at the end express his satisfaction and his hope that Laura would some time learn to sing like that. Then Nora tried omitting this feature of the lesson; and promptly the pupil's uncle appeared and asked her as a special favor if she wouldn't sing something before she went home. He listened with rapt attention to the old Irish melodies. Nora spent a considerable part of the interval between lessons in committing to memory and practicing other Irish songs, of a kind likely to please his taste rather than her own.

"Great! Great!" Patrick Maguire would exclaim, slapping his knee. "Say, Mrs. Corcoran, won't you give us that again?" And when she had complied, he would be likely to say, "I can't sing a note, but just to hear you, Mrs. Corcoran, makes me feel there's music in my soul."

It was inevitable that, having been first interested in the singing, he should next become interested in the singer. Nora had fully determined that this should result. When he began to escort her home after the lessons, she felt that they were approaching a basis on which she would be able to negotiate with him. But she was going to do nothing prematurely; she was going to be sure that the shock of surprise and disappointment would not flatten out the wave of sympathy. Besides, she realized that an application for pardon could hardly be considered until Dave had served a term proportionate to the offense which he had confessed. Perhaps by the next spring or summer, when he had been in prison a year and a half, it might be safe to make the effort. She thought that a year and a half would not seem an inadequate term for attempted robbery. Until that sufficient period of penance should expire she would abstain from any appeals; she would devote the interval to strengthening her hold upon Patrick Maguire's interest.

It had been a long time since she had been disposed to make herself as charming as she could. Now she recovered much of her old pleasure in exercising that facility. She flattered Patrick Maguire on his own account as shamelessly as she flattered him and Mrs. O'Brien about Laura. She had been hearing about Patrick Maguire — so it seemed to her — almost ever since she could remember. How then did it happen he was such a young-looking man? And so good-natured looking too? She always had thought of a political boss as a man who looked like this — and she thrust out her lower jaw, drew down the corners of her mouth, and swaggered back and forth across the room in an absurdly truculent manner.

Laura backed against the wall and looked awed; Maguire passed from a broad grin into a shout of laughter.

"Come down here, Maggie; come down here and look at this!" he called; and when Mrs. O'Brien appeared in the doorway he said to Nora, "Come now, Mrs. Corcoran, give it to us again."

"Oh, I could n't," Nora protested. "I was just being silly, Mrs. O'Brien."

"Go on, go on," urged Maguire. "It's her idea of what a political boss should be — the way she thinks I ought to look. Let's have it again now."

So Nora, with some reluctance, performed for Mrs. O'Brien's benefit, and Mrs. O'Brien was as entertained as her brother.

"You've got a comical way with you, Mrs. Corcoran, there's no doubt about it," she said. "To think you should ever have thought Patrick was that kind of a fellow!"

Nora was relieved that her conception aroused in Mrs. O'Brien amusement rather than hostility. She was still further relieved by other evidence, as time went on, that her increasing intimacy with Maguire was not disapproved by his sister. Having expected that Mrs. O'Brien would discourage the growth of social intercourse between them, she was somewhat puzzled as well as gratified by the woman's failure to display jealousy, or even vigilance. In fact, it could not escape Nora's notice after a while that as soon as Laura's lesson was at an end, Mrs. O'Brien usually had some mission that took her from the house, while Patrick Maguire continued to sit in the parlor and insist on being amused. If it had not seemed too incredible, Nora would have been disposed to think that Mrs. O'Brien was trying to make a match. But that was preposterous. It was inconceivable that Patrick Maguire's sister should be planning measures which, if successful, would either dispossess her of a comfortable home or at the least deprive her of the authority which she had long enjoyed in her brother's house.

So Nora concluded that she received such marked consideration only because Mrs. O'Brien had decided it was perfectly safe to let her have it, and because both mother and uncle were sincerely grateful for her recognition of Laura's extraordinary qualities.

One day when Maguire had chosen to walk with her after the lesson, they met Jerry Donohue. He saluted, looking straight at her and ignoring Maguire. Nora was rather pleased that Jerry should have seen her in such company. He had not been very attentive to her of late, and it would n't be at all a bad thing if some little jealous apprehensiveness should stir within him.

She felt a slightly vengeful satisfaction when he called on her the next day. Her mother was in the bedroom, lying down, so there was no particular reason why he should have talked so stiffly and formally as he did. About Dave and how handsomely the warden spoke of him, about the weather and how he enjoyed now being on duty at dawn, for he had heard a robin sing only day before yesterday in the park — and then abruptly — "I saw you walking with Patrick Maguire yesterday."

"Oh, yes," said Nora. "I walk with him quite often." After a pause, as she did not want to punish him too severely, she added, "I give his little niece music lessons, and sometimes, if he's going down street, he walks along with me. He's quite interesting."

"I have no doubt he would be if he was to tell all he knows," replied Jerry.

"He's very pleasant," said Nora. "Not at all uppish. And he's very nice with his folks."

Jerry made no response; his expression was glum enough to correspond with his thoughts. So she was getting ready to make a fool of herself over another scoundrel. And this time over a man who, if he had not actively connived at her brother's unjust conviction, had allowed his influence to be used to Dave's disadvantage. For a moment Jerry had an impulse to tell her this, but he was held back by the knowledge that if she called on him for proof he could not substantiate his statements. Although he was morally sure that Maguire had been at least a passive agent in the plot against Dave, he could convince no one of it who was disposed to disbelieve it. If he warned Nora against Maguire, she would probably think he was actuated by jealousy.

A twofold pride kept him silent. He would not speak against Maguire, lest she impute a mean motive to the speech; he would not speak for himself, because he was in no position to ask any girl to marry him; he could not see that he would ever be in a position to ask any girl to marry him. It happened to be one of those days when bills had come in and the cost of living for five people seemed almost more than he could bear.

Such thoughts were not of a kind to make a man hold his head up; and Jerry was unconscious how closely Nora was watching him.

"Jerry," she said in a wistful voice, "do you ever think much of what life might have been for us if — if the Purroy Works had gone on just the same as always?"

"No," he answered, and he did not mean to be cruel. "I find plenty to think of with life as it is."

"Yes, but don't you ever like to imagine things, Jerry?"

"Not that sort of thing. What's the use, when you're hungry, of imagining a dinner?"

"It might make you enjoy it all the more when you sat down to it."

"It might," admitted Jerry thoughtfully. "It might. But if the best that's ahead of you is a stand-up feed at a lunch-counter — how about it then?"

"I don't see why anybody should feel so hopeless as that."

Jerry was not stupid; he knew that she was going as far as she could in order to give him encouragement; she was trying to tell him, without being quite unwomanly, that whatever her acts had been, her feeling for him was still what she had once declared. But instead of being transported with elation, he was sensible of embarrassment and restraint — of a desire to stop her before she should go further, to stop her without meeting her halfway. He was still susceptible to her charm, but he was less sure of her character; and he had been sufficiently ripened by experience to know now that, though charm is a delightful and desirable quality in a wife, it is the greediest quicksand for happiness if not ribbed with sturdier traits. In the readjustment of values that two years had caused in Jerry's life, Nora no longer held the place that she had once occupied; that nature and circumstance would unite to raise her to it again, Jerry would himself have liked to be assured. For he had sentiment as well as common sense; if he could, indeed, recapture the full emotion of those past days and if then he could be free to act upon his impulses, how bright the world would seem!

Nora shed tears of resentment and humiliation after he had gone. She had virtually offered herself to him, and he had virtually spurned her. And now, perversely enough, it appeared to her that she loved him more than she had ever loved him — just because he had become strong enough and hard enough to treat her so!

XXIX

KATE PUTS UP HER HAIR: CLARA ARMSTRONG HAS
INCREASED HER KNOWLEDGE OF THE WORLD

GOING home from his interview with Nora, Jerry was
not very comfortable in mind. He had been less considerate of her feelings than he had ever been before,
and salutary though such treatment might be, he found,
after administering it, that his conscience troubled him.
She had been trying to be cheerful and he had managed to depress her spirits. That struck him now as almost inexcusable.

But it was irritating that with her talent and education she should be willing to drift as she was doing;
and it was even more exasperating that after the experience she had been through she should be so careless
in her choice of friends. Maguire's reputation was no-
toriously bad — except so far as women were concerned;
Jerry did not know what it might be in respect to them.
To be making the weekly or daily music lesson, which-
ever it was, a stepping-stone to friendly relations with
such a character seemed to indicate an incapacity for
values, a singular frivolity, a complete failure to have
learned by experience. She was as charming, as appealing as ever — and evidently as much in need of
protection. She was not the sort of woman made to
stand on her own two feet. He chafed at her short-
comings the more because he was not in a position to
guard her against the consequences of them.

On arriving at home, Jerry walked in upon a tableau, especially arranged for him because from the window Peter had seen him coming down the street. At first Jerry could not make out just what was the matter; the family were all placed round on chairs in the sitting-room, looking at him expectantly, with mirth and interrogation in their eyes. His mother sat in the middle of the room, with Peter on one side of her and Betty on the other, and their faces seemed almost to dance as they looked at him. He turned to Kate for explanation; and then, though she sat with her head down, very demurely mending stockings, he saw that she was quite a different Kate from the one he knew.

"Hello!" he cried. "Why, you've gone and put your hair up!"

Then they all laughed, as if there were something humorous about either the remark or the discovery. Kate laughed too as she lifted a rosy face and shining eyes.

"Does it make me look quite old, Jerry?"

"I should say so. Stand up and turn round, so that I can see you. — Yes, there —" as Kate obediently stood and turned before him. "You're dressed like a young lady too — not a little girl any more at all. Do you feel as different as you look?"

"No; only a little shy at having people think I've changed."

"The change is very becoming, so you need n't feel shy."

"Oh! Do you really like it, Jerry?"

"Yes, very much."

"Is n't that nice! Now I shan't feel half so shy about showing myself at school like this to-morrow."

"Of course you won't. Why, all the boys will be interested and all the girls will be jealous."

"If I thought that — But you see, Jerry, lots of the other girls have put their hair up, so I don't believe anybody will be much surprised."

Jerry smiled at her willful rejection of his little compliment. Her way of turning it off was rather clever too — so very innocent.

After supper Jerry had an hour before he had to go on duty; he took his place in the sitting-room with the rest of the family and began to review his notes on Blackstone. His mother was busy with her knitting; the others were studious as usual. Looking up from his notes from time to time and trying to fix them in his memory, Jerry found Kate's altered appearance an obstacle to thought. She sat where the light from the lamp fell full upon her hair, and until this moment he had never appreciated what beautiful hair it was. When it had been in a pigtail it had never displayed the sheen, the variety of light and color that glanced and sparkled from it now. He had always thought of it as just brown hair, and here he was discovering under the lamplight that it was red and gold and coppery as well, with waves and curls in it that he had never suspected. And now that it was all rolled up above her neck he was discovering for really the first time what a pretty neck she had. On the whole, he was discovering for the first time that she was quite grown up.

She had her head industriously bent while he watched

her; she was writing with pencil on a tablet held in her lap. Once she looked up as if to invoke an idea and encountered Jerry's eyes. She blushed and smiled, a deprecating smile that seemed to say, "Don't think I'm any different, please don't." Jerry's smile in response must have been reassuring, for in another moment her head was bent again and the pencil was traveling steadily back and forth across the page.

By nine o'clock Peter and Betty had been sent off to bed; Mrs. Donohue was yawning and dozing over her knitting, and it was time for Jerry to start on his patrol. When he rose, Kate gathered up her papers and rose too.

"My goodness, child, I wish you did n't have to be going out at this hour of the night!" It was the unvarying remark that Mrs. Donohue at this hour every evening addressed to her son. "I think I'll have to be going to bed; I do seem that drowsy." This also was as unvarying as a ritual.

The proceedings that followed had the ritual quality. Jerry and Kate moved certain chairs, clearing a considerable area in front of what appeared to be a tall oak wardrobe. Then Jerry pressed a spring in this piece of furniture, and the whole front of it descended majestically into the cleared space and revealed itself as a bed, all made up and ready to be slept in. Kate patted and poked the pillows, Jerry kissed his mother, and Mrs. Donohue said, "Dear me, Kate, I hate to be driving you to the kitchen with your studies. Don't sit up too long, will you?"

All these things took place as regularly as nine o'clock in the evening came round.

JERRY

On his way to the police station Jerry met four persons marching abreast, with arms linked together. The two on the flanks were young men of a tough and rakish type; the outside one gave place to Jerry grudgingly and defiantly. Their companions were a young woman about whose character there could be no question, and another young woman whom in the moment of passing Jerry recognized as the older Armstrong girl.

In that moment the Lesbian said, with a caressing intonation, —

"You're not going home yet, are you, dear?"

Replying with a cackle of laughter, Clara Armstrong chanted in a vinous voice, —

> "'Oh, we won't go home till morning,
> Till daylight does appear.'"

Jerry continued on his way, reflecting that Clara Armstrong, as well as Kate, seemed suddenly to have grown up.

XXX

THE longer that Nora postponed speaking to Maguire
about her brother, the more difficult it seemed to become. Several times she went to his house fully determined, if there was a favoring opportunity after the
lesson, to make her plea; indeed, she had rehearsed it
even to the inflections of her voice. Yet when the favoring opportunity arrived, her tongue clove to her mouth.

She was n't sure just why it was so impossible to speak.
Partly, of course, as she admitted to herself, it was pride
that balked her intention. It was harder to make the
disclosures about herself and Dave than it would have
been when Maguire was merely an employer, uninspired
with any special feeling of friendship. Whether he would
suspect the ulterior motive that had animated her or not,
he would be sure to think the less of her when he learned
just who she was. She was extremely reluctant to do
anything that might cause her to lose caste in an admirer's eyes.

There was another reason too, perhaps just as valid.
For Dave's sake she wished not to speak until absolutely
the most propitious moment had arrived. Once she
had spoken, if she failed to move Maguire, there was
no other resource; as long as she had not spoken, hope
flourished. Even when opportunity seemed to be favor-

ing, an instinct of prudence kept admonishing her, "Wait. It may yet be better."

But unexpectedly, most unexpectedly, the time came when it seemed that she must put her fortune to the touch.

She came one day in late April to give Laura her lesson; it was a day of balmy south wind and warm sunshine, and as she stepped along she was feeling unwontedly sanguine and happy. Surely she would be able to set her brother free; once people understood, they were ready to do what was right. She must speak to Mr. Maguire soon — perhaps this very day. A bright new ribbon tastefully arranged upon her old hat, indeed transforming the old hat, fortified her confidence and increased her courage.

With Laura she was patient, gentle, good-humored, even though the child was more trying than usual. The reek of a pipe permeated the house; no doubt somewhere Maguire was listening.

At the end of the lesson he appeared in the doorway, bearing in his hand, not a pipe, but a bouquet of mayflowers. He presented them to Nora with a certain ponderous courtesy.

"Oh!" said Nora. "Thank you. Are n't they lovely!"

She fastened them in her belt; meanwhile, Maguire observed, —

"Spring. They look springy. Nice day, don't you think, for an automobile ride?"

"A perfectly wonderful day for it," Nora agreed, hardly daring to think this was an invitation.

"I've got a new car; it's to be brought round in a

few minutes. You might come out and try it with me."

"Oh, I'd love to," said Nora.

"Can I come too, Uncle Pat?" asked Laura.

"Not to-day; your mother wants you upstairs. — Here — wait" — as Laura's expression became more ominous — "look here what I'm going to give you." He put his hand in his pocket and drew forth some coins. "You can have 'em if you don't make a fuss. And I'll take you out riding later to-day, maybe, if you're a good girl."

Somewhat appeased by the twofold bribe, Laura consented to go upstairs.

The car was large and luxurious. Nora in all her life had never ridden in anything so magnificent; she said so, and Maguire seemed pleased by the tribute. Neither had she ever been wrapped in such a costly fur coat as that which Maguire borrowed from his sister for her comfort.

"We'll run out along the river road; what do you say?" asked Maguire.

Nora assented, and then, a few minutes later, when she discovered just what route Maguire was taking, sat nervously rigid. They were going close by the penitentiary. Maguire pointed it out to her.

"State prison — got twelve hundred convicts locked up in there. Interesting place to see — take you over it some time. The warden is a friend of mine; he'll show you everything."

Nora's response was inarticulate. She felt as if she might be cringing and cowering in her seat; she hardly dared to steal a glance either at the building or at Maguire. If she had n't the courage now to tell him the truth, would she ever have the courage? She could not bring herself to the point; she felt miserably that she was disloyal to her brother, and her heart yearned to him, poor prisoner in a cell while she was speeding by, only a few yards from him, ecstatically free.

They left the gloomy building behind, and Nora had not spoken. She continued silent, wondering how she would ever dare to speak. Maguire, too, after pointing out a few other objects of interest, lapsed into silence.

When they had gone about fifteen miles from the city, they came to a park of woodland with an arched entrance that bore the name "Silver Grove."

"I always give a couple of picnics here every summer," said Maguire. "Want to come in and look round?"

He ran the car into the park and left it near the entrance. He and Nora walked along a woodsy path that led past a pavilion for dancing.

"Great place for the young folks," said Maguire. "Every picnic I give I feel I'm helping along some young couple. Gives 'em a chance to get acquainted. Many's the pair that's come here, you might say single, and gone away engaged."

"It's a funny thing you've never done it yourself, Mr. Maguire."

"Well, I never seemed to meet up with any one that quite fell in with my ideas. I've always had tastes in advance, you might say, of them I was likely to see. — This field here is where they play baseball. Pretty soon now we'll see the river."

Nora was not especially eager to see the river. She hoped the conversation would return to the interesting channel which it seemed to have abandoned. She was quite curious to learn how much he did like her, why he paid her such marked attention; purely out of curiosity she would be glad to know.

They emerged from the woods upon a bluff overlooking the river, a broad, muddy stream that flowed between sloping farm lands and white villages that showed in glimpses among trees.

"This is where the boys like to take the girls and sit," said Maguire. "They get such a fine view. It kind of makes them feel romantic, I guess."

"It is a fine view," said Nora sedately, yet full of wonderment.

"We might sit down a few moments on this bench," suggested Maguire.

He led her to a bench between two pine trees.

"I'm mighty sorry," he said after an interval of silence, "that you won't be teaching Laura any more."

To Nora, who had been preparing herself for something embarrassing yet pleasant, the cruelty of this announcement seemed only less emphatic than its crudity. Bitter disappointment, injured vanity, the collapse of all the hopes that she had been building on what she had fondly deemed her success, caused the blood to rush to her cheeks and the tears to spring to her eyes. She struggled for self-control and forced back the tears before she spoke. Yet there was a tremor in her voice as she said: —

"I — I did n't know that Mrs. O'Brien does n't want me to go on."

"It is n't that, but you see my sister's going to move away. Going to Baltimore to live. Going to marry a lawyer there."

The explanation was balm to Nora's spirit. She expressed her interest.

"Yes," said Maguire, "it's kind of romantic. Jack Moriarty wanted to marry her long before ever she married Ed O'Brien. It was a toss-up which of the two she'd take. Then after Ed died, Jack Moriarty waited what you might call a decent interval, and asked her again. She thought, though, she could never marry a second time. But Moriarty has stuck to it, and at last she has given in. Well, he's a good fellow, and I can't help feeling glad for them both, though of course it's going to be kind of lonesome for me."

There was an appreciable pause, and then he said slowly and distinctly, —

"Unless you could be persuaded to marry me."

Faced thus abruptly with the knowledge that she had been rather hoping to get at, Nora found herself at an utter loss.

"Why, Mr. Maguire, I never thought of such a thing." She glanced from him to the ground in honest embarrassment. "I — I don't know what I can say — except that I don't see how I can — and, anyway, I'm sure you could n't want it really."

"Now don't you make any mistake about that, Mrs. Corcoran. I'm accustomed to knowing what I want. I've considered this step more than a little. In fact,

I've talked it over with my sister. She feels just as I do, that it would be a fine thing for me. There's no manner of doubt in my own mind about that."

"I'm sure you just feel you need somebody to look after you when your sister goes, Mr. Maguire. I know that the thing for you to do is just to hire some good competent housekeeper — somebody that will be sure to make you comfortable. I never could; I'm no sort of a housekeeper."

"I can hire a housekeeper all right if it's necessary, but that ain't the point. I want to live with you, husband and wife. I've sat back and waited till I should see just the right woman. And you're it. I knew it pretty near the first time I heard you sing. You'd always pleased me, but then you got right a-hold of me. So you need n't to think I'm just asking you because I'm in need of a housekeeper."

"But you must have often seen women you might have married —"

"Not any I wanted to marry. It's this way, Mrs. Corcoran; as I said to you, I'm in advance of my friends in my tastes. It's only a high-toned woman that I could think of marrying, and I've not been by way of meeting high-toned women very often. I know one when I see her, now I tell you. And you're the highest-toned woman I ever knew."

Nora was touched by that crude compliment. It pleased her to feel that he regarded her as an ideal character, who was to be won only upon the loftiest ground — was not to be influenced by a consideration of the material advantages that he could bestow. If he viewed her in such a light — well, for once she would try to act in a manner befitting an ideal character. And without waiting to think twice and be afraid, she said: —

"Mr. Maguire, I'm sure you would n't feel as you do if you knew more about me — if you knew who I am. My brother is Dave Scanlan; he's serving a twenty-year sentence for murder and robbery. My husband was cruel to me and I left him, and my father, half crazed by what had happened to Dave and me, shot and killed my husband and himself."

"Scanlan!" muttered Maguire, knitting his brows. "Killed a storekeeper — was that it?"

"He did n't kill him," declared Nora. "I'm sure he did n't. There was another man with him, a man named Schlupfe, and Dave made a confession and told how Schlupfe had arranged the plot to rob the store, and how Schlupfe had done the shooting; but the jury would n't believe all that Dave said. I know he was telling the truth. Dave would n't — he could n't commit a murder. If the jury really believed he did it, they'd have found him guilty in the first degree, for according to the story Dave told there was nothing to excuse the shooting. And the judge would have had him put to death or sentenced to prison for life, at least, instead of for twenty years. But the man that was really guilty had a Congressman to defend him, and he got some witnesses to cast some doubt on Dave's story, — which was a perfectly straight story just the same, — and so the jury let this man off and put the whole thing on Dave — though if they'd had real convictions, as I've said, they'd have had the courage of them and brought in a first-degree verdict. Dave's lawyer felt there was some kind of political influence helping the guilty man — getting a Congressman to defend him and all. And I've been trying ever so long to get my courage up so that I could tell you all this, and ask you if you would n't look into Dave's case; and then, when you found how innocent of the murder he was, I thought maybe you'd be willing to use your influence and get him pardoned."

Once she had started on her speech she went ahead with it almost breathlessly; it was not for nothing that she had rehearsed it so often, and the declaration that Maguire had made to her supplied her with the confidence that she needed in order to put all the art of which she was capable into her appeal. Her voice, her eyes, her very attitude, as she sat with her arms straight at her sides and her hands grasping the edge of the bench, were of the most touching supplication. She could tell, even while she spoke, that she was making an impression; she could recognize the softness of pity in Maguire's eyes. She was unaware, however, of the truly magical impression that she was making — unaware that she had never before presented to the man so completely seductive and beguiling an aspect. When his emotions were engaged, he was but a soft-hearted wretch, and to see that lovely, high-toned lady in such distress, and to know that in enlisting Maxwell's services for Schlupfe he had remotely connived at the causes of that distress, made him feel all choky and pulpy inside.

"Don't cry, don't cry, Mrs. Corcoran," he besought her, for her eyes began to swim in tears. "I'll do what

I can; sure I will. It seems to me, now I think of it, I heard at the time that your brother got kind of a raw deal. But honest to God, I don't know what use I can be now, for the governor is of the wrong party and he'll not be likely to listen to me at all. Next autumn we'll have an election, and I'm hoping to get in a man I can do business with; and if I can — well, I'll do what I can, you may be sure of that, Mrs. Corcoran."

"Thank you, Mr. Maguire. I did n't realize about the governor; I thought you could always get what you wanted, no matter who was governor."

"Listen to that now!" Maguire laughed ruefully. "And it's what a good many think too — as if there was some arrangement by which I could always be pulling wires at the Capitol. But you may be sure I'll do all I can. And now, Mrs. Corcoran, do you realize what you've just said?"

"No; what was that, Mr. Maguire?"

"Well, that you have a feeling I'm always sure to get what I want. I suppose now that means you're ready to give it to me?"

"I guess you don't want it any longer, Mr. Maguire."

"Sure I do. Why not?"

"Considering all you've found out about me that you did n't know before."

"A strange thing it would be if that could make any difference. I'm asking you just the same and a little more so; Mrs. Corcoran, won't you be my wife?"

"I never thought to marry again, Mr. Maguire. I certainly never thought to marry you. So I don't see how I can say all at once."

"My sister never thought to marry again, but she's going to do it."

"Yes, but it's a man she came near marrying in the first place — one she may always have had a tender feeling for. And I've sometimes thought, if I ever did marry again, it might be such a man."

Consternation manifested itself on Maguire's plump face.

"You don't mean, Mrs. Corcoran, that there's somebody you're in love with?"

"Oh, no, I would n't say that. And I don't know that he has any thoughts of me any more. It may just have crossed my mind; that's all."

The tense expression of anxiety on Maguire's face relaxed, although his eyes remained clouded with dissatisfaction.

"Who is he? What sort of a job has he?" he asked.

"Oh, I could n't say, Mr. Maguire; it would be too mortifying to me if I told you and then he never took any interest in me after all."

"It's not in nature that should happen. You've put a great fear in my heart, Mrs. Corcoran. Come, now, when I'm telling you that you're the very soul I crave for, has it no meaning to you?"

"It has, indeed, and I don't know how it is you could ever have come to have such thoughts about me, Mr. Maguire. And I appreciate them, I do, indeed. More I can't say now; I can't say yes to you, and I would n't say no."

"If you were to stop calling me Mr. Maguire and were

to call me Patrick or even Pat, it might make you feel more as if you might marry me."

"I don't know as I could be so daring. But I'll try, Patrick."

"By the same token, it might be a help to me if I was to call you by some other name than Mrs. Corcoran."

"You might try Nora."

"The finest name that was ever given to a girl baby. Does this other man call you by it, Nora?"

"Yes, he does."

"Oh, my God, but I know what it is to be jealous!" cried Maguire.

Her failure to yield him immediately a favorable answer served only to intensify and inflame his passion. The intimation that she might perhaps be unattainable made her seem tenfold more desirable. His prayers were moving in their urgency, almost embarrassing; and yet he did not commit the vulgarity of spreading before her all that he could offer as a bribe. She was conscious of the reticence and respected him for it. He was trying to win her without having recourse to his material advantages. It was himself, not his possessions, that he was trying to present to her as worthy to be lived with. "Often and often I've thought what a grand thing it would be for me," he said, "to be going to operas and such with you, and have you teach me all about them. Often and often I've thought how grand it would be to have you taking me round and showing me what I ought to think about things."

He ran his car slowly back to the city, pleading with

her all the way. When they were passing the penitentiary he said: —

"Whether you decide to say no or yes, Nora, I'll do what I can for your brother. Honest to God I will. I kind of mind hearing that he had a raw sort of a deal."

Indeed, he was feeling bad about Dave; he had done a service for a henchman quite blithely, indifferent to the injustice that might flow from it.

Nora, unaware that his conscience had reason for being uneasy, almost could say yes to him after that speech. Almost, but not quite; for although she liked him now better than she had ever done before, he was n't, after all, Jerry Donohue.

XXXI

THE PRACTICE OF VARIOUS ARTS: WITH THE
PRODUCTION OF THE USUAL RESULT

LOOKING back upon her talk with Maguire, Nora felt
that she had every reason to be satisfied. First and
most important of all, she had achieved what she had
planned to achieve. Maguire's intervention on behalf
of Dave was as good as an accomplished fact; he would
do his utmost, whether his suit prospered or not. Certain
of that, Nora remained cool to his wooing. Having
married one man without loving him, she could hardly
imagine herself committing a similar blunder with another.

The truth was, as she acknowledged to herself, she
cared more for Jerry than she had done before her
marriage. She was unhappy because he came so seldom
to see her; still more unhappy did each visit make her,
because he never intimated the least desire to revive the
old relation.

Almost against her will she could not help showing
him sometimes how much she cared.

"You're so dull, Jerry," she complained on one occasion. "I believe you come to see me as a duty, just as
you might occasionally come to see mother if I were n't
here. Don't you get any more pleasure out of it than
that?"

"I suppose I am dull," he admitted. "You see, I 'm
planning to take the bar examinations in the autumn,

and I don't think about much else than problems of law."

"Of course that would make anybody dull," said Nora. "Don't let yourself get all dried up, will you, Jerry?"

"Oh, I dare say once I'm a lawyer I shall be as chipper as a lark," Jerry answered. "I'll be walking the street with a green bag in my hand, all stuffed out with papers and documents of the highest importance. And I'll have appointments with clients for every hour of the day, and an office with a mahogany desk and a telephone. — Nora," he said, suddenly changing his tone, "a dozen times a day it comes over me, the foolishness of it. Me trying to be a lawyer, and what good will it do me when I am one?"

"I'm sure you'll have clients and a big practice somehow," Nora said. "I don't know what will start people coming to you, but they'll come."

Then, just as she thought she had got him in a confidential, even a confessional mood, the most promising of moods, he disappointed her by rising and saying, "Well, I just dropped in on my way to the library, and I must be off to my studies."

"Oh, Jerry, don't go. Please don't go. If you only knew how much it means to me to see you!"

"That can't be, Nora."

"But it is. I have so little in life that's interesting and amusing; your visits are better than anything else. And you come so seldom and stay such a little while!"

She could be pathetic without sacrificing any of her charm. She leaned over the back of a tall chair and looked up at him with eyes the more lovely for being so appealing. The pose accentuated and made more alluring the pretty lines of her neck, the soft curves of her arms and shoulders and bosom, the warm color in her cheeks.

"Nora, I don't want to think about you too much," Jerry said. He stood with his hands behind his back, trying to harden himself against the impulses of the flesh; she was so pretty, so appealing. "If I thought about you now as I used to, it would only be interfering with my work, and it would do neither of us any good."

"Oh, Jerry, it would do me good if I could feel you thought about me that way again. Even if there was no chance of our getting married for years and years."

"Your marrying made a difference in my feeling, Nora. If I saw you a great deal and thought about you a great deal, I might want to marry you, just as I once did. But I'd rather not want that, and so I don't let myself think about you."

"Why don't you want to marry me, Jerry?"

"I'm in no position to think of marrying."

"Still you might *want* to, even if you could n't do it."

The reproach was half smiling, half serious.

"I'm afraid I should want to, and my reason tells me it would be a mistake. We'd not be likely to make each other happy."

"Why do you think that?"

"I could never feel sure of you, and I could n't be happy with a person I did n't feel sure of."

"Of course I don't wonder that you have that idea about me. But can't you see how it was, Jerry? Everything looked so hopeless, and I was foolish and believed that Charley Corcoran really cared for me. It seemed the easiest way out, and I was weak enough to take it. Don't you think that I've learned my lesson?"

"I can't help wondering. You're attractive, Nora, awfully attractive, but there's a question in my mind about you that never used to be there."

She flushed, but said humbly, tremulously, "What is that?"

"It's a question of your — your sturdiness. Whether you can be stanch and loyal to the things you believe in and the people you care for. It's just another way of questioning whether you have it in you really to believe in things or care for other people than yourself. It's not just your marriage that makes me wonder. It's the way you've treated Dave — so indifferent to him, as I look at it. And it's the way you seem not to have held steadily to any purpose or work in this last year and a half. Drifting, sort of — and tiring easily. — Well, you might tire easily of me. We might tire of each other."

"Oh, you're unjust to me; truly you are. I'm not indifferent about Dave — perhaps you'll know some time. And as for my not being true or loyal, Jerry, — that hurts, of course, but you have a right to say it. Drifting — perhaps I have been. But there's something you don't seem to understand — and I don't know how I can tell you."

"Never mind, Nora," Jerry said, trying to be sympathetic. "Don't feel that it's necessary to tell me anything."

"Oh, Jerry, how stupid you are!" Vexation was in

Nora's voice, and her eyes filled. "I *want* to tell you —
can't you see?"

"Oh, you want to," said Jerry, perplexed. "Well,
then, why don't you go ahead?"

"I will," she exclaimed, with sudden vehemence.
"Why am I drifting? What else does any woman do
who wants only one thing in life? What does any normal
woman do who's lonely and does n't have the life that
she craves? You reproach me with not having a purpose
in life; I suppose it's true. I have only desires and
longings, such as the normal woman has. A woman
can't have any special purpose in life unless her one big
woman's longing is fulfilled. At least I can't. You
would n't feel that I was drifting, that I had no purpose
in life, that I had no loyalty, if — if — No, you would n't,
Jerry."

She burst into tears, and flinging herself upon the
sofa, hid her face on her arms and sobbed.

Jerry stood aghast; then he came over and touched
her shoulder almost timidly.

"Don't, Nora, don't," he pleaded. "I did n't mean
to hurt your feelings; I did n't realize —" He kept his
hand on her shoulder. "Honestly, do you care for me so
much, Nora?"

"I never meant that you should know," she answered
through her sobs.

He bent and kissed her neck.

"Jerry, you must n't do that; you don't love me;
you've told me so."

"I have n't told you so," he said in a choking voice.
"Of course I love you."

[279]

Then Jerry was on his knees beside her, with his arms round her; she turned, showing him a face all lighted up with happiness, and while he kissed her he felt her straining him to her heart as she had never done before. And it gave him an emotion that he had never known before — of reckless exhilaration and brutality; while he crushed her in his arms she murmured in his ear a plea that intoxicated his whole spirit — "Love me, Jerry, oh, love me, love me."

"I love you," he answered. "Yes, I love you."

XXXII

MORNING THOUGHTS: A DISSERTATION ON LOYALTY

THE intoxication of rediscovered love carried Jerry through one evening. In the morning he awoke to feel only the shackles and the shame.

He was ashamed because he did not know whether he loved Nora or not; he was shackled by poverty and by duties if he loved her and by his word to her if he did n't. And in his slow dressing that morning, while he was lacing up his boots, and while he was fastening his high collar beneath his upstretched chin, he gloomily wondered why he had chosen so to complicate his life. It all seemed as unnecessary as it assuredly had been unpremeditated. A call that he had actually forced himself to make from a sense of duty — that it should have ended so! It was too astonishing.

He was conscious of a certain sense of relief as he reflected that in any event marriage was remote. And the moment that he began to feel relief because of that, a counteracting desire seized upon him. If he was bound to marry her anyway, he wanted to marry her now. Those kisses, that feeling of her body pressing against his and of her arms striving to hold him close and yet closer to her heart — they had roused the animal in him. He wanted more kisses, more embraces, and he wanted them passionately, without waiting.

At breakfast Kate tried, rather shyly, to enlist his interest. She asked him if he would do something for her, and with an effort at heartiness he answered, "Sure, I will. What's the big idea, Kate?"

Blushingly Kate explained that her graduation essay had been adjudged the best in the class and she had therefore been condemned to read it at the graduation exercises. And she wondered if Jerry would let her read it to him some time, and would criticize the way she did it.

"Of course, right now," said Jerry. "Only my criticism won't be worth much."

"It will be good practice for me to read it to you," said Kate. "For I shan't be any more afraid, reading it to the crowd, than I shall be, just with you."

"Afraid with me? Why?"

"Because I know it will seem awfully young to you, Jerry. You know so much and see so much, and I feel I'm very ignorant of life. And yet here I am, writing about it, and now I've got to read what I've written to a lot of people who know more than I do. That's why I feel that if I read it to you first I should n't so much mind the others."

"All right. Let's hear it."

Kate got out her manuscript and began to read. The subject of her paper was loyalty. It was a schoolgirl's dissertation, adorned with extracts from her favorite authors, and she read it with a schoolgirl's self-consciousness, hurrying a little over the passages that had caused her the deepest emotion. Her voice, usually tranquil, quivered a little under the stress of this disclosure of her thoughts; she did n't once lift her eyes from the page. Jerry watched her with an amused and affectionate interest; she sat with her neat little ankles crossed and her brown head bent over her manuscript, while with one hand she nervously kept gathering up and smoothing out a fold in her skirt. They were capable fingers that thus exercised themselves, and it was a pretty, well-shaped head that was bent over the manuscript, and the neat little ankles, now so sedately crossed, were often lively and twinkling enough.

"'We are loyal to our families, as a matter of course,'" read Kate. "'But there is a harder kind of loyalty that we must all try to achieve — the loyalty to ideas and ideals. If we do not achieve this loyalty, the caprice of the moment or the temptation of the hour may turn our steps forever from the path in which should lie the duty of a lifetime.' — Oh, Jerry," she exclaimed, "is it awfully silly? Don't you want to laugh?"

"No, not a bit. Quite the contrary."

"You mean you want to cry?"

"Now, Kate, go ahead and read your piece. I'm interested. I think it's fine."

So she continued: "'It is the readiness or failure to perform the nearest duties, to meet and master the obvious responsibilities, that is the test of loyalty. There is no real loyalty in one who shirks or evades. There is no real loyalty in one who is selfish. There is no real loyalty in one who shrinks from enduring or in case of need, giving pain. To every one probably must come some time a supreme test of loyalty, and only those will pass it who have borne themselves worthily in the daily little tests of loyalty. "To thine own self be true; thou canst not then be false to any man."'"

"By George, Kate, it's fine," said Jerry. "And you

doped it all out for yourself too. I don't see how you did it. Why, Socrates and Emerson have got mighty little on you."

"Oh, Jerry! No, but really — does n't it seem sort of — sort of pretentious and — well, young?"

"Young!" exclaimed Jerry. "It sounded to me like the wisdom of the ancients — words that might be coming out of a long white beard. You must have regular genius."

Kate was, of course, pleased that Jerry should think so highly of her production, even though she knew that his praise was excessive.

"It's because in a way it sounds so very old that I think it is probably very young," she said critically.

"Well," Jerry answered, "it hits me where I live. It reads me a mighty good lesson."

"I guess you're just about the last person in the world that needs it. You could n't be disloyal if you tried, Jerry."

"Whether you're right on that point or not, you're sound on the general principles. It's a fine essay and you need n't feel a bit bashful about reading it."

After Kate had gone off to school, Jerry sat for a few moments meditating on her words of wisdom. They did not contribute to his happiness. That sentence about the temptation of the hour turning one away from the duty of a lifetime — was he to be a living witness to its truth? He did n't know, he really did n't know. Nora and her kisses and her clinging arms seemed even more compelling when he thought about them than when he was surrendered to them.

JERRY

It was an odd thing that Kate should have evolved those aphorisms so pat to his situation. It was an odd thing that she should have got hold of such ideas — that unsophisticated, inexperienced young girl. Yet the whole essay showed clearly that she was still living in an ideal world; in that way it was the work of a young girl, simple, shy, and believing.

Jerry reflected on the contrast between Kate and Nora. He could not imagine Kate talking to any man as Nora had talked to him the night before.

XXXIII

On the morning when Jerry was meditating upon the singular applicability of Kate's monitory words to his own predicament, Nora felt impelled by the exuberance of her spirits, her sense of success and satisfaction, to go shopping. She had a tidy little sum of money now in hand, and there could be no better way of spending it than in the purchase of summer clothes — and no more propitious moment. So, with a sunny April face well suited to the sunny April morning, she took her way towards Bilbow and Slosson's department store; and as she walked it was natural enough that she should review the various circumstances that contributed to her satisfaction.

Best of all, of course, was the fact that Jerry loved her again. She had n't realized quite how much she wanted him to recapture his old sensations — until she felt herself once again in his arms. Then she had been carried away by a wild ecstasy, a rapture like nothing that she had ever before known, like none that Jerry himself had ever before inspired. She wondered, as she thought about it, that she could look back on it so calmly, that she could be doing anything so prosaic a few hours after it as going downtown to buy a suit, that she should not be given over to a sort of holy rapture and contemplation, instead of quite cheerfully trotting upon her agreeable errand. Well, she supposed that was the way of all true and passionate love — ecstasy and rapture, contentment and placidity, ecstasy and rapture again, cycle after cycle. Certainly it was all pretty nice — nicer than she had ever ventured to hope it might be.

If only they could get married now, without any more waiting! It subdued her happiness a little to think that they could n't, to feel that they were still under restrictions and disabilities. They would at least have to wait until next year when the new governor — surely there must be a new governor! — would be inaugurated and Maguire could take measures for Dave's release. If Maguire should find that she was pledged to another man, he might lose some of his enthusiasm for setting Dave free. She supposed that until that had been accomplished she would have to dissemble her real feelings, she would have to let Maguire think there might be a chance, a slight chance. She hoped he would be content to persevere if it were explained to him that it was a very slight chance — for if he would n't, rather than run the risk of losing the advantage of his influence, she would have to let him think there was a pretty good chance. And it would be awfully trying to herself, as well as mean to him, to have to do that.

Well, she could manage with Maguire; it would be nothing but a prolonged flirtation at the worst, and many girls indulged in such pastimes and thought nothing of it. She was too conscientious. Anyway, Maguire was no young and tender innocent.

Nora put him and the next ten months hastily out of her thoughts and tried to plan what she and Jerry could do after the new governor had pardoned Dave. Why could n't they get married then? Suppose Jerry were to contribute half his wages to their expenses; she did n't know what his wages were, but she thought that probably half the amount added to what she already had would be enough for their needs. The other half he could devote to his mother and those children that he had taken in and made his wards. His mother had some money, Nora was sure; there was the house that she owned out in Millvale. Mrs. Donohue and those children could get along very comfortably, no doubt, on half of Jerry's wages.

Nora was thankful that her mother's infirmity of temper had grown less as her physical infirmity increased. She and Jerry could live in the same house together now quite comfortably. They even seemed to like each other.

Really, when one began to consider the situation and apply common sense and imagination to it, the solution was simple enough.

It was too bad, though, that it had be to delayed for a year.

She hoped Jerry would come and see her every day.

In Bilbow and Slosson's suit department she wavered between a gray suit and a blue. She tried on each, and in each was almost convinced by the admiration of the saleswoman.

"Goodness!" said that person. "If I only had you to show off my suits for me I could sell twice as many as I do. You've just the figure, and things look so stylish on you. We've got two women here to walk round and show off clothes, but they don't put them on with the style that you do."

"Would you really give me a chance to do it?" asked Nora.

"I'm not the boss, but I'd be glad to advise Mr. Stratton to give you a trial. You might find it tiresome."

"Oh, no, it would be lots of fun to walk round in one pretty thing after another. I think I'll keep this suit anyway. Suppose you take me to see Mr. Stratton now, so that he can see just how I would show off a new suit."

The saleswoman arranged the interview, which resulted in Nora's being engaged as a model for a month, to display spring and summer costumes. She carried herself well, she was good to look at, she wore the standard size, and she could put on almost any color; Mr. Stratton told her that there was no reason why she should n't have quite a career as a suit model.

Nora went home, wearing her new suit and happier even than she had been when she was anticipating its purchase. Everything seemed at last to be falling just right for her. This occupation that was to be hers for a month was the most congenial possible. It very likely would lead to a permanent and attractive position with Bilbow and Slosson, if she cared to have a permanent position. Jerry might call it drifting if he liked, but it was drifting to some purpose. She would save every penny that she earned; there would be the less excuse then for their not getting married just as soon as Dave was free.

Two days later Mrs. Donohue took Kate to Bilbow and Slosson's to buy a dress for the graduation exercises.

After accomplishing this, Mrs. Donohue, who had not yet grown too old to enjoy seeing the newest fashions in clothes, suggested that they go into the suit department and look round. So the bright-eyed little woman in the antiquated clothes and bonnet and the shy girl, who was painfully conscious that her own clothes were more serviceable than stylish, passed into the room where a lady all in lavender and carrying a lavender parasol strolled back and forth in front of some spectators who murmured their approbation as she passed.

"Land sakes! If it is n't Nora Scanlan!" exclaimed Mrs. Donohue under her breath. She made directly for Nora, and Kate, not knowing what else to do, yet extremely reluctant to intrude upon a person of such grandeur, followed at her heels.

If Nora was annoyed by the interruption, she did not betray the fact. She explained hastily that she had to show styles to the ladies seated on the bench, but she thought they would be going soon; she hoped Mrs. Donohue would wait round for a few minutes. This Mrs. Donohue was quite content to do; she and Kate drew back and looked on with admiration while Nora resumed her graceful promenade. There was something quite exquisite in the way she held her head and carried her parasol, and in the serene and becoming dignity of her gait.

"She wears those clothes just as if she'd been born to them," muttered Mrs. Donohue admiringly.

The prospective customers, though interested, failed to purchase, and presently Nora was at liberty. She came and talked with Mrs. Donohue and Kate; she had never met Kate before. Her pleasant manner, quite as much as her impressive costume, fascinated the young girl.

"I know Jerry will think it's just a butterfly's way of earning money," Nora said to Mrs. Donohue. "But it was the only thing that offered, and it's quite hard work really. You tell Jerry for me that I guess I'm on my feet as much as any policeman."

"Now do be careful and don't get all played out," urged Mrs. Donohue.

"Oh, I shan't. I love dressing up so much that I don't seem to get tired. And I do have to put on such queer clothes sometimes as well as such pretty ones. Yesterday I had to pretend I was at the seashore and I walked about for an hour or so in the most fetching bathing-suit."

"Nora!" Mrs. Donohue was obviously scandalized. "Well, I suppose they didn't let any men in to look at you."

"Oh, men are always allowed to come in. But it was a very proper bathing-suit. Just pretty, that's all. Tell Jerry, if he ever has a chance and feels brave enough, to drop in; I'm sure he'd like to see me in such wonderful clothes."

"Aren't you afraid they'll spoil you for anything ordinary?"

"Oh, no; wearing them is just a pastime; I don't feel the need of always wearing such things. But when you put them on, it's quite restful, even though you're on your feet all the time; somehow at once you have a fresh point of view, you feel like a different person."

The forewoman approached.

"Now, Mrs. Corcoran," she said, "if you'll put on the blue linen sport suit, toque with cornflower trimmings, white silk stockings, and white kids."

"Yes, Miss Harris." And then, as Nora was about to move away, she said to Mrs. Donohue, "Do tell Jerry to come and see me soon — not here; of course I was joking when I said that. But some evening."

Mrs. Donohue promised to give Jerry the message.

"Did n't you like her, Kate?" Mrs. Donohue asked, as she and Kate took their departure.

"Yes. And oh, is n't she pretty! Is n't she lovely to look at!"

Mrs. Donohue beamed at Kate's unaffected enthusiasm.

"She is. And it's a wonder, for it's a hard life that she's had, with enough in it to line a body with wrinkles. But I expect she's happy now, and that makes all the difference. No doubt Jerry will be telling us some day soon that he and Nora have got things all fixed up to get married."

"Oh!" said Kate, masking emotion behind an intonation of mere interest. "I did n't know."

"There's no reason why you should, for neither Jerry nor I have wanted to talk about it. He was always in love with Nora, and when she married Corcoran it was a great blow to him. Well, I guess it was a good lesson to her and made her realize what she might have had. I dare say she'll be all the better wife for Jerry because of it."

Kate agreed that it was quite likely. But thereafter

she was silent, as one would be who had been abruptly despoiled of all the pleasant filaments of hope and love and longing in which one's heart had been tenderly wrapped, and had seen this web of innocent desires torn and tossed aside, never again to make a nest for any heart.

XXXIV

MRS. DONOHUE gave Jerry a description at supper that
evening of Nora's grandeur.

"Walking along the Avenue you'll not meet anything
so stylish in a day's march," she avowed. "You have no
idea, Jerry, how those clothes set her off. Nora always
was a pretty girl, but — well, I wish you could see,
Jerry, how handsome she looked. Did n't she, Kate?"

"Yes," Kate answered. "She's awfully good-
looking."

"She wants you to come and see her," continued Mrs.
Donohue. "Do go and call on her some day soon at the
store. She's there every morning and afternoon, and
it's all right for men to go into that department. I
really think you'd be interested to see how she looks in
such clothes."

"I'd just as soon see her in her own clothes," Jerry
replied.

"Well, yes, I suppose you would," agreed his mother,
with a knowing little chuckle.

Kate sat with downcast eyes; she felt that she must
appear not to understand these half-hidden meanings.

Jerry turned the conversation away from Nora and
asked Kate if she had found a satisfactory graduation

dress. Oh, yes; and Kate tried to brighten and show gratitude for such interest — but how difficult to do when your heart is sore and you are hardening your will for a decision of the utmost importance to you and yours!

After supper she sent Peter and Betty into her room to study their geography and then to Jerry and his mother she said: —

"I feel as if we ought to be planning a little for the future."

"I'll bet you've got a real idea up your sleeve, Kate," said Jerry.

"It isn't much of an idea, but I feel it's almost time for me to do something. I think I should like to learn typewriting and shorthand, and some day be a stenographer. I don't know how long it would take, but maybe if I were to start in at the Young Women's Christian Association — they have a school of stenography there — by next spring I might be able to get a place in some business office. Don't you think so, Jerry?"

"Yes; but that's not what we're aiming at." There was an expression of concern in Jerry's eyes. "A person of your talent, Kate, — you've got to have more of a chance. You're going to the Women's College next fall; we don't mean to let you waste your energy in pounding a typewriter."

"I'll try not to waste it. But you see, Jerry, just as soon as I can I want to feel that you and your mother are free of the responsibility for us."

"Nonsense, Kate. Why, we're just one family now. You mustn't talk like that."

"Yes, I must, Jerry. I don't believe you or your mother can ever know how I appreciate all that the Donohues have done for the Dobbinses." She smiled a little mistily.

"There you go again, talking as if we were n't one family!" cried Jerry. "We've got to tie our names together, that's all there is about it. Gerald Dobbins-Donohue, Katharine Dobbins-Donohue, Peter Dobbins-Donohue. Some class to a name like that! I'll see you're printed that way on the graduation programme, and then you'll stop talking as if the Dobbinses and the Donohues were separate clans."

"Would n't you have to get an act of legislature for that, Jerry, child?" inquired Mrs. Donohue anxiously.

Kate laughed. "He's just trying to give me a jolly, Mrs. Donohue. He's a great jollyer when he's once started."

"Yes, that he is; I mind sometimes he tries it on me," admitted Mrs. Donohue.

"But this is serious," Kate continued. "It does n't matter what you say, Jerry, or how good and kind you are to us, — and you've never been anything else, — I can't help realizing all the time that so long as you have to feel we're on your hands we're a handicap to you, and it's not fair you should be handicapped. And so long as I can't help feeling so about it, I can't be as contented as I ought to be. Now I'm old enough to take charge of Peter and Betty and support them until they're able to help themselves. At least I'm old enough to begin to fit myself to support them. And if I can get a place as a stenographer in a business office, I ought to earn ten dollars a week to start with; I'm sure we could get along on that — especially as Peter could earn a little money outside of school hours, selling papers or doing odd jobs. Anyway, I feel that's what I must do. You've given us so much I simply hate to ask for anything more; but the course in stenography will cost something — and I wondered if you'd feel able to let me take it?"

"I guess we can arrange that, if you're possessed to do it," Jerry said. "But look here, Kate; it's all nonsense that you should talk about taking Peter and Betty away and looking after them and supporting them. You can look after them and support them, if you insist upon it, right here at home."

"No; I should always have the feeling that we were hampering you. It is n't right that you should have to be considering us always; and as soon as I'm able to take care of the others, I should n't feel happy if I did n't do it. And I want to do it just as soon as I can."

"Have you got tired of us? Don't you like us any more, Kate?"

"Jerry, you can't think it's that!"

"If it is n't, I don't understand why you're so keen to leave us as soon as you can. Suppose you are earning ten dollars a week a year from now. That is n't much to keep a family of three on — and dress the way they'll want you to in any business office. And it does n't seem to me it's the best thing for Peter to turn him out on the streets to sell papers."

"It won't hurt Peter to have some responsibility. It is n't what we'd like to do, Jerry; it's what I feel we must do."

"Somehow I did n't realize you were one of these independent young women, Kate."

Her lip quivered before she replied, "Does any one enjoy being dependent? I'm grateful to you and your mother — grateful as I can be; but —" Her eyes filled; she could not go on.

"Never mind, Kate; I did n't mean to reproach you. Only it's quite a shock — and you must n't blame me for making a fight to keep you with us. Of course you must do what you think will be for your happiness. But you can't expect us to let you and Betty and Peter drop right out of our lives; and if it should turn out that things are too hard, why, you'll simply have to let us play mother and big brother again — won't she, mother?"

"Yes. Jerry's right about that, Kate."

"Of course I hope you won't forget all about us," Kate said. "But I'm sure that as soon as I get a position, if it pays me ten dollars a week, I can manage."

"Well, you're not going to get such a position right off; that's one comfort," Jerry said cheerfully. "I refuse to think of trouble before it comes. And you go ahead, Kate, and study typewriting all you want to. But I am sorry you've set your face against that college course."

He was both disappointed and disturbed; he felt even aggrieved at Kate's obstinacy. When he and his mother had become so fond of their adopted family, it was humiliating to discover that the adopted family had been secretly planning to sever relations. No matter how admirable the motive, the thing hurt. It would n't be the same in the house when Kate and Peter and Betty were gone. Besides, Jerry realized, with a shiver of apprehension rather than with a thrill of ecstasy, that the fulfillment of his pledge to Nora could not then be indefinitely delayed. The clear road to marriage that had been suddenly opened up before him — if he traversed it in his present mood it would be with reluctant feet.

His mother found an opportunity to enlighten him, when Kate had gone to help Peter and Betty with their lessons.

"I expect I'm responsible for Kate's decision," she said. "I would n't say I spoke with a purpose, but she is certainly a thoughtful and considerate child, to have made up her mind so promptly."

"What was it you said to her?" Jerry's tone was unconsciously severe, owing to the current of his thoughts.

"Now don't be cross with me, Jerry. I suppose you won't like it, but it was true enough, and it just came over me that it would be well to drop a hint to Kate — though I had no idea of her taking it up so. We were talking about Nora as we walked home from the store, and I told her — well, I told her a little about how you and Nora had once meant to get married, and how I was sure that now, of course, some time you and Nora would get married. I just felt it might be a good thing for Kate to realize —"

"Oh, mother, I wish you had n't said that."

"Why, Jerry? Of course you and Nora will some time?"

He sat silent and looked gloomily at the floor.

"I wish you had n't said it," he repeated at last, and in a tone so grave that she dared not question him.

After a few minutes, during which they both sat without speaking, he rose, put on his helmet, and went out. It was one of his free evenings, and he took his way to the law library. He walked slowly. It was indeed a clear road to marriage that had been opened before him — and how he wished that he loved Nora now as he once had done!

XXXV

A TALENT INSUFFICIENTLY APPRECIATED: AND A BRIL-
LIANT IDEA THAT IS NOT EVEN TO BE DISCUSSED

JERRY did not go to see Nora at Bilbow and Slosson's.
He did not go to see her at all for a week; and then one
evening passionate desire for her seized upon him; he
wanted again to feel her arms drawing him to herself, her
lips pressed against his. He hurried to her, and was
annoyed to find her mother in the room. Nora dealt
with the situation in a calm manner that left Jerry for
the moment abashed. "Mother," she said, "I think
Jerry has something he wants to talk about with me;
perhaps you had better go to your room." And Mrs.
Scanlan obediently withdrew.

Then — "Oh, Jerry!" Nora exclaimed, and came
towards him with face alight and arms outstretched;
again the sweetness of her kisses and her embrace, again
the passionate thrilling of his blood. "Jerry, Jerry, love
me, love me!" she murmured. "I love you, I love you,"
he answered; over and over again the antiphonal murmur — "Love me!" "I love you!" There were no reproaches for his absence and neglect, no questions, no
intimation of disappointment or distrust — only the
expression of love.

That evening for a long time they talked of nothing else; Nora looked happy, she looked prettier than
ever, she looked at Jerry with burning eyes; and

JERRY

Jerry spontaneously poured out the sort of yearning adoration for her voice, her hair, her eyes, that she had hoped would find expression on his lips. And Nora in return asked him if he could guess what had been hardest of all in her married life, harder even than her husband's cruelty and hate; and when Jerry answered that he could not guess, she said that it had been just this — thinking always and always about the man she loved. He did not question the truthfulness of that statement any more than he debated with himself the accuracy of some assertions of his own; passion encouraged the utterance of superlatives.

Yet Jerry, after the first intoxication had spent itself, realized the importance of finding some other ground for union than that merely of sexual attraction. He asked Nora to sing to him; and she sang — "Father O'Flynn" and "Kathleen Mavourneen," the songs that he had once loved to hear; he remembered her very phrasing in the old days, her girlish innocence and charm, and a certain mischief that used to glance from her eyes when she sang for him. The element of sexual attraction had existed, but she had been unconscious of it; and indeed his own imagination had transfigured it in making her the embodiment of a spiritual ideal. Now his imagination was unable to do that; he looked on her only with a heightened consciousness of sex; he suspected from the expression in her eyes that she looked on him with a similarly heightened consciousness.

He strove temporarily to put down this consciousness. He wanted most desperately to admire her for other reasons than the physical. He wanted to satisfy himself that there was between them the mental sympathy that he had formerly taken for granted.

"You sing so well, Nora," he said. "I always liked to hear you sing. I think you sing just as well as you ever did. And I suppose you've really not kept up your practice in the last few years."

"No, but I've done a little at it lately. If you like it, I shall be encouraged to do more at it."

"If only I had a pile of money you should have lessons from opera singers."

"I should n't let you waste your money in that way if you had it. My voice is n't good enough for that, Jerry, and I'm not ambitious to develop what voice there is. All I care about is singing so as to please you."

"You certainly do that. But I should like to feel that you were n't hampered in developing any talent you have; I should be so proud if only I could help you to develop it. And of course I never can."

"Well, don't feel badly about that." Nora laughed. "My best talent, I've decided, is for wearing clothes; and it's ever so much more fun than singing or the piano. And I get quite well paid for it too. Your mother saw me the other day; did she tell you?"

"Yes; you made a great impression on her and Kate. But you can't really like doing that kind of thing, Nora."

"I love it."

"I can understand a person's doing it because of being unable to get anything else to do and because of needing the money. I can't understand it for any other reason."

"You might if you came round some time and saw me, Jerry."

"How would that help me?"

"Why, I mean you'd see me looking my best. And you'd like that, would n't you? Would n't that make it seem worth while? Oh, yes, I love nothing better than decking myself out and parading round. Sometimes it seems hard when I love it so that my only opportunity for doing it is in make-believe."

"You would n't do it day in, day out?"

"Yes, if I could always have new and wonderful things to put on."

"I'm afraid you'll miss these new and wonderful things after you're married."

"Oh, I would go on wearing them just the same then."

"Nora! Of course you would n't!"

"Why not? You would n't have me, just because I was married, sit down with folded hands, would you, Jerry? It would be all the better that I could add something to our income."

"Not in that way. I should n't like to have you doing it in that way."

"In what way would you like me to be doing it?"

"Well, giving music lessons would n't be so bad. I'd rather not have you feel it necessary to do anything to earn money, but if you insisted on it, I should n't so much mind your giving music lessons."

"But I loathe giving music lessons and I love wearing pretty clothes. Why should n't I do what I like to do instead of something that I hate to do?"

"It seems to me it's keeping your mind too much fixed on a vain kind of thing."

"I don't know about that. It stimulates my imagination, and, besides, it's amusing to see the different people that come in to buy clothes, and hear them talk."

"Just putting on a lot of finery for the sake of getting other people to buy it can't stimulate your imagination in any worth-while way. And seeing people under such conditions — you can't get much that's worth while out of the best of them."

"Jerry dear, are you always going to be so bent on my intellectual improvement?"

She smiled cajolingly and even more cajolingly stroked his forehead and hair. And suddenly it all seemed priggish and preposterous, arguing in this way with such a delightful, hospitable, responsive, lovable little woman, and as suddenly he seized her in his arms; passion and desire again gained the mastery. "I love you," he asserted. "Oh, do love me," she pleaded. How else? For what was she made, if not to love and to be loved? How many young men, mistaking sentimentality for idealism, and overzealous to minimize the faults of one who has awakened passion and desire, have asked themselves that question and answered it with a glorious assurance! And how many young women who have been made only to love and to be loved disappoint their own and their husbands' reasonable expectations!

Jerry was perhaps different from most young men in that his moods of passion and desire, though hot and violent, were succeeded by emotions of disgust with himself. He found, as time went on, that although

Nora had the power to incite him to demonstrations of affection that were at the moment genuine enough, never simulated, he experienced no corresponding growth of affectionate regard for her in his imagination and his thoughts. On the contrary, when he was in what he chose to term his saner mood, the thought of his behavior in his passionate moments mortified him. If the love to which he gave expression was unaccompanied by any sense of spiritual kinship, did it not mean degradation for them both?

And Jerry could not long pretend to himself that between them there was a union of spirit. He did n't see how, with her brother's plight always in the background of her mind, she could be so consistently gay and untroubled. If it was a tribute to the happiness he had conferred upon her, it was disproportionate. Love and marriage ought not to wipe out all other ties and affections. How could any one who had passed through such experiences as Nora had done, whose father had died by his own hand and whose brother was in prison for murder, be so concerned with the light and frivolous things of life? Or even with the happiness of being in love? If she was a person of any depth of nature, she would sometimes show him the somber or at least the sober side of her character.

In one respect Jerry did her an injustice. He could not know of her sanguine hopes for Dave's early release; he could not know that these, as well as her happiness in loving and being loved, contributed to her gayety of spirit. She talked cheerfully sometimes of what they would do when Jerry was a lawyer and making a lot of money. They would live in a "swell" part of the city and have an automobile, and they would have their names in the society column of the Sunday newspaper. Would n't that be fun!

"Nora, what a silly girl you are!" exclaimed Jerry.

"Not silly at all, Jerrykins. I feel I'm just made for society, and I know you're going to be rich and get into politics and be a big man some day."

"I wish you would n't get such nonsense into your head. You'll be all the more dissatisfied with the kind of life you'll have to lead."

"What kind, now, do you think that will be?"

"That of the hard-working wife of a hard-working poor man."

"Talk as you will, Jerrykins, I know we'll be living on the Avenue one of these days."

"There's not an atom of reason for you to think so. As I've told you time and again, Nora, even after I pass my bar examinations I don't see my way ahead."

"Oh, I'm not worrying about that. You'll get a start, and that will be all you'll need."

"It's getting a start that bothers me."

"I may be able to fix that for you."

Jerry stared and then laughed. "Now what are you dreaming of?"

"I know a man who has influence. If I went and told him about you, I think maybe he'd give you a start."

"What man of influence do you know that you could go to like that?"

"Oh, well, I'm not telling you."

"Is it," Jerry challenged, "is it Patrick Maguire?"

"Well, what if it is?"

"I'd be a policeman all my life rather than do his dirty work for him. And I'd not want you to be asking any favors from the man — bad enough to have had to go to his house to give his child music lessons."

"It was n't his child."

On each side there was the silence of the aggrieved. Nora felt that Jerry was a victim of his silly prejudices and was ready to make her a victim of them too; Jerry was irritated by this evidence of Nora's incapacity to discriminate in the fundamentals of conduct.

Jerry's cavalier rejection of her clever proposal rankled in Nora's heart. It had been no random, thoughtless suggestion; she had received the idea as an inspiration and had built upon it an imposing fabric of future wealth and prosperity. She was contriving to keep on the best possible terms with Maguire; she seemed to have checked, for the time being, his romantic ardor and to be enjoying merely his admiring friendship; she had a feeling that such a settled old bachelor would not be broken-hearted at finally discovering that his suit was hopeless and would continue gladly to be the benevolent friend; she had conceived it to be quite possible that after Dave was out of prison and she had introduced Jerry to Maguire as her affianced, Maguire would say, "God bless you, my children," and act accordingly. At least she did not despair of bringing about this consummation by tactful management. Now to have Jerry kick over and stamp upon such a valuable basket of eggs — it was really too bad.

XXXVI

THE LAST WORDS OF RED SCHLUPFE PROVE TO BE
AMONG HIS BEST: A FAMILY REUNITED AT LAST

Two incidents — each bearing, as may appear later, in
a remote way upon Jerry's fortunes — are now to be
recorded. Rather, one of them shall be only hinted at
— glossed over as decorously as may be. It caused an
interchange of whispers between Mrs. Donohue and
Mrs. Bennett, some decently elliptical remarks by Mrs.
Donohue to Jerry, and a pious understanding between
the second floor and the third floor that a knowledge of
shameful facts should be kept, as far as possible, from
the young. In short, the older and prettier Armstrong
girl had, to use the unexceptionable phrase employed
by Mrs. Donohue and Mrs. Bennett in discussing the
matter, "gone to the bad." Occasionally she returned
from her life of gay and apparently prosperous adventure to pay a brief call on her family; Mrs. Bennett had
a glimpse of her on one of these occasions and Mrs.
Donohue upon another. "She was looking," Mrs. Donohue observed to Mrs. Bennett with satisfaction, "like
the painted Jezzie that she is." They wondered what
kind of a reception the family gave her. Mrs. Bennett
thought that the family must at least be cool to her.
Mrs. Donohue disagreed. "Proud of her, more like.
That's what I should expect of such a bad lot."

Interest shifted suddenly from the Armstrongs to
Dave Scanlan. In a running fight with two policemen

Red Schlupfe, who had been interrupted in a burglary job, was shot down; the bullet, passing through his lungs, inflicted a mortal wound. To the priest who was with him when he died he made a full confession of his part in the Walsh murder and confirmed the truth of all that Dave had declared on the witness stand.

Jerry carried the news of the confession to Nora and her mother, and on this occasion, at least, had no reason to feel that Nora was indifferent to her brother's fate. "Oh, Jerry, is it true, is it true?" she cried; and when he assured her that it was, she danced round the room, embracing and kissing first her mother and then Jerry, and then her mother again, while Mrs. Scanlan, overcome with emotion, wept and quavered, "Oh, Nora dear, oh, Nora dear!"

"Can't we get him out right away, Jerry?" Nora asked; her eyes were shining and eager. "Right away, to-morrow?"

"I'm afraid not as quickly as that."

"Why not, when everybody knows now he's innocent? What right have they to keep him in a day longer?"

Jerry gently reminded her that robbery or attempted robbery was no light offense, even if Dave was now exonerated of the murder.

"I'll go and see Mr. Trask to-morrow," he said. "He'll know the best way to go about it. I do feel, Nora, that we'll get Dave out soon; and then what will you be?"

"The happiest woman in the world, Jerrykins." She gave him another exuberant hug and kiss. "Oh, won't it be splendid, splendid, splendid!" She danced again up and down the room. "And now nobody can ever even think he may have done it, Jerry. Is n't that fine too! I feel almost grateful to that villain Schlupfe. How lucky that he had just that much religion in him at the last!"

Trask lost no time in petitioning for a pardon for Scanlan. He prevailed on Mrs. Walsh to sign the petition; and when in the course of a month Dave appeared for examination before the Board of Pardon and Parole, by whose report the Governor's decision would presumably be influenced, Trask and Nora and the priest to whom Schlupfe had confessed appeared also. The members of the Board were impressed by Dave's attitude of contrition, by Nora's plea, and perhaps too by her personality, and by the priest's assurance that Schlupfe's dying statement could not have been in any vital respect untrue; they recommended to the Governor that he pardon Scanlan; and two weeks later the Governor signed the pardon.

On a bright May morning Trask and Jerry and Nora were waiting in the corridor just outside the guard-room when Dave, a free man, emerged. He looked pale and very clean; his eyes wore a bewildered, deprecating expression; and when Nora ran to him and clung to him and kissed him, he made only a furtive little response and stood almost passive; one would have thought him stolid but for the tears that crept quietly out of his eyes and slipped down his cheeks.

In Trask's automobile Mrs. Scanlan was waiting; Trask and Jerry stood by while she gathered her son into her arms.

There was a hall bedroom that Dave was to have

on the floor above Nora and her mother. And there was a job as well as a bedroom waiting for him. Trask had induced his friend Murray to give Dave a chance; and Murray had been the more willing to do it because of a feeling that he had been unduly harsh with Trask's other protégé.

"He turned you down when you were suspended," Trask said to Jerry. "Afterwards, when he got all the facts, he had remorse. If Scanlan will show he's steady and hard-working he'll get ahead."

"I know he will be all right," said Jerry.

"Just keep an eye on him for a while. Keep him from getting morbid and discouraged."

Trask left them all at the door of the boarding-house. Mrs. Scanlan and Nora and Dave each tried to thank him as in turn they shook hands with him; but after making a beginning each one of them choked up and could not speak. Dave found his tongue only after he had got into the house and was sitting on the sofa with Nora and his mother on either side of him.

"If I did n't have you two to keep me straight, I'd keep straight for Mr. Trask," he said. "He's a white man, he is."

"Yes. Oh, is n't everybody good this morning, Jerry!" cried Nora.

She sprang up and flung her arms round Jerry, and then called to her brother: —

"It's all right, Dave; don't look shocked. Jerry is n't a bit shocked — are you, Jerry?"

"No, I'm getting to like it. Nora's bound that you shall have a brother somehow, Dave."

"She seems to have got me a pretty good one this time," Dave answered. He rose and shook hands with Jerry and then gave his sister a kiss. "I guess now we're all going to get busy and forget what's past."

Jerry was touched by Nora's impulse to share her happiness with him — to demonstrate it by running to his arms. When he had left the reunited family and was walking home, he thought of that little incident with pleasure. There was Nora at her best, an adorable Nora, a Nora brimming with sweet emotions, joyous trust, and happy hopes. If there was sometimes another Nora, what did it matter? This was the real, with the sunshine in her eyes and the soft caresses in her finger tips; this was the Nora that through the storms and trials of life must finally emerge.

XXXVII

IN WHICH JERRY FINDS THAT THE SITUATION IS SIMPLI-
FIED: AND KATE SHOWS HERSELF TO BE A CREATURE
OF STEEL

IT was not long before Jerry realized that his prospects
for an early marriage had been improved by Dave's
release from prison. Before that had taken place, Jerry
had felt that marriage, no matter how much he and Nora
might desire it, must remain a remote possibility. He
could not marry her and leave his mother to live alone;
Nora could not marry him and leave her mother to live
alone; and to marry and have both mothers live with
them — well, that would not be a promising experi-
ment, even if his mother were willing to make it, which
she never would be.

But Dave's release had simplified the situation. Dave
would be able now to take care of Mrs. Scanlan; and
after Kate and Peter and Betty had started upon their
independent career, there would be absolutely nothing to
prevent Jerry and Nora from getting married and taking
Mrs. Donohue to live with them. It was clear enough to
Jerry; and in discovering that marriage, instead of being
a thought to play with, had been suddenly brought forward into the realm of immediate actualities, he felt a
tremor of dismay. He would have liked not to consider
it at all until he had passed his bar examinations and
got some kind of a start towards the practice of his new
profession. It was the most inconvenient time to have

to be bothered by plans of marriage and arrangements for an entire readjustment of life.

Even more disturbing to Jerry was the ominously determined preparation on Kate's part for the withdrawal of her little family from the roof that had sheltered them. Although their departure was not and could not be imminent, there was a dispiriting feeling of imminence and inevitability in the air. Kate told Jerry with unconcealed satisfaction that the Commercial School practically guaranteed to find you a place if you had taken the full course in stenography and had shown proficiency. And after one month at it she reported that the instructor was most encouraging. Jerry wondered jealously how she could be so enthusiastic and so happy; it was almost ungrateful of her, it certainly was selfish. Of course young things were always excited by any prospect of change; but still, if her affections had gone out to him and his mother as his had to Peter and Betty and even her selfish little self, she could n't be so gay and sanguine over the prospect.

He hardly ever had any conversation with her; she was always studying or writing. And in her silent abstraction she seemed to Jerry to grow by degrees more and more distant; a person that he had once known intimately was being curiously transformed before his eyes into a person that he did n't know at all. The girlhood stage was passing; womanhood was blossoming. Kate gained in interest and attractiveness for Jerry as she gained in mystery. Often he watched her when she was unaware of it, and wondered what was going on in that well-shaped, well-poised little head.

To some of the processes he got a clue one day and embarrassed her by so doing. He brought up from the letter box on the ground floor a large envelope addressed to Kate and bearing the name of a New York magazine. She was standing in a window when Jerry handed it to her and he did not see that the color came at once to her cheeks. Even so, it was rather tactless of him to say jocularly, "Writing for the magazines, Kate?"

"I tried, but I guess they did n't want it."

She opened the envelope and drew out a slip that she glanced at and then passed over to Jerry.

"Of course I did n't really expect anything more — but I could n't help hoping —"

"They might have written you a letter anyway!" Jerry exclaimed indignantly. "I'll bet it was good too. Let me read it, will you, Kate?"

"No, I don't think I could. I know now that it's poor. I would n't want you to see it."

"Anyway you must keep on trying. That's what you ought to be doing. Much better than grubbing along in some business office."

"But it does n't look as if I could even grub along by writing, Jerry. I did hope I could get something accepted once in a while; it would help. But of course I don't intend to let writing interfere with my main work."

"How are you getting on with that?"

"Pretty well now. Typewriting I don't have much trouble with, and I'm able to take simple dictation if it is n't too fast. They feel quite sure I'll get a position as soon as I've finished the course."

"Whatever the position is, don't be in a hurry to leave us, Kate. Don't leave until, what with your writing and your regular work, you can count on at least eight hundred a year."

"No; I think that the only way to do is to start out and be independent when you mean to be independent. It won't do me a bit of harm to feel the spur of necessity."

"It won't do you a bit of good either," grumbled Jerry.

It made him the more unhappy the more he thought about it. He had become so attached to Peter and Betty and they to him that he felt it was positively cruel to compel a separation. Kate was a creature of steel to treat them all so. Why did she insist? Merely to ask himself the question caused him to have uncomfortable thoughts. What else would the proud, high-spirited girl do after receiving such an intimation of his designs and desires as his mother had given Kate?

And why had his mother conveyed that intimation? She was not ordinarily addicted to the performance of gratuitous and officious acts. She was not in the habit of indulging in idle gossip. The ironical truth penetrated to Jerry's mind. His mother had acted with deliberate intent, foreseeing the pressure that she would be putting upon Kate; Jerry suspected that one purpose and only one had actuated her — to provide, so far as she was able, that nothing and no one should stand in the way of her son's happiness.

XXXVIII

NORA FEELS THAT SOME THINGS IT IS BAD LUCK TO DO:
AND MAGUIRE IS CERTAIN THAT NOTHING CAN EVER
BE PINNED UPON HIM

HOWEVER wisely or regretfully Jerry might reflect upon
the complications that precipitate surrender to passion
had introduced into his life, he was not able to with-
stand the allurement of Nora's face, Nora's form, Nora's
voice. He could see flaws in her character, he could
criticize the course she was pursuing and disapprove of
her ideas; but when he was with her, he never failed to
feel longing and desire, to exult in the evidence of his
attraction for her, and to assure himself that he would
find her ultimately as pliant in mind as in body. That
she was not so at once was the odd factor that made
their relations so difficult, so gusty. A curious perversity
in clinging to wrong notions, and an equally curious resentment against Jerry for upholding right ones, char-
acterized her. She returned again and again to the
dispute over the propriety of her securing and Jerry's
accepting such aid to his advancement at the law as
Patrick Maguire might be disposed to furnish. She
annoyed Jerry by her depression over the fact that now
that the spring season was past and she was no longer
needed at Bilbow and Slosson's as a model, she was
deprived of the daily pleasure and excitement of dressing
up in fine clothes. She exasperated him by her unwill-

ingness to take up a worthier vocation and by her expectant interest in the fall styles and the new opportunities connected therewith that Bilbow and Slosson had promised her.

Often the evening that began with caresses ended with coolness.

But the forces that drove the two asunder seemed less strong than those that were pulling them together. If they parted on the verge of a quarrel, each one was soon anxious to bring about a resumption of affectionate relations. And in that very fact, thought Jerry, lay the most hopeful promise for the future.

He told Nora of Kate's plans and showed her how they cleared the way for marriage. Of course, if Kate and her family found the struggle too hard, he and his mother must help them; even that responsibility he ought to be able to bear as a married man without too desperate results for his wife.

Nora, listening, agreed — "Oh, yes, Jerry."

"You won't mind if my mother lives with us, Nora?"

"It would be nicer if we could be all by ourselves, would n't it?"

"I 'm sure you would n't find mother at all hard to get on with."

"I can't help thinking that anybody else's mother would be hard, in a way. Or if I did n't find her so, I would probably jar on her — which would be just as bad."

"Mother and Kate have always got on all right."

"Oh, yes, a mousy little girl. I 'm afraid she would n't find me so easy."

"I don't feel that I could leave mother to live alone —"

"What do you expect my mother to do?"

"I thought that she and Dave —"

"And suppose that Dave wants to get married some time?"

"Things could be adjusted somehow when that time came."

"What makes you think that your mother would be willing to have me come into her house?"

"Willing! Why, she looks forward to it."

That assertion mollified Nora. "Does she truly? Of course that would make it better. If she liked me a lot, and would always let me do just as I pleased —"

"She would."

"Do you think so? Of course I really would n't mind, Jerry, — at least not very much. I only thought it would be nicer if we could be just our own two little selves."

Encouraged by the successful termination of this skirmish, Jerry pressed for an assurance that Nora would marry him just as soon as the departure of Kate and Peter and Betty made him free to get married. She asked how soon that would be; and bearing in mind what Kate had told him, he gave her an approximate date.

"Oh, no, I think I'd better not promise," Nora said. "After what happened before, I think it's bad luck for me to make a definite promise of that kind."

"But there is n't anybody else now that — that you could make such a mistake with?" Jerry asked suspiciously.

"You silly boy!" Nora covered her confusion and her blushes by embracing him and letting him kiss her as long as he would.

The truth was, she had Patrick Maguire very much on her mind. Maguire's consternation over having been unable to contribute in any way to Dave's release had been quite appealing. He took her out in his automobile and gave vent most plaintively to his disappointment.

"Not that I begrudge your brother his freedom a bit earlier than what we expected," he said. "But I was looking forward to having a hand in it. I was hoping to make you feel a little grateful to me, Nora. I was hoping it would be the means of making you care for me a bit more than you do now. And now he's out, and I feel that the little hold I had on you is clean gone, and you may be ready to chuck me now at any minute."

"You would n't think I was being nice to you just till you should help me to get Dave out!" said Nora. "Why, I can't help liking anybody that shows me he likes me."

"Liking's not the word I want to hear, and no more is it the word I'm for using to you," Maguire replied. "I've got to keep on till you feel more than that about me."

"But if I can never feel more than that about you?"

"Then till you're willing to marry me on liking alone."

"If I did that, you would n't be happy."

"Not so happy as I'd be if you went the whole hog with me. But I'd be good to you and proud of you, and I guess, when you found I was n't a bad sort of a husband, you'd feel you could make me a pretty good sort of a wife. I'd be willing to take you on those terms. I would n't feel it was much of a gamble."

"Would n't it be quite a gamble for me?"

"I don't see in what way. I don't drink, I ain't bad-tempered, and I'm well enough fixed. Seems to me the girl who takes me is getting a pretty sure thing. Not so many possibilities, maybe, as in a young chap that's handsome and got his way to make — and not so many chances for an upset, neither."

"Of course I know you've got influence and all that," said Nora. "But are n't there a good many people that think — that disapprove of you?"

"Sure. Surest thing you know. I've got enemies — plenty of 'em. Mostly among the respectable folks too. I guess my wife would be frozen out of the blue-blood circles. But say — it's quite a gamble you're taking if you're waiting to marry into one of them, Nora."

He smiled at her quizzically. He had stopped the car under an apple tree that overhung a country road; he could n't be bothered with the steering-wheel during such a serious conversation as this.

"I was n't thinking of such people," Nora answered. "Just ordinary nice people. I was wondering what they think of you. You see, I've heard —"

"You mean, there's a lot of people that think I'm a grafter — a kind of high-grade crook. Well, I suppose that's a good deal a matter of opinion. I'll say this for myself: no one has ever pinned anything on me, and no one ever will. I've stowed away some money. How did I get it? By grabbing it pretty much wherever it was in

sight — same as any business man. I used what knowledge and power I had to get me money. I had knowledge and power that were useful to public service corporations, and I've got all I could out of 'em. Just the
way a public service corporation needs, we'll say, a
banker to float it, and the banker takes it out of that
corporation in return — which is the same as saying out
of the public — according to his knowledge and power.
The banker's graft is respectable, and mine ain't, but
from my point of view there's no particular difference
between 'em. Of course, that ain't the usual point of
view, but it's mine."

Intricacies of finance it was impossible for Nora to
understand, and she therefore did not urge him to be
more explicit. But she did put to him a question that
went straight to essentials.

"If all the things you've done could be proved against
you, would they put you in prison?"

"No," he replied, after considering a moment. "I
don't believe so. You see, that's a thought I've always
had in mind — to fix things so that nothing could be
pinned on me. Of course, if everything was shown up,
there would undoubtedly be some fellows that would be
liable to a jail sentence; but I would n't be one of 'em."

"Oh, that's the worst thing you could say about
yourself!" Nora exclaimed. "If you're that sort of a
man, I don't feel that I like you at all. A kind of a big
spider drawing people into his web — getting other
people into trouble and keeping clear of it yourself —"

"Say, hold on, Nora," protested Maguire in an aggrieved voice. "You don't understand. It's just like I

[323]

was general of an army, see? I station my colonels and
captains and lieutenants and so on, and I give 'em a
plan of campaign — in which there's nothing necessarily criminal for anybody, you see. Then each one of
them understands that he has a part to play, and at the
proper time he has to deliver the goods. Well, the time
comes, and the goods are delivered, and it's up to each
man how it's done. I may hear.things that make me
think some men have broken the law to produce the
results; but that was their lookout. Other men produce
the results without breaking the law."

"It looks to me as if you were drawing a pretty fine
line," Nora said disapprovingly. "Why do you go on
doing that sort of thing? Are n't you rich enough?"

"Just about. I've had about enough. A man can get
away with it and be prosperous for a certain number of
years, just as I've done, but if a fellow stays at it too
long, he'll overplay the game and the reformers will get
him. Some of the men that have been working for me, I ·
don't mind telling you, are a little too raw in their
methods. I don't stand for that. I've been thinking
I'd draw out before this coming mayoralty campaign; I
have a hunch it would be the wise thing to do — not be
mixed up in it at all. I can get along without the excitement of politics. I'd like to settle down and farm it in
the country; and we might have our town house in the
winter, and you'd get society that would be nice people
who'd worked their way up in the world and got some
education — not the blue-blood circles, but just about
as good. I tell you what, Nora, I'd be just as nice to
you as any husband would know how to be."

She avoided then, she avoided at other similar interviews, giving him a definite answer. She was pledged to
Jerry, and vowed, in all likelihood, to a life of poverty;
but there was a pleasurable excitement in being confronted by the temptation to acquire sudden wealth.

If she had been profitably occupied with some work
or had happened to have some cause very much at
heart, the temptation to dally with temptation might
not have existed. But now that Dave was no longer a
cause to work and scheme for, she had nothing but herself on which to fix her thoughts. She had even, with the
expiration of her congenial term of duty at Bilbow and
Slosson's, no regular daily task to keep her contented.
She was drifting again, and she had begun to question
herself more sharply than ever before about her re-
quirements for happiness. Wearing those good clothes
at Bilbow and Slosson's every day and then suddenly
having to give up wearing good clothes altogether —
that experience had shown her how much clothes meant
to her — how she needed them for her soul. It was n't
only good clothes that she needed; what was more vital
to her was to feel that she had a chance to emerge from
her humble and distasteful surroundings into a larger,
brighter, more amusing life. As the wife just of a policeman, she could never hope to emerge. If Jerry became a
lawyer, there might be a chance — but only if he was a
successful lawyer. And she could n't see how he was
ever to get a start; if only he would n't be so obstinate,
if only he were willing to grasp at opportunity wherever
and however offered! Suppose the dream of the law
came to nothing, suppose they just starved along, al-

ways, as they would certainly have to do at first. And with Jerry's mother always with them. A nice little woman enough, but what a restraint she would put upon the temper!

Then, when the whole future was looking just as drab and dull as it is ever possible for the future to look, along would come Jerry and take her in his arms. And he was so splendid and sparkling-eyed, had such a shining and confident smile, and was so tall and strong and handsome, that the future at once took on the gay colors of the moment; it seemed too foolish to have misgivings about what Jerry would achieve. If a fat, homely little pudge of a man like Maguire, starting with nothing and with no special brains either, could have worked up to a big automobile and plans for a farm in the country and a house in town, why, surely, Jerry! — And she did love him so!

XXXIX

IN the city the activities preliminary to a quadrennial municipal election had begun. Jerry's interest was aroused one day early in June when he read in the newspaper that Roger Trask had taken out Republican nomination papers for the office of District Attorney. His interest was intensified when it appeared that John Maxwell was hoping to be the candidate of the Democratic city machine for the mayoralty. There were contests for all the nominations; for two months within each party the rival candidates campaigned sharply; but after the September primaries each party boasted in the grandiloquent language peculiar to political campaigns that it would present to its opponent a united front. Trask won the Republican nomination for District Attorney; the Democrats named Maxwell as their candidate for Mayor. Notwithstanding the Democratic professions of harmony, there was dissatisfaction even within the machine. The news that Patrick Maguire had resigned the presidency of the Ward Fourteen Maguire Club and announced his retirement from politics furnished a first-page sensation for all the local newspapers. They speculated variously upon its significance; and those hostile to the local Democratic machine were not convinced by his assertion that personal reasons

[327]

alone governed his course and that he would enthusiastically support the entire Democratic ticket.

Whether Maguire supported it or not was a matter of
little concern to Jerry; what did concern Jerry was the
fact that the Chief of Police, Dolan, succeeded Maguire
as the dictator of the local Democratic machine. The
word was passed round that the police force must do
everything possible to insure Maxwell's election and
Trask's defeat. Jerry knew that padded voting-lists
were being prepared; it was common gossip among the
patrolmen that on election day "colonizers" in great
numbers were to move from booth to booth and vote
over and over again under the names of persons who
were dead or had never lived. Jerry also heard it frequently said that the eagerness of the Democratic machine to raise funds was hardly second to its eagerness
to win the election.

"It's a crime, the way they're shaking down the
tenderloin," Sheehan said to him. "The Chief does it in
person. Won't trust that graft to anybody else. Tells
the poor devils this election is life or death to them, and
they ought to be willing to pay high for the protection
they'll have afterwards. He has no mercy on 'em at all,
except that he tells 'em that when Maxwell is Mayor
they'll soon get it back."

"I shouldn't think he'd have the nerve," was
Jerry's comment.

"Well, nobody would dare to testify against him. He
could break any man. Of course I only tell you what the
fellows are saying under their breath; I'm not in the
Chief's confidence. But I know there's an awful lot of

money being coughed up by the underworld these days. And by the saloons and breweries. I bet there's a whole lot of it that does n't go to what you might call the legitimate expenses of the campaign."

"Sure," said Jerry. "I don't suppose Dolan lets much that he collects get away from him."

In September Jerry took his bar examinations. Two weeks later he received word that he had passed. He was jubilant over it until he carried the news to Nora; she contrived after a while to make him feel that it was a rather empty achievement. She asked him what his plans were now; he had none, except that he meant to go to Mr. Trask for advice.

"Well," she said, "I hope he'll be able to do something for you. For if he won't and you refuse to let me ask Mr. Maguire to help you get a start, I don't see that you'll be much better off than you were before."

Jerry was silent; it really was n't very nice of her to hark back to Maguire. It was n't very nice of her to be so unenthusiastic over his accomplishment — a thing that might mean much to them both.

To tell the truth, she was in a bad humor that evening; a trivial episode of the day, a thing that had indeed been a minor success on her part, had rasped her nerves. She was again at Bilbow and Slosson's, exploiting their fall styles; she had that morning put on for show purposes the most striking and becoming clothes that she had ever worn. Surveying herself in the mirror, from head to toe, she had been enraptured; "lovely" was the only word to describe what she saw. She had not believed she could look so beautiful. A vulgar rich woman had been enchanted, had literally bought the clothes off her back, defying the timid suggestions of the saleswoman. Nora saw her own glorious and proper setting made the permanent possession, the grotesquely unbecoming possession, of another. As she looked at the infatuated purchaser of the beautiful, inappropriate garments, she felt injured and disdainful. Was it for such results that she exercised her talent and made herself charming? How happy she could be if she could own such clothes instead of merely enticing other people to buy them! How hateful to see them bought by such unworthy people!

She could not explain all this to Jerry; he would have been unsympathetic. He was displeased with her anyway for resuming her work as model at Bilbow and Slosson's. She thought he ought instead to be congratulating her on her spirit; it was hard work, and if he had been generous enough to look at it from that point of view, she was earning money for him as well as for herself. For she was putting it all aside for their wedding.

"Oh, Jerry," she said, breaking quite abruptly in upon his morose silence, "I do hope you'll get a start that will make you rich some day. Sometimes I don't feel as if I could be really happy in this world without being rich."

"I'm glad you put in 'sometimes.' If you always felt so, there would be no use in our even thinking about getting married."

"Perhaps we'd better not think about it." Her eyes flashed with sudden anger, and then as suddenly softened. "Oh, Jerry, what's the matter with us both? We didn't use to talk to each other like this. I don't mean to be snappish. But if you would only be cheerful and confident always, as you used to be, — if you'd say when I talk as I just did, 'Why, of course we're going to be rich,' whether you really thought so or not, it would help so much. I would n't mind a great deal if we never were, if only you made me feel always hopeful and expectant and seemed so yourself. That's the way you used to be."

"I'll try, Nora."

"I don't want you to try; I want it just to bubble out of you, as it once did."

"It will, it will. I'll be a regular Old Faithful and spout regularly —"

"Now, Jerry, don't call yourself Old Faithful; it's too depressing; I don't want to feel that I'm marrying that — even if I am."

"It's the name of the world's greatest geyser, silly," Jerry reminded her. "Its quality of bubbling rather than of faithfulness was what I had in mind to emulate."

"Now that's the way I like to have you talk, Jerrykins." She rewarded him by perching on his knee and putting an arm round his neck. "Oh, I can be so sweet to you when you're nice, and so horrid when you're glum!"

That evening as Jerry was about to enter his house, a woman came up to him and said, rather timidly, "Officer Donohue? Is this Officer Donohue?"

"Yes."

"Clara Armstrong — she's a young friend of mine — she told me I'd better see you." The woman was agitated, and kept glancing up and down the street apprehensively. She was not a young woman; she might have been pretty once. Clara Armstrong and a few other young girls lived with her. It was a very quiet, respectable sort of house, but the extortion was too much for her. Chief Dolan kept coming down on her every little while, and now, rather than meet his last demand, she was going to quit. But she would like to see that man punished, he was such a nasty brute; she was mad enough so that she was willing to take some punishment herself if she had to, so long as she could get him punished too. Clara Armstrong had told her that Officer Donohue and the Department had not been on good terms, and so she was confiding in him. She had been ordered to hand over five hundred dollars in currency to Dolan day after to-morrow. He was to call at her house for the money. Could n't Officer Donohue be there and arrest the Chief when he received it?

Jerry questioned her for a long time. He finally promised to go to her house at five o'clock the next day; he would then tell her what to do.

XL

JERRY'S expectation of getting advice from Roger Trask
was disappointed. Trask, he found, was out of town for
two days. He would have to determine for himself what
action he should take.

He got Sheehan on the telephone at Station 10, and
made an appointment to meet him during their lunch
hour.

Sheehan listened attentively while Jerry repeated the
woman's story.

"Well," Sheehan said, "what did you think of
doing?"

"There are two or three things I might do," Jerry
answered. "I suppose the most obvious would be to
take the woman to the Police Commissioner and let
him deal with the case when he'd heard all the facts."

"If you did that, most likely nothing would come of it.
The Commissioner wants to keep his job and he'll do it
only if the Maxwell-Dolan outfit win the election. He'd
probably tip the Chief off, and then it would end in your
being framed up. To get results, you need the backing of
those that are hostile to Dolan, not friendly with him."

"Yes; I wanted to have Mr. Trask's help, but he's
away. Now what do you think of this? The *Standard's*
hostile to Dolan and Maxwell all right. How about the
Standard's getting in on it and having witnesses of its

[333]

own there when Dolan is caught? There'd be no chance then of hushing the thing up."

"Now you have pretty near the right idea," said Sheehan with enthusiasm. "Plenty of witnesses, and publicity, plenty of it, afterwards — that's the thing. If it can be managed."

"Will you back me up — help me to make the arrest?"

"You talk with the *Standard* first, and then I'll tell you what I'll do."

It was not difficult to get access to the private office of Mr. Finlay, the publisher of the *Standard*. He was a man with sandy beard, aquiline nose, and keen blue eyes; he slid his large capable hands nervously back and forth along the arms of his chair while Jerry talked.

"If we can pull this thing off," he exclaimed when Jerry had finished, "it will be the greatest stroke for good government in this place — why, it will mean the end of that Young Turk crowd that's got hold of the city machine. We'll beat 'em all, from Maxwell down. Now we don't want to make any false moves. What time has Dolan set for handing over the money?"

"He's to be there for it between five and six to-morrow. I'm going round at five this afternoon to make the preliminary arrangements. It might be well for you to come with me or send some man you can depend on who will be there to-morrow as a witness."

Finlay rang and told the boy who responded to send in Mr. Bridewell.

"He's the best reporter we have," Finlay said to Jerry. "Absolutely safe, and keeps his head."

Bridewell appeared, a clean-cut, fair-haired young man, with a pleasant smile. As Finlay outlined the plot to him, a glint of eagerness and excitement came into his eyes.

"Officer Donohue thinks that you and he had better go down there this afternoon and set the stage for the proceedings to-morrow," Finlay concluded.

"I'm certainly lucky to come in on a story like this," said Bridewell. "Have you thought at all about the money that's to change hands?"

"Not particularly. Why?"

"Wouldn't it be a good idea for the *Standard* to furnish the woman with the money — every bill marked so that you and I can identify it?"

"Excellent," agreed Finlay. "Tell her, Mr. Donohue, that we'll supply the funds; she's not to use any money except what you or Mr. Bridewell will hand her to-morrow. You'll have to be pretty circumspect, entering and leaving that house; you don't want to have Dolan get wind of your plans and disappoint you."

"He's pretty self-confident — not likely to take more than ordinary precautions," Jerry said. "But we'll be careful."

Late that afternoon Jerry, Sheehan, and Bridewell met at the house and rehearsed the parts that they were to perform the next day. Under the stairs in the front hall and opposite the door into the parlor was a closet in which Jerry and Sheehan were to conceal themselves; leaving the closet door ajar, they could hear without seeing or being seen. The woman was to get the Chief into the parlor before passing the money to him. In that room a high-backed sofa set across a dark corner would furnish a hiding-place for Bridewell, if he got down behind it on his hands and knees. The woman was all alone in the house; she explained that she had got rid of the other occupants by telling them that the police had notified her to expect a raid within the next two days.

At four o'clock the next afternoon Jerry and Sheehan arrived; a few minutes later came Bridewell. He gave the woman five hundred dollars in five packets of ten-dollar bills; he showed Jerry and Sheehan the letter "F" written in a fine hand on the middle of the topmost bills of the packets. "It's written on every bill," said Bridewell. "Mr. Finlay put it on and stands ready to identify his writing."

When at last the doorbell rang, the three men noiselessly took their places. Inside the closet Jerry stood nearest the door; Sheehan was behind him leaning over his shoulder.

They heard the woman say, "Well, I've got it for you, Chief, but I don't know how we're all going to live from now till election."

She led him into the parlor while she talked.

The Chief was in a good-humored mood; his collections had been prospering. "Oh," he said, "you'll just have to get on with a few less silk petticoats and lingerie; you folks are too luxurious in your habits."

"I wonder what you do with all the money you raise this way," said the woman in the cajoling manner of which she was past mistress.

"Well, we've got to use a lot of it to elect a mayor who'll be good to you folks," replied the Chief.

JERRY

"I certainly wish you success in that. — Here it is,
Chief, — one, two, three, four, five hundred, all in ten-
dollar bills. Is that right?"

"That's right."

Just a moment longer Jerry and Sheehan waited, in
order to give him time to button the money inside his
coat. Then Jerry flung the closet door open and sprang
out, followed by Sheehan. The Chief, a powerful and
active man, leaped at Jerry; the two went down in a
furious grapple; Sheehan fell upon the Chief and choked
him until he surrendered. Jerry snapped handcuffs on
his wrist.

"Don't do that, for God's sake!" said the Chief.

"I would n't take chances with you without 'em,"
answered Jerry.

"Look here!" cried the Chief, breathing heavily.
"You men have got me all wrong on this. I came here
trying to get evidence against this house. I —"

"Pretty thin," said Sheehan. "You're caught with
the goods on you — pockets full of marked money."

Bridewell, hitherto unnoticed by the Chief, came forward. "Every bill marked with the letter 'F'— and I
can testify to the transfer."

"Who are you?" demanded the Chief.

"I represent the *Standard*, and I'm lucky to have got
in on this thing. The full story will be on the presses in
an hour."

"Did you make a note," said Jerry, "of his statement
as to how the money was to be used?"

"To elect a mayor who'd be good to the folks he was
robbing? I did that."

JERRY

The Chief cursed Jerry and Sheehan and the woman, and then was silent.

Sheehan telephoned for the patrol wagon. Bridewell waited to see the dramatic departure. There was a bit of discipline that exceeded his expectations and that he was obliged to record in his narrative with a note of admiration for the Chief. When the driver of the wagon saw who the handcuffed prisoner was that was descending the steps, his face did not change its impassive expression; he brought his hand up and saluted. And the Chief, with head erect, raised his free hand and returned the salute. "The incident suggested," moralized Bridewell, "that he might have been a great Chief of Police if he had only been honest."

An hour later, Bennett, setting up the story that had just come to him, was thrilled to find it recorded the exploit of his neighbor of the second floor. And it was from Bennett and not from Jerry that Mrs. Donohue and Kate and Peter learned of the notable performance of their hero, for Bennett raced home in his supper hour, just to tell them. Mrs. Donohue and Kate discussed eagerly what the most probable reward for such an achievement would be; Kate thought that Jerry was the logical successor now to the Chief of Police; Mrs. Donohue, while admitting the plausibility of Kate's suggestion, secretly hoped that her son, now that he was a lawyer, as well as a policeman, would be made Police Commissioner.

XLI

THE story of Chief Dolan's arrest as printed in the *Standard* was a rude blow to Democratic hopes. Maxwell and his fellow candidates for office issued immediate and impassioned disclaimers of complicity in the Chief's alleged design to raise a campaign fund by extortion. They reserved final judgment until his guilt was proved, but they assured the public that should he be found guilty, no one would denounce more heartily than they a private enterprise of so shameful a character. Nevertheless, the episode put them on the defensive at the outset and gave their opponents a tactical advantage of which Trask, and White, the Republican candidate for Mayor, made the most. Trask declared his intention, if elected District Attorney, to probe to the bottom of the blackmail scandal; he was not satisfied that it was merely a private undertaking of Dolan's by which Dolan alone was to profit; it was to be remembered that Dolan occupied a conspicuous place in the local Democratic machine, that the mantle of the ex-boss Maguire had in fact descended to him, that he had been particularly active in getting Maxwell nominated, that there had long been only too good reason to believe the Democratic machine maintained itself in power by methods akin to those which had been exposed, etc. Solemn as-

[339]

severations of innocence and expressions of pious indignation on the one side, and from the other counterblasts of invective, satire, and innuendo furnished entertainment for the public during the next six weeks.

Meanwhile, under the surface a contest for the possession of Dolan was waged between the two forces, and Dolan himself, through his attorney, was trying to make the best terms for himself that he could. Trask was approached with the suggestion that in the event of his election to office he should guarantee immunity to Dolan in return for a full confession. It was hinted to Trask that if he rejected this proposal, Dolan would press for an immediate trial; Mulkern, the District Attorney, being a member of his own political machine and a candidate for reëlection, would not be likely to make things hard for him. Trask replied that before taking up the question of immunity he must hear from Dolan himself just what he proposed to tell and whom he proposed to incriminate. Thereupon negotiations with Trask ceased, and Dolan's trial was pushed through before the election. He pleaded guilty, declared that his ill-advised attempt to swell the campaign fund had been entirely his own, and that none of the candidates for office, none of the party managers, had been cognizant of it. Mulkern expressed his willingness, in view of Dolan's past excellent record and acknowledged services to the city, to have him let off with a light sentence; Dolan's lawyer made an eloquent plea for his client; the judge, an appointee of a machine-picked governor, sentenced him to pay a fine of a thousand dollars and to serve three months in prison. Maxwell went about the city vociferating that the outcome of the trial was a complete vindication for himself and the honorable men who were on the ticket with him; he appealed to the voters to rebuke the contemptible efforts of the opposition, an opposition that for the first time in any mayoralty campaign had been so malignant as to impugn the character of a nominee for that important office. The Maxwell supporters and newspapers insisted that their candidates were the stronger for the attack that had been made upon them; they predicted victory by an overwhelming majority. But the best-informed among them admitted privately that the outlook was far from good. If Maguire would go actively to work for the old party, they might pull through; the leaders labored with him until he suddenly disappeared from the city. That action of his disheartened them. The circumstances of the disappearance, to be presently set forth, disarmed criticism; nevertheless, the leaders felt that he would not have let personal affairs jeopardize party success if he had foreseen the possibility of success; in their vernacular he was a wise guy; he meant not to injure his prestige by participating in a losing fight. Moreover, for the execution of the rather coarse work of election day the services of Dolan as Chief of Police had been absolutely indispensable. The Police Commissioner, highly disturbed by the turn that events had taken, named in Dolan's place a man of no piratical tendencies whatever, a sober and diligent police officer from whom nothing was to be hoped.

Both Kate and Mrs. Donohue found the Police Commissioner's action disappointing. But they looked forward confidently to some startling recognition of Jerry's qualities, some brilliant opening for his talents, now that he had performed so important an act in the line of duty. That he was not long going to remain a patrolman they were assured; Jerry himself admitted that. He had sought Trask's advice, as he had told Nora that he intended to do; and Trask had asked him to continue on the police force till after the election. Then, however that turned out, Trask would find a place for him in some law office. Meanwhile, it would be of the utmost advantage to a prospective district attorney if Jerry could ferret out evidence that would convict the ringleaders of the machine that had for so long misgoverned and plundered the city. "They've bought off Dolan now," Trask said. "I can't prove it, but I'll bet he held 'em up. He wouldn't have taken it all on his own shoulders just for love."

Jerry did not prove, it must be confessed, a talented detective. He opened up a number of clues, but lost them in the maze of intrigue to which they all led; he heard stories and received hints of information from some of his fellow policemen who, under Dolan's régime, had been afraid to talk; but none of them did more than indicate and suggest. Going back of the immediate campaign, Jerry secured many legends but little real proof of the knavish methods of the Maguire machine, of the tributes that Maguire had exacted from all sorts of men and corporations in their need; Maxwell, so far as he could ascertain, had been above the necessity of making money out of politics and for that reason had been the more useful protégé for Maguire. The mass of information and conjecture that he accumulated might be valuable some time, and he gathered it diligently and digested it as well as he could; but he had to confess inability to bring to account the persons who for years had exerted a baneful influence on public affairs.

With one of these persons, he was annoyed to find, Nora continued upon friendly terms. On the Sunday after Dolan's arrest, Maguire drove Nora up to her door in his automobile just as Jerry came briskly along the sidewalk. Nora was embarrassed and said good-bye to Maguire rather hurriedly; he, on the other hand, seemed in no haste to depart. He shut off his engine in spite of her good-bye and waved his hand genially to Jerry.

"Quite a stroke of yours, Officer," he said. "Quite a hit you've made, getting on the front page of the papers."

Jerry ignored him, and turned to follow Nora, who was opening the door.

"I can't see you now, Jerry; you must n't come in now," she said under her breath. Maguire, seated in his car, was watching them.

"You must see me now," Jerry answered, and he entered with her and closed the door.

"You — you treat me as if I had no rights," Nora cried angrily. "I'm tired; I did n't want to be bothered with you now."

"You've given me some rights, and I propose to stand on them, whether it bothers you or not," Jerry replied grimly. "I think we've got to come to an understanding once for all about Maguire."

"Come upstairs," said Nora, after a pause. "We can't stand talking here."

She led the way up to the sitting-room. Jerry walked past her to the bay window and looked out. Maguire was still waiting in his car; he saw Jerry in the window, waved to him again with a smile that might have been good-humored or might have been derisive, and then, starting his engine, moved rapidly away.

"Do you let him take you on automobile drives?" asked Jerry.

"Yes; sometimes."

"How does it happen that he asks you?"

"Because he finds me pleasant company, I suppose."

"My question may have sounded insulting. I did n't mean it so. All I meant was, how do you and he happen to have established such friendly relations?"

"In the first place, through my teaching of his niece. Then, when I had come to know him a little, I asked him one day to help me to get Dave pardoned. He promised to do what he could when a new governor was elected. Then, when Dave was pardoned without his having been able to do anything about it, he just kept on being nice to me."

"He wants to marry you, does n't he?"

"Yes."

"Have you ever told him definitely that you could n't marry him — that you were going to marry me?"

"Not definitely — not just that. But I've hinted to him there was some one else that I cared very much about."

"Still, Maguire thinks his chances are pretty good — thinks they're improving?"

"I can't be sure, Jerry, what he thinks."

"Aren't you treating him exactly as you treated Corcoran when you had promised to marry me? And aren't you treating me now exactly as you treated me then?"

"You can't say that, Jerry. I haven't married Mr. Maguire."

"If you didn't feel in the back of your head that you might marry him, you would have put a stop to his courting of you."

"Why should I? He's not so young and inexperienced that I need to be tender of him. I think you're very mean to be so cross with me, Jerry. You leave me alone for days together, and I need some amusement. I don't see any harm in accepting an invitation to go out in a friend's automobile. I don't see any harm even in letting him try to persuade me to marry him. He can't do it, for it's you that I love, Jerry; it's you that I mean to marry."

She looked at him with soft eyes; she spoke with a note of plaintiveness in her voice.

"Then why don't you tell him so?"

"Because it amuses me to see him and ride in his automobile occasionally, and if I were to come out as you want me to it would be the end of all that. Can't you understand, Jerry, how much I need the amusement, and how harmless it is? I see you hardly once a week, and I see nobody else that gives me any fun. When we're married and I'm seeing you every day and feeling that I'm really doing something for you every day, I won't need any outside excitements. But just now I do need them, and Mr. Maguire supplies about all that I have."

"You must find other resources and they must n't include flirtations," said Jerry firmly. "You tell me, Nora, that you love me; now you must prove that you do by giving in to my wishes."

"Why should n't you prove your love by giving in to mine?"

"In this matter it's impossible. I want you to-night to write to Mr. Maguire, telling him that you are engaged to marry me and that his attentions to you must cease."

Nora was silent. Then she came and took Jerry by the arm and said, "Now, Jerrykins, don't stand up any longer and scold and scold as if you were a great big nasty school-teacher. Sit down and talk to me." She pushed him down on the sofa and then perching herself on his knees passed an arm round his neck. "Why do you treat me like a naughty little girl, Jerrykins? I'm not a naughty little girl; I'm a nice little girl. And of course I'll do anything you say, only don't you think you're rather unkind to poor little me?"

She stroked his cheek with the soft hand that had crept round from behind his neck. She looked at him with eyes that were both mischievous and reproachful.

"No," Jerry said, "I'm not being unkind, Nora. And I'm just asking you to do what is really the kindest thing to Maguire."

"Oh, hum!" said Nora. "So it's Mr. Maguire's feelings that you're anxious about — that they should n't be hurt, or anything of that sort. Jerrykins dear, I wonder if I really do love you when you ride a great high moral horse. Especially when you ride it so ferociously right at me."

She continued to stroke his cheek and to look into his face with her mischievous, whimsical eyes and her faintly challenging smile.

Suddenly his arms were round her. "There, then!" he exclaimed among the kisses. "Of course I love you — and you've got to love me. And — you've got to do what you're told. Do you understand, you teasing little thing?"

"Yes." She sighed and gave him another kiss. "Are n't you the hard-hearted fellow, Jerry! Shall I write the letter now?"

"I wish you would."

"And then you could take it and drop it in the box for me?"

"Nothing certainly could be safer than that."

She sat down at her writing-table, and Jerry watched her while she wrote and felt a new and sweeter tenderness for her. What a winning little person it was that could give in so gracefully!

She handed him the note for his approval. It was as follows: —

DEAR MR. MAGUIRE:—

I feel that I must tell you I am engaged to be married to Mr. Gerald Donohue. Try not to feel disappointed. I think we had better not see each other any more.

Sincerely yours,
NORA CORCORAN.

"Just right," said Jerry.

She sealed and addressed and stamped the note and handed it to him again.

She deserved and received more petting; he vowed to himself that although mounting the high moral horse had succeeded well this time it was a performance to be avoided in the future.

He had but a few more minutes with her; patrol duty summoned him. He dropped her letter in the first mail box that he passed and had a moment's pleasure imagining Maguire's emotions upon receiving it.

Then Jerry smiled, remembering that the encouraging bit of news that he had meant to give Nora he had never delivered. Yet it was important, too, quite as important as the matters that had caused him temporarily to forget all about it. He had intended to tell Nora of Trask's assurance that after the election he would find a place for him in some law office. She would be so relieved to know that the question of getting a start need no longer cause them anxiety!

XLII

WITHIN five minutes of the time when Jerry had left the
house, Nora wished that she could recall the letter. It
was a brutal note to send to one who had been kind to
her. And to send it was reckless as well as brutal, for it
meant that she was cutting herself off from a friend;
already Nora was conscious of a sense of insecurity.
Hitherto she had known that if she wearied of adventures in idealism, or decided after a more careful survey
of the prospects that it would be an error to marry one
who had only love and hope to offer, she had but to
stretch forth her hand and she would be reverently conducted to the flowery meads of luxury — her fit and
proper home. As it had been at least pleasant and
cheering to think that there was still this resource open
to her, so it was depressing now to reflect that the resource existed no longer. And while she thought about
it, the wrath of the helpless invaded her. What an act
of folly she had committed in a moment of docility!
And how mean and selfish Jerry had been to prescribe
the step that she had taken!

She looked at her hands lying idle in her lap; pretty,
shapely hands they were. She held one of them up and
examined it critically; those well-manicured finger nails
would soon be ruined if she had to be cook and house-

[349]

maid of her own establishment. How she would like to
have a wrist watch and a diamond ring! Although it
would be an unjustifiable extravagance, she might some
day buy a wrist watch, it was not wholly beyond her
means; but the diamond ring she had for some time
recognized to be procurable from only one source and in
only one way, and now she had caused an agreeable
possibility to vanish. Pearl earrings too; alas, for pearl
earrings, become suddenly unattainable! Alas, for the
house on the Avenue, the automobile, the name in the society column of the Sunday newspaper! Jerry scoffed at
her dreams and was unwilling to make even the small-
est concession by which they might eventually, perhaps,
come true.

Dave and Mrs. Scanlan returned from an afternoon of
trolley riding in the suburbs and wandering in the park.
Over the cold tongue and cold biscuits and prunes that
constituted the Sunday supper they recounted to Nora
and the landlady and Miss Sims, who had a room in the
adjoining house and came in for meals, their adventures.
Such crowds everywhere — and the cars that jammed!
— Mrs. Scanlan had been so lucky as to get a seat,
though; both going and coming some man had got up for
her — an old man going out, she hated to take it from
him, and a nice, pleasant-appearing young man coming
in; well, it was a comfort to be at home again. But the
park was lovely, the shrubs and flowers and the swans
on the lake — such greedy birds as they were for crusts
and crumbs! The Zoo was the best of all, and the little
brown bears were so comical. Dave was urged to tell
about the little brown bears; Miss Sims was especially

interested. There was an old stump of a tree with a branch horizontal at the top, and one little bear got up there and then kept pushing the other little bear down when he tried to climb, and growled and pretended to bite him, and the other little bear growled and pretended to bite too. But the funniest was when they hit each other; you had to laugh; they were just like kids. Miss Sims could see how funny it must have been; she laughed over Dave's description of it. Miss Sims knew all about Dave's past and had managed to convey to him her appreciation of the fight he was making to redeem himself. She was young and alone in the world, a frail, blue-eyed, pale girl with high cheek-bones and a small chin; she was assistant to the cashier in a big furniture store. After supper she and Dave went off to an open-air sacred concert; she was in a continuous state of inarticulate emotion at finding how much of good there still was in him. The landlady cleared away and washed the dishes; Sunday nights, when her maid-of-all-work was out, she had to perform this task, and usually Nora was good-natured enough to assist her. But this evening Nora did not offer her services, and the landlady felt aggrieved and sat out on her doorstep with her knitting instead of going upstairs and asking Nora if she wouldn't play one or two pieces for her.

Nora passed a quite unhappy evening. She thought more about Patrick Maguire than about Jerry. She thought of the appeals that Maguire had made to her that very afternoon; in the light of what she had just done, how piteous they seemed! He had besought her not to keep him in suspense, he had forced her to admit

that she really liked him, he had been almost pathetically elated by that admission. And he had been anxious
to assure her that he was not involved in the blackmail
scandal; it was the kind of thing he had never stood for;
and he had drawn out of politics because he had seen
there was a gang in control that was bent on using those
methods. The opposition might try to implicate him, it
probably would, because it had always hated him, but
he had nothing to fear. And she need n't have anything
to fear either; if she married him she might be sure he
would never mix up in any dirty work. Wearisome almost had been his repetitions, assurances, and avowals;
they poured out of him while he ran his car along country roads and while he sat with her under some trees by
the edge of a lake.

She imagined him tearing open her letter with eager
expectancy, and then —! How could she feel anything
but compunction for him and pity for herself.

And as the evening passed, it was the selfish rather
than the generous emotion that absorbed her consciousness; it was her future as a poor man's wife rather
than Maguire's future as a disappointed and lonely man
that she contemplated with dismay.

The next morning, still unreconciled, and finding
strangely little solace in a becoming hat of red velvet
and an equally becoming costume of dark red broadcloth
trimmed with coonskin, she strolled along the spacious
aisles of the fourth floor of Bilbow and Slosson's. As
usual, the young women who presided over the millinery
and lingerie counters gazed at her enviously, the floor-
walker with the neat black mustache and emotional

dark eyes greeted her with affability, and the customers whom she passed turned their heads to follow her with interest. But these demonstrations failed to provoke in her the usual agreeable reaction, the new costumes and dresses displayed upon the forms failed to win her critical scrutiny, the persuasive perfumes that the discreet and subtle management caused to permeate this aristocratic section of their establishment failed to give pleasure to the most fastidious of her senses. Even the survey of herself in the long mirrors at the ends of the aisles was mechanical, abstracted, indifferent.

Patrick Maguire emerged from the elevator and came towards her. Nora blushed and trembled when she saw him; as they approached each other, walking slowly, she pressed a hand to her throat; her heart was jumping and battering. Maguire looked grave and determined; he lifted his pea-green Fedora hat and replaced it on his head without a smile.

"I got your letter," he said, as he turned and walked with her. "After getting it, I had one or two things to attend to, and then I came round here at once. It does n't go, Nora, it does n't go."

"What do you mean?" she asked faintly.

"You 're going to knock off work here and come out with me while I tell you."

"I can't possibly do that."

"Oh, yes, that 's what you 're going to do. And I can't wait for you to change your clothes either; what you have on will do very well. So just tell whoever 's in charge that you 're going out and don't know when you 'll be back."

Nora laughed nervously. "You must think I want to lose my job."

"You won't lose it. Tell 'em you'll buy the clothes you have on; that's true enough. They suit you well; I like you in them, and I'll buy 'em for you."

"I wouldn't let you."

"Oh," said Maguire with a faint smile, "I guess you will."

The forewoman came bustling up, puzzled, interested, and pleasant. "Oh, Mrs. Corcoran," she said, "Mr. Stratton has just sent up word that you're to have a holiday. So you're excused, of course. What a nice day for it!"

"A holiday!" cried Nora. "I don't want it. I haven't asked for it. I —"

"Now don't you form the habit of rejecting everything that's offered to you, Nora," interposed Maguire. "You'll go awful wrong if you adopt that for a policy." He turned to the forewoman. "Mrs. Corcoran's going to keep these things she's got on. Just charge 'em to me — Patrick Maguire; Mr. Stratton will tell you it's all right."

"It is not. I won't hear of such a thing."

"Now, now, what did I just tell you about the awful mistake of rejecting what's offered to you?" Maguire's voice was soothing; he winked at the forewoman. "Come on now; we don't want to waste any more time. Of course you're going to keep these clothes."

"Why, of course, Mrs. Corcoran." The forewoman employed the honeyed manner that she exhibited only to customers of distinction. "They're so lovely on you;

good gracious, I wish somebody would make me such a present."

"You might just as well wear them, Nora," urged Maguire. "If you don't, they'll be sent round to your house. Why not wear them and increase the pleasure of your holiday?"

"That's right too," agreed the forewoman.

"I must say —" began Nora; but Maguire interrupted with a remark to the forewoman, who interpreted it correctly as a dismissal.

"Just see that it's charged to me, will you, please?"

"I must say," repeated Nora, as the forewoman withdrew, "this is the strangest kind of an answer to that note."

"Sometimes," said Maguire, "it's necessary to take radical measures."

He summoned the elevator; Nora entered it without protest. She had no idea he could be so decisive, and she was interested in discovering now what his intentions were.

In the automobile he glanced at his watch. "Eleven o'clock. Too bad you should have had to miss so much of your holiday. But after getting your letter I had things to do that prevented me from coming earlier."

"Tell me, how were you able to get me this holiday?"

"Oh, Bilbow and Slosson will do anything for me, within reason. I fixed matters for them so that they could throw a bridge across Exchange Alley to their new building; it meant getting special legislation through the City Council. And I never held 'em up for it — not to any great extent."

He made no allusion to the letter, but when he had driven out beyond the suburbs he stopped the car and drew a small box from his pocket. He handed it to her.

"There's one of the things I had to do," he said. "See how you like it."

She opened it with a premonition of what she should find. Yet she was unprepared for the splendor that she uncovered — a ring in which was set a magnificent diamond.

"It's very handsome," she said. She looked at it a moment longer and then held it out to him.

"Put it on," he said. "See how it looks on your finger."

"Oh, all right."

She began to take off her right glove.

"The other glove," he suggested. "It's on the left hand that it's worn."

"Anything to oblige you. Of course I don't bind myself in any way."

"Of course not."

She slipped the ring on her finger and held it up so that the light played on it.

"Does it happen to fit?" he asked.

"Yes, it's just about right."

"Of course if it were n't and you liked the stone, it could be set in a ring of the right size."

"You don't expect me to accept such a gift."

"I would n't have bought it if I had n't expected you to accept it."

"It's out of the question. I should take a ring like that only from the man I was engaged to."

"Well, let's not argue the point. Just wear it to-day, to celebrate the holiday. Don't you like to see it on your finger?"

"It's perfectly wonderful," she admitted.

"Feeling and seeing it on your hand will give you pleasure to-day, won't it?"

"Yes, I suppose it will."

"That's all that's necessary."

He started the car and drove on without further speech. His silence and his air of purposefulness seemed to Nora formidable; this ride became exciting; she was unable to think of things to say, because she was so keenly expectant and apprehensive. Indeed, she could n't tell whether it was expectancy or apprehensiveness that agitated her.

Maguire observed that she did not put on the glove that she had taken off. She kept her bare hand in her lap and frequently spread out the fingers and set new colors to flashing in the stone. Frequent sidelong glances told Maguire that she was more interested in looking at the ring than at the objects along the road.

Presently he stopped the car again, out in the open country. He produced another little packet and handed it to her. "See what you think of that."

Opening it, she discovered a pair of earrings, into each of which was set a large and lustrous pearl. She looked at Maguire with consternation.

"Goodness!" she cried. "Are they real?"

"Sure," he answered, with a note of injured sensitiveness in his voice. "Do you think I'd be giving you imitations?"

"You must n't, must n't *talk* of giving me such things."

"All right, I won't *talk* of it," he said indulgently. "But just put them on. They'll help you to enjoy your holiday."

She sat gazing at the pearls with rapt eyes; she held them in her hand reverently. Never before had she touched anything so rare, so rich, so fabulously expensive. As she looked at them, they seemed to have the power almost of putting her into a trance.

Out of something very like that Maguire's voice, gently insistent, summoned her.

"Put 'em on, Nora; let's see how you look with 'em on."

She laid the precious things carefully in her lap and began to unpin her veil. "I wonder," she said, "if you're crazy or am I?"

"There's nothing crazy about me," Maguire rejoined. "I should n't wonder if sometimes you went a little off your head."

He watched her attentively while she affixed the ornaments to her ears.

"You know how to do it just by instinct," he remarked. "I don't suppose I could get one of those things on if I was to stand in front of a looking-glass. You certainly are a picture."

She smiled at him. "Do they look well on me? How I wish I could see myself."

"You will; that's part of it," was his somewhat enigmatic answer. He waited till she had carefully arranged her veil again and then said, "Now shall we toddle along?"

JERRY

They went bowling down the road at the leisurely rate of twenty-five miles an hour. At least it seemed a leisurely rate of travel in that smooth-running, comfortably cushioned car.

As they proceeded, silence again fell between them. Nora wondered when the next wayside stop would occur and what act of presentation would signalize it. If there was to be another stop and the principle of climax was observed, it could hardly be less than a diamond tiara or a pearl necklace. She began to feel there was something magical about the creature; certainly he was superb in both audacity and opulence. She could comprehend now as she had hitherto been unable to do his power over men. No longer could she think of him with a tinge of disparagement in her liking; with a compassionate sense of his ineligible qualities. He revealed himself as formidable and romantic; it was a bewildering discovery to make.

There was no other wayside stop, and to a fairly well-satiated Nora this was hardly a disappointment. On the contrary, she was glad when, upon entering a town that was the seat of a small college, they turned into the grounds of the attractive inn.

"We'll lunch here," said Maguire. "You'll have a chance to see how you look."

He left her at the entrance while he drove off to put up the car. When he rejoined her, she was seated in a chair on the veranda; her veil was pushed up and the earrings showed in their full splendor. He smiled at seeing how her eyes sparkled.

"What did you think?" he asked.

"I hardly knew myself," she acknowledged. "I want to have another look before we go."

He smiled; a few minutes later she caused him to smile again. On the way to the dining-room they passed the inn parlor, and Nora espied an oval mirror in a gilt frame on the farther wall. She could not resist its lure; she slipped into the room, the four ladies who were playing bridge stopped their game to gaze at her; she went up to the mirror and stood in front of it for some moments, patting and pretending to arrange her hair. The four ladies watched her with pleasure, for they saw a slim, graceful figure, appropriately clothed, a face youthful and happy, merry, whimsical eyes, pretty lips parted in a smile; and they accepted the pearl earrings and the big diamond sparkling on the white hand as the proper appurtenances of such a handsome, high-bred young woman. Maguire, who had followed Nora into the room, waited blandly for her to finish.

"Are n't you the little humbug!" he said when they were once more on their way down the corridor to the dining-room. "But it was worth looking at, was n't it?"

"I liked it," she admitted. "Do you think anybody else would?"

He laughed indulgently at such obvious, such guileless coquetry.

She was quite surprised to find how well he seemed to understand her and how much sympathy he had with what Jerry was accustomed to make her feel were her weaknesses. A thought entered her mind and enchanted her with its brilliancy. Perhaps what would be weaknesses in one condition of life might be graces in another.

With this flash of insight to guide her, she felt that she understood herself completely.

Not until they had finished luncheon and Maguire had lighted a cigarette did he embark upon the theme of themes.

"Well," he said, pushing back his plate and folding his somewhat stubby forearms on the table, "are you having a good holiday?"

"Oh, yes," she answered.

"No reason why you should n't have every day a holiday like this."

"You forget the letter I wrote you. The reason is in that."

"I can't take that seriously, Nora. I know you don't love him. You may think you do, but I know different. If you did, you could n't be enjoying yourself so much to-day. You could n't have kept me going all this time as you've done if you loved him. I knew you did n't love him when he happened along yesterday just as you were getting out of the machine; I could tell by the look on your face. I saw the look on his face, too, and I'm not so awful sure he loves you. Maybe when you two are alone together you work each other up into thinking you're in love. But there's nothing real about that, you know. Maybe you're the kind of person that could never really be in love with anybody. I'm not sure that you ain't."

"If you really thought that, you could n't care anything about me," said Nora, quite outraged.

"That's the funny thing, I do. I'll do the loving, and you'll do the appreciating. That makes a good team.

Satisfactory to both. Some day, maybe," — Maguire
spoke slowly, — "something may happen that will
make you do some loving too. But I don't hardly expect
it for myself."

Nora dropped her eyes and let them rest on the
sparkling ring.

"What did you do after you got my letter?" she
asked presently.

"I thought about it for a little while. Then I went
out and bought those jewels."

"You decided you could bribe me into marrying you?"

"Bribe's an awful coarse word, Nora. I've been in
politics a lot, and I've never got so I like the sound
of it."

"But that's really what you did think, is n't it?"

"I would say," replied Maguire, speaking slowly,
"that I wanted to bring home to you what you'd be
missing in one case, what you'd have in the other. I
wanted to start you thinking more carefully about the
future than you'd been doing. These things that you're
wearing to-day, just to oblige me, they're only symbols,
you know. There's a whole lot that goes with them.
You ought to think before you get married what you're
going to make of your life. If you face and realize the
possibilities that I can offer you, and then decide that
just because you love Donohue you'll be contented and
happy with him and won't ever regret turning your back
on me, why, all right; I've nothing more to say. Only I
want to be sure you've looked over the ground first.
Donohue's a patrolman, and he's honest — a nice
young chap. He'll do the best he can for you, but a

policeman that's honest — he'll never be able to do much."

"He's a lawyer now," struck in Nora. "He's just passed his bar examinations."

Maguire smiled. "More than half the lawyers in this city don't make a patrolman's wages. He'll quite likely be better off if he sticks to the uniform."

"He's bright enough; he ought to make a good lawyer."

"There are a lot of men who pass their bar examinations of whom that might be said and who can't pay office rent."

"If he could only get a start!" sighed Nora. "That's all he needs, I'm sure."

"That's all that hundreds of good men need and never get."

"I suppose you could help him to it if you wanted to," Nora said musingly. She twisted the ring back and forth, making the diamond sparkle and dance.

Maguire studied her through narrowed eyelids.

"I suppose I could," he replied. "But why should I?"

"If you love me so much you ought to want to do all you can to make me happy. And if I decided to marry Jerry Donohue, I should think you'd like to help him along all you could."

"You've got funny ideas about a man's love."

"Have I? I supposed if you really loved a person, you were willing to sacrifice yourself for that person, and do everything you could to make her happy."

"Within limits. A man is bound to want some response for all his sacrifices."

"But think what a pleasure it would be to you to see me blissfully happy and feel you had helped to make me so."

Her eyes twinkled, yet he could not be sure that she was teasing him. He regarded her in meditative silence.

"And," she continued, "think how mean you'd feel if you saw us struggling along, two worthy people, and yet never gave us the little boost that we needed."

"I tell you, Nora," Maguire said seriously, "I don't know just what I'd do in such circumstances. I suppose if I found things were going hard with you I'd try to help out. Yes, I suppose I'd do that."

Suddenly Nora's eyes, that had been mischievous and twinkling, swam in tears. "You are nice; you do love me," she said. "And I don't see why you do, after the way I've treated you."

"I find plenty of reasons for it. We each of us can give the other something; we'll get on better and better as time passes."

"If I were to change my mind now and say I'd marry you, I think you'd despise me; you'd know I had been influenced by your presents and I wouldn't seem a nice person to you any longer."

"It wouldn't make the slightest difference in my feelings; in fact, I've already anticipated all this. I was afraid the registry might be closed by the time we got back this afternoon, so after my visit to the jeweler's I went round there." He drew a long envelope from his coat pocket, took out the enclosure, and handed it to her.

She unfolded it, glanced at it, and gasped.

"Is it a joke?" She looked over the paper at him incredulously.

"Joke, no. It's a marriage license."

She glanced at it again, saw again his name and hers — "Of all the — impudence! How did you dare?" Her cheeks were blushing, but her eyes twinkled and a smile plucked at her lips.

"After buying diamonds and pearls, that was n't taking any chance at all," responded Maguire with a grin. "I know the registry clerk intimately, and I swore him to secrecy. Now would you like to hear the rest of my plan?"

She hesitated just a moment. "Yes."

"Go back to the city just as fast as the automobile will take us — well, not quite that, for I don't believe in being reckless even over such a thing as this —"

"You don't!" interjected Nora. "I'm glad to hear it."

"We'll round up your mother and brother" — Maguire was reckless anyway of her interruption — "go straight to the priest, and take the night train for Chicago. We'll stay there a few days — long enough for you to fit yourself out with all the clothes and fixings you want; and then we'll make for California; we'll take in the Grand Canyon and the Yosemite and anything else you say; and we'll go from one big hotel to another and stop in each place as long as you like. Then, when you feel ready for it, we'll come home and start in to make a home. What do you say?"

He had spoken with suppressed excitement, his words tumbling out faster and faster as he proceeded. Now he hung over the table and looked eagerly and confidently into her face.

She looked for a moment into his, dropped her eyes, raised them again, inhaled a long breath, expelled it in a sigh, and then said, quite plaintively, "Oh, dear, I wonder — Are you sure you want me, Patrick?"

He reached out and covered her hand with his. "I'm sure."

One moment more she hesitated while she searched his face.

"Well, then," she said, "it's yes."

Maguire gave her hand a long squeeze. Then he rose.

"Now," he said, "I'll get the automobile."

XLIII

MRS. GLEASON, the landlady, frequently came in to sit
with Mrs. Scanlan in the afternoons. The fact that
Mrs. Scanlan's daughter had two suitors had not es-
caped her notice, and she was interested in getting such
information as she could in regard to their wooing. But
this was not the only interest prompting her visits. She
enjoyed eliciting details about the tragic past of the
Scanlan family; she was quite skillful in persuading
Mrs. Scanlan to dwell on the gradual demoralization of
her husband, on Nora's unhappy marriage, on Dave's
disgrace; she particularly delighted in hearing all that
Mrs. Scanlan could tell of the night when Michael Scanlan had killed his son-in-law and himself; her questions
stimulated Mrs. Scanlan's memory and she was able to
recall many small happenings of that fatal evening
which gave color to her narrative. The tragedy seemed
now so far in the past that Mrs. Scanlan, instead of
resenting questions about it, was rather gratified by the
interest that inspired them; it awoke in her a sense of
importance that was usually dormant, and at times she
became animated, almost dramatic, in her recital.

Now Mrs. Gleason had led her through the story
again, this time making the treatment that Nora had
suffered at the hands of Corcoran the subject of special
inquiry. When it appeared that there was nothing more

to be derived, the landlady observed sympathetically: —

"It's certainly a sad tale, Mrs. Scanlan, and I do hope there's some comfort ahead. I'm thinking one thing, at any rate, and that is that Mrs. Corcoran will not go down to her grave wearing that mean fellow's name."

"No, it's true enough she won't," agreed Mrs. Scanlan. "I expect it won't be long now before she changes it."

"Do you think she'll be Mrs. Patrick Maguire?"

"Oh, no. He's just a friend of hers. There's nothing at all between them."

"Now I'm sorry to hear that. I was hoping maybe he'd asked her. Why, he's got millions, so they say."

"I don't know as that would make any difference to Nora."

"It would be a strange thing if it would n't. There's mighty few young girls that it would n't make a difference to; and a woman that's been through what your daughter has — well, it's a sure thing to me that if she does n't marry him it's because he never asked her."

"You can think about that as you like," returned Mrs. Scanlan, with a flash of her old-time spirit. "I don't inquire into matters that don't concern me, and it's a good rule for every one."

"Oh, I was n't meaning to pry into anybody's affairs, Mrs. Scanlan. It's a thing I never do, I do assure you. I've kept a boarding-house too long ever to be accused of that. If I've seemed to take an interest in your daughter's goings-on, it's no more than I'd do for anybody whose welfare I had at heart. No more, I do assure you."

JERRY

Mrs. Gleason plied her knitting-needles with redoubled vigor. She was making a sweater, and now with an injured expression of the mouth devoted herself to counting the stitches. Mrs. Scanlan, also with an injured expression of the mouth, rocked silently, empty-handed.

Unmistakably there was the sound of an automobile stopping in front of the house. Gathering up her work, Mrs. Gleason hastened to the bay window; Mrs. Scanlan was not far behind her.

"It's the two we've been talking of!" exclaimed Mrs. Gleason. "He's coming in with her, Mrs. Scanlan. I never before saw her in those clothes or that hat."

"No more did I," said Mrs. Scanlan.

"They look awful expensive. I don't suppose it's an elopement; they'd hardly be coming back so soon if it was that. Still, secret marriages — sometimes they're kept secret a long time."

"There's nothing of that sort, you may be sure."

"Well, maybe not. But it's the parents that are the most surprised at the doings of their children."

The door opened, and Nora entered, followed by Maguire; they looked smiling and happy. .

"Mother, I've some great news for you," said Nora, coming forward and putting her arm round Mrs. Scanlan's waist. "I'm going to marry Patrick Maguire this very evening."

Mrs. Scanlan was speechless and unresponsive while her daughter kissed her and Maguire smiled and bowed. Not so Mrs. Gleason; her voice soared triumphantly.

"There, now, I was n't so far off. When I saw you

[369]

two getting out of that automobile, I says, 'I wonder if it's an elopement; I wonder if there's been a secret marriage,' I says. Well, sudden is next thing to secret, and taking your folks by surprise is next door to eloping, so I don't see but what I hit it pretty near right."

"But, Nora, I thought —" began Mrs. Scanlan.

Her daughter promptly checked her.

"Yes, mother, but it's all settled now. Here, Patrick, you and mother had better kiss each other."

Maguire performed his part of the ceremony with sprightliness and gallantry, but Mrs. Scanlan submitted as one dazed and still unreconciled.

"It ain't what I expected; that's all I can say," she remarked mournfully.

"Now, Mrs. Scanlan," said Maguire, "don't you be afraid that your daughter's drawn the same kind of a ticket in this lottery that she did before. I'll promise you she has n't. And if it's a shock to you now, I'll guarantee it won't be a disappointment to you in the long run."

Nora's mother could not mistake the ring of genuineness in the speech. "It all seems so strange," she said. "But if Nora's happy, it's all right — and she looks happier and handsomer than I've ever seen her."

"I am," declared Nora. "It's the wedding presents, mother; have you noticed Patrick's wedding presents? He's just covered me with them."

Mrs. Gleason at once began to chant a hymn of stupefaction which dealt with each article and ornament in turn. Mrs. Scanlan, more subdued, more inarticulate, was hardly less appreciative.

JERRY

"Oh, it's a pleasure to plaster things onto Nora,"
Maguire said. "I expect to do it a lot. Say, she wears
things like a queen, don't she?" He allowed himself a
moment's rapt gaze, and then in his brisk efficiency
manner enunciated the following: "Now it's half past
five. I've got to have an hour to make arrangements.
But I'll be back here by seven to take you all to Father
Cleary's house, and by that time, Nora, you must be all
packed and ready to start. After the wedding we'll have
a little supper at the Wallace House — be pleased to
have you join us, Mrs. Gleason."

"Oh, indeed, if I don't intrude!" cried the landlady, in
a transport of delight.

"We'll have to go right from the hotel to the station," continued Maguire. "Our train leaves at nine.
We're starting for California, Mrs. Scanlan."

"I'm ready to believe anything," replied Mrs. Scanlan in a tone of resignation. "It's all so strange — so
different from what I expected."

"I'll be back in a little more than an hour," repeated
Maguire. "And by that time, Nora, you'll have to be
all packed and ready. But you don't need to take much,
you know; we'll get all the things you need in Chicago."

"If it ain't like dreamland!" ejaculated Mrs. Gleason,
as Maguire withdrew. "Well, Mrs. Corcoran, you certainly are one who don't have just a run of ill luck. I'm
sure, considering what you folks have been through, I
can find it in my heart to congratulate you."

Nora made no acknowledgment of this magnanimous
speech. "Mother, I guess you'd better get ready for the
wedding while I'm packing up my things," she said

[371]

abruptly. "I hope Dave will be home in plenty of time. Goodness, there are so many things to do and so much I want to tell you."

Mrs. Gleason moved towards the door. "I must be getting ready for the wedding too," she remarked. "At least I hope I'm invited to that, Mrs. Corcoran, as long as Mr. Maguire was so good as to invite me to the wedding supper?" Simpering, she awaited a favorable response, which was somewhat brusquely forthcoming. She then took her departure; and Nora flew to her mother's arms and cried, "Oh, mother, he's the nicest man; you've no idea how nice and kind he is."

"Nicer and kinder than Jerry?"

"Perhaps not, but he's different, and I'll be happier with him and Jerry will be happier without me. I'm sure of it."

"Does Jerry know?"

"Not yet. Mother, you must begin to get ready, and so must I."

"Do you think you're treating Jerry right, Nora?"

"I'm sorry for that, but it has to be. We've had so many differences that he won't feel badly — not long."

Mrs. Scanlan was unused to playing the part of conscience to Nora. Her questions had been prompted more by bewilderment than by doubt; the decisiveness of Nora's replies made her feel that all must be for the best. But Dave, who had come in just as his sister had completed her preparations, manifested strong disapproval; at first he was flatly incredulous, then he was hotly indignant.

"But no longer ago than yesterday you were telling

[372]

me that you and Jerry were soon to be married!" he
cried. "What's got into you, Nora? You're throwing
over a good man to tie up to a rich one — that's what
you're doing. You made one mistake throwing over
Jerry Donohue; mind that. If you do it again, you'll
deserve no better than what came to you last time."

Nora kept her temper. "I'm not making that mistake
again, Dave, though it's no wonder you should be
afraid of it. Patrick Maguire has as kind a heart as
Jerry himself. If it seems to you I've changed my mind
all of a sudden, I can only say it's been a long while that
I've been wondering if I ought n't to change it. Now
it's done, and I've no misgivings at all. I'm happier
than I've been all these months that I've looked forward to marrying Jerry."

"I doubt if you'll be happy long, Nora."

"You would n't doubt it if you knew Patrick."

"His reputation's not of the best."

"He's quit politics. He's not going to do anything of
that sort any more. You ought to be willing that a man
should make a fresh start, Dave."

His only reply to that was a look of bitterness and
reproach. Instantly she felt contrition; she knew that
she had been unkind. She ran to him as he stood leaning
against the mantelpiece, his hands in his pockets; she
clung to his arm and pleaded with him.

"Forgive me, Dave; I ought n't to have said that.
Forgive me, and be nice to me — the night I'm to be
married."

"Oh, I can forgive you. But how about Jerry?"

"I suppose he'll find it hard. But I know I'm not the

kind of wife he wants, and truly, Dave, he's often as much as told me so. I think we both only loved each other sometimes."

"I wonder how long you've been loving Maguire all the time."

Nora was silent.

"You'd better reconsider, Nora."

She shook her head. "No, Dave. You can't understand, but I'm just as sure as I can be that what I'm doing is right for all of us."

"Do you think it's right not even to let Jerry know?"

"I think it's better."

"You're just going to let him find it out for himself?"

She hesitated. "I suppose I ought to send him a note. I'll write him a note now, Dave. And please, no matter how disapproving you feel, be nice to me and go and get ready for the wedding."

"You'd better change your mind before it's too late."

"Nothing could make me change now, Dave."

He looked at her steadfastly for a moment, shook his head, and walked away. She heard him ascending the stairs to his little room.

As she sat down at the table where she had written the note to Maguire the day before, she thought, "Poor Jerry! It will be quite a shock to him, I suppose. But he won't feel badly very long; he's too much interested in other things." So without any sentimental dawdling or waste of words she wrote to Jerry that she was marrying Patrick Maguire that evening. "He's a good man, and he loves me, Jerry, — and he can give me what I want. I'm doing it suddenly because it seems to me the best way for all of us — no, I'll be honest and say because Patrick suggested it and because I felt it would spare me worry and debate in my own mind. I don't suppose you can ever forgive me, and I know it's a mean way to treat one that I like as much as I do you, Jerry."

She had just finished the letter when her mother entered the room, attired in the black silk dress that Nora had bought for her out of her earnings at Bilbow and Slosson's.

"You never looked nicer, mother," said Nora, giving her a kiss. "Now you must be just as happy as you are nice."

"It's so hard to realize. Such a change to have come in a few minutes. It's the way all the big changes in my life have come — no warning at all. Well, I hope this will be a pleasant one — not like most of the others."

"Indeed it will. And isn't it strange how what you and father used to hope for is coming true, long after you thought the chance of it had passed?"

"How do you mean, Nora?"

"Why, don't you remember how you and he used to count on my marrying a rich man? And now I'm doing it."

"Somehow it don't mean to me now what it might have once."

"Why, mother, it's going to mean a lot to you; wait and see. And it's going to mean a lot to me too — not just because he's rich."

"Indeed, I hope so, Nora."

But Mrs. Scanlan's tone was that of resignation

rather than enthusiasm, and a shadow crossed Nora's face; why could n't Dave and her mother show a little happy excitement?

There was a knock on the door and Miss Sims entered. She at least showed happy excitement. Mrs. Gleason had told her; she felt she must just run in and say how wonderful she thought it was. So much romance in it — getting married the same day you were engaged! It was beautiful.

Nora kissed her; and tears of happiness stood in Miss Sims's eyes. "Sister," that kiss had seemed to say.

Dave appeared, and then a few moments later Mrs. Gleason, with her plump figure encased in lavender foulard and with a lavender hat mounted upon her auburn hair. Still in an exclamatory mood, she bestowed compliments and congratulations as lavishly as if she had not already released a shower of them. While she was paying homage to Mrs. Scanlan's dress, Miss Sims was about to slip away, but Dave signaled to Nora with his eyes.

So Nora said, "Oh, Miss Sims, don't go. Do stay and come with us to the wedding."

"Oh, thank you, Mrs. Corcoran. Oh, thank you, I should love to."

The delicate tinge of pink that covered the girl's countenance from the small chin to the high cheek-bones and the wide forehead made her look almost pretty, emphasized the innocence and sensitiveness of her face. Nora noticed it and with a quickened sympathy stepped forward and kissed her. The young girl's eyes shone, and she glanced at Dave with a radiant smile. Nora

[376]

noticed that, too, and thought it fortunate that fate had thrown Dave and this good, sweet, little girl together. In this happy hour Nora wished to forecast and promote the happiness of those about her. She saw for Dave and his quiet wife a peaceful, contented life and growing prosperity; Patrick Maguire would assist them to that. She saw for her mother a serene old age, free from worries and cares; Patrick Maguire would provide for that. She might even have concerned herself for a fleeting moment with Mrs. Gleason's future, but the sound of a motor-car stopping in front of the house made thoughts about the landlady impossible. Dave reached the window and announced, "It's your man, Nora."

Maguire came upstairs; he was still wearing his gray-green suit, but he had a white carnation in his buttonhole and carried a bouquet of lilies of the valley, which he presented to Nora. She introduced him to Miss Sims, with whom he shook hands cordially, saying, "Pleased to know you, Miss Sims. Pleased to have you get into the taxi with us — lots of room for everybody."

"Oh, thank you ever so much." Surely no one could doubt, looking at her face, that this evening was full of happiness for Miss Sims.

Welcoming the wedding party into his study, the priest was jovial and merry; he congratulated Nora on having broken down the defenses of so well established a bachelor as Patrick Maguire.

The marriage ceremony was brief; after pronouncing the pair man and wife Father Cleary gave a hand to the bride and then to the bridegroom. Patrick kissed Nora and turned to face the others. Miss Sims had been heroically stifling sobs, Mrs. Scanlan looked as if she had been shedding tears, but Mrs. Gleason glowed with exuberance and rapture. She clapped her hands in a dainty and refined manner and cried, "Splendid! Splendid!" She kissed the bride and was all ready to bestow a similar salute upon the groom, but he did not give her an opportunity; she concluded that though he might be a leader in politics he was a shy man with the ladies.

Crowding again into the taxicab, bride and groom and wedding guests were speedily transported to the Wallace House. There in the palm room they sat down to a dinner which the head waiter — instructed by telephone — had specially ordered for them; he paid them personal attention, two of his subordinates hovered over them, champagne brimmed and bubbled in their glasses, the other diners gazed at them with wonder, a stringed orchestra discoursed music from a balcony. Mrs. Gleason soared more and more freely on the wings of her elation. She poised her glass aloft with many a challenging smile, pledging the health now of Mrs. Scanlan, now of Nora, now of Mr. Maguire; at intervals she drummed on the table to show how perfectly she could keep time with the orchestra, and when, as fortunately happened twice, they rendered a selection with which she was familiar, she gayly supplied the words. Miss Sims hardly spoke; she was dazzled by so much brilliancy, but she had an anxious, an apprehensive eye for Dave and the champagne. He saw the expression on her face, smiled, and shook his head reassuringly; and later, when no one was looking or listening, he caught her hand under the table and told her that she need n't be afraid; he was n't ever again going to let drink make a fool of him, not even if Maguire was to order up all the wine of France and stand it before him. Mrs. Scanlan, watching her daughter and Maguire, felt more reconciled; he had kind eyes, she thought, and looked at Nora as if he loved her. And what the priest had said to Nora about him had been encouraging. Nevertheless, her enjoyment of this festivity was clouded by thoughts of Jerry, and by thoughts, too, of Nora's wedding journey to the ends of the earth. So many things might happen, railroad wrecks, automobile accidents — it was dangerous to go so far from home and for so long a time. And she herself was so ailing and feeble — quite likely she would never see her daughter again after this night. Then Maguire beguiled her into drinking some champagne, and Mrs. Gleason beguiled her into drinking some more, and after that she felt quite cheerful. As for Nora and Patrick, they were so happy and showed it so plainly that people at the neighboring tables wondered what was the cause. They looked at each other and laughed; Patrick told humorous stories that made everybody else laugh. But finally he announced that they must start for the train.

Again two taxicabs were requisitioned. At the station Mr. Maguire's party was permitted to pass through the gate and sit for a few minutes in the stateroom that Patrick had reserved. Mrs. Scanlan and Miss Sims felt that they were being introduced this evening into realms of luxury. Mrs. Gleason's exclamation, "Now, is n't this cozy!" seemed totally inadequate.

Nora drew Dave aside for a moment.

"The letter to Jerry," she said. "It's on the table, Dave, at home. Will you mail it?"

And when he had said yes, Nora added, "If you see him, try — try to make him feel not too hardly towards me, Dave."

"I'll do what I can," Dave answered.

Then the good-byes had to be said, and again the sobs had to be stifled and the tears winked back. Mrs. Scanlan kissed Nora and kissed Maguire, murmuring into his ear, "Be good to her," and receiving in answer a long, firm pressure of the hand. Dave kissed Nora and shook hands with Maguire. Miss Sims kissed Nora and shook hands with Maguire. Mrs. Gleason, sober because the evening's gayeties were at an end, kissed Nora and — shook hands with Maguire. Shy and obdurate he was to the last.

A few moments Dave and the three women stood on the platform and waved and looked at Nora through the window, while she waved her handkerchief and kissed her hand to them. And then slowly the train pulled out of the station, and Nora and her husband were alone.

A little after nine o'clock that evening Jerry stood on Mrs. Gleason's steps and rang the bell. In his impatience it seemed to him that the maid was even more slow-footed than usual in responding. He was impatient because he was snatching just a few moments from patrol duty, which took him within a block of the house; he was impatient just to look in on Nora; he was impatient because her sweet submission to his dictation on the preceding evening made him wish to show her now a greater deference, a truer ardor; he could atone whole-heartedly for the neglect with which she had reproached him. He was eager, too, that she should hear the bit of news, so promising for their future, that he had omitted to convey the night before.

He did not ask the maid if Mrs. Corcoran was in; he had seen the light in the second-story windows and so went springing up the stairs. Dave opened the door to his knock.

Jerry said, "Hello, Dave; Nora in?" — and entered.

He saw Mrs. Scanlan and Miss Sims and the landlady; they looked at him in a manner that seemed to him strange, and they failed to reply immediately when he said, "I dropped in to see Nora for a few seconds. Is she in?"

After a moment Mrs. Scanlan was able to shake her head and murmur, "No."

Dave took up the letter lying on the writing-table and with a white face held it out to Jerry. "She left this for you," he said. "I was going to mail it."

Jerry looked at the envelope a moment before opening it. The eager expectancy that had been shining on his face faded; and he glanced at Dave with troubled, questioning eyes.

He read the note, and without speaking restored it to its envelope. He looked up; there was sadness but no throbbing passion in his voice as he said: —

"Has it happened?"

"Yes."

"How could it! How could you let her!"

"There was no stopping her. She was off with Maguire in his automobile all day, and when she got home she told us. I talked with her, but her mind was made up. She did feel badly about you, Jerry, but she said it was really the fairest and best thing for you in the long run."

There was a moment of silence, during which Jerry felt himself under the pitying scrutiny of four pairs of eyes. He put the note in his pocket and said with a smile in which there was no mirth: —

"Nora and I certainly seem fated not to get married to each other."

Yet as he patrolled the streets on that fine October night, there was no despair and very little bitterness in his heart. His spirit seemed unbecomingly elastic under what should have been a crushing blow. Instead of feeling angry because he had been tricked and cheated and cast aside, or miserable because the girl he loved was forever lost to him, he was conscious of a vast relief, a new sense of freedom. No more petty and baffling struggles with a will that yielded as perversely as it opposed, no more waste of time and manhood in persuasion through kisses, no more anxious contemplation of the future. He knew now — what he had never quite had the courage to admit — that to him Nora would have been a drag rather than a help.

He smiled at the ironical thought, "How badly mother will feel about this!"

XLIV

THE enormity of Nora's offense nearly prostrated Mrs. Donohue; she had no words with which to characterize such faithlessness. Jerry had difficulty in convincing her that he was not heart-broken.

"Really, mother, you need n't waste any sympathy on me," he said to her when, after an invective against Nora, she began to pour forth words of lamentation, consolation, and compassion. "I've often and often not been a bit sure that I was in love with Nora, and when I read her note, after my pride stopped smarting, I came pretty near feeling glad. I guess I 'm not made so that I can love anybody — except you, of course. I guess I'm too selfish at bottom."

"You need n't tell that to me, child. Oh, I know how it is when a great blow falls; at first you feel that you 'll be brave and you stand up under it so that everybody wonders how you can. Then, after a while, when everybody else no longer feels the shock of it and when people think you 're getting over it yourself, that 's the time when it begins to take hold of you. You 'll be feeling this thing a month from now, Jerry, child, far more than you do to-day."

"Don't you believe it," Jerry answered. "I have n't really been in love with Nora, and a month from now

[383]

I'll pretty nearly have forgotten that I ever thought I
was."

"Oh, you'd put the best face on it, no doubt about
that. Just as you did before. But there's no deceiving
your mother about it, no more now than then; and it's
sore and sorry I feel for you, my poor boy."

It was of no use to protest; his mother insisted on
viewing him as a tragic figure, a man of blighted life.
And that she transmitted this conception to Kate, with
a full explanation of the cause, he had no reason to
doubt. It seemed to him that Kate and Peter and
Betty crept round more quietly than ever, that they
tried to leave him to himself, possibly with the design
of not intruding upon his grief, and that an unnatural
hush brooded over the house. If he tried to enliven the
domestic circle with jokes and laughter, he was sure to
invite a sympathetic, comprehending look from his
mother and to detect constraint in Kate's responses.
In the evenings when he was at home it was a quiet and
studious household, with Kate the most studious of all.
She was working feverishly over her stenography and
was making no attempts at writing. In her notebook
she constantly transcribed mysterious symbols; sometimes she drew Peter into her room and had him read
aloud to her while she took down the words. Jerry could
hear the drone of Peter's voice, even though the door
was closed, and now and then Kate's interruptions —
"Not so fast, Peter; let's have that again." One evening he suggested to her that some variety in dictation
was advisable and offered to relieve Peter of his task;
she assured him it would be a great help if he would.

She gave him the textbook and he read from it several typical business letters; afterwards she read her notes to him and made a quite accurate rendering.

"Pretty smart, Kate, pretty smart," he said. "I guess no one would dictate much faster than I was reading. And can you spin it off on the typewriter at a good speed? Well, you're a clever one, that's all I can say."

"Of course, I'm pretty familiar with just the letters in that book," she replied.

"Then I'll give you a new one. We'll write a letter to Mrs. Bennett, upstairs. Now begin: 'Dear Mrs. Bennett: Please send your baby down to talk with me in the evenings. They're all so busy on our floor that they don't give me any social life any more. It isn't only that they're busy; it's as if there was a funeral just over or just coming, I don't know which, but any way it's kind of doleful' —"

"Oh, Jerry, you've got clean away from me."

"No matter; we'll change it a little — 'A funeral just over or just coming, and somehow they manage to make me feel as if it was mine.' Get that, Kate?"

"Yes." She did not look up, though her color had risen.

"'I bet this is a pretty neat-looking letter I'm sending you, and when my law practice gets so I can hire a stenographer I hope I can hire one that will write as good as this.' Get that, Kate?"

"'Write as well as this.'" Kate made the final jottings. "My teacher says that a stenographer should correct her employer's English when it's so bad as to be illiterate."

There was a shy twinkle in her eye as she glanced at him.

"That's a swift come-back," he acknowledged. "But I can't let you think a member of the bar is illiterate. I was trying to slip something over on you, to see what you'd do about it."

"Now you know. According to my teacher, some men will discharge a stenographer for correcting them, and others will make her their private secretary."

"I hope you draw one of the right kind. For I don't believe you'd ever let anybody's sloppy English go without fixing it up — a person with your talent for writing."

"I think I'd make just as few alterations as I could," said Kate, looking pleased. "I wouldn't want to spoil the individuality of a letter."

Kate and Jerry held various similar discussions; Jerry found it entertaining to draw her out, to hear her comments on the teacher and on the pupils, to get her views about the world of business that she was preparing herself to enter. In all this he took a mischievous sort of pleasure, for he felt that if Nora's marriage had definitely settled any one thing, it was that the Dobbinses should continue to live with the Donohues and that Kate should go to college instead of getting a job as a stenographer. It would hardly be possible to send her until the following year; meanwhile, she was acquiring some knowledge which would be useful to her anywhere. Jerry could not conceive that his philanthropic purposes could now be balked; as the condition that had driven Kate to prepare for an independent life no longer existed, she could, no doubt, be persuaded to forego the plunge, to do instead the thing that was so obviously best for Betty, Peter, and herself. If a life of independence still seemed a goal to strive towards, she would see that it was wise to qualify herself for work in which her natural gifts would have freer play than would be theirs should she be content with only a common-school education. Jerry believed that he could say, "Now, Kate, I know exactly why you were so possessed to rush out into the world and earn your living. But the thing you expected me to do never came off, and so you need n't be in any haste." He believed that if he said just this and then dilated on Kate's duty to her brother and sister and herself, the Dobbinses would not be lost to the Donohues immediately. The prospect of keeping them in the family cheered Jerry immensely, and was only one of several factors that gave zest to life at a time when his mother suspected that gloom enveloped his soul.

For another thing, the election went in all respects as Jerry had hoped it would do. Maxwell was badly defeated; Trask was victor over Mulkern by a huge majority; the old Democratic city machine, if not smashed, was seriously disabled. Two months intervened before the new administration entered upon its duties; Trask invited Jerry to pass that interval in his office as an assistant, and offered him a salary a little larger than that which he had been receiving as a patrolman. Plunging into the new work with ardor, Jerry had almost at once an opportunity to demonstrate his capabilities. Trask turned over to him a case that was scheduled for early trial, and Jerry went into it with such thoroughness and single-mindedness that he was unaware of the interest with which his employer was watching him. He collected an impressive array of judicial decisions supporting his client's contention, he was indefatigable in seeking out witnesses, and he showed skill and soundness in sketching the argument. When he submitted the result of his researches, Trask said to him, "I think you'd better try this case." That had been more than Jerry had hoped to do; he tingled with excitement, and in the evenings returned to the office and paced the floor preparing for his first forensic effort. It was successful, so successful that immediately Trask gave him another and more complicated case to work out. And here again Jerry's preparation proved so painstaking and showed such a grasp of both details and principles that Trask said, "I can't do better than let you go into court with it."

During the trial Trask stopped in to ascertain if his assistant needed help. Jerry was cross-examining a witness; and after five minutes Trask went away satisfied. He had seen revealed what he had believed he should find — the power of personality impressing itself on judge, on jury, on witness; Jerry's straightforward, honest, definite manner, his mental alertness, and his imposing physical vigor made him a formidable cross-examiner. He won his case, and Trask congratulated him and added mysteriously, "You've passed the test."

What he had meant by that Jerry learned when Trask appointed him Assistant District Attorney. With a salary of three thousand dollars a year and work enough to keep him busy every minute, Jerry felt that the days when he had wondered how he should ever get a start at the law were very far away.

So prosperous a condition seemed to warrant an alteration in the family's mode of life. They could continue in their lodgings until April, when their lease of the apartment expired, but then, Jerry determined, they should move to a more dignified neighborhood. One evening he invited suggestions. His mother thought it would be nice if they could live somewhere near the park. Betty, in heedless rapture exclaimed, "Would n't that be lovely!" But Peter and Kate were silent.

"What do you say, Kate?" Jerry asked.

"I have n't anything to say, Jerry. It's awfully good of you to think of us, but you know we're going to look out for ourselves pretty soon."

"Oh, that's —" began Jerry, and then he flushed and stopped. It would n't be so easy, this explanation. "Kate, I guess you and I must have a little heart-to-heart talk. Mother, don't you want to go up and visit Mrs. Bennett for a while? And Peter, you and Betty can go and study in the other room."

Mrs. Donohue accepted exile amiably. She lingered for a word of admonition. "Now, Kate, don't you be stubborn. Jerry's told me what he wants to do for you, and I'm sure I approve. Things are n't as they were once, you know."

With a meaning nod she withdrew. Peter and Betty took their books and went into Kate's room. Kate closed her notebook and sat with downcast eyes, waiting, while Jerry paced to and fro with his hands behind his back. Finally he began, with somewhat less poise of manner than he was already accustomed to display in the courtroom.

"Of course I know what put the idea of launching out for yourselves into your head. Mother gave you a hint that I was wanting to get married, and you felt that you and Peter and Betty might be preventing me. Whether there was ever any reason for that belief or not, you must know that the situation's altogether different to-day." He hesitated for a moment, and then, as Kate did not speak, he continued, "And I'm glad it is. I knew, off and on, that I did n't love Nora enough, and she knew, off and on, that she did n't love me enough. There's nobody now that I'm the least bit interested in; and you and Peter and Betty are part of the family, and I want to have you get the advantages that I'd give you if I was really your brother. There's a college education ahead for every one of you. You won't let pride stand in the way, will you, Kate?"

"But what is a person without pride, Jerry?" She looked up at him with clear eyes, even though there was a puzzled frown on her brow. "What you offer us is the life of a parasite, and if I agreed to it I should be throwing away the pride that is all that makes me a real person — real to myself anyway. Besides" — she smiled, and the puzzled frown vanished and a livelier light shone in her eyes — "the fact that you're not interested in any one now has no special significance for the future. By next week or next month you may be in love with some woman — and not just off and on."

"You don't understand me," cried Jerry. "I shall

probably never marry. I shall be much too busy to
fall in love, — and I think I'm not capable of any very
permanent feeling about a woman."

Kate laughed; she sprang up and tucking her arm
inside his patted his hand while she walked with him
to and fro.

"You're capable of anything that's normal and
human, Jerry. Just anything. You're capable, too, of
any sacrifice. Put yourself in my place. If I go out into
the world now to earn a living, in two or three years,
provided I show intelligence and capacity, I ought to
be earning a better living. On the other hand, if I allow
you to support us and to send me to college, I may suddenly discover that I'm impeding your life and that
some other woman looks on Betty and Peter and me as
blocking her happiness. Of course, as soon as I discovered that, I should at once have to break away and stand
on my own feet, and I should be less fit to do it then
than I am now — or shall be soon — besides having lost
the time when I might have been getting a start. Now
suppose this should n't happen. Don't you know that
I should always suspect that just because of us you
were not letting it happen? For you see, Jerry, I know
you pretty well. And I know you're capable of any
sacrifice."

"You've got me all wrong, Kate. I'm not self-sacri-
ficing, and I'm too selfish and too comfortable, just
as we are, to fall in love. You see, I'm urging you to do
what I ask because it would be for my satisfaction and
comfort — not because it would be a fine thing for you."

"I'm not going to let a keen lawyer draw me into an

argument." Kate gave his arm a final pat and dropped it. "I don't doubt, Jerry, that we'll leave you and your mother with tears in our eyes, but it's got to be done, and you and she must make your plans for April without reference to us. By April I expect to have a job."

"I had no idea, Kate, you'd be so difficult to manage." Jerry's glance was half reproachful, half admiring.

"Oh, I can be granite when I have to be," she answered with a smile.

When Mrs. Donohue returned from visiting Mrs. Bennett, she found Jerry pacing the floor and dictating notes for a brief to Kate; Peter and Betty had already gone to bed.

"Now I hope to goodness you've got it all fixed up," said Mrs. Donohue, and her tone indicated that indeed she had no doubts about the matter.

"No, it's not to be fixed up," Jerry replied. "And the worst of it is, she's convinced me she's right, so I can't do anything more by way of persuading her."

"But I can't understand!" wailed Mrs. Donohue, and she gazed from one to the other in amazement. "Jerry, child, could n't you make her see. Don't you know we *want* you, Kate?"

Reluctantly and without pretending to comprehend the reasons presented to her, Mrs. Donohue bowed to the superior intelligence of the young.

"What must be must be," she said with resignation. "But it certainly will take all the pleasure out of moving — which is little enough — to feel that we're losing you and Peter and Betty, my dear."

Partly because of this feeling, partly because Jerry

had very little time for house-hunting, the question what they should do in April dragged on from week to week unsettled. And the longer it dragged on, the less disposition there was to settle it.

"Perhaps Kate won't get a job right off," Jerry said to his mother. "We can stay on here as tenants at will, and we'd better do that until Kate feels that she and her family must leave us."

Meanwhile, he and Kate were helping each other professionally; often he brought work home at night and dictated to her, and she presented him with typewritten copies of his utterances the next day. It was good practice for her, because it familiarized her with legal phraseology; Jerry profited by the arrangement, for it enabled him to turn out more work than he could otherwise have done. He found Kate almost as rapid as his office stenographer and a good deal more intelligent; sometimes she ventured a hint or a criticism, and it was always worth considering. The more he worked with her, the more confidence he came to have in her judgment, the more respect for her character; more and more did he feel that she was a good person to work with. That she had a reciprocal feeling about him was suggested by the rapid improvement in her work; Jerry was himself amazed by it. Such facility and cleverness, with fingers and with mind — he saw it developing almost magically under his eyes. And as he became more impressed by this, his senses awoke to other aspects of the girl; she was good to look at in her absorbed moments and inspiriting when she was aroused; sometimes there was deep thoughtfulness in her eyes, sometimes there

was admiration, sometimes raillery; as she was deft with
her fingers and quick of mind, so was she swift and lis-
some in all her movements; and the more that Jerry
watched her, the more did she amuse and please and
interest him.

On an evening in March Jerry came home to hear the
announcement that he had known was some time inevitable. Kate had a position. She was going to work the
following Monday in the office of a stockbroker who
had applied to the school for a stenographer. Although
she was very cheerful about it, Peter and Betty were
subdued, and Jerry suspected that Kate might be less
exuberant really than she seemed. It was a stormy
night, with wind and rain beating against the windows;
but the little rooms were cozy and snug, and the little
family, sitting together, engaged in their separate tasks,
formed a circle which it was hard to think was soon to
be broken. As if by tacit consent they all avoided a discussion of the subject that was uppermost in their
minds — where and how Kate and Peter and Betty
would now live.

"Have n't you some dictation, Jerry?" Kate asked.
"I need all the practice I can get, before next Monday."

Jerry produced papers from his green bag, Peter and
Betty withdrew to another room where their studies
should not be disturbed, Mrs. Donohue continued to
knit. But she grew drowsier and drowsier while Jerry,
pacing to and fro, delivered his slow monologue, and at
last she gave forth unwittingly sounds indicating that
for her at least it was bedtime. So Kate and Jerry made
the folding-bed ready and went out to the kitchen to

finish their work. They were still at it when Betty and Peter called good-night to them.

"I guess that's enough for this evening," Jerry said at last. "Tired, Kate?"

"No, not a bit." She sighed. "I wish my new employer were a lawyer; my training with you would be so much more valuable if he were. I don't suppose" — she spoke hesitatingly — "your office needs another stenographer, does it, Jerry?"

"I don't know about the office. But I need *you*, Kate." Jerry slipped his arm round her and gave her a kiss.

"Oh, Jerry!"

"Yes, I do." He kissed her again and laughed, her eyes were so wide and shining, her lips were opened in such a circle of wonder and — yes, of happiness. "You're the best little helper any man could have, and I can't have you living anywhere else than just with me."

Then he felt both her arms round him, felt her lips softly brush his cheek, and heard her say in a breaking voice, "Oh, Jerry, Jerry, my darling! And I do adore you so!"

XLV

FROM the Donohues' new suite of rooms it was only a short walk to the boulevard fronting the park. On Sundays Jerry and Kate usually took a stroll among the park gardens, and each time they would note with interest the progress made in the building of the new house on the boulevard, at the corner of their street. It was a large and handsome house in the Georgian style, built of dark-red brick, with buff trimmings.

"But I'm sure the people that are going to live there aren't as happy as we are, Jerry," said Kate as they passed it one day. She gave her husband's arm a squeeze, after glancing round and making sure that no one would see.

"I should say not," declared Jerry proudly.

"And however grand they are, I don't believe they have anything much nicer than our new parlor furniture."

"Especially when you think of the new tall clock." Jerry glanced at Kate with a twinkle of mischief in his eye.

"Yes," she admitted. "I must say I'm getting resigned to having it. For it does look awfully well. Of course, I never can like Mrs. Maguire — but it was a handsome present just the same."

"And quite a handsome letter she wrote you about me," suggested Jerry.

"Oh, yes. It sounded much nicer than she is."

"I shall always think she's pretty nice," Jerry said teasingly. "And if she had n't been as sensible as she is nice I should never have been as happy as I am."

"Truly true? I 'll try not to be jealous of her or hateful, Jerry. But I did feel glad I was n't at home when she called, and I could n't help being relieved that she was n't in when I called. Now that will probably be the end of it. People who live at the Wallace House are n't going to bother much with people like us."

"I'm not so sure. I have an idea Nora won't find many congenial friends among the persons her husband knows. She could n't help liking you, Kate, and I guess she'd like to have you for a friend. They'd hardly have sent us such a present otherwise."

"It's your friendship she cares about, not mine."

"I think it's both of us."

"Have you seen her at all, Jerry?" Kate eyed him so anxiously that he laughed.

"Not since she was married. I did n't even know she was living at the Wallace until the clock came, with the card giving her address." Jerry suddenly took off his hat and waved it to a policeman on the opposite sidewalk, who grinned and came across the street.

"Sergeant Sheehan, I want you to meet my wife," said Jerry. "She knows all about you."

"Indeed I do." Kate gave the sergeant her hand. "And I was so glad when Jerry told me of your promotion."

" You'll be springing up the ladder now by leaps and bounds," said Jerry.

Sheehan beamed with pleasure and answered, " Do you mind my saying, Donohue, that you'd be a better officer once you got yourself a wife? But you've done better for yourself in every way than I ever supposed you would. That's the plain Irish of it, now I'm telling you, Mrs. Donohue."

They all laughed cheerfully, and Sheehan with his white-gloved hand gave Kate his best salute before passing on.

At the apartment Jerry's mother welcomed the pair with the news that Mr. and Mrs. Bennett and the baby had called.

" Every time I see them I can't help wishing in one way that I was back at the old place; they're such nice folks, both of them, and I do love that baby. But they came to tell us of their stroke of luck. Mr. Bennett's been promoted; he's to be foreman of the composing-room, and they're thinking some of moving now. They were wondering if they might get into this building, and I told them of the flat that's vacant on the fourth floor. They're going to see the agent to-morrow. Won't it be splendid if we have them near us again! — Oh, and there's another matter they told me of. Clara Armstrong's living at home now. They say she's toned down so you'd hardly know her. Of course I was glad to hear it, though I'm free to say I never expected it."

" There are lots of pleasant things that you never expected and that yet have come true, are n't there, mother?" Jerry gave her an affectionate pat. " When

we left our house in Millvale that day, you never thought
that in a few years you'd be living in a place as fine as
this, with mahogany furniture on all sides of you and a
tall clock like a music-box."

And at that appropriate moment the tall clock rang
the Westminster chimes and then struck the hour.

No, Jerry's mother admitted that she had never
looked for such good fortune as had come to them. Yet
there was one little reservation in her heart, one small
grievance that she would always cherish, that she could
never quite forgive, even though, of course, it could
make no real difference in her feelings about anybody.
Her lips drooped and her eyes took on a far-away look
whenever she thought about it. The new furniture was
very handsome, though it was n't in all respects just
what she would have picked out if it had been left
entirely to her judgment; the chiming clock was very
magnificent — to think that such a thing should have
been given them by Nora Scanlan, but some people did
have luck and to spare in this world; the new pictures
on the walls were no doubt very fine, though if her taste
had been more freely consulted, she would have had
colored pictures instead of photographs. But the thing
that hurt was that the memorial dove was not to be
seen on the parlor wall. It was Jerry who had suggested
to her that perhaps the most fitting place for so intimate
a symbol of love and bereavement was her bedroom
rather than the parlor; oh, she knew who had put Jerry
up to that, for he had never been one to lack piety and
reverence. So now it hung over her bed and under the
crayon enlargement of her husband's photograph; and

sometimes when she looked at it tears would fill her eyes and she would wonder what would become of it when she was gone.

On a Sunday afternoon in October Jerry and Kate were passing the big new house on the corner of the boulevard, now all but completed, and saw the door of it standing open. "Let's go in and look it over," said Jerry.

They entered and wandered through the newly plastered rooms, and poked their heads into closets. They were admiring the large fireplace in what was presumably the dining-room when they heard footsteps along the hall; turning, they beheld Nora and Patrick Maguire in the doorway.

"Jerry!" cried Nora, with a ring of unaffected cordiality in her voice. Her face lighted with a smile that embraced Kate in its friendliness. "Mrs. Donohue, have you met my husband?"

"Pleased to meet you, Mrs. Donohue," said Maguire, coming forward genially and shaking hands. "Good of you to be interested looking over our new house."

Kate, furiously embarrassed, and thinking that there was sarcastic intention in the speech, flushed to the eyes and was silent. Jerry, hardly less confused, began, "We did n't realize it was your house —" And then Nora tactfully interposed, "Oh, did n't you? I'm sorry, for we hoped you had come in and were specially interested on that account. Now you must let us show you all over it; we 're really terribly proud of it. This is to be our dining-room; it's to be paneled in oak; we 're going to have a sideboard built into this wall. The fireplace is to be done in Dutch tiles. Patrick," — she turned abruptly to her husband, — "you take Jerry down and show him the cellar; I don't believe Mrs. Donohue will want to see that, but I know he'll be interested."

So Jerry and Maguire descended to the cellar, where Maguire pointed out the laundry and explained the heating arrangements and exhibited the coal-bins. Jerry pretended to be interested, and wondered how Kate was getting on.

When he and Maguire ascended to the first floor, neither Kate nor Nora was to be seen. "Gone upstairs, I guess," said Maguire. He conducted Jerry from room to room, and conscientiously described the character of each. Then before proceeding to the second floor he said abruptly: —

"You fellows in the District Attorney's office have managed to stir things up a good deal. You've driven the lame ducks to cover, and I guess you'll get a good many of 'em before you're through."

"It looks as if we should."

"I understand you're doing well. They tell me you're a smart trial lawyer. Nora wanted to know how you were doing, so I made some inquiries for her. That's what they give me to understand. But I tell you, Mr. Donohue; I don't care how smart you are, you can't pin anything on me."

"To tell the truth, I've been rather afraid I might be able to," replied Jerry. "But I have n't found anything yet."

"No, and you won't. — Now we'll go up and look at the second floor."

He showed Jerry the library, with its view of the pond through the golden maple trees of the park; he showed him the bedrooms and the bathrooms; and finally they looked into a room where Kate and Nora were standing together in the embrasure of a window. Maguire led Jerry away and remarked, "That room's to be the nursery."

"Oh!" said Jerry. He knew now that Kate and Nora were quite likely to be friends.

Maguire took Jerry up to the billiard-room at the top of the house. "I hope we'll have many a friendly game up here of an evening," he said. "Well, now, I guess you've seen it all."

Jerry expressed his admiration of the house and thanked the host for his courtesy. They found Kate and Nora waiting for them on the first floor.

"Don't you think, Mrs. Donohue, we'll have quite the house?" Maguire asked.

"I think it will be a wonderful house," Kate answered with enthusiasm.

"All the credit goes to her." Maguire jerked his thumb towards Nora. "Say, Mrs. Donohue, I'll have to tell you a story on myself, just to give you a line on my wife. When we were on our honeymoon, we stopped in Chicago so she could buy some clothes. Her trousseau, you know. And then she said to me, 'Before ever I get one single thing for myself, I'm going to buy clothes for you, and then I don't ever again want to see you in these things you're wearing,' she says. A green Fedora hat and a green suit it was, all very nifty, I thought. 'What's the matter?' I says. 'I've always kind of fancied myself in green.' 'It's one thing that's kept me in doubt whether I could ever come to care for you,' she answered. 'If I can be sure I'll never see you in a green hat or a green suit again, I'll feel more hopeful in my mind,' she says. So now she does with me and with the house as she pleases — which is no doubt the way you do with your husband and your house, Mrs. Donohue."

Kate laughed, quite at her ease now. "Yes, pretty much," she answered.

"Did you think to tell Jerry about Dave and Nellie?" asked Nora.

"No, I did not."

"The first thing that is going to happen in our new house is a wedding," Nora said. "Dave and Nellie Sims — we're going to make the wedding party a kind of house-warming. Just a few people — I hope you'll both be sure to come — and your mother, too, Jerry."

"Well," said Jerry to Kate when after bidding their entertainers good-bye they were walking homeward, "what do you think now?"

"Of course I can't help liking her," Kate answered. "And him, too. She's so attractive I'm afraid you can't help loving her still, Jerry."

Jerry laughed and looked into her eyes. "Oh, no, Kate, you're not a bit afraid."

THE END